'You won't have to shop around to find a more winning protagonist'
Ireland on Sunday

'Hilarious'
OK!

'Expect to laugh. A lot'
Company

'I almost cried with laughter'
Daily Mail

'A sure-fire, laugh-out-loud hit'
Sun

'High-octane, laugh-a-minute entertainment'
Woman & Home

www.penguin.co.uk

The Shopaholic Series

Starring the unforgettable Becky Bloomwood,
shopper extraordinaire . . .

The Secret Dreamworld of a Shopaholic
(also published as *Confessions of a Shopaholic*)

Meet Becky – a journalist who spends all her time
telling people how to manage money, and all her leisure
time spending it. But the letters from her bank manager
are getting harder to ignore. Can she ever escape this
dream world, find true love . . . and regain the use of
her credit card?

Shopaholic Abroad
Becky's life is peachy. Her balance is in the black –
well, nearly – and now her boyfriend has asked her
to move to New York with him. Can Becky keep the
man *and* the clothes when there's so much temptation
around every corner?

Shopaholic Ties the Knot
Becky finally has the perfect job, the perfect man and, at
last, the perfect wedding. Or rather, *weddings* . . . How
has Becky ended up with not one, but two big days?

Shopaholic & Sister
Becky has received some incredible news. She has a
long-lost sister! But how will she cope when she realizes
her sister is not a shopper . . . but a skinflint?

Shopaholic & Baby

Becky is pregnant! But being Becky, she decides to shop around – for a new, more expensive obstetrician – and unwittingly ends up employing Luke's ex-girlfriend! How will Becky make it through the longest nine months of her life?

Mini Shopaholic

Times are hard, so Becky's Cutting Back. She has the perfect idea: throw a budget-busting birthday party. But her daughter Minnie can turn the simplest event into chaos. Whose turn will it be to sit on the naughty step?

Shopaholic to the Stars

Becky is in Hollywood and her heart is set on a new career – she's going to be a stylist to the stars! But in between choosing clutch bags and chasing celebrities, Becky gets caught up in the whirlwind of Tinseltown. Has Becky gone too far this time?

Shopaholic to the Rescue

Becky is on a major rescue mission! Hollywood was full of surprises, and now she's on a road trip to Las Vegas to find out why her dad has mysteriously disappeared, help her best friend Suze and *maybe* even bond with Alicia Bitch Long-legs. She comes up with her biggest, boldest, most brilliant plan yet – can she save the day?

Christmas Shopaholic

Becky is hosting Christmas for the first time. With her sister Jess demanding a vegan turkey, Luke insistent that he just wants aftershave again, and little Minnie insisting on a very specific picnic hamper will chaos ensue, or will Becky manage to bring comfort and joy at Christmas?

Wedding Night

Lottie is determined to get married. And Ben seems perfect – they'll iron out their little differences later. But their families have different plans . . .

My Not So Perfect Life

When Katie's ex-boss from hell books a glamping holiday at her family's farm, Katie plans to get her revenge on the woman with the perfect life. But does Demeter really have it so good? And what's wrong with not-so-perfect anyway?

Surprise Me

Sylvie and Dan have a happy marriage and are totally in sync. But when they introduce surprises into their relationship to keep things fresh, they begin to wonder if they know each other after all . . .

I Owe You One

When a handsome stranger asks Fixie to watch his laptop for a moment, she ends up saving it from certain disaster. To thank her, he scribbles her an IOU. Soon, small favours become life-changing.

For Young Adults

FINDING AUDREY

Audrey can't leave the house. She can't even take off her dark glasses inside. But then Linus stumbles into her life. And with him on her side, Audrey can do things she'd thought were too scary. Suddenly, finding her way back to the real world seems achievable . . .

For Younger Readers

The Mummy Fairy and Me Series

Ella's family have a big secret . . . her mummy is a fairy! She can do amazing spells with her Computawand to make delicious cupcakes, create the perfect birthday party and cause chaos at the supermarket. But sometimes the spells go a bit wrong and that's when Ella comes to the rescue!

Prepare for magic and mayhem in this sweet and funny new series for young readers.

Christmas
Shopaholic

sophie
kinsella

BLACK SWAN

TRANSWORLD PUBLISHERS
Penguin Random House, One Embassy Gardens,
8 Viaduct Gardens, London SW11 7BW
www.penguin.co.uk

Transworld is part of the Penguin Random House group of companies
whose addresses can be found at global.penguinrandomhouse.com

Penguin
Random House
UK

First published in Great Britain
in 2019 by Bantam Press
an imprint of Transworld Publishers
Black Swan edition published 2020

A CIP catalogue record for this book
is available from the British Library.

ISBN
9781784166403 (B format)
9781784165277 (A format)

Typeset in 11/14pt Giovanni Book by Jouve (UK), Milton Keynes.
Printed and bound in Great Britain by Clays Ltd, Elcograf S.p.A.

Penguin Random House is committed to a sustainable
future for our business, our readers and our planet. This book is made from
Forest Stewardship Council® certified paper.

To Kim Witherspoon

From: Store Manager
To: Becky Brandon
Subject: Re: Enquiry

Dear Mrs Brandon

Thank you for your email.

I was delighted to hear that you are planning to do 'loads' of your Christmas shopping at Hector Goode, Gentlemen's Outfitters.

I am also pleased you wish to purchase the 'Campbell' coat for your husband, Luke.

However, I am afraid I cannot tell you if the coat is going to be reduced in price before Christmas.

With all best wishes for a happy festive period.

Yours sincerely

Matthew Hicks

Store Manager
Hector Goode
Gentlemen's Outfitters
561 New Regent St
London W1

From: Store Manager
To: Becky Brandon
Subject: Re: Re: Re: Enquiry

Dear Mrs Brandon

Thank you for your email.

I do appreciate that it will be 'really annoying' if the 'Campbell' coat is reduced by half after you have purchased it.

I also understand that you don't want to leave it too long in case it sells out and you end up 'running around in a panic on Christmas Eve'.

Nevertheless, this is not information I can give out.

With all best wishes for a happy festive period.

Yours sincerely

Matthew Hicks

Store Manager
Hector Goode
Gentlemen's Outfitters
561 New Regent St
London W1

Dear Mrs Brandon

Thank you for your email.

No, I cannot give you a 'tiny hint'.

I'm sorry you feel that Christmas shopping has become a game of 'who blinks first'.

I do agree, it was easier when there weren't any sales till Boxing Day and 'everyone knew where they were'.

Nevertheless I wish you a happy festive period.

Yours sincerely

Matthew Hicks

Store Manager
Hector Goode
Gentlemen's Outfitters
561 New Regent St
London W1

ONE

OK. Don't panic. Don't *panic*. I've got 5 minutes 52 seconds before my basket expires. That's loads of time! All I have to do is quickly find one more item to bump up my total to £75 so I'll get free delivery.

Come on, Becky. You can find something.

I'm scrolling down the BargainFamily site on my computer screen, feeling like a NASA operative keeping cool under unspeakable pressure. The onscreen timer is in my peripheral vision, ticking down steadily beneath a heading that reads, *Your Basket Will Expire Soon!* But you can't give in to timer-fear when you're shopping on discount sites. You have to be strong. Like tungsten.

Shopping has really changed for me over the years. Or maybe I've changed. The days when I was a single girl, living in Fulham with Suze and going round the shops every day, seem *ages* ago now. Yes, I used to spend too much. I'll freely admit it. I've made mistakes. Like Frank Sinatra, I did it my way.

(Except 'my way' involved stuffing Visa bills under the bed, which I bet Frank never did.)

But I've learned some important lessons, which have genuinely changed the way I go about things. Like, for example:

1 I don't use carrier bags any more. They used to be my biggest joy in life. Oh my *God*, the feel of a new carrier bag . . . the rope handles . . . the rustle of tissue paper . . . (I still sometimes go and swoon over my old collection at the back of the wardrobe.) But now I use a Bag for Life instead. Because of the planet and everything.

2 I'm totally into ethical shopping. It's like a win–win! You get cool stuff *and* you're being virtuous.

3 I don't even spend money any more. I *save* money.

OK. So obviously that's not exactly, actually, literally true. But the point is, I'm always looking for a good deal. I see it as my responsibility as a parent to procure all the items that my family needs at the most cost-effective prices possible. Which is why BargainFamily is the *perfect* place for me to shop. It's all reduced! Designer labels and everything!

The only thing is, you have to be a fast shopper, or else your basket expires and you have to start again. I'm on £62.97 already, so all I need is another item around 12 quid. Come on, quick, there *must* be something I need. I click on an orange cardigan, £13.99, RRP £45, but when I zoom in I see a horrible lacy border.

White shirt?

No, I bought a white shirt last week. (One hundred per cent linen, £29.99, RRP £99.99. I must remember to wear that, actually.)

I click on my basket to double-check on what I've already got, and a pop-up window bursts forth, announcing *You've Saved £284 Today, Becky!*

I feel a flash of pride as I survey my items. I've saved a whole £284! I've got an adorable bunny rabbit dressing gown for Minnie and a fantastic DKNY jacket, down from £299 to £39.99 in clearance, and a huge rubber ring shaped like a flamingo, which we can use next time we go on holiday.

And OK, yes. I *could* theoretically check out now and pay £5.95 for delivery. But that's not prudent. I'm not a former financial journalist for nothing, I know these things. It's far more economically sound to find yourself something else that you need, and get the free delivery.

Come on, there must be something. Tights? Everyone needs tights.

Oh, but I'm always bumping up orders with tights. I have so many black opaques, they'll last me till I'm 105. And those tartan patterned ones I clicked on last week were a big mistake.

I click on 'Homewares' and scroll down the items quickly. Silver antelope sculpture, was £79.99, now £12.99? Hmm, not sure. Scented candle? Oh God. No. I can't buy another one. Our whole house is like one big scented candle. In fact, Luke said the other day, 'Becky, is there any chance of buying a candle called "Fresh Air"?'

I'm just squinting at a bread bin shaped like Big Ben when a pop-up appears in front of my eyes – *Your Time Is Running Out, Becky!* – and my heart jumps in fright.

I *wish* they wouldn't do that. I *know* my time is running out.

'I know!' I hear myself saying out loud. 'Don't stress me out!'

Just to reassure myself, I click back on my basket again – and my heart stops. The flamingo ring is sold out! Sold out!

Noooo! I was too slow! Argh. The trouble with discount websites is, you can't see the people snatching bargains away from you. Now my heart really is thumping. I'm *not* losing my jacket, or Minnie's dressing gown. I need to fill this basket and check out, pronto.

'Mummeee!'

Minnie's voice hails me from outside the door, immediately followed by Luke saying, 'Minnie! Darling, leave Mummy alone when she's doing her mindfulness. Sorry, Becky,' he calls through the door. 'Didn't mean to disturb you.'

'Er ... that's OK!' I call back, feeling a tiny stab of guilt.

I know Luke thinks I'm sitting here peacefully doing my mindfulness meditation. And I was. In fact, it's still running in the corner of the screen, so in a way I *am* doing it, except I turned the volume down so I could concentrate on shopping.

It's become a bit of a routine, my mindfulness. I come into the study and turn on the meditation and it keeps me mentally well-balanced. And just occasionally I log on to a shopping site, too.

The thing is, the stock on the BargainFamily site changes every day, so it makes sense to check out 'Deals of the day'. Minnie needs a new dressing gown, so I started with that – and then how could I *not* buy a DKNY jacket for £39.99? I mean, that's an insanely good bargain and it'll last me for ever. Which meant that obviously I had to add some other items to get the free delivery. That's when I turned down the volume of the mindfulness guy. He's nice, but he's a bit serious and he distracts you from the task in hand.

Anyway, shopping *is* mindfulness, if you ask me. I've forgotten about all my other worries right now. I'm in the moment. I'm in the zone.

I glance at the timer and my stomach flips over. Two minutes 34 seconds before my basket expires. Come on, Becky . . .

Hastily I click on Accessories. That's the answer. You can't have too many accessories, can you? And I could always give one as a present.

I swiftly scroll down a page of boring clutch bags, weird-looking hats and nasty-looking gold necklaces. Every time a page loads, I feel a burst of optimism, but then my spirits fall. There's nothing. What's wrong with me? Am I *that* fussy?

I'm starting to think I'll have to admit defeat and pay the delivery charge for the first time in my life, when the next page loads. And something catches in my throat. Can that be . . .

Are my eyes playing tricks on me?

I'm staring at a turquoise printed gossamer silk scarf. Surely it can't be . . .

Denny and George? On BargainFamily? *Seriously?*

Blinking in disbelief, I read the description. *Silk scarf, was £239, our price £30.*

Thirty quid for a Denny and George scarf? *Thirty quid?*

I scroll down and there are two more underneath. All 100 per cent silk. All stunning. All 'Limited stock'. Shit. I need to hurry!

Without pausing to consider further, I start clicking. *Buy. Buy. Buy. View Basket. Check Out.* I feel like a virtuoso pianist, hitting all the right notes, at the top of her game. And I've made it with twenty seconds to spare! My basket is intact! My credit card details are stored, this should take no time . . .

Your password is not secure.

A pop-up has stopped me in my tracks and I stare at it breathlessly. What's the problem now? I peer at the screen, reading the rest of the message.

Would you like to change your password? We suggest C?/ x887dau.

I bet they do. Well, they can just sod off. My password is fine. Carefully I type in *Ermintrude2*, and a final *Complete.*

I lean back in my chair, panting as a new message appears on the screen. *Congratulations! You saved £879 today!*

I mean, it just shows. A penny saved is a penny earned, which means I've just effectively earned £879. In one online shopping session! If I made that every day, it would be . . . I shut my eyes, trying to calculate. Well, anyway, a six-figure salary. I think sometimes Luke doesn't appreciate this fact about me: that I'm quietly generating our family thousands of pounds, all the time.

The only thing is, now I should buy something ethical. This is a habit that my sister Jess got me into. (Half-sister, really.) Jess is very right-on and frugal and we were once having a lively debate – well, argument – about shopping. I was saying it supported the economy and she was saying the economy didn't deserve to be supported. And then she said, 'I mean, Becky, if you just shopped ethically, once in a while . . .'

And that spoke to me. In fact, it made me feel stricken with guilt. I *should* shop ethically. We all should! So I started a little habit – when I've been on a shopping spree I try to buy something ethical, too. Like those people who buy trees to make up for flying on planes.

I log on to the Ethical Consumer Today site and peer at the home page. The only trouble is, I've already bought nearly everything from this site. I've got the beeswax candles and Fairtrade coffee and all the yoga bracelets . . .

Wait. New product! 'Organic spicy falafel mix.' Perfect! You can't have too much organic spicy falafel mix, can you? I quickly order eight packets (free delivery), complete my purchase with one click and sit back with satisfaction. I'll tell Luke we're going to have Falafel Night every Tuesday, which we should do anyway, because it's healthy.

At the thought of Luke, I reach forward and increase the volume of my mindfulness meditation, and it's just in time, because the door opens, right as the mindfulness guy is saying, 'Let go of your worries.'

I turn round to Luke and give him a calm, mindful smile.

'Hi!' I say.

'I thought I'd give you a heads up,' Luke says apologetically. 'We need to leave for the restaurant in about fifteen minutes. How's it going?'

'Good,' I say. 'Really good.'

'You look radiant.' He surveys me admiringly. 'Kind of . . . I don't know. Serene. Content.'

'I feel content!' I beam back at him.

Three Denny and George scarves for £30 each! How could I *not* feel content? I'll give one to Suze for her birthday and I'll save one for Minnie . . .

'I'm so glad you've found this for yourself,' says Luke, dropping a kiss on my head. 'I used to be sceptical about all this meditation business, but you've convinced me.'

'It's just a question of applying your mind to what really *matters* in life,' I say wisely, as the doorbell rings.

Luke goes out to answer it and I hear a series of thumps from the hall. A few moments later, the front door closes and Luke's head reappears round the door.

'Some deliveries for you,' he says.

'Ooh!' I light up. 'Deliveries!'

I love the way online shopping just *comes* to you. I hurry out to see three boxes and a plastic ASOS package in

12

the hall. Excellent! I was hoping my ASOS delivery would arrive in time for this evening. I grab the package, slit it open with the scissors I keep in the hall for exactly this reason, and out slither four navy satin jumpsuits.

'Wow,' says Luke, staring down at the sea of navy satin. 'That's a lot of . . . whatever they are. Did you need that many?'

'I'm not going to keep them *all*,' I say, as though explaining remedial algebra to a fairly promising student. 'You don't keep them *all*. You try them on and keep one and send the rest back. And they were half-price,' I add for good measure, ripping open the size 12 Long and holding it up. 'Total bargain.'

Luke is still frowning perplexedly. 'But did you really need to order four?' he says.

'I didn't know what size I needed,' I retort. 'And I didn't know if I needed Regular or Long. Don't blame *me*, Luke,' I add, warming to my theme. 'Blame poor sizing standards in the fashion industry which penalize the innocent consumer.'

'Hmm. What about those eight cushions?' says Luke, his gaze turning to yesterday's delivery, stacked against the skirting board. 'Sizing issues there, too?'

'I couldn't see the colours properly online,' I say defensively. 'I had to order them all to have a proper look. I'm only keeping two, I'll send the rest back tomorrow. Free returns. And do you know how much I saved on them? £52!'

'Becky, I would pay £52 for our house not to look like a bloody depot,' says Luke, eyeing all the boxes and packages filling the hall. 'All we need is a guy in a brown overall with a forklift truck.'

'Ha ha,' I say, rolling my eyes sardonically.

'And when are you going to send back those statues?' Luke gestures at the life-size statues of Aphrodite and Hermes which are standing at the bottom of the stairs, still half wrapped in brown paper. 'We've had them a week. They're grotesque!'

'They're not grotesque,' I say defensively, 'they're *avant garde*. And I can't send them back because they're ethical.'

'*Ethical?*' Luke stares at me.

'They were made by a disadvantaged youth group,' I explain. 'Upcycled from bicycle parts and fridge components.'

I have to admit, they're pretty monstrous. And I didn't realize they would be so big. But how can I send them back? If I do, the youth group will be devastated. All their self-esteem will vanish and it will be our fault for not being open-minded about their statues.

'Well, they're giving Minnie nightmares,' says Luke flatly. 'I had to put a bag over Aphrodite's head.'

'I think she looks more sinister *with* the bag over her head,' I counter. 'She looks scary. She looks like a hostage.'

'She looks even more scary when she's gazing at you with her cold metal eyes.' Luke shudders. 'Could we not just have given some money to the youth group?'

'That's not how ethical shopping *works*, Luke,' I say patiently. 'You have to *buy the stuff*. Anyway, I need to try these on. When are we leaving?'

14

'Eight minutes,' says Luke. 'And counting.'

I dash upstairs, clutching the packages, and quickly try the first jumpsuit on. Hmm. Too long. I grab the Regular and put that on instead – then stare at myself in the mirror. At last!

What happened was, last week I was watching a TV show and saw this really cool jumpsuit. So of course I instantly stopped concentrating on the show, grabbed my laptop and started googling jumpsuits instead. It took me a while to find one that wasn't sold out – but here we are!

I survey myself, trying to be fully objective. It's a great fabric. The navy colour is elegant and the flared trousers are really flattering. It's just the front that I'm peering at uncertainly. Or rather, the lack of front. It's even more revealing than the one on TV.

Can I get away with a jumpsuit slashed to the navel?

Can I?

Am I too old?

No. No! Fashion is timeless. You should be able to wear what you like, when you like. All the old rules are gone.

They wear outfits like this on the red carpet, all the time, I remind myself, trying to bolster my own confidence. Ribs are the new cleavage. Besides, it's not *indecent*. Not strictly speaking. I mean, you can't see my nipples.

Not quite.

And OK, so I'm not heading on to the red carpet, I'm heading for dinner with Mum and Dad at Luigi's of Oxshott – but I can still wear something fashion-forward, can't I? People will call me The Girl in the Iconic Jump-suit. They'll look at me in awe as I sashay past, wishing *they* could wear something so daring.

Exactly.

Defiantly I grab a red lipstick and start applying it. I can do this. I can style it out. Go, Becky.

TWO

The November air outside is all crisp and chilly and I can smell the tang of a bonfire. Across the road they've got fairy lights up already. It'll be Christmas before we know it. At the thought, I feel a warm, happy sensation spread through me. Christmas is just so . . . *Christmassy*. The tree. Presents. The Nativity set we've had for ever (except we lost Baby Jesus years ago, so we use a clothes peg instead). Carols playing and Mum pretending she made the Christmas pudding. Dad lighting a fire and Janice and Martin popping in for a sherry in terrible Christmas jumpers.

The thing about our family Christmas is, it's always the same. In a good way. Mum always buys the same things, from the crackers to the Waitrose chocolate roll. Now we have Minnie, we all get even more excited – and this year she'll be old enough to really understand it. I'll buy her a cute Christmas onesie and we'll look out for Father Christmas in the sky

17

and leave out a mince pie for him . . . Basically, I can't *wait*.

Luke's dad and sister are going to Florida for Christmas and, to be fair, they invited us along. His mum, Elinor, is going to be in the Hamptons, and she invited us, too. But we've declined both invitations. We both want a nice, normal, happy family Christmas.

As I buckle Minnie into her car seat I look back at our house and feel a familiar tweak of disbelief at how life has changed for me and Luke over the last year or so. Once upon a time we lived in central London and I worked at a department store called The Look. We knew where we were heading and everything seemed settled.

Then we went on this massive, life-changing adventure to California – and while we were away The Look went bust. And openings for other personal-shopping jobs were pretty thin on the ground. At the same time, my best friend Suze had decided to expand her gift shop at Letherby Hall, the stately home where she lives. (It was more of a gift 'cupboard' till then.) I was having a glass of wine with her one evening, and bewailing the fact that I couldn't find a job, while she was bewailing the fact that she couldn't find anyone to help run the gift shop – and asking me for all my ideas – when the solution hit us.

So now I'm an employee of Letherby Hall Gift Shop! Not only that, Luke and I have moved out of London to the village of Letherby. We're three minutes away from Suze, living in a house owned by a family who have gone to Dubai for two years. We've rented out our

London house. Luke commutes to his job and Minnie has joined the village school with all of Suze's kids. It's perfect! The shopping isn't *that* brilliant in Letherby – but you can get everything online, next-day delivery. So, it's all good.

Mum and Dad are thrilled, too, because 1. Letherby isn't too far from Oxshott, where they live, and 2. our rented house has off-street parking. Off-street parking is, like, my parents' religion. That and double-glazing. And 'good quality' curtains.

(Though Mum and I don't exactly agree on what 'good quality' curtains means. We discovered this when she dragged me to a curtain exchange place and tried to make me buy some wadded blue flowery curtains which were 'a *fraction* of what they'd cost new, Becky love, a *fraction*'. At last I said, 'Actually I might get blinds' and she looked devastated and said, 'But these are such good quality!' and I said, 'But they're gross.' Which I shouldn't have done.

I mean, it was fine. Mum was only offended for about half an hour. And every time I visit her I say, 'Those curtains look *great* in the spare room, Mum, and the matching duvet is *gorgeous*.')

As we pull up in front of Suze's massive front door, Minnie starts wriggling with excitement. She loves having sleepovers with Suze's children so much I almost get offended. I mean, what's wrong with home?

'Wilfie!' she's already yelling, as he appears in the drive. 'Wilfie! I'm here, I'm here! Let's play monter tucks!'

'Monter tucks' is Minnie-talk for 'monster trucks'.

Minnie, Wilfie and his twin Clemmie spend hours happily running monster trucks up and down the endless corridors of Letherby Hall. I've even bought Minnie her own monster truck to keep there.

I've also made sure to mention this fact when I email Jess, who's living in Chile at the moment. Jess and her husband Tom have applied to adopt a child, rather than add to the world's population problem, and meanwhile Jess is always lecturing me about bringing up Minnie in a gender-neutral way and sending me books called things like *The Zero-Carbon Child*.

So last week I wrote her an email – 'I'm really encouraging Minnie in non-gender-aligned play' – and attached a photo of Minnie clutching a truck, wearing a pair of Wilfie's jeans. (She'd fallen in the mud and had to change out of her frilly skirt.) Jess wrote back: 'That's sound thinking, Becky, we have to fight the sexist stereotypes, but couldn't you find trucks crafted from sustainable wood?'

I haven't got back to her about that yet. (I did ask Luke if he could whittle a monster truck for Minnie out of sustainable wood, and he just looked at me.)

Nor have I mentioned to Jess Minnie's massive collection of dolls and sparkly fairy wings, or the way she begs to wear a pink dress every day. Because you don't have to tell your frugal, vegan, principled sister *everything*, do you?

I just manage to kiss Minnie goodbye before she hurtles into the house with Wilfie, carrying her little backpack with all her overnight stuff. Next moment, Suze arrives in the drive, wearing yoga leggings and a sweatshirt, her blonde hair piled up and secured with a bulldog clip.

'I'll just make sure Minnie's OK,' says Luke, heading into the house.

'Thanks so much for having her, Suze,' I say as I hug her.

'Any time!' says Suze. 'And give my love to your parents.'

'Of course.' I pause, before adding casually, 'Hey Suze. You know how you have that sculpture-park bit in the garden here?'

I've suddenly remembered the North Lawn at Letherby Hall, which is littered with metal orbs and carved bits of stone and stuff. It's open to the public and has loads of room in it and is the perfect solution.

'Yes?' Suze looks a bit surprised. 'What about it?'

'Well, I wondered if you'd like an art donation?'

'An *art donation*?' She stares at me.

'Yes, two statues. Very avant garde,' I add carelessly. 'If you can transport them, then you can have them for free.'

'Statues?' Suze peers at me in bewilderment – then her face suddenly changes. '*Not* those two monstrosities in your hall.'

Drat. I didn't think she'd seen them.

'They're not monstrosities,' I say defensively. 'They're Art. When did you see them, anyway?'

'When I dropped Minnie back home the other day. Bex, they're vile. Why on earth did you buy them?'

'Because they're made by a very deserving youth

group,' I say loftily. 'And I think they have artistic merit, *actually*.'

'Well, good for you,' says Suze. 'I hope you enjoy them. Although if you think they're so great, why is there a bag over the head of one of them?'

Oh God. I can't keep up the pretence any longer.

'Suze, *please* have them,' I beg in a rush. 'You've got so much room. You could hide them behind a tree and no one would even see them.'

'No way.' Suze folds her arms. 'Just send them back.'

Honestly. Wasn't she listening?

'I can't send them back! They were made by a *youth group*!'

'Well, give them to someone else.'

'Who?' I say desperately.

'Dunno.' Suze shrugs. 'But they're not coming here.'

I'm about to plead their case further when Luke appears out of the house.

'All set?' he says to me.

'What are you wearing?' says Suze, glancing at my navy satin legs. 'Is that a new pair of trousers?'

'Jumpsuit,' I say smugly.

'Ooh, I want one of those!' says Suze at once. 'Show me!'

I automatically start unbuttoning my coat – then pause.

'It's a bit . . . adventurous.'

'Great!' Suze gestures at me to carry on unbuttoning, but my fingers don't move. For some reason, I'm feeling apprehensive about revealing my whole outfit.

'I mean, it's quite out there,' I add, playing for time.

22

'Sounds fab!' says Suze enthusiastically. 'Go on, Bex, show me!'

Even Luke is looking interested now.

Ribs are the new cleavage, I remind myself. Then, almost defiantly, I throw open my coat and say, 'Ta-daah!'

I feel the November evening air on my chest, and silently thank God for my silicone, stick-on 'mini bra replacements', although if either of them falls to the floor I will *die*.

No one seems able to speak. Luke's jaw has actually dropped. Suze takes a step back, and she blinks about twenty times.

'Wow,' she manages at last. 'That's . . .'

'Is there a part missing?' enquires Luke, deadpan. 'In the front-ish area?'

'No!' I say defiantly. 'It's the look.'

'Well, I think you look amazing.' Suze rallies. 'It's really cool, Bex.'

'*Thank* you. What?' I add, turning to Luke.

'No. Nothing. Great. Let's go.' His mouth twitches a tiny bit. 'I'm sure your parents will be blown away.'

Luigi's is one of those lovely warm, cosy restaurants that hit you with the scent of garlic and wine as soon as you enter. Our table is waiting for us – although Mum and Dad aren't there yet – and as I let my coat slither from my shoulders I feel insanely cool. This jumpsuit is *fantastic*. I should get it in every single colour! I can see my reflection in the windows as I walk to the table, and I can't help shimmying along like a model, watching the satin ripple and shine.

I even mentally itemize my outfit as if I'm in a magazine, which is an old habit of mine. Coat: Topshop. Jumpsuit: ASOS. Shoes: See by Chloe. Bracelet: model's own. (Can't remember where I got it.)

A teenage girl sitting with her parents is gaping at me, wide-eyed, and I smile kindly back. I remember what it was like to be a suburban teenager, looking enviously at sophisticated women with amazing clothes. An old man nearby splutters his soup as I pass, but he's probably never even heard of Miranda Kerr, so he doesn't count.

I have sticky 'fashion tape' attaching the jumpsuit to my skin so I'm not worried about anything popping out, I'm just loving my fashion-forward moment. As our waiter draws out my chair I smile at him gracefully before sinking down into it and—

Shit.

Shit. Oh my *God*.

It gapes. When you sit down. It gapes.

To my blood-chilling horror, as soon as I sat down, the satin ripped away from my fashion tape (which is *not* 'fully secure in all emergencies', they're *liars*). The entire neckline has concertinaed into a kind of horizontal letterbox shape, and you can see my—

Oh God, oh *God* . . .

My hands have instinctively grabbed the neckline back into place, but I've only got ten fingers. There's still far too much flesh and tape and silicone on view. The waiter, after one aghast glance at my chest area, has hastily dropped the leather-bound menus on the table and backed away. I'm frozen, my whole body stiff with

24

stress. Did anyone notice? Is the entire restaurant staring at me? What do I do now?

I lift my eyes desperately, to see Luke regarding me quizzically.

'Is that the look?' he says. 'Sorry, I know I'm not as fashion literate as I might be.'

'Ha ha, very funny,' I mutter furiously.

It's a cocktail-party jumpsuit, I've realized. Not a sitting-down jumpsuit. They should have made this clear on the website. They should have added a caption: *Suitable only for standing/posing with shoulders well back/ laughing at witty quips.*

'Luke, I need your jacket,' I add in an agitated undertone. 'Quick, pass it over.'

'Don't have one.' He shrugs. 'Sorry.'

He *what*?

'How can you not have a jacket?' I demand. 'You always have a jacket!'

'Because you told me not to wear one,' Luke replies calmly.

'What?' I stare at him. 'No I didn't!'

'Yes you did. Last time we went out for supper you said, "You always wear a jacket, Luke. It's so boring. Why don't you mix it up a bit?"'

Oh right. Actually, that does ring a bit of a bell. Maybe I did say that.

'Well, I hereby retract it,' I say frantically. 'You should *always* wear a jacket, in case I have a wardrobe malfunction.'

'Always wear a jacket.' Luke pretends to make a note on his phone. 'Anything else?'

25

'Yes. Give me your napkin. Quick!'

Thankfully the napkins are really big and made of posh red damask material. I knot three together to make a kind of bikini top, tie it tightly around myself, then look up breathlessly. On the plus side, I'm decent. On the minus side, what do I *look* like?

'Super-hot,' says Luke, as though reading my mind.

'Shut up.' I glare at him.

'I'm serious. You do look hot.' He grins at me. 'Bravo.'

'Darling!' Dad's voice greets me and I turn to see my parents coming through the restaurant. Dad's wearing a linen jacket with a paisley handkerchief in his top pocket, and Mum is in a pink floral two-piece which I recognize as belonging to Janice, our neighbour.

Mum and Janice are always swapping clothes to 'refresh' their wardrobes. Janice is about two sizes smaller than Mum but it doesn't put them off – Mum just leaves half the buttons undone, while Janice cinches everything in with a belt.

'Becky, love! How are you? How's Minnie?' Mum hugs me tight, then peers down at me. 'That's an unusual outfit! Is that what they call a "handkerchief top"?'

'Er . . . kind of.' I avoid Luke's gaze and add quickly, 'Shall we have a drink?'

Already an elderly waiter is bringing over a sherry for Mum, plus a gin and tonic for Dad. They *know* my parents here. Mum and Dad have lived in Oxshott since before I was born, and they come to Luigi's about twice a month. Mum always orders the special, while Dad always looks at the menu for ages, as though expecting to see something new, before ordering the Veal Marsala.

'Luke.' Dad shakes Luke's hand before hugging me. 'Good to see you.'

'We have *so* much to talk about!' says Mum. 'What are you two having?'

We order our drinks and the waiter pours out water while Mum twitches impatiently. I can tell she's got things she wants to discuss, but she never says anything in front of waiters, not even at Luigi's. I don't know what she thinks, that they'll immediately go off and text the *Oxshott Gazette* the latest gossip: *Bloomwoods intending to buy new lawn mower but can't decide on brand*?

'So!' says Mum as soon as the waiter moves away. 'I don't know *where* to start.'

'Christmas,' says Dad.

'Christmas.' I beam at him. 'I can't wait. I'll bring the crackers. Shall we get the ones with the nail-clippers and things or the ones with wind-up penguins?'

I'm expecting Dad to answer 'Wind-up penguins,' because last year he won the wind-up-penguin race and was ridiculously pleased about it. But to my surprise he doesn't answer immediately. He looks at Mum. In fact, he looks *shiftily* at Mum.

I have very acute parental radar. I know when something's up. And almost at once I guess what it is: they're going away for Christmas. A cruise. It's got to be a cruise. I bet Janice and Martin talked them into it and they've already bought their pastel outfits.

'Are you going on a cruise?' I blurt out, and Mum looks surprised.

'No, love! What makes you think that?'

Oh, right. So my parental radar isn't quite as acute as I thought. But then, why the shifty look?

'Something's going on,' I assert.

'Yes,' says Dad, with another look at Mum.

'Something to do with Christmas,' I say, feeling Sherlock-Holmes-like in my deduction abilities.

'Well, Christmas is *one* factor,' allows Mum.

One factor?

'Mum, what's going on? Not something bad?' I add in sudden fear.

'Of course not!' Mum laughs. 'It's nothing, love. Just that we've agreed that Jess can move into our house. And Tom, of course,' she adds. 'Both of them.'

Tom is Janice and Martin's son, and he and Jess are married – so we're all kind of related now.

'But they live in Chile,' I say stupidly.

'They're coming back for a few months,' says Dad.

'Jess never told me!' I say indignantly.

'Oh, you know how cautious Jess is,' says Mum. 'She's the type to keep back news till it's one hundred per cent confirmed. Look, here are your drinks.'

As our drinks are deposited on the table, my mind can't help racing ahead in speculation. Jess's emails to me are quite short and curt, and Mum's right: she's the type to keep news back. Even brilliant, exciting news. (She once won a big geology prize and didn't tell me and then said, 'I thought you wouldn't be interested.')

So could this be because – Oh my God! As soon as the waiter has gone, I say excitedly, 'Tell me! Have Jess and Tom adopted a child?'

At once I can see from Mum's expression that I've misfired again.

'Not yet,' says Mum, and I see Dad wince slightly.

'Not quite yet, love. The wheels are still turning out there. Bureaucracy and so forth. Poor Janice has given up asking.'

'Oh,' I say, deflated. 'I thought maybe ... Wow. It takes a long time, doesn't it?'

When Jess showed me a photo of an adorable little boy, ages ago now, I thought we'd meet him really soon. But that adoption fell through and we were all a bit devastated. And since then, Jess and Tom have been pretty cagey about their prospects.

'They'll get there,' says Dad with a determined brightness. 'We have to keep the faith.'

As Luke pours tonic into his G&T, I'm picturing Jess and Tom, out in Chile, waiting and waiting for news of a child to adopt, and my heart squeezes. I really feel for Jess. She'd be a *brilliant* mother (in a strict, vegan, recycled-hemp-clothes kind of way) and it seems so unfair that adoption takes so long.

Then my thoughts turn to Suze and my heart squeezes again. Just after we got back from the States, she had a miscarriage, which was a shock to all of us. And although all she ever says about it is, 'I'm so lucky already ... it wasn't meant to be ...' I know she was crushed.

As for me, we'd love another baby, but it just hasn't happened.

By now my heart is feeling squeezy all over. Life's weird. You can *know* you're the luckiest human being in the world. You can *know* you don't have anything to complain about. But you can still feel sad because you don't have that one extra little person in your life.

'Cheers!' says Luke, lifting his glass to everyone, and I hastily smile. 'And here's to . . .' He hesitates. 'What exactly?'

'That's what I'm trying to tell you,' says Dad, after we've all sipped our drinks. 'Jess and Tom are coming back to the UK for a while. Janice was fretting about giving them space . . . and the upshot is we're offering them our house for a few months.'

'They'll be next door to Janice, but not on *top* of her,' puts in Mum. 'And Janice won't have to cook chickpeas every night. Poor love, she was getting quite agitated about it! I mean, Janice is as vegan as anyone, but she does like a boiled egg for breakfast.'

'How long are they back for?' asks Luke, before I can ask Mum if she knows what 'vegan' actually means.

'Well, this is the thing!' says Mum. 'Till January at least. Which means we won't be able to host Christmas. So we thought, Becky . . .' She pauses and turns to me with a flourish. 'Now you're in your lovely house, maybe it's time for *you* to host Christmas!'

'*Me* host Christmas?' I stare at Mum. 'But . . .'

I feel as though all this time someone has been gently playing 'Hark! The Herald Angels Sing' on a vinyl record in the background – and now someone's scraped the needle off, into stark silence.

I don't host Christmas, *Mum* hosts Christmas. She knows how to do it. She knows how to unwrap the chocolate roll and put it on a doily and sprinkle icing sugar on it.

'Right.' I swallow. 'Wow. Host Christmas. That's pretty scary!' I laugh to show I don't really mean it. (Although I half do.)

'You can do it, love.' Mum pats my hand confidently. 'Get a good turkey and you're halfway there. I've invited Janice and Martin,' she adds, 'and Jess and Tom, of course. I mean, we're all family now, aren't we?'

'Right.' I take a gulp of G&T, trying to get my head round all this information. Jess and Tom are coming back, and we're hosting Christmas, and—

'Wait a minute.' My head jerks up as my thoughts rewind. 'So when you say you're offering Jess and Tom the house, do you mean you're having them to stay? Or . . .'

'We're moving out for a bit,' says Dad, his eyes twinkling. 'We're having an adventure, Becky.'

'*Another* adventure?' I say, and exchange looks with Luke. After our trip to the States, I would have thought my parents had had enough adventures to last them for ever.

'A change of scene.' Mum nods. 'We got back from America, and it made us think, love. We've lived in the same house for all these years. We haven't tried anything else. And Dad's always wanted to keep bees.'

'It's always been a little dream of mine,' says Dad, looking a bit embarrassed.

'If not now, then when?' chimes in Mum.

'Wow,' I say, digesting this. I mean, it's true: my

31

parents haven't really experimented much. Good for them, branching out. I can just see Dad pottering around in a little country cottage with a bee hive and an orchard. We can come to visit and Minnie can pick apples and I can buy a drifty linen 'apple-picking' skirt from the Toast catalogue . . .

Actually, I'm really into this idea.

'So where are you looking?' I ask. 'You could move to Letherby. There must be some cottages to rent. In fact, yes! There's a thatched cottage for rent on Suze's estate!' I almost choke with excitement as I suddenly remember. 'It's adorable. Move there!'

'Oh, love.' Mum exchanges amused looks with Dad. 'That's not really what we're after.'

'Letherby is suitable for you and Suze,' says Dad kindly. 'But we want somewhere with a bit more buzz. And I'm not talking about the bees!' He laughs at his own joke.

Buzz? My parents?

'So where are you moving to?' I say, baffled. 'Dorking?'

'Sweetheart!' Mum peals with laughter. 'Did you hear that, Graham? Dorking! No, love, London. Central London.'

'Not *central* London,' Dad immediately contradicts her. '*East* London.'

'Graham, you're talking nonsense. East London *is* central London these days. Isn't it, Becky?' Mum appeals to me.

'Dunno,' I say, perplexed. 'Where exactly are you talking about?'

'Well!' says Mum knowledgeably. 'It's this super little area. Very tucked away. We came across it when Dad was showing me where his old office used to be. It's called . . .' She pauses for effect. 'Shoreditch.'

Shoreditch? I gape at her, wondering if I've heard wrong. Shoreditch, as in . . .

Shoreditch?

'It's on the tube,' Mum is saying. 'Just a bit north of Liverpool Street. You'll be able to find us quite easily, love.'

'I know where it is,' I say, finding my voice. 'But Mum, you can't move to Shoreditch!'

'Why not?' Mum looks affronted.

'Because Shoreditch is for young people! It's where hipsters come from! It's all craft beer and sourdough bread. It's . . .' I whirl my hands hopelessly. 'Not you.'

'Well!' says Mum indignantly. 'Who says it's not us? I should say we'll fit in perfectly! Your father's very fond of beer.'

'It's just . . .' I try again. 'It has a vibe.'

'A "vibe"?' echoes Mum, rolling her eyes. 'What a lot of nonsense. Oh, Carlo, I'm sorry,' she adds to a hovering waiter. 'You'll have to give us a moment. And then you *must* tell us how your daughter's doing on her gap year.' She twinkles at Carlo, before taking a deep gulp of her drink and glaring at me huffily across the top of it.

'Look, Mum, of course you can live anywhere you like,' I backtrack. 'But don't you feel like you belong here?' I spread my arms around the cosy restaurant. 'You know all the waiters. You know their families. You know the Veal Marsala. Shoreditch is . . . Shoreditch.'

'Perhaps I don't want Veal Marsala any more,' says Dad suddenly. 'Perhaps I want . . .' He hesitates, then says self-consciously, 'smashed avocado.'

He lifts his chin almost defiantly, and I blink back at him. Dad wants smashed avocado?

'Avocado?' says Carlo, perking up. 'Avocado and prawns to start? And then the Veal Marsala?'

I'm aware of Luke stifling a laugh and shoot him a look, although to be truthful I feel a bit hysterical myself.

'Anyway, we've found an apartment,' says Mum defensively, 'and it's available immediately. It has lovely fitted blinds, Becky. All included.'

'Views over the city,' puts in Dad with satisfaction.

'And a "wet room",' says Mum proudly. 'So practical for the older person.'

'There's a cooperative bee hive on the roof,' adds Dad happily. 'And a hot tub!'

'Does it have off-street parking?' I can't resist asking, and Mum shakes her head pityingly.

'Love, don't be so suburban. We'll be using Uber!'

I don't know what to say. My parents are moving to Shoreditch. I'm actually a little envious, I suddenly realize. I wouldn't mind an apartment with a hot tub and views over the city.

'Well, bravo!' I lift my glass. 'Here's to a whole new lifestyle!'

'I think it's great,' says Luke warmly. 'Good for you, Graham and Jane. Can we come and visit you in your flash new pad?'

34

'Well, of course!' says Mum, whose indignation has already died away. 'We'll have a nice house-warming party with nibbles. It'll be super.' She beams around the table – then suddenly her gaze narrows. She peers at my chest intently for a few seconds, before looking up in astonishment.

'Becky, love! I've just noticed something! Your top matches the napkins!'

From: Jess Bertram
To: Becky
Subject: Christmas

Hi Becky

I gather you know the news of our return. We're really looking forward to coming back to the UK and seeing family. Your parents have been very generous with the offer of their house.

Also: thanks so much for hosting Christmas. We're really looking forward to it. Obviously we're hoping that it reflects our non-consumerist, sustainable values. I'm sure we'll have a lot of fun.

Jess

Hi Becky

Yes, I'm still vegan and Tom is, too.

Jess

From: Jess Bertram
To: Becky
Subject: Re: Re: Re: Re: Christmas

Hi Becky

No, we don't have a 'day off from being vegan' on Christmas Day as a 'little reward'.

As for presents, no, there is nothing I'm 'hankering after'. Tom and I will be exchanging non-tangible gifts in the spirit of creating a minimal footprint on our ravaged Earth.

If you can't shake off the pressure to buy pointless items simply to follow 'tradition', could I suggest that they are sustainable, non-consumerist, locally sourced presents that reflect the true principles of fellowship rather than the hollow pleasures of shopping?

Looking forward to a festive day.

Jess

THREE

As I arrive at school the next morning with Minnie, my head is in a whirl. Though I'm not sure whether my biggest preoccupation is that 1. Mum and Dad are moving to Shoreditch, or 2. I've got to host Christmas for the first time ever.

It's just one day of the year, I keep telling myself. It's no big deal. I mean, what's the worst that could happen? (Actually no. Let's not start that thought process.)

Anyway, it's fine, because I've already begun. I've looked on Pinterest and found a million lists on 'How to host Christmas'. I've ordered two tickets for the Christmas Style Fair in Olympia. I'll go with Mum and get some inspiration. Plus I'm going to start my Christmas shopping *now*. It's only November. There's loads of time!

I take Minnie into the cloakroom, help her hang her coat up, then head towards the classroom. At once I see Minnie's friend Eva, together with her mum, Petra – and my heart slightly sinks.

'Look!' exclaims Minnie, wide-eyed. 'Look at dah drum! It's 'normous!'

Petra is holding a massive tribal drum, made out of twigs and canvas and decorated with ribbons. Eva starts beating it with her hand while Petra beams smugly around and Minnie gawps. Did they *make* that?

I close my eyes briefly, then open them again. I love the village school, and I love Minnie's teacher, Miss Lucas, but does she *have* to be such a craft nut? She's always coming up with 'fun, optional activities' which aren't optional at all, because everyone does them. This weekend it was 'Make a musical instrument from items around the home'. I mean, *what*?

Minnie and I put some dried beans in an empty jar, and I thought we'd done really well – but this is on a whole other level.

'*Such* a fun activity,' Petra is gushing to Miss Lucas. 'The whole family got involved!'

'I'm so glad!' Miss Lucas beams. 'Creativity is *so* important. Minnie, did you make a musical instrument?'

'We made a shaker,' I say, trying to sound confident.

'Marvellous!' enthuses Miss Lucas. 'Can I see it?'

Oh God.

Reluctantly, I reach into Minnie's book bag and pull out the shaker. I was going to paint it or something, but I forgot, so it's basically a Clarins jar. I can see Petra's eyes widen, and Miss Lucas seems momentarily stumped, but I keep my chin high. She said 'items around the home', didn't she?

'Super!' says Miss Lucas at last. 'We'll put it next to Eva's drum in the display!'

Great. So Eva has a tribal drum and Minnie has a Clarins jar.

Thankfully Minnie doesn't seem to mind – but I'm feeling hot all over. Next time, I'll ace the craft project, I promise myself. I'll make something drop-dead amazing, even if it takes me all weekend.

'Bye, Minnie, darling.' I kiss her and she runs happily into the classroom.

'Tarkie, careful!' Suze's piercing voice makes us all turn and I gasp. What the *hell* has Suze got there? It's a complicated arrangement of tubing and funnels and duct tape, and it's taking both her and her husband Tarquin to carry it, while the children trail behind.

'Lady Cleath-Stuart!' exclaims Miss Lucas. 'Goodness!'

'It's a euphonium,' says Suze breathlessly. 'It plays three notes.'

Suze loves art and craft and she's always been brilliant at it. She's always getting her children to make papier mâché figures and pasta collages and leave them drying all over the kitchen. So I'm not surprised she can knock up a quick euphonium from household items.

'Suze!' I say. 'That's amazing!'

'Oh, it's nothing really,' says Suze modestly. 'Shall we carry it in? Tarkie, be careful round the corner . . .'

'Shit.' A low voice behind me distracts my attention. 'Shit, *shit*.'

I swivel away from watching Suze manhandling her homemade euphonium, to see a mum called Steph Richards peering in dismay out of the window at the road below. 'Bloody traffic warden's coming,' she says.

41

'There wasn't anywhere to park, I *had* to go on a zigzag. Harvey, darling, let's quickly get you into class.'

Her voice is strained, and her face is lined with worry. I don't know Steph very well, but I do know that she had Harvey on her fortieth birthday (she told us once at a parents' event). She has some monster job in Human Resources, is the major breadwinner of the family and always has a crease in her brow. She has a Yorkshire accent and once told me she grew up in Leeds but moved down for uni and never went back.

'Don't worry,' I say impulsively. 'I'll go and divert the traffic warden. Take your time with Harvey.'

I dash out of school and sprint along the street, which is always crowded with cars at drop-off time. I can see the traffic warden making his way along the road. And there's Steph's car, illegally parked.

She won't get a ticket, I vow. I won't let it happen.

'Hello! Officer!' Panting hard, I reach him when he's still three cars away from Steph's. 'I'm *so* glad you're here!'

'Yes?' The traffic warden gives me a discouraging look, which I ignore.

'I wanted to ask you about the rules for parking on Cedar Road,' I say brightly. 'If there's a double yellow line and there's a sign saying "No stopping between six and nine" but there's a white zigzag as *well* . . . what are the rules for motorbikes?'

'Huh?' The traffic warden peers at me.

'Also, what does "loading" actually *mean*?' I add, blinking innocently. 'Suppose I'm moving house and I've got six sofas to transport, and some really big pot plants – I mean, they're more like trees, really . . . what do I do?'

'Ah,' says the traffic warden. 'Well, if you're moving house, you may need a permit.'

I can see Steph hastening along the street, clicking in her businessy heels. She passes me, but I don't flicker.

'A permit,' I echo, as though fascinated by every word he's saying. 'I see. A permit. And where would I apply for that?'

She's reached her car. She's bleeping it open. She's safe.

'Or, actually, you know what?' I add, before the traffic warden can reply. 'Maybe I'll just look online.' I beam at him. 'Thank you *so* much.'

I watch as Steph pulls out of the dodgy parking space, drives along a few metres, then draws up alongside me on a newly vacated spot, her engine running.

'Thanks,' she says out of her window, with a wry grin. She's really thin, Steph, with dark hair and the kind of translucent skin that gives away when you're exhausted. Which I'm guessing she is from the shadows beneath her eyes. Also, her foundation needs blending in at the jawline, but I don't like to say so.

'No problem,' I say. 'Any time.'

'Mornings are a nightmare.' She shakes her head. 'And it doesn't help with half the mums turning up with the bloody London Symphony Orchestra. I know Suze Cleath-Stuart is your friend, but a *euphonium*?'

I can't help laughing – then immediately feel disloyal to Suze.

'You know what "instrument" I made with Harvey?'

Steph continues. 'A margarine tub and a wooden spoon to hit it.'

'We filled a jar with beans,' I volunteer. 'I didn't even paint it.' I meet her eyes and we both smile – then, to my dismay, Steph's eyes suddenly fill with tears.

'Steph!' I exclaim in horror. 'It's only art and craft. It doesn't *matter*.'

'It's not that. It's : . .' She hesitates, and I can see the distress pushing at her face, as though it wants to burst out. 'Harvey doesn't know, OK?' she continues in a low, trembling voice, her eyes flitting around. 'But Damian's left us. Three days ago. Walked out, no warning. Harvey thinks he's gone on holiday.'

'*No.*' I stare at her, aghast. I don't really know Steph's husband, Damian, but I've seen him with Harvey a couple of times, so I can picture him. He's older than Steph – a paunchy guy with close-set eyes and a grey beard.

'Yes. Sorry,' she adds. 'Didn't mean to land that on you. Not what you expect on the school run.'

'It's not . . . You didn't . . .' I flounder desperately. 'Do you want to talk? Go for coffee? Is there anything I can do to help?' But Steph's shaking her head.

'I've got to go. Big meeting. And you already did help, Becky. Thanks again.' She gives me a wan smile, then puts her car into gear.

'Wait,' I say before I can stop myself. I grab a tissue from my bag, lean into the car and blend her foundation. 'Sorry,' I add. 'I just had to.'

'No. Thanks.' She shoots a wry look at her reflection in the mirror. 'Make-up's not top of my agenda right now.' She hesitates, then adds, 'Could you keep it to yourself? About Damian, I mean. You know what school gossip's like . . .'

'Of course,' I say fervently. 'I won't tell a soul.'

'Thanks. See you, Becky.'

She drives away and I watch her, feeling as if I'd quite like to bash her husband's head, hard. I think I'd do a pretty good job of it and I even know what I'd use: my new Zara bag. It's got really sharp corners.

As I arrive at work I'm longing to share Steph's awful news with Suze, but I promised I wouldn't. And anyway, Suze isn't here yet. So instead, I quickly scroll through my emails, feeling a tad wary as I see the ones from Jess, headlined *Christmas – a few more points*.

I don't know why I'm wary, really. Jess and I have exchanged some friendly emails and she's already said she appreciated that we weren't vegan and understood if we wanted to eat a turkey on Christmas Day. (Although on another level she didn't understand it at all and never would.)

But it's also become increasingly clear that she thinks tinsel is evil and glitter is monstrous and fairy lights are the work of the devil. How are we going to decorate the Christmas tree? And what about Mum's light-up plastic reindeer?

I love and admire my sister Jess with all my heart. She's steadfast and honest and she only wants to do good for the world. When she's not researching rocks in Chile, she's always off volunteering for really unglamorous charities, like she once spent a whole week digging latrines. (When I exclaimed, 'Oh my God, Jess!' she just looked puzzled at my shock and said, 'Someone's got to do it.')

She's kind of serious, but when she cracks a smile you feel like she's made your day. Basically, she's awesome. It's just that I do find it a *tiny* bit hard to live up to her principles.

Anyway, it'll be fine, I tell myself yet again. It's only Christmas. It'll work itself out.

Putting my phone away, I head into the Letherby Hall Gift Shop and glance around, checking that everything looks OK. We sell clothes, cushions, greetings cards, boxes of toffees . . . a bit of everything. It's fairly random really, but I've been trying to organize it into themes and displays, and I'm really proud of my *'hygge'* table. It has blankets, scented candles, tins of hot chocolate, Letherby organic cotton pyjamas and some alpaca hoodies in a lovely soft grey.

I pause to tweak the display lovingly, then look up to see Suze striding in, in a pale blue Letherby tweed mini skirt which looks *amazing* on her. (It was my idea that we should all wear the merchandise. Mainly because if anyone can make a tweed skirt look hot, it's Suze.)

'Hi!' I say. 'Amazing euphonium!'

'Oh, thanks!' Suze's face brightens. 'Don't you love Miss Lucas? She has such wonderful ideas for craft projects!'

'I suppose,' I say reluctantly. 'Although there are quite a *lot* of craft projects, don't you think?'

'But they're such fun!' enthuses Suze. 'I should have been a primary school teacher. I love all that stuff.'

She unlocks the till and neatens a pile of leaflets on local walks. Then she clears her throat. As I look up I notice her long legs are twisted around each other. In fact, she looks really awkward. What on earth is up?

'By the way, Bex,' she adds in a super-casual voice, 'I'll take the statues, after all.'

'What?' I stare at her.

'I'll take the statues. We'll have them here.'

'You'll *take* them?' I say in astonishment. 'Just like that?'

'Yes!' she says evasively. 'Why not? It's no big deal.'

'Suze,' I say, narrowing my eyes. 'What do you want?'

'Why would I *want* something?' she retorts hotly. 'God, Bex, you're so suspicious! I'm just volunteering to take your statues. I went to have another look at them, and I thought, "Actually, they're quite impressive."'

'No you didn't!' I retort disbelievingly. 'You're softening me up to ask me a favour.'

'No I'm not!' Suze turns bright pink.

'Yes you are.'

'OK!' She suddenly cracks. 'I am! Bex, you have to ask us for Christmas. Tarkie's Uncle Rufus has invited us to his castle in Scotland and I just can't do it. I can't!'

She looks so despairing, I stare at her.

'What's wrong with Tarkie's Uncle Rufus? It can't be that bad, surely?'

'It's *awful*,' says Suze desperately. 'He doesn't believe in heating and his housekeeper runs freezing cold baths for everyone each morning and there's no cornflakes for breakfast, only haggis, and all the children have to peel potatoes all day.'

'The *children*?'

'He thinks it's good for them. He brings in extra potatoes for them to do and if they leave any peel on he shouts at them.'

'Wow.'

'Exactly! And he phoned last night to invite us. My parents are going to be in Namibia, so he knew we weren't going to theirs, and I didn't know *what* to do. So I said, "Gosh, Uncle Rufus, that sounds lovely, but actually, my friend Becky's mother has already invited us for Christmas Day." You don't have to actually *have* us,' she adds hurriedly. 'Just be our excuse. And I'll take the statues,' she finishes breathlessly.

'Actually, Mum's not hosting Christmas this year,' I inform her.

'Oh God.' Suze's face falls. '*Don't* tell me you're going away or something. Can I still tell Uncle Rufus we're spending it with you?'

'Even better, you can *actually* spend it with us!' I say with a flourish. 'Because guess what? *I'm* hosting Christmas!'

'*You're* hosting Christmas?' Suze's face freezes in a stunned rictus.

'Don't look like that!' I say crossly. 'It'll be great!'

'Of course it will!' Suze hastily recovers herself. 'Sorry, Bex. I was just a bit . . . surprised. Because you're not exactly . . .'

'What?' I say suspiciously. 'I've hosted parties, haven't I? And they haven't turned into fiascos, have they?'

Actually, now I think about it, most *have* turned into

some sort of fiasco. But still, Suze doesn't need to look like that.

'Nothing!' Suze backtracks. 'It'll be lovely! You'll do it brilliantly! But how come your parents aren't hosting?'

'OK, get this,' I say with relish, because I've been longing to share this news with Suze. 'Jess and Tom are coming back to the UK for a bit!'

'Wow!' says Suze in excitement. 'Does this mean their adoption's gone through?'

'No,' I say, temporarily halted. 'Not yet. Although it won't be that much longer,' I add, determined to be positive. 'I'm sure of it. Anyway, they're going to live in Mum and Dad's house while they're here . . . and my parents are moving to a flat in Shoreditch!'

'Shoreditch?' Suze's eyes widen in shock. 'Your mum and dad?'

'I know! I said, "Why Shoreditch?" and Dad says he wants smashed avocado.'

'Smashed avocado?' Suze looks so gobsmacked, I can't help giggling. 'Does he know you can get avocados in Waitrose in Cobham?' she adds earnestly, and that sets me off again.

'Good morning, girls!' Irene, our other sales assistant, comes bustling up, dressed in Letherby tweed trousers and a merino wool jumper.

Irene is in her sixties and very sweet. She's worked for the gift shop ever since it was basically just a cupboard with a few boxes of fudge, and she still remembers 'mad' Lord Cleath-Stuart, who was Tarkie's great-great-uncle and commissioned the pink-tiled hall with the erotic murals that no one ever mentions.

'Good morning, Irene!' Suze greets her. 'How were things in the shop yesterday?'

'Very good,' says Irene, nodding. 'Nothing to report. Oh, except that a customer asked me to say hello to you, Becky.'

'To *me*?' I say in surprise. Usually it's old family friends of Suze's, called things like Huffy Thistleton-Pitt, who pop in to say hello.

'He said he understood that you worked here and seemed very disappointed not to see you,' Irene nods. 'Asked me to pass on his regards. What was his name now?' Her brow crumples deeply. 'Arnold? I wrote it down somewhere, I wonder where . . .'

'Arnold?' I frown. I don't know anyone called Arnold.

'Arnold was the *surname*. Or was it Irwin?' she adds thoughtfully.

'Irwin?' I shake my head. 'Doesn't ring a bell.'

'He was a young chap,' Irene elaborates. 'Your sort of age. Striking.' She looks at me expectantly, as though I'll say, 'Oh, the striking guy. Of course, *him*.'

'Well, let me know if you remember,' I say kindly. 'If not, no worries.'

Irene wanders off again and Suze grins. 'A striking guy, huh, Bex?'

'I wouldn't trust Irene's taste,' I retort, rolling my eyes. 'It was probably my old geography teacher.'

'Was he striking?'

'His dandruff was pretty striking,' I say, and we both start giggling again.

'So anyway,' says Suze, composing herself. 'We didn't finish talking about Christmas. Tell me what I can do to help. Let me know the plan. Except we *must* go to the morning service at St Christopher's,' she adds, 'because the vicar's written a special Christmas carol medley and he's really proud of it. Can that fit in your plan of the day?'

'Of course!' I say. 'Definitely! I mean, I haven't exactly *got* a plan of the day yet,' I add, feeling the need to be honest. 'Or any kind of plan. But it's early days.'

'Oh, totally,' Suze agrees at once. 'The most important thing when you host Christmas is, have enough booze.'

'Mum said the most important thing was the turkey,' I counter, already feeling a bit anxious.

'Oh, well, the *turkey*,' says Suze airily. 'The turkey goes without saying – wait.' She interrupts herself, suddenly looking stricken. 'If Jess is coming, do we all have to be vegan?'

'No, it's fine, we can eat turkey,' I reassure her. 'And I'll buy Jess and Tom a vegan turkey.'

'A vegan turkey?' Suze goggles at me. 'Does that exist?'

'I bet it does,' I say confidently. 'There's vegan everything. Oh, and by the way, Jess thinks we should give each other sustainable, non-consumerist, locally sourced presents that reflect the true spirit of fellowship rather than the hollow pleasures of shopping.'

'Right.' Suze stares at me, looking a bit shaken. 'Wow. I mean . . . good point. Definitely. We should only buy local things. It's, like, vital for the planet.'

'Absolutely.'

'Totally.'

Silence falls between us and I feel like we're both re-appraising our Christmas lists.

'I mean . . . Harvey Nichols is *quite* local, isn't it?' says Suze at last. 'Compared to some places.'

'Compared to, like . . . Australia.'

'Exactly!' Suze looks relieved. 'I mean, some people go on ridiculous shopping trips. My cousin Fenella once went on a Christmas shopping trip to New York.'

'That's so un-green,' I can't help saying a little censoriously. 'Let's agree, we'll only shop locally at, you know, Selfridges and Liberty and places.'

'OK,' says Suze, nodding earnestly. 'We'll do that. Only local shopping. Ooh, what are you going to get Luke?' she adds. 'Have you got any ideas?'

'I'm sorted,' I say, a little smugly.

'*Already?*' Suze stares at me.

'Well, I haven't actually bought it yet,' I admit, 'but I know exactly what I'm getting him. We were in Hector Goode and we saw this lovely coat and Luke said he liked it. So I said, "Well, maybe a little elf will get it for you!"'

'Lucky thing,' says Suze enviously. 'I have *no* idea what I'm going to get Tarkie! Why haven't you bought it yet?'

'I wanted to see if it was going to be reduced,' I explain. 'But the shop people won't tell me. They're *so* unhelpful.'

'*So* unhelpful,' agrees Suze sympathetically. 'What about waiting till Black Friday?'

'It might sell out. So I've decided I'll order it tonight—' I stop mid-stream as two women in Puffa jackets enter the gift shop and approach them, smiling. 'Hello! Welcome to the Letherby Hall Gift Shop. Can I help, or are you happy to browse?'

The pair of them totally ignore me. A lot of people do that, I've noticed, but I always just smile even more brightly.

'*Hygge*,' says one, looking dubiously at the sign. 'What's that?'

'Oh, I've heard of that,' chimes in her friend. 'Only, isn't it all nonsense?'

Nonsense? I gaze at her, feeling insulted. How dare she call my lovely table nonsense?

'*Hygge* is a Scandinavian word,' I explain as charmingly as I can. 'It means cosiness and warmth ... friendship over the cold winter ... lighting lots of candles and making yourself feel good. Like Christmas,' I add, suddenly resolving to host a totally *hygge* Christmas. God, yes. I'll have a million candles and woolly throws and warming glasses of glogg. (Glug? Glygge?)

As the women walk away I start making a mental list – *candles, throws, glogg* – then realize I really need to start writing this stuff down. I'll buy a special Christmas-planning notebook, I decide. And a gorgeous new festive pen. Yes. And *then* it will all fall into place.

FOUR

That evening I sit down on the sofa with my brand-new Christmas-planning notebook and pen. (Both from the Letherby leather range, 15 per cent staff discount.) Minnie's quietly playing with her tea set before bed, so I've got time to start on my master list.

I write down *Christmas* on the first page and look at it with satisfaction. There. Started. People get in such a flap about Christmas, and there's no need. It's simply a matter of itemizing the tasks you need to do, calmly completing them and ticking them off. Exactly.

Briskly I write down: *Buy vegan turkey.*

Then I stare at the page. Where am I going to find a vegan turkey?

OK, maybe I'm doing this wrong. Maybe what I need to start with is a very simple task which I can accomplish straight away. I write down *Buy Luke's present*, and open my laptop. I'll order it in two minutes, tick it off, and I'll be on the way.

I find the web page for the coat and squint at the

photos. It's lovely. It's perfect! It comes in navy and grey, I notice. Which would Luke prefer? I try to imagine him in the navy one . . . then the grey one . . . then the navy one again . . .

'Hi, sweetheart.' As I hear Luke's voice, I put an arm across the screen, look up – and freeze. Luke's standing in front of me, in exactly the same navy coat that's on my screen. How did that happen? Did I somehow will it into being? Am I *psychic*? I suddenly feel like I'm in one of those films with tinkly wind chimes and weird stuff going on.

'Are you OK, Becky?' he says, surveying me curiously.

'Luke . . .' I falter. 'Where did you get that coat?'

If he says, 'But I've always had it, darling,' in a toneless voice, I will seriously freak out.

'I bought it today.' He swings it around. 'Nice, isn't it? I'll take it to Madrid the day after tomorrow.'

'You bought it *today*? But . . .'

My shock has been replaced by indignation. Luke bought it for *himself*? How could he? No one should ever buy anything for themselves in November or December, *just in case*.

'What?' says Luke, looking puzzled.

'That was going to be your Christmas present!' I say reproachfully. 'You knew it was.'

'No I didn't.'

'Yes you did! We saw it in Hector Goode a month ago, remember?'

'Of course I remember.' Luke peers at me as though I'm mad. 'That's why I went back to buy it.'

'But I told you I was going to get it for you for Christmas!' I erupt in frustration. 'You should have *waited*!'

55

'Becky, I remember our conversation very well,' says Luke calmly. 'You didn't mention Christmas presents once.'

Honestly. Luke is so *literal*. It's a major character flaw of his, actually. I often tell him so.

'I was subtle! I said, "Well, maybe a little elf will get it for you"! What did you *think* I meant by "a little elf"?'

'Look, Becky,' says Luke, looking amused. 'Don't fret. This can still be my Christmas present. I love it. Thank you very much.' He drops a kiss on my head, then heads to the door, but I'm not mollified.

'You can't have your Christmas present in November,' I call after him. 'You have to have something to open on Christmas Day.'

'Get me some aftershave,' says Luke over his shoulder.

Aftershave? Is he for real? *Aftershave?* Aftershave is the most unimaginative present for a man you could ever choose out of a 'Presents for Dad' catalogue full of golf tees and bad ties.

On the other hand . . . it's quite easy.

I turn to my Christmas planner and after *Buy Luke's present* I add *Aftershave*. But I won't get the same one he always uses, I decide as I write. Ha. I'll get a fab new surprise aftershave.

Then I turn my attention to Minnie, who's playing by the fireplace with her adorable little tea set. She's handing out cups to all her teddies and pouring out 'tea' from the dinky teapot.

'Minnie, poppet,' I say. 'It's going to be Christmas before too long, and maybe, if you're good, Father

Christmas will bring you a present! What d'you think you would like?'

'I would like . . .' replies Minnie, still engrossed in her tea party, '. . . a hamper. Please,' she adds as an afterthought. '*Pleeeeeease* I want a hamper.'

I stare at her, puzzled. A *hamper*? Like . . . a Fortnum's hamper full of smoked salmon? A laundry hamper?

Then my eye falls on the tea-set box, which advertises other products in the range. Of course! She's been begging me for ages to buy the full picnic hamper with plastic glasses and napkins and pretend food. Well, that's easy enough.

I quickly log on to the website where we got the tea set and search 'picnic hamper'. It's gorgeous, with a gingham lining and little knives and forks and even a sweet little vase of plastic flowers. There are only five left in stock, so thank God I asked her about this early enough. Plus my details are already stored on the site, so it takes me a minute to buy it. Done!

As the email arrives in my in-box – *Confirmation of your order* – I feel a jab of pride. I've started Christmas shopping! I grab my Christmas planner, write *Get Minnie present*, and tick it off. Ha! I'm so on top of things. I just need to continue like this, in a calm, orderly way.

Except, of course, as soon as you want to be calm and orderly, life decides to trip you up. By 7.30 a.m. the next morning, I'm not remotely calm *or* orderly. I'm rushing hectically round the house, helping Luke look for a vital set of papers that he needs for a meeting and has gone 'missing'.

'Did you put them in here?' he says, yanking out the drawer of the dresser in the hall.

Immediately I bristle. Why's he blaming me? Why would I put some boring old set of papers anywhere?

'No,' I say politely. 'I didn't.'

'What about in here?' He reaches for the cupboard doors of the dresser. 'What do we keep in here, anyway?' As he speaks, he opens a door and a deluge of canvas bags falls out.

'That's nothing,' I say hastily, rushing forward to stop him, but it's too late. Damn.

'What on earth is this?' says Luke incredulously, looking at the mountain of bags at his feet.

'Just . . . er . . . some bags,' I say.

'What bags?'

'Bags! You know, bags! Maybe your papers are in the kitchen. Let's go and look.'

I'm trying to hurry him away, but Luke doesn't move. He stares at the massive, tangled pile of bags for a moment, then starts pulling them apart and reading the slogans on them.

'Bag for Life. Bag for Life. Tote for Life. Greener Bag. Tesco. Waitrose . . . Becky, what the *hell*?'

OK. So the truth is, I do sometimes buy a Bag for Life and then forget to take it out with me next time and have to buy another one. Which is not ideal, because I've ended up with a cupboardful.

But I've often found with Luke that attack is the best form of defence.

'I try to buy bags for life,' I inform him loftily, 'because I'm a responsible consumer and I've given up on plastic

58

bags. But you're suggesting I should use plastic bags instead and choke the oceans? Well, that's an interesting insight into your moral compass, Luke. Very interesting.'

Luke's mouth twitches and I lift my chin defiantly.

'I'm not saying you should use plastic,' he says calmly. 'I'm suggesting you use one bag, for life. The clue's in the name, my love. "Bag for *life*", not "Bag for one use, then stuff it in a cupboard and buy another one".'

He opens the other dresser door, and an even bigger mountain of totes falls out. Shit. I was hoping he wouldn't see those.

'Oh my *God*,' he says, looking genuinely appalled. 'Becky, how many bloody "bags for life" do you need? How long are you planning to live?'

'They'll come in handy one day,' I say defensively. 'Anyway, you haven't found your papers. You're just procrastinating.'

At that moment, Minnie comes into the hall, pushing her dollies' Moses basket on wheels. Luke glances down at it, then does a double-take.

'There they are!' he exclaims, and grabs a stash of papers out of the Moses basket.

'That is miiine, Daddy!' says Minnie crossly, trying to snatch them back. 'It is for my *barkit*.'

'Barkit' is Minnie-talk for 'basket'. And yes, I know we ought to correct her pronunciation, but it's so *sweet*. I mean, she can talk. She's perfectly articulate for her age (Miss Lucas said so when I consulted her). It's just that she misfires on a few words, like 'monter' and 'barkit' and 'raffodils' for 'daffodils'.

'They're not for your barkit, poppet,' says Luke to

59

Minnie. 'They're important papers for Daddy. Here you are.' He tucks a Bag for Life around Minnie's doll Speaky, in the Moses basket. 'And there's plenty more of them.' He kisses Minnie's head, then straightens up. 'So I'm picking up Minnie from Suze's?'

'If that's still all right.' I nod. 'I'll head into town straight after work. I'd better crack on with the Christmas shopping.' I heave a slightly brow-beaten sigh. 'It's quite a tall order, hosting Christmas, you know.'

'I know,' says Luke, looking suddenly concerned. 'Becky, I'm really willing to help. I have to travel a fair bit before Christmas – but just give me jobs to do and I'll do them.'

'OK.' I nod. As he kisses me, his top lip feels a bit prickly and I blink in surprise. 'Haven't you shaved today?'

'Oh,' says Luke, looking a bit self-conscious. 'Ah. I'm growing a moustache.'

'A *moustache*?' I stare at him.

'You know, for Movember,' he explains. 'For charity.'

'Right!' I quickly plaster on a smile. 'Of course. Good for you!'

I'm not massively keen on moustaches, truth be told. But doing it for charity is really worthwhile, so I must be supportive. 'It looks great already,' I add encouragingly, and kiss him again. 'It really suits you. See you later!'

'Have fun shopping,' Luke replies, and I stare at him, a bit offended. Wasn't he listening?

'I'm not shopping, I'm *Christmas shopping*. It's totally different. It's *work*. I have a list *this* long.' I make a dramatic gesture. 'Presents, decorations, food items, extras . . .'

'Extras?' Luke crinkles his brow 'What are extras?'

'They're extras! You know. *Extras.*'

I can't actually think of any extras right now, but I know they exist, because every guide to hosting Christmas talks about 'all those last-minute extras'.

'But wait.' Luke suddenly frowns in memory. 'Becky, haven't you *done* your Christmas shopping? At that country fair in the summer? Yes! You bought five hand-made leather cushions and said they would be perfect for Christmas presents. Bloody heavy cushions,' he adds with a grimace. 'I lugged them around all that day. Where are they?'

My face has gone hot. I'd kind of hoped he'd forgotten about those.

'We were asked for items for the school bring-and-buy sale.' I try to sound casual. 'So I donated them. I thought it was the right thing to do.'

'You just gave them all away?' He stares at me.

'It's a good cause!' I say defensively.

I won't add, 'Also, I realized they were rubbish cushions when I tried to put them on the sofa and they all slid off.'

It was all the stall-holder's fault for having such a nice face. He lured me into buying his stupid cushions, *and* a leather elephant.

'Well, look . . . couldn't we do all this online?' suggests Luke. 'If we sit down together with a laptop we could blast through it. Or give me a task. I'll order decorations. Take me five minutes.'

Luke? Order decorations? Is he mad? Last time he ordered decorations he got six vile purple baubles and then, when I complained, he said, 'Well, I think they look nice.'

'No, it's OK,' I say swiftly. 'I need to see them properly, in a shop. And anyway, we need to support the British high street.'

'Well, couldn't you go somewhere closer than Selfridges?'

'I don't mind.' I give a slightly martyred sigh. 'Someone's got to put the effort in. See you later.'

FIVE

Oh my *God*, I've missed shopping. And London. And all of it.

As I push my way in through the heavy doors of Selfridges, a Letherby Hall Gift Shop tote bag slung over my shoulder, I feel dazzled. Selfridges is so *twinkly*! It might only be November but the festive season has truly arrived. There are Christmas lights and garlands everywhere. There are huge red baubles decorating the escalators. Carols are playing and the air is warm and scented and I don't know where to start. I'm feeling a mixture of euphoria and panic, almost. Where do I go? Up? Down? I haven't been shopping for *ages*.

I mean, I've shopped online, obviously. But that's a whole different activity. In fact, I think they should invent a different word for it. Online ordering isn't really shopping, it's *procuring*. You *procure* stuff online. But you don't get the buzz of actually stepping into a shop and seeing all the gorgeous stuff, feeling it, stroking it, being seduced by it.

I take a step forward, just breathing in the atmosphere. Living out of London is fab in many ways – but I do miss this. I miss passing shiny exciting window displays every day. I miss stopping to stare at an awesome Chanel jacket. I miss ducking into Anthropologie on the way somewhere and deciding to see what's new in Zara, and finding a bargain in Topshop.

On the other hand, it's forced me to be efficient. The thing about living out of London is, you have to make the most of every trip in. You basically have to rush around and buy everything you can think of, because who knows when you'll be in town again?

Luke and I don't exactly agree on this theory. But then that's no surprise, as we don't agree on the meaning of 'efficient'. Luke once said that buying the entire stock of TK Maxx's discount Clarins range wasn't 'efficient', it was 'ridiculous'. But he knows nothing. Doesn't he understand how much money I saved? And time! That's all my skincare needs sorted out, practically for my whole life. And it only takes up two boxes in the garage. Hardly anything.

(The only tiny issue – which I haven't mentioned to Luke because he doesn't need to know every little detail of my life – is that when I was putting them in the garage, I came across a box full of pots of discounted L'Oréal moisturizer that I'd forgotten about. But that's OK, because you can't have too much moisturizer. It's a staple item.)

I suddenly realize I'm standing motionless in the Selfridges perfume hall, and give myself a little mental shake. Come on, Becky. Focus. Christmas shopping. I get out my 'to-do' book and look down the list – and at once feel daunted. I got slightly carried away last night, writing down ideas. There are about a hundred entries, from 'New fairy lights that don't buzz' to 'Festive place mats?' to 'CHOCOLATE!!!'

Where do I start?

A man with a massive bushy moustache passes by and I find myself distracted by the sight of him. What if Luke grows a moustache like that?

No. He won't. Don't be stupid. And anyway, it's for charity. I must be positive. I take another step forward, trying to focus. Come on. I'm in the perfume hall. I'll find Luke an aftershave. Yes. Good plan.

There's a guy dressed in black nearby promoting some new men's fragrance called Granite. I take a cardboard slip from him – but the smell makes me choke. It's a real mystery to me, the way so many expensive perfumes in this world are vile. Most of them smell as if someone just mixed together all the scents that no one buys, shoved the mixture in a new bottle and gave it a new name like Celebrity Pow!

Luke has always worn Armani aftershave, but I want to get him something *different*. I'll head to Prada, I decide, glimpsing the counter in the distance. You can't go wrong with Prada, can you?

But after three minutes at the counter, I'm feeling even more bewildered. There's so much *choice*. I sniff at L'Homme Prada, and Luna Rossa, and Marienbad. Then I go back to L'Homme Prada – and a nice man behind the counter called Erik starts spraying samples on card strips for me to smell.

But by the time I've got eight strips lined up in front of me, I've lost track. Erik keeps talking about amber notes and hints of leather, and I keep saying, 'Oh yes,' but truthfully it all just smells like aftershave.

'Could you spray this one again?' I say, gesturing at Desert Serenade. 'In fact, could you spray them all again? And is there one that's a bit like Babylon but not quite so . . .' I wave my hands vaguely.

'Excuse me.' A deep voice interrupts me and I turn to see a guy in a grey coat and blue scarf frowning at me impatiently. 'Are you going to take all day?'

'I'm buying aftershave for my husband,' I explain, as Erik starts spraying all my strips again.

'Well, could you please just hurry up and buy it?'

'No, I couldn't "just hurry up and buy it"!' I retort, nettled by his tone. 'I need to choose the right one.' I sniff Desert Serenade again and wince. 'No. Definitely not.'

'Oh, you're one of *those*,' says the man with a dismissive eye-roll, and I glare at him indignantly.

'What do you mean "one of *those*"?'

'Girls who insist on choosing new aftershaves for their blokes for Christmas.'

'My husband *asked* me to buy him aftershave for Christmas, actually,' I say coldly. 'Not that it's any of your business.'

'Maybe he did,' replies the man, unmoved. 'But he meant, "Buy me the aftershave I always wear."'

'No he didn't.'

'Yes he did.'

'You don't even know my husband!' I glower at him.

'I don't need to. No one in the history of mankind

has ever successfully chosen a scent for another person. L'Homme Prada Intense, please, 100ml,' he adds to Erik. 'I'll pay over there.'

Erik hands him the glossy box and the guy walks off, saying 'Have a good Christmas' over his shoulder.

Hmph. People are so rude. I turn my attention back to Erik and smile at him. *He* understands me, at least.

'I've narrowed it down,' I say, waving three strips of card at him. 'These are my options.'

'Great!' enthuses Erik. 'Good choices! I'm sure he'll love them!' He looks at the strips of card, then adds helpfully, 'So you should really try them out on his skin? Because it's all about body chemistry?'

Oh, for God's sake. *Now* he says this? What if they all smell totally vile on Luke's skin and make him gag? Or make me gag?

I hate to admit it, but Annoying Mr Blue Scarf has a point. Giving aftershave isn't the easy option after all. It's the impossible option. Either you buy an old favourite which requires no effort and is really lame. Or you go out on a limb and choose something new which he probably hates but has to say he likes. And your whole life you don't know if he was just being polite, until on his deathbed he suddenly croaks, 'I always hated L'Homme Prada!' and conks out.

(You know. Worst-case scenario.)

'Did you want to make a purchase?' Erik interrupts my thoughts, and I blink at him. I don't want to buy an expensive mistake, but I don't want to give up, either.

At that moment, Annoying Mr Blue Scarf walks past, towards the exit, and shoots me a sardonic grin.

'Still at it?' he says. 'You should have a coffee break.'

'Some people are happy to go the extra mile for their husband's Christmas present,' I reply frostily.

He raises his eyebrows, looking amused, and heads out of the door. I watch him go, feeling a bit ruffled – but the little exchange has only fuelled my determination. I *can* blow Luke away with a perfect new aftershave. I just need to be scientific.

'So, I was wondering,' I say, flashing my most charming smile at Erik. 'Do you have any little sample bottles?'

As I let myself into our house, three hours later, I feel a quiet pride. No one can say I wasn't thorough. I smelled every single aftershave in that bloody place and now my Letherby Hall Gift Shop tote contains thirty-one sample bottles of aftershave, which I must hide from Luke. I must also hide the big glossy Selfridges shopping bag slung over my—

Oh. Too late. Here he is.

'How did you do?' he says, coming forward with a sympathetic smile. 'You look exhausted!'

'I'm OK,' I say bravely. 'Not bad.'

'Let me take that for you.' Luke reaches for the Selfridges carrier. 'What's in there? Decorations? Presents?'

'Oh, um, just Christmas stuff,' I say in vague tones, holding tightly on to it. 'I'll put it away.'

Before he can quiz me any more, I hurry up the stairs.

'So, did you tick a lot of items off your list?' Luke's voice follows me. 'Did you make good progress?'

'Er . . . kind of!' I throw over my shoulder. I hurry

into our bedroom and shut the door. I dump the bag of aftershave samples on the bed, then turn to the glossy carrier. I survey it for a moment, then reverently pull out a tissue-wrapped package. As I rip the tissue off, I hear myself inhale deeply. I can't quite believe what I'm holding. An Alexander McQueen dress, 70 per cent reduced just because it has a pulled thread on the back! I'm going to look awesome on Christmas Day!

And OK. So I know 'Buy new dress' wasn't on my original to-do list. But everyone knows the key to successful shopping is being flexible and spotting opportunities. I was heading towards the Christmas department, absolutely intending to buy decorations, when I happened to pass through the fashion department. And I happened to see a discounted designer rail, where the most amazing Alexander McQueen dress was waiting for me. It's got gorgeous ruffled sleeves and sequinned stripes and the only *slight* issue – teeny-weeny point – is that it's a bit too small for me.

Just a tad. A smidgen.

Here's the thing: it was the only one they had and it was 70 per cent off and I couldn't *bear* not to buy it. Plus, it's not like I can't get into it. It's just a bit . . . tight. But you don't need to breathe much on Christmas Day, do you? Or move your arms much. And I'll probably lose some weight before then.

Perhaps. Oh God . . .

I peer anxiously at the dress, which seems to be shrinking as I look at it. Even with the discount, it was expensive. I *can't* not fit into it on Christmas Day.

Maybe I should go on a health kick before Christmas, it occurs to me. Start exercising and drinking green juice or whatever. Then I'll lose weight and get into the dress – and the bonus is, I'll be healthy, too. Perfect!

I gaze at the dress lovingly for a few more seconds, then stash it away in the wardrobe and get my notebook out of my handbag. I write 'Buy new dress for Christmas Day' and tick it off with satisfaction.

Then I turn towards the bed and survey my bag of aftershave samples. I have a plan which will definitely work – it just requires Luke to fall asleep and stay asleep. I hide the bag in my bedside cabinet then head downstairs, trilling in my most innocent voice, 'Luke! I feel like celebrating! Let's have some more wine!'

Three hours later, I'm lying in bed, staring at the ceiling, seething with frustration. I never knew it took Luke so long to fall asleep. What's *wrong* with him?

I keep prodding him very subtly to see if he's dropped off, and he keeps saying 'Huh?' or 'What?' to which I say 'Sorry, just stretching!'

Finally he opens his eyes and says irritably, 'Becky, I've got an early flight to Madrid and I'm knackered. Could you stop doing bloody yoga in bed?'

So I leave off for a bit, silently drumming my fingers with impatience, until at last he genuinely seems to be asleep and doesn't even stir when I say urgently, 'Luke, I think I can hear a burglar!'

Then I worry that I really *can* hear a burglar, so I creep downstairs clutching a high-heeled shoe as a weapon, turn all the lights on, wander around, find no burglar, turn them off again, check on Minnie and come back to bed.

I feel pretty knackered myself by now. But I have a plan to execute. Silently I get the bag of aftershave samples out of the bedside cabinet and remove four tiny bottles. I spray a little of Royal Oud by Creed on Luke's neck, under his left ear. I dab the Luna Rossa by Prada under his right ear. Then I mark them both in discreet felt-tip L and R, so I won't lose track. I spray his right wrist with Quercus and his left wrist with Sartorial, and mark those Q and S. I inhale the scents in turn, and scribble scores in my book. So far, Sartorial is winning. It's gorgeous.

Luke is sleeping so peacefully, I think I can risk one more. So I take another sample called Pacific Lime out of the bag. I lean over to spray it discreetly on his chest – but just as I'm pressing the nozzle, a huge moth flies out of nowhere, making me shriek in shock and fling my arms up.

'Argh!' Luke sits bolt upright, clutching his eye. 'Becky! Are you OK? What happened?'

He's blinking at me, still half asleep. Suddenly I see that his eye is wet. Shit! I sprayed his eye with Pacific Lime! But maybe he won't notice.

'I'm fine,' I say breathlessly. 'Sorry. Just a moth.'

'Fuck. *Ow*. Something's up with my eye.' He's still clutching at his eye, which is starting to look red.

My heart is gripped with horror. Oh God, please don't say I've blinded my husband. I can see the *Daily World* headline: *Irony As Wife Blinds Husband In Bid For Perfect Present*.

'Let me get you a wet cloth,' I say desperately. 'Can you see? Is your vision blurred?'

I rush to the bathroom and bring back a dripping flannel. I hastily plaster it on to Luke's face and he curses.

'I'm all wet now!'

'Better safe than sorry,' I say, gazing anxiously at his eye. 'Is it feeling better? How many fingers am I holding up?'

'Four,' says Luke curtly, and my heart falls.

'Wrong!' I say in dismay. 'Oh my God, Luke, we need to get you to hospital!'

'I'm not wrong!' snaps Luke impatiently. 'One, two, three, four. Use your eyes.'

I peer at my own hand and suddenly realize I *am* holding up four fingers. Oh, right.

'I'm fine.' Luke blinks a few more times, then peers at me blearily. 'But what the hell *happened*? I was fast asleep.'

'A moth,' I say quickly. 'Just a moth.'

'A moth woke you up?' he says incredulously.

'Er . . . it was a really big moth. Why don't you go back to sleep?'

I'm hoping Luke might lie down again, but his gaze falls on his wrist. He stares at the Q for a few seconds, as though trying to make sense of it.

'Someone wrote Q on my wrist,' he says at last.

'Wow!' I say, trying to sound surprised. 'How weird. It was probably Minnie. Anyway, it's late . . .'

'And S on my other wrist,' says Luke. He suddenly gets out of bed and heads to the mirror. 'What the *fuck*?'

72

He's staring at the letters on his neck. A moment later he swivels round to survey the bed and I see his eyes fall on the pen, which I left right there on the duvet. I'm an *idiot*.

'Becky?' he says ominously.

'OK, it was me,' I admit in a rush. 'I was trying out aftershaves on you while you were asleep. For your Christmas present,' I add meaningfully, hoping his face might soften and he might say, 'Oh darling, you're so thoughtful.'

But he doesn't.

'It's one a.m.,' he says, with the air of someone trying to keep his temper under control. 'And I've got bloody *writing* all over me. I mean, did you think I wouldn't *notice*?'

'You always shower first thing.' I can't help sounding proud of my plan. 'And it's a washable pen. I knew it would all just come off and you'd never even realize.'

'Well, that's something,' grunts Luke, heading back to bed. Then he stops, his eyes focusing on the pen again. 'Wait. You used a Sharpie. That's permanent.'

'No it's not.'

'Yes it is!'

'Only the black ones are permanent,' I explain. 'I used a blue one.'

'The blue ones are permanent too!' Luke erupts. 'Look.' He grabs the pen and brandishes it at me, his finger jabbing at the word. '"Permanent".'

What?

I grab the pen from him and peer at it. Oh my God, he's right. It *is* permanent. I never knew that. I've been

73

using Sharpies all these years, and I never realized! That's quite funny, actually . . .

Then I look up and see Luke's expression and gulp. Maybe it's not that funny.

'I have L and R on my neck,' says Luke in an uber-calm voice. 'On the wrong sides. And tomorrow I'm meeting the finance minister of Spain.'

'Right. Sorry.' I swallow hard. 'Um . . . you could wear a cravat?'

Luke doesn't even bother to reply. (I mean, I don't blame him.)

'I'm really sorry,' I say again in my humblest voice. 'I just wanted to get you the perfect Christmas present. And since we're talking about it,' I add hopefully, 'do you prefer any of the aftershaves? I like the one on your left wrist.'

I look at him expectantly, but Luke makes no move to smell his left wrist.

'I like the aftershave I always wear,' he says. 'Shall we get some sleep?'

Search history

How long does it take to grow a moustache?
Most attractive moustaches
Moustaches bad for the health
Sex with moustache
Lose three stone by Christmas
Lose one stone by Christmas
Online personal trainer
Online personal trainer not bossy
Exercise wear
Sweaty Betty
Lululemon
Flattering leggings
Magic leggings
Drop two sizes with just leggings
Chocolate diet

SIX

The next morning, Luke is distinctly on the grouchy side. I say 'morning', but it's more like the middle of the night. I would have thought that being the boss of your own company would mean you *didn't* have to get up at silly o'clock to catch planes, but apparently it doesn't work like that.

I kiss him goodbye, wincing slightly at the furry texture of his new moustache. (It's for *charity*, I keep reminding myself.) I watch as his taxi pulls away and wave, trying to look as loving and apologetic as I can. Then I head into the kitchen and slump on a chair.

I feel fairly grouchy myself. I didn't get enough sleep either, and I feel awful that I nearly blinded Luke. The whole thing was a total disaster. I spent *ages* collecting all those aftershave samples – and all for nothing. Luke doesn't want a new aftershave. He wants the same old thing. It's totally against the spirit of Christmas! Imagine if Father Christmas opened his letters and they all said, 'Dear Santa, please give me the same old thing.' He'd go into a decline.

As I switch on the kettle, I remember that annoying guy in Selfridges, telling me that my husband didn't want a new aftershave. I hate that he was right – and I stand by my reply. Some people *are* happy to go the extra mile for their husband's Christmas present. So the coat didn't work out and the aftershave didn't work out. I'm undeterred. I feel all the more determined to find something that will make Luke's jaw drop.

(In a good way. Not because it's a purple mohair jacket. Although to be fair, I kept the receipt for that purple jacket, and I *still* think it suited him. It was all Mum's fault for exclaiming 'Dear God!' in such appalled tones when he tried it on. Sometimes I don't understand how I came from such a fashion-illiterate family, I really don't.)

As I drop Minnie at school I look around for Steph in case she wants a chat or anything – but I can't see her, so I head to work. I make myself a coffee, then lean against the cash desk, looking around the shop for present inspiration. But I've already given Luke the hip flask and the gentleman's handkerchief set and the caramel sea salt chocolate. (Well, OK, that was mostly for me.)

I heave a gusty sigh, cursing myself. I should never have bought him the hip flask. I should have mentally earmarked it for Christmas.

'Are you OK, Bex?' Suze comes up, peering at me in surprise.

'Didn't sleep very well,' I say morosely. 'Actually, Luke and I had a row.'

'What about?'

'Christmas presents and stuff,' I say vaguely.

I won't mention that I drew on Luke with a Sharpie, it sounds a bit weird.

'Oh, Christmas presents.' Suze rolls her eyes sympathetically. 'We had a row, too. Tarkie wants to give the children each a lamb but I want to get them a piglet. Who wants a lamb when they could have a piglet?' She looks at me expectantly.

'Er . . .' Personally, I wouldn't want either, but that's probably not the answer Suze is hoping for.

'Does Minnie want a piglet?' Suze's eyes suddenly light up. 'Shall I get her one too?'

A piglet? In our garden? Oinking everywhere and making a mess and growing into a massive hog? I love Suze to bits, but there are certain areas of life where we really don't see eye to eye.

'I don't *think* so,' I say carefully. 'She's not really a piglet girl. In fact, the only useful thing I've done so far for Christmas is buy Minnie's present,' I add. 'She's desperate for a picnic hamper, and I've already ordered it.'

I'm expecting Suze to exclaim 'Well done!' or ask to see it online, but instead she looks doubtful.

'You've ordered it already?'

'Yes. Why?'

'Hmm.' Suze twists her mouth up. 'Isn't that a bit early? What if she changes her mind?'

Changes her mind? That hadn't even *occurred* to me.

'She won't,' I say, more confidently than I feel. 'She's wanted that hamper for ages.' But Suze just shakes her head.

'They're totally fickle. I call it "the swerve". They say, "I really want a pogo stick, it's all I want, please, please,

78

please can I have a pogo stick?" Then, three days before Christmas, they go to a friend's house and see a talking mermaid on a TV ad and suddenly they want that instead. But it's already sold out,' she ends in gloomy satisfaction. 'So you have to find it on eBay at three times the price.'

'Minnie won't change her mind,' I insist. 'She loves that hamper.'

'You wait,' says Suze, sounding like a grizzled old fisherman predicting a storm. 'She'll see a talking mermaid on telly and the hamper will be toast.'

'Well, she's not *allowed* to see a talking mermaid,' I say crossly. 'I'm banning the telly until Christmas.'

'Yeah, right,' scoffs Suze. 'Are you going to move to an Amish village?'

I'm about to retort, 'Maybe!' and google Amish villages (*are* there any in Hampshire?) when Irene comes up, holding a piece of paper out to me.

'Oh, Becky!' she exclaims. 'Good news. I found the name of the young man who was asking after you.'

'The *striking* young man,' puts in Suze, grinning at me.

'Exactly.' Irene beams innocently. 'It was . . .' She reads off the piece of paper. 'Craig Curton.'

I stare at her, feeling a bit gobsmacked. Craig Curton?

'D'you know him, Bex?' says Suze with interest as Irene hands me the piece of paper.

'Actually, I do,' I say. 'Actually . . .' I hesitate. 'He's an old flame.'

'An old flame?' Suze stares at me, agog. 'I never heard about him! When was he?'

'Ages ago.' I make a brushing-away motion. 'At uni.'

I'd completely forgotten about Craig Curton. Or at

79

least, not *forgotten* about him exactly, but I can't say I've thought about him much.

'He's *very* striking, Becky dear,' puts in Irene, her eyes bright. '*Very* handsome.' She heads off to greet a customer and Suze grins wickedly at me.

'Irene's got the hots for your old boyfriend. Is he a super-model or something?'

'I think Irene must have quite low standards,' I say, giggling. 'He's actually a bit weird-looking. You know, dyed black hair and really pale and awful teeth. He was in a band,' I add hastily. 'That's why I went out with him.'

'Well, I'm googling him,' announces Suze, grinning. 'I have to see this Greek god for myself.'

'He's not a Greek god.' I roll my eyes. 'In fact, I don't know why I went out with him, even if he *was* in a band.'

I wait for Suze to reply but she's staring down at her phone, looking a bit stunned.

'You know what, Bex?' she says slowly. 'He *is* a bit of a Greek god. Unless it's a different guy. Is this him?'

She holds out her phone and I jolt in shock. That guy is gorgeous. That *can't* be Craig Curton.

I stare down at the image, trying to make sense of it. OK, I can just about see that it's Craig. An older Craig. But his hair, which used to be weird and shapeless, is now tumbling down to his shoulders in dark shiny waves. And his teeth have been done. And he's tanned. And look at those *arms*.

'He's amazing,' says Suze flatly.

'He's changed.' I find my voice. 'He's . . . he didn't look like that. Nothing like that.'

80

'What does he do?' Suze scrolls down the page, which is some kind of professional network. 'Musician,' she says, sounding a little awe-struck. 'His latest release is called "Love Underneath".'

'Really?' I try to grab for the phone, but Suze snatches it back.

'I haven't finished looking!' she says. 'Last year he released "Honest". He recently toured Germany with Blink Rage. Who are Blink Rage?'

I have no idea who Blink Rage are, but I'm not going to admit that.

'Haven't you heard of Blink Rage, Suze?' I say, a little pityingly.

'Hi, Becky.' A raspy male voice greets me from across the shop and both our heads jerk up and I nearly die of shock.

It's him. It's him. He's here. And we're googling him. Fuck.

'Hi!' says Suze in a weird squeak, dropping her phone with a clatter. 'Hi. Welcome to the . . . Hi!' As he gets near she grabs her phone and hastily turns it over – but not before we've all seen his face filling the screen.

My face goes instantly red. This is *so embarrassing*.

'Hi, Craig,' I say, trying to sound nonchalant. 'Hi. We were just . . . Hi. What a surprise! It's been . . .'

'Years,' he nods. 'Unreal, right?'

He sounds just like a rock god, with that raspy voice. And he looks like one too, with his long hair and battered leather jacket and a skull tattooed on his earlobe.

He greets me with a kiss on each cheek, then he steps back and just looks at me with an easy, confident smile.

That's new, too. He never used to smile like that at uni, he used to read me depressing pieces out of the paper and tell me I should be more engaged with the struggle.

'This is Suze,' I say, and Suze says, 'Oh, hi!' She shakes his hand, then gazes at him with moony eyes, twiddling her hair as if she's about fourteen.

'You came back!' Irene's delighted voice chimes in and I turn to see her hurrying over. 'How lovely!' To my horror, she turns to me and mouths, *Very striking!* in a totally unsubtle way.

Oh my God. Could we be more uncool?

'So. Um . . . What brings you here, Craig?'

'I live here now,' he says in the same leisured, easy way.

'You *live* here?' I say in astonishment.

'I've rented Lapwing Cottage.' He addresses Suze. 'I'm your tenant.'

'Oh.' I can see the light dawning on Suze's face. 'I didn't know Lapwing Cottage had been rented out!'

Trust Suze not to know she's rented out a cottage on her own estate. She and Tarkie have got so much property and investments and stuff between them, she can't keep track. We were once eating lunch at a local café and they kept bringing us complimentary slices of cake and being really nice to us. We had no idea why – until Suze suddenly realized that she was the landlord, she'd just forgotten.

'Is it OK?' she adds anxiously. 'If there are any problems, talk to Gordon, our estate manager, he runs all that kind of thing.'

'It's great,' says Craig. 'It's charming. Old world. Rustic.'

'So, how did you know I work here?' I demand.

'One of those crazy small-world things,' he says easily. 'I rented the cottage online. Wanted a bolthole from London. A place to write songs. Chill out, you know? Then I'm in the village shop getting some supplies and I see a postcard: *For sale, three garden spades, never used, apply Becky Brandon née Bloomwood*. I think to myself, "There can't be two Becky Bloomwoods." So I ask the guy and he tells me you work here. What are the odds?'

'Wow,' breathes Suze.

'So I have a question,' Craig adds, fixing me with his dark gaze. '*Three* garden spades?'

'They were on sale,' I say, feeling a bit defensive, 'so I bought a few. Our garden's quite big and I thought we might need several. Only it turned out we don't.'

'Sounds like you.' He looks amused. 'Well, I must be going. Nice to see you, Becky. We should have a drink some time. What have you been up to all these years?'

'Oh . . . er . . .' My mind has immediately gone blank. What *have* I been doing all this time? I can't think of a single thing. 'Loads of stuff,' I say feebly. 'You know.'

'Cool.' He nods. 'You've got a kid, I hear.'

'Yes, a daughter. Minnie.'

'Nice.' He turns to Suze. 'One more question. Would it be OK if I hired a hot tub for the garden?'

'A hot tub?' Suze looks taken aback.

'I have a thing for hot tubs.'

He smiles, showing his dazzling new teeth, and I have an immediate vision of him in a hot tub with his hair all wet and glistening and his chest all hairy and Ross Poldarky.

I mean, he never used to look Ross Poldarky, but I bet he does now.

'A hot tub,' says Suze, sounding utterly flustered. 'Gosh. Of course! I mean, we don't usually, but . . . if you want . . .'

'Cool.' He nods again. 'And I'll be having a Christmas party, I should think. I'll send you both invites.'

'Oh!' says Suze. 'Thanks!'

'Well, see you.' He lifts a hand in farewell and heads out of the shop with a lope. He didn't used to walk like that. He's picked it up from somewhere.

I look at Suze, who breathes out.

'Wow,' she says.

'Yes,' I say, still feeling a bit flabbergasted. 'Well, there you go. That's my ex.'

'He's really cool.' She eyes me suspiciously. 'Bex, were you really cool at uni?'

I'm tempted to say, 'What are you talking about? I'm really cool now!' But this is Suze I'm talking to.

'I was a *tiny* bit cool,' I say honestly. 'Like, for about half a term.'

'Were you in the band, too?'

'I . . . um . . .'

I clear my throat, trying to decide how to answer. The band is actually a sore point, because I *should* have been in it. I bought this amazing pink bass guitar and I learned loads of notes, and Craig said I could have a go. But after the first rehearsal the rest of the band ganged up and said I wasn't good enough. It was so unfair. They wouldn't even let me play the tambourine.

'I was his creative inspiration,' I say at last. 'It was

pretty collaborative. Good times,' I add in a careless, rock-chick manner.

'So why did you two break up?' says Suze, agog.

'The band got a record deal and they dropped out of uni to make an album.'

'No way!' Suze's hand flies to her mouth. 'That's amazing! Would I know it?'

'Well, no,' I admit. 'What happened was, they all went off to this place in Devon to record it—'

'Did you go too?' interrupts Suze.

'No.' I feel an old flicker of resentment. 'Mum and Dad wouldn't let me drop out. Anyway, they went off to make this album, but they kept fighting about it. And then one of them hit another one and the police got called. So then all their parents drove down and made them stop recording and go back to uni.'

'Oh,' says Suze, looking disappointed. I can tell she was hoping for an ending more along the lines of, 'And then they sold out Wembley!'

'Craig had a massive row with his parents,' I continue. 'He refused to go back to Bristol. And then the band fell apart.'

'What did Craig do?'

'Took a year off and went to Manchester. But by then I'd already broken up with him.'

'Because of the band,' supplies Suze, a little breathlessly. 'Because they all thought you were Yoko.'

'Kind of.' I hesitate, feeling I should be honest. 'Also, he wasn't very hot then. In fact, he was a bit annoying.'

We've talked quite enough about my old boyfriend, I

decide, so I move away to adjust a display of jumpers in a businesslike manner. But Suze follows me, oblivious.

'And now here he is, living in Letherby,' she says, wonderingly. 'That must be weird for you.'

'No it's not.'

It is a bit, but I'm not admitting that.

'It must be a *little* weird,' persists Suze.

'It's not weird at all,' I say firmly. 'Why would it be weird?'

'I mean, he's quite different from Luke,' muses Suze, ignoring my protestations. 'Are you going to go to his Christmas party?'

'Dunno,' I say after a pause. 'Are you?'

'Of course!' she says eagerly. 'We have to go! I bet it'll be awesome, all musicians and cool people.'

At that moment there's a clatter as a customer knocks over a pile of toffee tins, and we abandon the conversation. And as I'm stacking them back up, I try to absorb this strange new fact of my life. Craig Curton is living in Letherby. And he looks so *different*! His arms. His hair! It's so swooshy and thick, and that stubble really suits him . . .

By mistake I knock over the toffee tins again, and as Suze looks round I hastily say, 'Oops!'

'Distracted, Bex?' says Suze, lifting her eyebrows meaningfully, and I lift my chin in dignity. Of course I'm not distracted. At least, I'm not admitting it to Suze.

But oh God, I can't help it, I feel as though seeing Craig has opened up a window into the past. Memories of uni are piling into my head. Those jeans I used to wear. And that lipstick. What was I *thinking*?

86

I was quite awestruck by Craig, when we first got together. I thought he was really intellectual because he talked about Schopenhauer and drank a brand of gin I'd never heard of. But now, from my position of maturity, I can see that I shouldn't have been so impressed. I mean, anyone can drink gin and talk about German celebrities. I was talking about Heidi Klum just the other day.

Anyway, it was all a long time ago. We all went out with weird people when we didn't know any better. When I first met Luke he was going out with a totally snooty girl called Sacha de Bonneville, so *he* can talk. (Why am I having an argument with Luke about this in my head? I have no idea.)

I put the last toffee tin back in place and shake back my hair. It's just one of those strange, random coincidences. And Suze is right: if Craig throws a Christmas party we should go. Maybe there'll be famous people there. Or maybe he'll play some new song and we'll be the first to hear it.

Maybe he can get us VIP tickets to his next concert! I feel like I suddenly have a whole new status symbol which I can drop casually into conversation. 'Well, of course, I used to date a rock musician . . . ', 'Well, of course, I was always his inspiration . . . ', 'Well, of course, he wrote a song about me . . . '

And then I freeze. Oh my God. What if he *did* write a song about me?

Search history

Craig Curton

Craig Curton Becky Bloomwood

Craig Curton lyrics

Craig Curton songs inspired by unnamed mystery woman

Craig Curton celebrity friends

Sacha de Bonneville

Venetia Carter

Talking mermaid

Heidi Klum

SEVEN

By the next morning I've googled the lyrics of every single song I can find written by Craig Curton. I've listened to snippets of them all and peered at the videos and I *still* can't work out if any of them are about me.

I'm definitely not in his best-known song, 'Lonesome Girl'. It starts off: 'She's mesmerizing,' and at first I thought, 'Ooh, that could be me, I'm quite mesmerizing.' But then it continues: 'She's everywhere, she's in the air, feel the pain, know the pain.' What pain? Anyway, I'm not lonesome. So. Not me.

Then there's a song called 'Girl Who Broke My Heart', but she's got 'French lips, French kisses, French soul, French heart.' So I'm guessing that's not me either.

I'd better not be the inspiration for the woman in '23rd Century' because it says, 'What will you learn from her?' and the answer is, 'Hate, only hate, twisted hate.' Which isn't exactly very cheery.

In fact, none of Craig's music is cheery. It's quite thrashy and shouty and the lyrics are depressing. It's far

89

better to watch his videos with the sound off. (I probably won't mention that to him.)

I've also followed him on Instagram, and he's pretty cool. He doesn't ever seem to wear anything except leather, ripped T-shirts, studded boots and stubble. His Instagram feed is full of photos of him in smoke-filled bars with girls lounging about – and all the girls are very beautiful, with nose rings and tattoos and electric-blue eyeshadow. He always did like parties. I remember that. When we were going out I went to more parties than in the whole of the rest of my life. I don't think I did a *single* bit of work.

Even when we weren't partying, we kept pretty extreme hours. I remember we used to stay up way into the night, burning joss sticks, lying on the floor and staring at the ceiling. Craig would play the guitar softly and talk about South American politics, which was really important to him. I didn't know *that* much about South American politics – but I was doing a Spanish module at the time, so I would casually drop in Spanish phrases like '*Que pena!*' I felt special, as though we were solving the world's problems, along to a great acoustic soundtrack—

'Excuse me!'

An elderly woman's voice penetrates my memories and I blink back to reality. I'm standing on Jermyn Street, surrounded by Christmas shoppers, blocking the entrance to a shop. Oops.

'Sorry!' I say, and as I step away I feel a stab of guilt. OK, I need to stop thinking about my ex. Focus, Becky, focus. Christmas shopping is my task, I've taken the day off especially. *Christmas shopping.*

I take a few steps forward, looking around all the decorated shop fronts, getting myself back in the zone. There are twinkly Christmas lights all around, which helps, and I can hear 'Last Christmas' being piped from somewhere. (I love that song.)

Last night I skimmed through a few Christmas magazines, which really got me in the Christmas mood. God, I love glossy-magazine land. You turn the pages in a happy stupor, staring at amazing decorations and women laughing while they drink champagne in sparkly tops, and you think, 'Oh my God, I want *all* of this and I definitely need a new sequinned top and I really hope Mum buys that Christmas pudding with the orange inside.'

But this year, of course, it's me buying the Christmas pudding. I'm in charge. I sometimes feel a little weak at the responsibility that has been handed to me. However, thankfully the magazines were full of useful tips – for example, the 'must-have bauble' this year is a silver llama with glittery hair and WORLD PEACE embroidered on its side in pink. To be honest, I hadn't realized there was such a thing as a 'must-have bauble'. But there it was in every magazine, so I've ordered six. We're going to have the most on-trend tree ever!

The magazines also said you should book your supermarket delivery early, so I did that, too. In fact, I did it twice. I've got one delivery arriving on 23rd December with the turkey and all the important stuff – and then a second one arriving on Christmas Eve, in case I forget anything. Talk about organized!

I was getting a bit wired by that point, but then I read this brilliant article called 'Don't try to solve ten problems at once!' It said the answer to stress-free Christmas shopping was prioritizing and doing one thing at a time. So today I'm focusing again on one simple task: find a present for Luke.

But *what*?

I feel so uninspired. I've already been round all the department stores and OK, I've seen nice things – but nothing that made me think, 'Yessss!' So then I came to Jermyn Street because that's menswear central, isn't it? Only now that I've wandered about a bit, I realize that all the suits need to be tailored, which is too complicated . . .

Ooh. Hang on a minute.

I stop dead and stare upwards. I've just spotted the most amazing dressing gown in a window. It's navy blue, decorated all over with cheetahs, and it looks like it's made of some gorgeous silk. It looks like the kind of thing a movie star would wear. In a movie called *The Dressing Gown*.

I enter the shop, which is called Fox and Thurston and has lots of waistcoats and boaters and jaunty socks. There's a section at the back with dressing gowns, and I head there straight away. And there it is! It looks even more sumptuous up close, and Luke could definitely do with a new dressing gown.

Casually I examine it, but I can't see a price tag. So I swiftly move away and get out my phone. My new rule in posh shops is: don't ask the price but google it. Then you can gulp in private, instead of under the snooty gaze of an assistant.

I call up the website for Fox and Thurston and click

on Unique Dressing Gowns. I scroll down various dressing gowns and suddenly spy the navy one. It's called Cheetah Cloud and it's made from hand-woven Chinese silk, and it costs . . .

What?

I stare at the figure in disbelief. £4,000 for a dressing gown? No *way*. The belt on its own is £350, I notice, and clamp my lips tight so I won't giggle. Who wants a dressing-gown belt on its own?

'Hi!' A very thin, pretty girl with swooshy blonde hair is approaching me with a smile. 'Can I help you?'

For a split second I don't quite know what to say – but then a brilliant idea hits me.

'Oh, hello there,' I say in a businesslike way. 'My name's Becky Brandon, née Bloomwood.' I extend a hand. 'I work in brand representation. Would you be the right person to talk to on a business matter?'

The girl's eyes widen and she says, 'I'd better get Hamish.' A few moments later, a guy with a beard, dressed in red chinos and a striped waistcoat, comes striding up to me.

'Hamish Mackay,' he says. 'I'm the manager. How can I help you?'

'Hello,' I say, shaking his hand confidently. 'My name's Becky Brandon, née Bloomwood. I'm a brand ambassador consultant and I just wondered who your brand ambassadors are, currently?'

'Right,' says Hamish, shooting me a curious look. 'As far as I'm aware, we don't have any brand ambassadors.'

'*Really?*' I feign shock. 'You know, all the big brands have them. I think it's short-sighted not to avail yourself

of this wonderful opportunity.' I can see Hamish opening his mouth to protest, so I quickly press on. 'Luckily
enough, I have a client on my books who's available and
I think would make a very fine ambassador for you. Very
good looking, very dapper, very high profile in the world
of finance. He's exactly who you need right now.'

'I'm sorry, *what* is this?' says Hamish, looking puzzled.

'It's an arrangement,' I explain smoothly. 'All you
would supply is a few items of clothing, maybe a suit
and dressing gown, for example, and in return, he
would wear the clothes in a variety of high-profile situ-
ations. It's a win–win. Works every time.'

There's a pause as Hamish peers at me. Then he says,
'What's your name again?'

'Becky Brandon, née Bloomwood. I can take an item
or two with me now, if that's easier,' I add casually,
reaching for the dressing gown. 'Why don't I do that
and send over the paperwork later? I know this particular gentleman has some very high-profile events coming
up and you'll definitely want him to be wearing these
garments.'

'A *dressing gown*?' says Hamish incredulously, eyeing
it in my arms. 'How's he going to wear a dressing gown
at a high-profile event?'

Oh. I hadn't quite thought that through.

'Well . . . what *is* a dressing gown these days?' I retort
boldly. 'Call it a "dressing gown", call it a "smoking
jacket" . . .'

'It's not a smoking jacket,' Hamish interrupts me. 'It's
a dressing gown.'

'All the old rules are over,' I continue, ignoring him.

'My client might sling this garment casually over his black tie . . . he might go for the dress-down look . . . he might layer it over a coat . . .'

'Layer a dressing gown over a *coat*?' says Hamish, looking repulsed.

'Why not?' I say defiantly, trying not to picture the moment where I tell Luke he has to layer a dressing gown over his coat.

'That's a very expensive garment,' says Hamish, removing the dressing gown from my arms. 'Please don't touch it any more. What's this guy's name?'

'Luke Brandon of Brandon Communications,' I say proudly, and something clicks in Hamish's eyes.

'So this guy's your husband?'

Drat. I should have taken a pseudonym.

'Perhaps he is,' I say, lifting my chin. 'But that's irrelevant. We're utterly professional—'

'And you're just trying to score some free clothes,' he continues, unmoved.

I stare at him, offended. Free clothes? What a nerve! They should be *delighted* that Luke would wear their clothes.

'It seems you fatally misunderstand the principles of the brand-ambassador concept,' I say loftily.

'No, I think I understand exactly.' Hamish seems amused. 'Nice try.'

Hmph. He's not going to give me the dressing gown, is he? I might as well quit while I'm ahead.

'Well, if that's what you think,' I say with my most dignified air, 'then I will leave you always wondering what could have been. Always thinking: "*Was* Luke

Brandon our perfect brand ambassador . . . ?" You will repent at leisure for giving up this opportunity; I can only pity you.'

Tossing my hair back, I head for the exit, half hoping he might exclaim, 'Wait! You're right! Here's the dressing gown!'

But he doesn't. Pah.

I close the door behind me and stomp along the street, feeling quite grumpy. What am I going to do now? I'll go to Fortnum's and have a cup of tea, I decide. I probably need a bit more blood sugar or something. I'll have a scone, too.

I've been walking without paying much attention to where I'm going, so I turn my steps back towards Piccadilly. And I'm striding along, glancing automatically into shop windows as I go – when something attracts my eye. I stop dead in shock and my heart catches in my mouth.

Yessss! I've found the perfect thing!

First of all, it's luggage.

Luggage.

I've always had a soft spot for luggage, ever since the day that Luke and I tried out suitcases together, when we hardly knew each other. (They were actually for Sacha de Bonneville, it turned out, but let's not go there, and anyway, who married him? Exactly.)

Second of all, it's beautiful. It's like a suitcase that opens up into a wardrobe with all hangers and compartments and things. (I feel like it has a special name but I can't think of it right now.) It's made out of amazing dark brown leather and is *so* elegant.

Then, as I lean closer, I feel a jab of disbelief. It's lined with silky material with a repeat pattern of 'LB'. Luke's initials! And there's 'LB' engraved on the side. And – oh my God – a brass 'LB' charm dangling from the handle.

I gaze at it in bewilderment. How can something so perfect just be waiting for me? Did the Christmas Present Gods see me coming?

I raise my head to see which shop I'm at, but it's not a shop. It's in the window display of . . . what on earth *is* this place? I stare confusedly at the façade of what seems to be a house. It's a white stucco building with a large painted front door.

Then I spot a discreet metal sign to one side of the front door: *LONDON BILLIARDS*, and underneath in smaller writing: *The London Billiards and Parlour Music Club, est. 1816*. Oh right, of *course*. It's a club. This entire area of London is stuffed with posh London clubs. Luke is a member of one, actually, and he's taken me along a few times, but it's deathly. There's no music and they don't even do mojitos.

(To be fair, Luke finds it quite deathly too, but he says it can be useful for business. Why it's useful to sit in an ancient armchair and eat potted shrimp I don't know, but there you go.)

Anyway. Doesn't matter what it is. The point is, I want to buy their suitcase-thingy. Without further hesitation I press the metal doorbell and a moment later I'm buzzed in. As I push my way in, I find myself in a hall with old patterned tiles, a staircase with red carpet and a man sitting behind a desk who looks about ninety-three and is talking on an old-fashioned telephone. He puts his hand over the receiver and says, 'One minute, young lady,' then resumes talking.

Since he's busy, I wander over to the other side of the hall and peep through a pair of massive wooden double doors into a large room. It has a marble mantelpiece and lots of ancient armchairs, just like at Luke's club. But oh my God. Luke's club seems totally vibrant and down with it, compared with this place. For one thing, it's half empty. And for another, everyone here looks as if they're ninety-three. Even the young people look as if they're ninety-three. I've never *seen* so many leather elbow patches.

As I watch, a shrivelled waiter pushes along a wooden trolley covered with bottles. He pauses by an armchair and leans down to address one of the young ninety-three-year-olds.

'Sherry?' he intones funereally, and I bite my lip to stop myself giggling. The waiter looks older than anyone, in fact I'm amazed he can lift the sherry bottle.

'Young lady?' I turn to see the man at the desk summoning me, and hurry over.

'Hello!' I say with a friendly smile. 'My name is Becky Brandon, née Bloomwood. I saw your wonderful suitcase-thingy in the window and I would very much like to buy it. Please,' I add hastily. 'Thank you.'

The man behind the desk sighs a weary sigh.

'Young lady,' he says.

'Becky,' I put in.

'Becky,' he echoes with disdain, as though he's never heard the name 'Becky' before and doesn't care for it. 'I'm afraid the portmanteau on display—'

'Portmanteau!' I can't help interrupting. 'I *knew* it had a name!'

'I'm afraid it is not for sale. It is the prize in our Christmas raffle.'

A *raffle*? That's just typical.

'Well, can I buy a ticket for the raffle, please?' I ask. 'In fact . . . several tickets?'

I'll buy as many tickets as I can afford, I instantly decide. I mean, someone's got to win, haven't they? And why shouldn't it be me?

'The raffle is only open to members,' says the man discouragingly.

'Oh,' I say, deflated. 'Right. I see.'

How do I get round this? Could I ask one of the ninety-three-year-olds to buy me twenty tickets, maybe? I could compliment his elbow patches and take it from there . . .

'How much are the tickets?' I ask casually. 'Just out of interest.'

'Twenty pounds,' says the man, and I stare at him, appalled.

Twenty pounds? *Twenty pounds?* For one raffle ticket? That's not right. It's against the laws of raffles. If I were a member of this club I would be complaining.

'Was there anything else?' says the man, raising his eyebrows.

Honestly, he doesn't need to sound so snotty. I'm tempted to say, 'Yes, actually I'm a Sherry Inspector and I've come to see if your trolley's up to scratch.'

'I suppose not,' I say at last. 'Thanks, anyway. So why are you called London Billiards?' I can't help asking. 'What happened to the Parlour Music bit?'

'The parlour music declined,' says the man disapprovingly, although whether he disapproves of parlour music or of the fact that it declined is hard to tell.

They could do with a bit of parlour music round here, if you ask me.

If the parlour music was Beyoncé, and the parlour was a disco.

'Well, 'bye then,' I say. 'Good luck with the billiards.'

I head unwillingly towards the door, my eyes fixed on the portmanteau. It would be so perfect . . . *so perfect* . . . And then suddenly a new thought strikes me.

'Excuse me,' I say, striding back to the desk. 'Could you please furnish me with the name and details of whoever made the portmanteau?'

I'm quite pleased with 'furnish me with'. It sounds suitably pretentious.

I can tell the man is trying to think of a reason to say no, but can't quite manage it.

'Very well,' he says at last. He opens a ledger, leafs through the pages, squints at a name, then laboriously writes it out on a slip of paper. It's someone called Adam Sandford and his address is in Worcestershire.

'Thank you *so* much.' I beam at him.

This is even better. I'll commission Luke his own special portmanteau!

There's no time like the present, so I send Adam Sandford a quick email, standing on the street. Then, feeling satisfied with myself, I decide to go to Hamleys toy shop. I cut through the Burlington Arcade, which is full of the most gorgeous twinkly trees and massive red baubles, and on to Regent Street, all lit up with angels.

As I get near the iconic red banners of Hamleys, I feel a spring in my step. A machine is pumping bubbles into the air outside the shop, Christmas music is blasting through speakers and two elves in stripy tights are handing out shopping baskets. I'm about to take one when I feel a buzzing in my pocket and pull out my phone. It's him! Adam Sandford has replied already!

But as I read his words, my delight evaporates.

Dear Mrs Brandon née Bloomwood

Thank you so much for your enquiry regarding the portmanteau. I would be delighted to craft one for your husband, but I'm sure you will understand that it is a time-consuming process to make such a bespoke item, and that I have a waiting list. I estimate I should have one ready for you in approx. 36 months. Would that suit?

Yours kindly

Adam Sandford

Thirty-six months? Three *years*? What good is that?

'Excuse me!' says a woman holding about six Hamleys carrier bags, and I quickly turn away. I walk along disconsolately, thinking hard. Now I've seen that portmanteau, every other present idea for Luke seems really lame. Should I go and visit Adam Sandford? Or ask him to recommend another portmanteau maker? But why would he recommend a rival? Unless maybe his son went into the trade . . .

And then, out of the blue, the answer hits me.

Twenty minutes later, I'm standing outside The London Billiards and Parlour Music Club, est. 1816 again. Here's my plan: I'm going to join the club and enter the raffle. And if I don't win, I'll persuade the person who *does* win to sell it to me. Perfect! You probably need referees or whatever to join the club, but I'm sure I can busk that. OK. Let's go.

Straightening my back, I enter the club and stride up to the desk, where the same ninety-three-year-old man as before is sitting. He eyes me dubiously, but I draw breath before he can say anything.

'Hello again! My name is Becky Brandon née Bloom-wood and I would like to join The London Billiards and Parlour Music Club,' I announce grandly. 'My referee is Tarquin Cleath-Stuart, whose ancestor founded bil-liards in 1743.'

This might not actually be true, but they'll never know, and I can easily make Tarkie go along with it.

'His name was Billiard Cleath-Stuart,' I embellish for good measure. 'Hence the name "Billiards". My next referee is Danny Kovitz, the international designer, also a renowned supporter and campaigner for billiards.'

I'll get Danny to make a T-shirt with *I ♥ billiards* on it. It'll be fine.

'My third referee,' I begin, but the man lifts a hand. He doesn't seem to be at all impressed by my list of ref-erees, in fact he seems to be waiting to get a word in.

'Young lady,' he says testily.

'Becky,' I correct him.

'Young lady,' he repeats with emphasis. 'The London Billiards and Parlour Music Club is only open to gentlemen members.'

I stare at him, the wind taken out of my sails. Gentlemen members? That is *so* unfair.

Ooh. Shall I identify as a man? Shall I say, 'Actually it's not Becky, I forgot for a moment, it's Geoff'?

No. Because that would let them off the hook. They should let women join. Why *can't* women join?

'Well, I would like to dispute that,' I say briskly. 'As a woman who is passionate about both billiards *and* parlour music, I feel it is discriminatory of this club to exclude me. To whom may I write on this matter?'

The man gazes at me frostily for a few moments.

'The chairman is Sir Peter Leggett-Davey,' he allows at last. 'You may write to him at this address.'

'Thank you so much,' I say, making a small bow. 'I am, sir, yours, etc.'

I'm not quite sure what I meant by that, but it just popped out.

'Goodbye,' says the man in final tones.

'Goodbye,' I echo, and whirl round, intending to make an impressive exit, only I bash my bag on his desk by mistake and have to add, 'Oh, oops, sorry.'

As I head out on to the street, I'm already composing letters to Sir Peter Leggett-Davey in my head – and I give a most almighty jump when I feel a hand on my arm and hear a voice exclaiming, 'Young lady, you were tremendous!'

I wheel round to see an elderly man gazing at me with shining eyes. He's tall and thin, with liver spots and longish silver hair and a violet paisley cravat tucked into his shirt.

'I heard you speaking and I *couldn't* agree more!' he says emphatically. 'This club is in the Dark Ages! I've been trying to find some like-minded woman to challenge the rules, only my niece wasn't interested.'

'Oh, well I'm interested,' I say. 'Definitely.'

'I'm Edwin,' says the man, clasping my hand and shaking it. '*Delighted* to meet you. Might I buy you a quick drink and discuss your campaign for membership?'

'You mean . . . in there?' I point back inside the club.

'Of course! As my guest. Female guests are allowed, at least.'

'Well, OK!' I say, beaming at him. 'Thanks. Only it'll have to be quick, because I've got to go Christmas shopping.'

'Oh, just a snifter,' says Edwin, nodding conspiratorially. 'Absolutely.'

He leads me back into the club and signs me in under the disapproving gaze of the old man while I smile smugly. Then he ushers me into the massive grand room with the old chairs and the mantelpiece and the sherry trolley.

'Now, let's find somewhere nice to sit,' he says, peering around. But the place seems to have filled up. Every chair seems to have a trousered leg poking out from it, or a newspaper visible over the top.

'Lord Tottle?' says a man in an apron, coming over to us. 'Everything all right?'

'All the chairs are full,' Edwin says fretfully. 'No one's moving. In fact, Baines over there looks quite dead. You *must* stop the members dying in their chairs, Finch.'

'You come this way, my lord,' says Finch soothingly, and he leads us into another room, where he establishes us by the fire. 'Shall I send the sherry trolley over?'

'Good God, no,' says Edwin, looking appalled. 'We want the good stuff. Can I tempt you to a gimlet, Becky?'

'Yes!' I say, taken aback. 'Fab! Thank you!'

It isn't even noon yet, I realize. But maybe a gimlet will help me do my Christmas shopping. In fact I'm sure it will.

'Finch is on our side,' murmurs Edwin, as Finch moves away. 'We've been pushing for a decade, you know. Never managed it. But I have a good feeling this time. I think you'll make it. I'll be your proposer, of course, and I'll find you three seconders from the club, which is what you need.'

'Oh, thanks.' I beam at him again.

'I know the Cleath-Stuart family,' he adds conversationally. 'Never knew that about inventing billiards.'

'Oh well, it's just a legend,' I say hastily. 'In fact, it's more of an urban myth.'

Finch deposits our drinks on the table, and Edwin lifts his up in a toast.

'To your membership!' he exclaims. 'Now, if it's not too much to ask, might I draft your letter to Sir Peter? I know exactly what to say to press his buttons, the pompous wretch.'

'Of course! Thank you.'

'And then the matter will go to the AGM in December.' Edwin eyes me over the top of his drink and I notice he has the most amazing pink enamelled cufflinks. 'Could you speak out at a meeting, Becky? I'm very happy to draft your speech, if you could perform it with gusto?'

'Definitely,' I say firmly.

'Marvellous.' He touches my glass with his again. 'I'll send you the details and we'll fight them together. I'm a friend of the disenfranchised, my dear, always have been, and I will be very glad if we can prevail. And it's splendid to find such a keen supporter of billiards as yourself,' he adds, his face lighting up. 'So unusual. So refreshing.'

Oh right. I'd forgotten about the billiards bit.

'Well,' I say after a pause. 'You know. I mean, *billiards*. It's just so . . .' I spread my hands expressively. 'What's not to love?'

'Precisely!' Edwin says enthusiastically. He crosses his legs and I notice he has violet socks to match his cravat. 'To find another aficionado is always a delight.'

'I just have one question,' I say, trying to sound casual. 'When will the raffle be held?'

'The raffle?' Edwin looks puzzled.

'The Christmas raffle. I saw something about it in the lobby?'

'Oh.' Edwin's brow clears. 'That. Yes, that's usually straight after the AGM. We have mulled wine and whatnot. Festive cheer.' He twinkles at me. 'Let's hope *we're* the ones with the cheer, m'dear!'

I beam back at him happily and swig my gimlet. This

is all falling nicely into place. I'll go to the AGM, read out whatever brilliant speech Edwin writes for me, join the club, enter the raffle and get the portmanteau. And Luke will be totally blown away. Ha!

I'm still glowing as I arrive back at Letherby station. I've had a fantastic afternoon. Not only did I make major strides towards getting Luke an awesome present, I went back to Hamleys and found a fabulous fluffy unicorn that Clemmie will adore. I'm so ahead of the game!

I'm supposed to be picking Minnie up from Suze's house, but I decide to pop home first and hide the unicorn. It's pretty enormous, but I can just about manhandle it—

'Becky.'

As I hear a familiar raspy voice I jump, and turn round. Craig is loping towards me out of the station, dressed in the same battered leather jacket as before and black jeans covered in some sort of graffiti.

'Oh, hi!' I exclaim, shifting the unicorn to see him properly. 'Craig! How are you?'

'We must have been on the same train and didn't know it.' He smiles at me over the unicorn. 'Here, give me something to carry.'

'Oh. Thanks.' Awkwardly I hand over the unicorn. He peers at it curiously, then falls into step with me as we head along the main street.

Craig walks with a different rhythm from Luke – in fact, everything he does has a different rhythm. He's far more measured. And he won't be rushed. I'm remembering that now. (I used to find it really annoying.)

He lights a cigarette, then looks at me. 'You want one?'

'No thanks,' I say. I watch as he inhales and blows out a cloud of smoke, then add, 'How are you finding Letherby?'

'It's just what I need,' he says musingly. 'A bit of quiet, you know? Somewhere totally sleepy, middle of nowhere, nothing going on. Perfect.'

I feel a bit defensive on Letherby's behalf. There's not exactly *nothing* going on here. There's the village shop and Suze's shop, and there's the Lamb and Flag, which does a really good Sunday lunch. But I don't point that out, I just say, 'That's probably what you need.'

'Telling me.' He nods heavily. 'I've just been on tour for two months solid. Before that I was in Kiev for six months. I mean, you know the scene in Kiev.' He glances at me. 'The partying's insane.'

Kiev? The only thing I know about Kiev is chicken Kiev. But I'm not admitting that.

'Oh, Kiev!' I nod, trying to sound world-weary and experienced. 'God, yes. That scene. Extreme. It's like . . . crazy!'

'It's the new Berlin.' Craig blows out another puff of smoke.

'Yes,' I agree fervently. 'That's what I always say, too. It's the new Berlin.'

'Now, Tbilisi,' continues Craig thoughtfully. '*That* has a great scene.'

'Tbilisi!' I nod enthusiastically. 'Totally. Awesome. It's the new Kiev,' I risk.

Where's Tbilisi again?

'So you've been?' Craig looks at me with interest. 'When did you go there?'

'*Go* there?' I echo, playing for time, and crinkle up my eyes as though trying to remember. 'Hmm. Actually, *was* it Tbilisi . . . or Tenerife? Anyway, are you still in touch with the others from the band?' I add hastily, changing the subject.

'Jeez, no.' Craig looks surprised at the idea. 'I lost touch with those losers. But hey, Becky.' He focuses on me as though for the first time. 'A bunch of us are going to Warsaw at the weekend, check out a new club. The guys from Blink Rage, a few others . . . You want to come?'

I stare at him, gripped. *He's inviting me to go partying in Warsaw with Blink Rage?* For a moment I'm there, wearing electric-blue eyeshadow and amazing shoes (which I would need to buy), jumping around to some banging song in a nightclub, and people are calling me The Girl with the Great Eyeshadow, except in Polish . . .

And then I blink and remember that Minnie's got ballet on Saturday. And I've promised Suze to look after her three children all day Sunday while she and Tarkie go to some family friend's memorial service. And we're having a supermarket delivery.

'It sounds amazing,' I say regretfully. 'But I have commitments. Another time, maybe?'

'Sure,' says Craig in that easy way of his. We walk on a little longer, then he says casually, 'I always used to think about you, Becky. Used to wonder what you were up to now.'

'Me too,' I say at once. This isn't strictly true, but I can hardly say, 'Actually I forgot all about you.' We walk a few more steps, then I add carelessly, 'So, am I what you expected?'

'Hmm.' Craig considers for a moment, then looks up. 'Honestly? I thought you'd be more edgy.'

I stare at him, stricken. More edgy?

'I'm edgy!' I say, trying to laugh lightly. 'God! I'm *so* edgy.'

'Really?' says Craig quizzically. 'Because what I'm seeing is a sleepy village, husband, kid, *tweed* . . .' He looks down at the unicorn. 'And whatever this is.'

'It's a unicorn,' I say, and he raises his eyebrows.

'There you go.'

'That's only part of who I am!' I say, a bit flustered. 'I'm still totally edgy. I'm like . . . whatever. Bring it on. Smash it. Radical.'

Oh God, what am I *saying*? No one says 'radical' except million-year-old hippies.

'It's fair enough.' He shrugs. 'People settle down. They have kids, go soft.'

'I haven't gone soft!'

I try to push my hair back into an edgier style, wishing I had a tattoo to casually reveal.

'Cool.' Craig smiles, but I can't tell if he's humouring me. We reach the turning down towards his cottage and pause on the pavement.

'Shall I carry this home for you?' he says, nodding at the unicorn.

'No, don't worry, I'll be fine now.' I take it from him. 'Thanks. And, you know, count me in next time you go to Warsaw!' I add. 'I *do* still party, I *am* still edgy—'

'Oh, Mrs Brandon!' A cheerful voice greets me and I look up to see Jayne, the school nurse, walking along, dressed up for an evening out. 'What a super unicorn!' She strokes the white fluffy mane admiringly. 'Now, I'm glad I've bumped into you, because I didn't see you at pick-up. I'm sorry to say, there's a case of nits at school.'

Nits. Of all the things she could mention, *nits*?

'Oh dear,' I say hurriedly. 'Well, thank you—'

'So we're asking if all parents could check their children's hair tonight. Remember, the eggs are *white*, but the lice are *brown*.' She smiles brightly at Craig. 'Hello!'

'Hi,' says Craig, looking amused. 'Well, I guess I'd better leave you to it. See you, Becky.'

He lopes off and I feel a burst of frustration. It's not fair. No one looks cool when they're talking about nits. Not even *Kate Moss* could look cool, talking about nits.

At last Jayne finishes telling me how to use a nit comb and we wish each other a good evening. Then I continue on my way home, still clutching the unicorn, feeling ruffled. I know it was only a passing comment, but Craig's judgement has really got under my skin.

From: Myriad Miracle
To: Becky Brandon
Subject: Your New Subscription!

Hi Mrs Brandon (née Bloomwood)

Welcome to the Myriad Miracle Training System™!

Congratulations on choosing to turn your life around with our renowned Lifestyle and Health program, devised by experts.

With our high-tech 'Exer-Monitor'™ our team will be able to monitor and guide your daily routine, observing your activity levels with our interactive app. We'll blast you with fun motivational messages, nutritional tips and a daily 'Exercise of the Day'.

Every day!

You've chosen Ultra Miracle, the highest level of the program. Awesome! This means that as well as emailing you our weekly analysis of your exercise, nutrition and mindful activity, we'll support you with unlimited texts and the opportunity of Skype real-time sessions.

Mrs Brandon, you are a very special person. Enjoy life. Enjoy health-seeking. Enjoy the success of Myriad Miracle.

Yours sincerely

Russ Danbuster
(Founder)

EIGHT

I'm still edgy. I *am*. Kind of. Aren't I?

All the way to Shoreditch the next day, I can't stop thinking about that conversation. I can't stop remembering Craig's pitying look. As we get out of the car, I'm so preoccupied, I can't help saying, 'Luke, do I look edgy?'

'No, you look lovely,' he replies absently, and I feel a jerk of dismay.

'So you're saying I look crap,' I say morosely, and Luke's head jerks up.

'*What?*' He stares at me. 'Becky, I just said you look lovely. How the hell can you twist that into "I look crap"?'

'You said I wasn't edgy. Edgy's *good*.' I try to impress this point on him. 'It's *good*.'

'Oh,' says Luke, sounding baffled. 'Then yes, you do look edgy. If I saw you in the street, I'd say, "Wow. That's one edgy person."'

Hmph. He's not taking it seriously, is he?

As we walk along towards the building, I look critically

at my own reflection in car windows. I mean, OK, so I'm not a student any more. I don't party every night any more. But is it worse than that? Am I totally uncool?

My new satin jumpsuit is pretty edgy, I remind myself – I must wear that more often. (If I can find stickier 'fashion tape'.) But on the other hand, look at the block-heeled boots that I'm wearing today, with my skinny jeans. They're comfy. They're practical. They're 'busy working mum' boots, I realize, with a pang of horror. I have to throw them away! I have to take action! Edge myself up, before it's too late.

'Hey, Luke,' I say casually as we turn the corner. 'We should go to Warsaw one weekend. Don't you think?'

'*Warsaw*?' Luke looks puzzled – then his brow clears. 'Have they opened a new shopping centre there?'

'No!' I say, a little offended. 'I meant we should take in some of the clubs. There's a great underground techno scene,' I add nonchalantly. 'You know LL Dee is DJ-ing at Luzztro this weekend? She's been on fire this year, apparently.'

'I'm sorry, who?' says Luke, looking mystified, and I feel a flare of frustration. Here I am, trying to be edgy, and my husband's never even heard of LL Dee!

I mean OK, I'd never heard of her either till I went on Google last night, but at least I made the effort.

'I'm quite surprised you haven't heard of LL Dee, Luke,' I say. 'Your business is in communication. You should be *aware* of the world.'

'I'm in financial PR, my love,' replies Luke politely. 'Techno DJs aren't really my remit.'

Honestly. Luke can be so narrow-minded. I glance

114

over at him, about to tell him so – but I'm halted by a pang of dismay. It's about the thousandth pang of dismay I've felt since he came back from Madrid with his moustache looking so . . . moustache-like.

I'm trying to be open-minded, I really am. I keep reminding myself it's for charity. I just wish charity hadn't ever had the idea of moustaches.

It's not yet fully grown and I keep surreptitiously peering at it, to see which way it might develop. Will it be one of those big bushy caterpillar type ones? Or all thin and stringy? I keep googling *moustaches* to find one I like, but all I've found so far are ones I *don't* like.

'Look at dah wabbit!' Minnie interrupts my thoughts, pointing excitedly at a woman with pink hair, power-walking towards us with a buggy. 'It's in dah pushchair, Mummy! In dah *pushchair*!'

I do a double-take and realize that Minnie's right – the woman's pushing a live rabbit in a buggy. Oh my *God*. I watch the woman go by, then exchange glances with Luke. You definitely wouldn't get that in Letherby.

I've only been to Shoreditch a few times before and it still feels exotic to me. It's more like the meatpacking district of New York than London, all red-brick buildings and graffiti and interesting-looking shops everywhere and people pushing rabbits in buggies.

My parents live in an edgier place than me, it suddenly hits me. Oh God. That's against the laws of nature, surely? Parents should be *less* cool than their children.

Should we quickly move to Shoreditch, too? Or somewhere even edgier, like Dalston? I'm tempted to get out my phone and google *edgy postcode London really cool*. But even as I'm considering it, I know I don't really want to. Minnie's so happy at her school and it's fab being so near Suze. And anyway, I can be edgy in Letherby, can't I?

'Are those presents both for your parents?' asks Luke, glancing at the gift bags in my hand.

'The champagne's for my parents, but this one's a welcome-home gift for Jess,' I say, lifting up the smaller, squarer bag. 'Herbal body lotion.'

'A present for Jess!' exclaims Luke, looking amused. 'Isn't that a risky venture?'

'It's vegan,' I explain. 'And it's made by a collective. She's *got* to like it.'

I know why Luke looks amused. Just a few times in the past, I've slightly misjudged what to give Jess. Like the time I gave her this new high-tech mascara and instead of saying, 'Ooh, fab, thanks!' like any normal person would, she gave me this massive lecture about the environmental cost of cosmetics.

But today I'm giving her the worthiest present in the world. It's vegan and it's eco *and* it's a sludgy green colour. I actually feel quite smug.

'Here we are.' Luke comes to a halt and peers at a set of double doors. 'The Group.'

This is what my parents' new building is called: The Group. It looks like an old factory, with black metal window frames and brick arches, and a mural of elephants. As I stare up at the façade, I can't help feeling impressed.

'Well,' says Luke. 'Good for your parents. This looks great.'

116

'It's amazing!'

' "Live, work, chill",' Luke is reading off a sign. ' "Co-living for today." Is there a buzzer?'

I'm just searching around for a set of buttons when the doors open and Mum comes bursting out.

'You made it! Welcome!' she cries excitedly. 'Janice and Martin are already here, and Jess, of course, and Dad's making espresso martinis!'

Espresso martinis?

I'm about to say 'Since when did Dad know about espresso martinis?' when I suddenly clock what Mum's wearing. She's in a pair of orange baggy trousers that look like they belong to a Buddhist monk, together with a T-shirt with the slogan *Bitch Don't Kale My Vibe*.

She . . . what?

As Mum catches me gawping at her outfit, she beams.

'Aren't my new trousers super, love? I bought them from a stall in Brick Lane. So comfortable. Now, let me show you around our new home!'

She sweeps us through a lobby with exposed bricks and metal rivets everywhere, plus neon signs reading *Work*, *Play* and *Chill*.

'So, this is one of our "chill" areas . . .' She pushes open a door to reveal a room full of beanbags and low-slung sofas. It's dimly lit, soft music is playing and a young guy with dreadlocks seems to be asleep in the corner. Minnie makes an immediate dash for one of the beanbags, but Luke swiftly leans in and scoops her back out again.

'Sorry to disturb you, Kyle!' Mum says in a stage whisper, and closes the door again. 'That beanbag's wonderful,' she adds. 'Super for taking the weight off my bunions! Now, let me show you the "garden hangout" . . .'

Before I can reply, she's whisking us down a little corridor and pushing open a door to a cool-looking terrace. There are plants hanging from baskets, a couple of outdoor sofas and a firepit.

'Wow!' I say in admiration.

'It's a nice space,' says Mum complacently. 'The bees are on the roof. And look, there's a bicycle rack for Dad to store his unicycle.'

'His *what*?'

'He's joined a local circus skills workshop,' she beams. 'Great fun. And now here's The Hub.'

She leads us to another door and ushers us into a big light space with skylights and a huge central wooden table. About ten people are typing at laptops, most with earphones in, and a few lift their hands in greeting, saying, 'Hey, Jane.'

'Hey, Lia,' replies Mum cheerily. 'Hey, Tariq. This is my daughter Becky, her husband Luke and my granddaughter Minnie.'

'Hi,' I say, lifting a friendly hand and smiling at all the faces.

'Love,' murmurs Mum into my ear. 'A little piece of advice? No one says hi here. It's a bit "old hat". Everyone says hey.'

'Oh right,' I say, discomfited.

'What businesses are based here?' enquires Luke, looking round at all the laptops.

'Lots of startups,' says Mum. 'In fact, Dad and I might

launch a little startup, we thought,' she adds brightly. 'In our spare time. It's very much "the thing".'

'Great!' says Luke, his mouth twitching a little. 'Good idea.'

'But now let's go upstairs,' says Mum, chivvying us out of The Hub and towards an old-fashioned clanky lift. 'We're having drinks and then we've booked a table for brunch. Jess is so excited,' she adds. 'She's *dying* to see you.'

'Did she actually say that?' I ask in astonishment, because Jess doesn't normally say gushy things.

'Well, maybe not,' confesses Mum after a slight pause. 'But I'm sure that's what she *meant*.'

OK. I'm just saying, *some* people, if they were seeing their half-sister for the first time in ages, might rush over and hug them. But I'm used to Jess by now. As Mum shows us into the flat, Jess looks up from her drink, lifts a hand and says 'Hi, Becky' in her flat, calm voice.

Honestly. Does she think I'm going to say 'Hi, Jess' in the same low-key way and that will be the sum total of our greeting?

'Jess!' I hurry over to give her a massive hug, even if she doesn't want it. She feels skinnier and musclier than ever, her skin is tanned and her hair has been bleached by the sun.

'Where's Tom?' I look around. 'Is he here?'

'No,' says Jess.

'How come?' I ask in surprise – and I'm disconcerted to see Jess flinch.

Jess never flinches. She's like granite. Is something up?

'Tom had a few things he needed to tie up in Chile,' she says stiffly, her eyes averted from mine. 'You know he's been working with a charity out there? He's coming over as soon as he can. Obviously he'll want to see his parents, so . . .'

She trails away as though she can't think what to say next, which is pretty unusual for her, too.

'Oh right,' I say. 'Shame you couldn't travel together.'

'I'd already agreed to give a series of lectures in London on igneous rocks,' replies Jess impassively. 'The dates were agreed.'

'Right.' I nod wisely as though I know what igneous rocks are. 'Well, anyway . . . welcome back!'

'Aunty Jess!' Minnie clasps her round the legs and Luke comes over to kiss her too, and Jess's cheeks glow a little as though she can't help being pleased. Maybe she just needs to be jollied along a bit.

'How was your flight?' I ask. 'Are you jetlagged? I got you something to say welcome back . . .'

I hand Jess her present and as she starts to unwrap it I look around the flat, taking it in properly. It's got floor-to-ceiling windows, a teal velvet sofa and amazing light fittings everywhere. And there's Dad, in faded jeans and a long-sleeved grey marl T-shirt, mixing espresso martinis at the copper cocktail bar, while Janice and Martin sit on industrial bar stools.

I can't help gaping at Dad, just like I gaped at Mum. My dad never wears a long-sleeved T-shirt. He never wears jeans. The most relaxed look I've ever seen him in before is a golf-club polo shirt.

'Happy new home, Dad!' I say, giving him the champagne and kissing him. 'This is amazing!'

'You like it, Becky?' Dad beams.

'It's so *different*!'

'It's very different, isn't it, love?' says Janice in a tremulous voice. 'Very different.' She's wearing a particularly swirly floral two-piece with a pleated skirt and looks quite incongruous, perched on her industrial bar stool, looking around nervously as though she's found herself in the middle of the Gobi desert.

'Espresso martini, Martin!' says Dad cheerfully and hands him a cocktail glass. Martin stares at it dubiously, then takes a small sip.

'Quite refreshing,' he says after a pause.

'Minnie, darling, here's some juice for you . . .' Dad gives her a beaker and she beams happily, sits down cross-legged and starts to sip. 'And a gin and tonic for you, Janice, was it? Now, what sort of gin?'

'What *sort* of gin?' Janice's eyes swivel about uncertainly as though it's a trick question. 'Um . . . Gordon's?' she whispers.

'Janice!' chides Dad. 'Be more adventurous! We went to an artisan gin tasting the other night. This one is Japanese.' He brandishes a bottle at Janice. 'Try this.'

'Lovely, I'm sure!' says Janice, looking disconcerted. She watches Dad slicing up a cucumber, then adds, 'We missed you at the bridge club. Everyone was saying, "What a shame the Bloomwoods aren't here."'

'We're going to start poker nights!' says Mum, breezing over to the bar and opening a bag of beetroot crisps.

'Poker!' says Janice. 'Goodness!'

'Thanks, Becky,' comes Jess's voice behind me, and I turn to see her holding the bottle of sludgy green body lotion.

'What do you think?' I ask eagerly, studying her face for signs of pleasure. 'It's vegan and the bottle is recycled glass, and the box is made from sustainable cardboard.'

'I saw that.' She nods expressionlessly. 'Thanks.'

I feel a tweak of frustration. Couldn't Jess just *once* exclaim, 'Oh my God, I love it!' and fling her arms around me?

'I know you're anti-consumerist and everything,' I add. 'But I thought this would be OK because it was made by a women's collective.'

'Yes. I read the label.' Jess nods. 'It's a good initiative.'

I stare at her impassive face, willing her to say more. I *know* it's really pathetic of me, but I want her approval. I want her to say, 'Wow, Becky, it's the perfect present!'

'You have to admit, it's an environmentally friendly choice,' I say with a light laugh. 'Ticks every box. I mean, it's pretty perfect, isn't it? Nothing you can object to.'

'Well,' says Jess, then stops.

'What?' I narrow my eyes at her.

'I appreciate it, Becky. It was very thoughtful and generous of you. You're always generous. Thank you.' She puts it down on a side table. 'So, what's your news? How's Minnie getting on at school?'

She's dodging the question.

'What?' I demand. 'What's wrong with my present? Why isn't it perfect? Tell me!'

Jess sighs. 'Well, the packaging is problematic. But you must realize that.' She gestures at the plastic film on the box.

'It's fully recyclable,' I say in bewilderment. 'I checked. It says, "Fully recyclable".'

Jess just gives me a blank stare. 'We can't recycle our way out of the plastic pollution catastrophe that's devastating our planet in its thoughtless surge of consumerism,' she says. 'Although thanks again,' she adds as an afterthought. 'As I say, it was thoughtful of you.'

I can feel my shoulders slumping. *Great*. Every time I think I'm green enough for Jess, she goes even greener. I'm going to get her something so green for Christmas, she won't know it, I silently vow. I'll get her . . . leaves.

A buzzer sounds, and Mum picks up an entry-phone receiver. 'Hello? Oh, Suzie! Come on up! Third floor!'

'You're going for the facial-hair look, I see, Luke!' says Dad in a jovial voice. 'Very "now". What do you think of Luke's moustache, Becky?'

My head jerks up and I realize everyone's looking at me. Shit. OK, I need to be supportive.

'I think it's a brilliant charity effort,' I reply, dodging the question, 'and everyone must sponsor Luke.'

'We can get you some moustache oil for Christmas, Luke!' says Janice, and my smile turns to a rictus of dismay. *Moustache oil?*

'It'll be gone by then,' I say, a little too quickly.

'Well,' says Luke, stroking his upper lip self-consciously. 'That was the idea. But if you like it, Becky . . .'

Like it?

'Do you like it, love?' says Mum, with interest.

Argh! I feel totally put on the spot. I don't want to say anything negative, but how can I say I like it? Husbands and wives should *not* discuss moustaches in polite company, I instantly decide. It should be a major breach of etiquette.

'You said it looked great the other day,' adds Luke.

'Right,' I say, my voice a little shrill. 'Yes. I did say that, didn't I?'

'So!' says Mum, handing me and Luke espresso martinis. 'Speaking of Christmas, shall we discuss arrangements?'

'Let's wait for Suze,' I say. 'The Cleath-Stuarts are coming for Christmas Day, too.'

'Oh good!' exclaims Mum. 'It's going to be such a lovely day. Just think, Graham! No cooking, no decorating . . . Becky's going to do it all!'

'*All?*' I echo in slight alarm.

I know I'm hosting Christmas, but doesn't Mum want to do some? Or like . . . most?

'Becky, love, we don't want to get in your way,' says Mum in generous tones. 'It's your Christmas.'

Before I can say, 'I don't mind sharing,' the doorbell to the flat rings and Dad swings the door open.

'Suze, my dear!' he exclaims. 'Welcome to our new home.'

'Wow,' says Suze, her eyes like saucers as she ventures in, peering around. 'Just wow. This flat! And Jess, you're here, and Jane, your outfit is amazing, and . . . Oh my God, Luke!' she says, as though this is the biggest surprise of all. 'You've got a *moustache.*'

'Becky likes it,' says Janice eagerly, and Suze's gaze swivels to me in astonishment.

'*Really?*'

'For now,' I amend quickly. 'I like it for now. You can like things for a bit. You can really like them and then . . . not like them quite so much.' I clear my throat. 'That can be a thing.'

'Huh,' says Suze, looking mystified. 'I never thought—' She stops dead. 'I mean, absolutely. Good for you, Luke. It's . . . It's just . . .' She seems to be struggling for words. 'Wow!'

As we walk along Shoreditch High Street to the restaurant where we're having brunch, Minnie holds my hand and we fall into step with Suze and Jess while the others walk further ahead.

'Have you *seen* what your mum's T-shirt says?' demands Suze, as soon as Mum is out of earshot. She sounds on the brink of hysteria, which is pretty much how I feel, too.

'I know!' I say. 'Thank God Minnie can't read!'

'And espresso martinis.'

'And *circus skills*.'

Dad showed us some tricks on his newly acquired diabolo, just before we came out for brunch. We all clapped and said 'Encore!' and Janice only shrieked once, when the diabolo nearly hit Martin on the head.

'I think everyone should retire to Shoreditch,' says Suze firmly. 'It's the way to go.'

Jess has been walking along silently, but now she

says, 'It's really generous of Graham and Jane to give me their house. They didn't need to.'

'Oh, they wanted to,' I say quickly. 'They're having a great time here! It's an adventure for them. When do you think Tom will come over?' I add casually, to make conversation – and at once Jess flinches, exactly like she did before.

'Not sure,' she says. 'As soon as . . . He'll . . .' She stops as though to give herself time. 'Not sure. I'm not sure.'

OK. That was a weird response. Jess's jaw is rigid and her gaze is fixed ahead. I glance at Suze, and I can see she's a bit puzzled, too.

'How's Tom's work in Chile going?' I venture.

'Yes. Good.'

'Any news on the adoption?' I ask, even more cautiously.

'No, none.' Jess's face closes up and I see her hands clenching into fists.

I have an anxious feeling in my stomach. My sister is even more monosyllabic than usual. Her eyes have darkened with misery. And OK, I know we're only half-sisters, but we definitely have a psychic connection. (We once built exactly the same kind of cupboard, hers for rocks, mine for shoes.) I feel I know her – and right now I'm pretty sure something's wrong with her and Tom.

I glance at her anxiously, longing to fling my arm around her and say, 'Jess, what's up? Is it Tom? He's always been a bit weird, you mustn't mind that.' But I'm not sure how well she'd respond. She's not the chattiest person in the world. I'd better take it slowly.

'By the way, Suze,' says Jess, her eyes still fixed straight ahead, 'I haven't seen you since your . . . loss. I was sorry to hear about it.'

'Thanks,' says Suze, her eyes darkening a little, too. 'It was . . . you know. One of those things.' She glances at me and I give a half-smile, half-wince.

We walk on a short way in silence and I'm pretty sure we're all thinking about children. I'm thinking wistfully, 'I wonder if Luke and I *will* ever have another baby?' But then instantly I feel bad for wanting anything more than Minnie, and I squeeze her hand tightly, just to prove it to her.

Then it occurs to me: maybe Jess isn't thinking about children at all, she's thinking, 'How am I going to break it to everyone that Tom and I have split up?'

The thought makes me feel cold – but at the same time, it's not really a shock. It must be difficult for them, living so far away. And both working hard. And Tom surrounded by lots of sexy young charity workers in khaki hotpants (I expect). Maybe he's fallen in love with one of them.

Or has Jess fallen in love with a guy in khaki hotpants? Or a *girl* in khaki hotpants?

I mean, anything's possible.

I glance at Jess again, wondering whether to press her on the subject. But after all, she's only just arrived back, and the whole family's around. I'll take her out for a drink some time and talk privately to her, I decide. Just us girls, all nice and relaxed. She'll open up then.

'Bex, you must be really out of shape!' says Suze. 'You're breathing so hard!'

127

'Oh.' I look up in a daze. 'No, I was thinking about . . . you know. *Things*.'

I wonder if Jess will divine my empathetic, sisterly thoughts – but she just gives me an impassive look and says, 'You should try high-intensity workouts, Becky. You usually dodge cardio, don't you?'

Instantly all my empathy melts away. Dodge cardio? I don't dodge cardio!

'Actually, I've got a new online personal trainer,' I say loftily. 'I'm on a bespoke exercise programme.'

'Wow!' says Suze. 'I didn't know you were doing that.'

'Well, I bought this new dress for Christmas,' I explain. 'Alexander McQueen, 70 per cent off.'

'Alexander McQueen!' Suze opens her eyes wide.

'Exactly! But it's just a teeny bit too small. So I thought, I'll hire a personal trainer and fit into the dress, *plus* it's good for my health. Win–win.'

Jess frowns.

'How much is the fitness programme?' she says. 'Surely this is all ending up far more expensive than just buying a dress that fitted you in the first place, or, even better, using a dress that you already had in your wardrobe?'

I'd forgotten about Jess's habit of asking annoying questions and then staring at you without blinking. Next she'll be saying, 'Why don't you just do a hundred press-ups every day?' or 'Why don't you live on potatoes and water?'

'You can't put a price on health,' I say briskly. 'It's an investment.'

At that moment Mum waves at us from a restaurant entrance and calls, 'Here we are! This way!'

'Wait,' says Suze. 'Before we go in, Bex, I just need a word about . . . something. Jess, do you mind? Maybe you could take Minnie in?'

Suze waits until Jess has disappeared into the restaurant, holding Minnie's hand. Then she turns to me and says in an undertone, 'What do you *really* think about Luke's moustache?'

'Hate it,' I mutter back. 'But I'm being supportive.'

'Got it.' Suze nods, then as we enter the restaurant she gives Luke a dazzling smile.

'By the way, Luke,' she says. 'Fab moustache!'

It seems to take about an hour for us all to order brunch, partly because Janice can't pronounce 'chia' and Martin doesn't want turmeric in his mango smoothie, whereas Mum wants extra shots of spirulina in everything, even her cup of tea. Dad orders smashed avocado on sourdough in an over-casual, self-conscious kind of way and Mum says to me, 'He has avocado every day, Becky! Every single day!'

But at last our waiter has gone and we're all sipping coffees and juices and Minnie's crayoning in her *How The Grinch Stole Christmas* colouring book. I'm just telling her that grinches don't *have* to be green, they can be pink (we haven't got a green crayon) when Mum taps a fork on her saucer for attention.

'Now, everyone,' she says, 'I'd like to welcome you to Shoreditch and thank you all for coming to see our new home!'

We all applaud lightly and Mum beams around the table.

'And now,' she continues, 'I'm going to hand you over to Becky, who is hosting Christmas for us all this year. Becky, this is *your* Christmas, love. It's *your* day. We won't interfere at all. Do it any way you like! As long as we watch the Queen's speech.'

'As a republican, I'll be boycotting the Queen's speech,' says Jess at once, raising her hand. 'But I understand that you want to support the monarchy in its repressive and toxic traditions. Just tell me when it's over.'

'As long as there's a turkey,' says Martin with a nervous laugh. 'I do like a turkey on Christmas Day.'

'Martin's sister once made *fish pie*,' says Janice in a pained whisper, as though confessing to a murderer in the family. 'Fish pie on Christmas Day! Can you believe it?'

'Of course we'll have a turkey,' I say. 'And a vegan turkey for Jess,' I add proudly.

I've found a vegan turkey online, made from soybeans and mushrooms. It's in the shape of a turkey, with legs and everything!

'Thanks, Becky,' says Jess, looking pleased. 'That's really good of you.'

'And stuffing,' says Martin. 'I do like plenty of stuffing. And pigs in blankets . . .'

'Bread sauce,' says Dad.

'I like Brussels sprouts with chestnuts,' says Janice. 'There's a super Delia recipe, Becky. I'll send it to you.'

'No, no, no.' Mum shakes her head. 'Brussels sprouts don't need any fussing. Just boiled with a bit of butter.'

'I don't eat butter,' puts in Jess at once.

'We'll have all of that,' I promise. 'And Christmas pudding and Christmas cake and . . . er . . .'

What else is there? My mind's gone blank.

'Crackers!' says Suze. 'I'll bring crackers. Unless, Jess, do you want to bring crackers?'

'Christmas crackers are problematic,' says Jess without a flicker. 'The toys inside are forgettable bits of plastic tat that contribute to the choking of wildlife and destruction of our eco-system. But I'll bring some if you want,' she adds.

'Right.' Suze looks a bit shellshocked. 'Or we could maybe . . . not have crackers?'

'I'll find some eco crackers,' I say hurriedly.

'Martin and I were thinking we should have a piñata!' puts in Janice brightly. 'The children would like that.'

'A piñata?' I echo, puzzled. 'Is that a Christmas thing?'

'Martin and I have been watching *Christmas Around the World*, love,' Janice informs me. 'It's an afternoon show on BBC2. Very educational. And the Mexicans have a piñata at Christmas time! So why not us?'

'Well,' I say, a bit flummoxed. 'Er . . .'

'We want to do Santa Lucia, too,' continues Janice. 'You put candles on your head and wear a white robe and sing Swedish songs.'

'Lovely!' agrees Mum with enthusiasm. 'Let's have an international Christmas!'

'That's cultural appropriation,' says Jess disapprovingly.

'It's not if you borrow from *all* cultures,' Mum counters. 'Then you're being fair.'

'Christmas trees are a German tradition,' chimes in Dad knowledgeably. 'Prince Albert brought them over.'

'Christmas trees are problematic,' says Jess, but I'm not sure anyone's listening.

'Jesus wasn't British,' puts in Janice. 'I don't mean to sound disrespectful or anything, but he wasn't.' She looks around as though waiting for someone to disagree.

'Well, obviously Jesus wasn't British—' Luke begins.

'There you go, then!' says Mum triumphantly. 'We can have a piñata! Becky, you can get one, can't you, love?'

'Er . . . of course!' I say. I grab my Christmas notebook out of my bag and write down *piñata, candles, Swedish songs??*

'Christmas trees are problematic,' repeats Jess, more loudly. 'A better alternative would be to decorate an item already found within the home, such as a broom.' She turns to me. 'You can decorate it with recycled materials such as old tin cans, hammered into festive shapes.'

A *broom*? I'm not hanging a broom with old tin cans and calling it a Christmas tree. I'm just not.

'I'm sure we can make some sort of ecologically appropriate tree work somehow,' says Luke firmly, seeing my face.

'What about presents?' demands Suze. 'Does anyone have any requests, because I never know *what* to get.'

'I'm going to give everyone a makeover on the day as my present,' says Janice brightly. 'There, the surprise is ruined, but at least you know you'll look beautiful!'

My jaw falls slightly and I exchange glances with Suze.

'Wow, Janice!' says Suze. 'That sounds . . . What exactly do you mean?'

'I'll give all the girls one of my special contouring make-ups,' says Janice happily. 'And the men will have a facial scrub and polish. I'm going to bring all my kit.'

'Right,' I say faintly. 'Um, fab!'

I've had one of Janice's special contouring make-ups before. First she drew stripes on me as though she was marking up a motorway. Then she tried to use Sellotape to give my eyeshadow 'nice crisp lines' and I lost about four layers of skin.

But anyway. It's very kind of her and maybe she's improved.

'And guess what? Jess and Tom are giving us all zero-waste presents!' says Janice proudly. 'Jess has already told me all about it, haven't you, love? So imaginative.'

'What are you giving us, Jess?' I say, unable to keep a challenging note out of my voice.

I know I shouldn't – but I want to catch her out. Whatever it is, I'm going to find something 'problematic' with it. Even if it's a hemp basket from a charity shop, I'll shake my head sorrowfully and say, 'Oh Jess, but what about the wasteful electricity used up in the charity shop?'

'Well,' says Jess after a pause. 'I guess I can tell you without totally giving it away. Tom and I would very much like to give you each . . . a word.'

I stare at her, the wind knocked out of my sails. A *word*?

'You mean, a wooden word that you put on the mantelpiece?' says Mum, looking puzzled.

'No, simply a word,' says Jess. 'We will say the word aloud to you and that will be our gift.'

'Gosh,' says Suze, looking a bit stunned. 'That's . . . I've never . . .'

'Bit difficult to wrap up,' says Dad jovially.

'It will be wrapped in significance,' replies Jess without flickering, and Dad coughs.

'Of course it will!' he says.

'What word are you giving us?' I demand, finding my voice.

'That would give away the surprise,' says Jess. 'We want to give each of you a different word, according to . . .' She looks around the table and hesitates. 'Well, anyway. That's what we want to do.'

I stare at her, intrigued. What word is she giving me? I'm desperate to know. It better be a nice word.

Oh God. It better not be 'Visa bill'.

No, I'm OK. That's two words.

'Hey Bex,' says Suze in my ear, and I look up to see she's come round to perch beside me, holding her coffee cup. 'A word, huh?'

'I know,' I say with a tiny eye-roll. 'Trust Jess to win on the virtuous-present front.'

'Well, I was thinking. Shall we give each other zero-waste presents this year, too? You know, instead of being hollow consumers and all that?'

Suze surveys me expectantly and immediately I wish I'd thought of it.

'Yes!' I agree enthusiastically. 'Only, what? Not a word, because that's copying Jess.'

'No. But maybe . . .' She thinks for a moment. 'We could write a song for each other? And perform it as the present?'

'What?' I say in horror. 'Suze, are you nuts?'

'Or we could make something out of found objects.' Suze's eyes light up. 'That could be fun.'

Fun? I'm trying to think of a tactful way to tell Suze that it sounds the least fun ever, when inspiration hits me.

'I know!' I say in excitement. 'We'll just give each other something that we already own. It's green and it's easy and the present will actually be a *nice* thing.'

'Oh my God!' exclaims Suze. 'Brilliant idea, Bex!'

There's a short silence. My mind is already roaming excitedly over Suze's wardrobe. She's got so many amazing clothes. What if she gives me her purple embroidered coat?

No. She wouldn't. It's too precious. But *maybe* she would . . . ?

I suddenly notice the same distant look on Suze's face.

'Suze, tell me what you'd like,' I say. 'Whatever it is, it's yours.'

'No!' she protests. 'I'm not going to *ask* for anything. That's not the Christmas spirit.'

'Just give me a hint,' I suggest.

'No! I'll be delighted with *anything* you give me, Bex. Doesn't matter what.'

But as she sips her coffee, her face is again preoccupied. What's she thinking about? My new silver pumps. Or . . . no. My leopard-print bag?

Argh. This is impossible! Maybe I'll give her more than one thing.

'Mango smoothie, soy latte, smashed avocado on

135

sourdough . . .' A waiter interrupts us and we all look up.

'I'd better get back to my seat,' says Suze. 'Bon appetit!'

The waiter starts putting down drinks and plates, and I pick up my pen again. I'd better make a few more notes in my Christmas notebook, before I forget everything. I write down *Suze present, stuffing, bread sauce, eco crackers, eco tree (NOT broom)*. Then I pause.

I don't know how to make bread sauce, I realize. It's always just appeared on the table in a jug, every Christmas. How do you make *bread* into a *sauce*? And where will I find an eco tree?

I'm staring ahead with a furrowed brow when Luke pulls a chair up beside me.

'All OK?' he says.

'Fine!' I say automatically, but I've suddenly remembered pigs in blankets, and scribble it down in my book. Then I write *vegan pigs in blankets???* Is that a thing? Without quite meaning to, I heave a great sigh – then look up to see Luke watching me.

'Becky,' he says in a low voice. 'Don't fret. None of this really matters. If we don't manage to get hold of pigs in blankets, Christmas won't collapse.'

'I know.' I give him a grateful smile. 'Still, you know. I want everyone to be happy . . .'

'They will be,' he says firmly. 'Minnie, poppet, can I borrow your book for a moment?'

He takes Minnie's Grinch book and flips to the page where all the Whos are holding hands and singing, not caring that the Grinch has nicked all their stuff. I love that page.

'*This* is Christmas,' he says, pointing at the happy line of Whos. 'Remember? Friends and family gathered together, celebrating. Not presents, not piñatas, *people*.'

'I know, but—'

'Whatever the Grinch can steal, that's not Christmas,' asserts Luke firmly.

I turn his words over in my head. *Whatever the Grinch can steal, that's not Christmas.* I love that. I'll just have to try to keep it in mind. I gaze at the book for a moment longer – then impulsively give Luke a kiss.

'You're right,' I say. 'Thank you.'

I really do love my husband. Even with his moustache.

Messages

Janice
Becky, here's the recipe for Brussels sprouts with chestnuts. They're delicious! Janice xxx

Mum
Don't listen to Janice, love. Brussels sprouts don't need messing about. Just trim them and simmer them. Easy. Mum xxx

Suze
Bex, I'm not actually that keen on Brussels sprouts, could we have broccoli instead? Suze xxx

Bex
Hi Jess!
I think your idea of giving us all words for Christmas is really amazing!!! I was wondering if you wanted a suggestion for my word? Because if so – just a thought – you could give me 'edgy'.
Bx

Bex
Or 'cool'.
Bx

Bex
Or 'The Girl in the Blue Eyeshadow'. I know that's more than one word, but I mean, they're free, aren't they?
Bx

Jess
Becky, I'm not going to tell you what your present is. Jess.

From: Myriad Miracle
To: Becky Brandon
Subject: Fitness questionnaire!

Hi Mrs Brandon (née Bloomwood)

Thank you for your completed online fitness questionnaire. We hope you're excited to embark on your new Myriad Miracle Training System™ program!

However, we think you may have misconstrued some of the questions and request that you resubmit them for our analysis.

QUESTIONS FOR RESUBMISSION

12. What is your specific aim?

We would expect a fitness or wellbeing goal rather than 'Squish into Alexander McQueen dress'.

13. Do you have any particular areas of concern?'

We would expect an area such as 'body fat percentage' or 'cardio fitness', rather than 'zip'.

We look forward to receiving your amended questionnaire.

Happy health-seeking!

Debs
(membership assistant)

NINE

I am still edgy. I *am*.

I'm staring at myself in the mirror before work on Monday morning, tweaking my Letherby tweed suit, which I've just 'distressed'. I was inspired by my friend Danny Kovitz, the designer. He can take a sack, gather it in places, fray a hem or two . . . and make it look like an amazing dress. So I thought I'd do the same thing. Only I'm not sure I've created *quite* the same effect.

I've unpicked a couple of seams, shredded the hems with my nail scissors and added some brooches. I also tried to gather the jacket with some stitches, creating new shape and line – except I created a weird bulge instead. I might unpick that quickly.

'I'm off, Becky,' says Luke, striding into the bedroom, holding his briefcase. He stops dead at the sight of me. 'Wow,' he adds cautiously. 'You look . . . different.'

'It's edgy,' I say quickly. 'I've distressed it.' Then I realize he's peering at my face. 'Oh, my eyeshadow?' I add carelessly. 'Yes, I thought I'd go for a stronger look.'

On the way back from Shoreditch, I popped into Boots and bought a make-up palette called 'Ultimate Drama' and I've just followed a YouTube tutorial called 'Edgy Blue-Black Look'.

I mean, OK. It's quite dramatic for a Monday morning. But then, why *shouldn't* Monday mornings be about bold eyeshadow?

'Uh-huh,' says Luke slowly. 'Is that a blue streak in your hair?'

'Only a tiny one.' I shrug.

'And what's this music?' asks Luke curiously, tilting his head to listen to the beat thumping through the room.

'Spittser,' I say casually. 'You know, the DJ? He's awesome. He was DJ-ing in Gdansk last night. Shame we couldn't have been there.'

I got all that off a website last night. And I downloaded the 'ten essential underground clubbing tracks'.

'*Gdansk*,' echoes Luke, looking perplexed. 'Becky . . . has anything brought on this sudden interest in Eastern European clubs?'

'It's not *sudden*,' I contradict him. 'I've always been into edgy music, you know that.'

'Last Christmas you made us all listen to *Abba's Greatest Hits*,' Luke reminds me.

'I'm eclectic,' I say frostily. 'People can be eclectic, you know.'

Luke's mouth is twitching, but I'm going to ignore him. I put a leather cuff on over my tweed jacket and look at myself with satisfaction. Meanwhile Luke's eyes have drifted downwards to my new black boots.

'Now, *those* are great,' he says.

'Oh, these?' I shrug carelessly.

I'm not sure I can actually walk in these boots, but they're the edgiest things I've ever possessed. I got them online, next-day delivery. They have killer heels, eyelets, metal rivets *and* little chains swinging on the backs of them.

'They're hot,' says Luke, still transfixed.

Ah. Right. These boots have clearly made an impression. Luke's voice has got deeper by about five notches, and when at last he meets my gaze, his dark eyes are gleaming.

'Glad you like them,' I say, and preen a little.

'Oh, I like them.' He nods slowly.

Luke has a real thing for boots. I should have put these on last night. And now, just the way he's looking at me makes me catch my breath. I stare back silently and feel my heart start to beat harder.

I've often thought I should write *Becky Brandon née Bloomwood's Guide to Marriage*. I could jot down helpful observations here and there. And my first observation would be that love in marriage is like one of those wavy graphs where the pen keeps zooming up and down and you can't predict it at all.

Obviously I love Luke all the time, like constant thumpy background music. But those exhilarating guitar solo moments when I suddenly think, 'Oh my *God*, I want you *now*' seem to come at random. (Is this just me? I must ask Suze.)

And this is a perfect example. Last night we had a nice supper *à deux* in the kitchen, which should have been all romantic. But all I could do was stare at Luke's upper lip and think, '*Why* did you have to grow a moustache, couldn't you just have made a donation?' Whereas now, this morning, when we're in a rush and need to leave, all I can think is 'I don't care about the moustache, you're my total love God.' In fact, I feel quite hot and flustered. It's the way he's looking at me, all purposefully.

'What time are you back?' I ask huskily. 'Do you have any late meetings?'

'I'll cancel them,' says Luke, his eyes not leaving mine. 'If you keep those boots on.'

'Mummy!' Minnie comes running into the room, breaking the mood. I blink a couple of times, then shoot a rueful grin at Luke. 'Mummeeee!' She clutches my hands and pulls at them. 'Where is my *darden-on-a-tray*?'

'Don't worry, sweetheart,' I say. 'It's all ready.'

'I must dash,' says Luke, giving me a similar rueful look. 'See you later. Oh, and the school just sent an email,' he adds as he leaves the room. 'Something about a nit check?'

Honestly. Every time I try to do anything edgy, the school has to bring up nits. I swear they're doing it on purpose.

As I grab my trench out of the hall cupboard I decide I'll wear my trainers to walk Minnie to school and bring my edgy boots in a bag. *Not* because I can't walk in these spiky heels, but simply because the road gets a bit muddy in places. Also, I need to do about seventy thousand steps today, to make up for a few steps I haven't quite accomplished recently.

143

Ooh, I wonder if sex counts? That burns calories, doesn't it?

As we walk along, I'm half listening to Minnie chatter about getting a hamper for Christmas and half keeping an eye on the 'winter garden on a tray' balanced in my other hand. Every time I glance at it I sigh inwardly. I totally meant to ace the next craft project, but I forgot about it till we got back from Shoreditch and I had to run round the garden hastily gathering a few twigs and berries. It doesn't look like a 'winter garden on a tray', it looks like 'random crappy stuff on a tray'.

As I'm helping Minnie hang up her coat, I see Steph enter with Harvey and I wait so that we head towards the classroom together. Her face is pale and strained, but she gives me a wan smile.

'Nice garden,' I say, although hers is even worse than mine, just a clump of muddy grass, with a brown leaf balanced on top.

'Yup,' she says shortly. 'Whatever. Oh *God*.'

I follow her gaze and my eyes widen. Suze has already arrived and looks radiant as she holds up the best 'winter garden on a tray' I've ever seen. (Out of three total.) It's got moss and branches and snow and acorn figures having a picnic. How long did *that* take?

'Goodness!' Miss Lucas is exclaiming. 'How wonderful, Lady Cleath-Stuart! Is that a real bird's nest?'

'We found it in a tree,' says Suze. 'It was already abandoned,' she adds hastily.

'A real bird's nest,' echoes Steph in disbelief, and I can see her gazing at Suze's garden with a kind of exhausted, wistful look.

144

'Oh, Bex!' says Suze, turning to leave. 'Didn't see you there—' She breaks off and gapes at me. 'Your *eyes*.'

'Thought I'd try a new look,' I say carelessly. 'What do you think?'

'Um . . . yes!' says Suze, after a pause. 'Very . . . D'you want a lift to work?'

'No, don't worry, I'll walk. I need to do some steps.'

'Cool. Well, see you there. Hi, Steph!' Suze adds as she passes and Steph mutters, 'Hi,' while quickly turning so that her earthy, cloddy garden is hidden from sight.

Luckily, Minnie and Harvey don't seem to have noticed how superior Suze's garden is. (The brilliant thing about children is, they have no idea about anything.) Also, to give her credit, Miss Lucas looks just as delighted with our gardens as she did with Suze's one.

'Harvey!' she says. 'Minnie! What lovely winter gardens!'

'Yup,' says Steph again, in an undertone that only I can hear. 'Ours has been shortlisted for the Turner Prize.'

I shoot a quick grin – then notice that her eyes are glistening. Oh God. It's the horrible bastard husband, I know it is, only I can't ask her about it, standing here in the school corridor.

'Now, I'm glad I've caught the pair of you,' Miss Lucas says. 'We've just cast our Nativity play, and both Minnie and Harvey are going to be kings!'

A king! I can't help beaming at Minnie in delight.

'The costume is very simple,' Miss Lucas adds cheerfully. 'Here's the pattern . . .' She hands each of us a big

145

envelope and my smile freezes. Pattern? As in, *sewing*? 'Just use a simple running stitch,' Miss Lucas continues blithely, 'with perhaps some pin tucks. If you *did* want to add some embroidery or ribbon, that would be wonderful, but it's not at all essential.' She smiles at us brightly.

Pin tucks? *Embroidery?*

I remember clearly looking around this school, and I don't recall the head teacher saying, 'Of course, if your child comes here, you *will* be expected to be proficient at pin tucks and embroidery.' But I can't say anything. Minnie's looking up at me expectantly.

'No problem!' I hear myself replying breezily. 'I expect I'll add some sequins too, and some extra hand-stitched detail.'

'Wonderful!' Miss Lucas claps her hands together.

Steph, meanwhile, has made no response, just shoved the envelope in her tote, her eyes distant. When we've said goodbye to the children and are heading out again, she says, 'See you then, Becky,' and quickly ducks into the Ladies' before I can reply. I stare after her a bit anxiously – then follow her in. I just want to make sure she's OK.

There are quite a few mums in there, as there always are. No one's there because they actually need the loo, they're just gossiping. Steph makes her way to one of the two sinks, stares at herself miserably in the mirror, then starts redoing her eye make-up. I decide I'll give her a moment to finish, then draw her aside for a supportive word.

She's struggling to do her make-up, though, because

her eyes keep watering and she keeps having to wipe it all off. After a bit, a woman I don't recognize peers at Steph and says, 'Excuse me . . . are you OK?'

'Me?' Steph jumps like a scalded cat. 'Yes, I'm fine. Fine!'

She gives me a desperate look in the mirror, then quickly heads into a cubicle. Without pausing, I hurry into the one next door. I want to text her, but the signal in here is rubbish. If I whisper, everyone might hear . . . if I knock on the wall, everyone will definitely hear . . .

In sudden inspiration I get out a pen from my bag and find an old receipt. It's for three No7 serums from Boots which were on special offer. Ooh. Where did I put those, again?

Anyway. Not the point. I write on it, *Are you really OK? Love Becky xx* and pass it under the cubicle wall.

A few seconds later it comes back and Steph has written underneath: *No. Not really.*

Knew it.

I write, *Let's go and talk. In your car? x* and send it back. Almost at once comes her reply: *Yes please. Thanks. X*

Twenty minutes later, I've heard more about Steph's life, her husband Damian's life and their last, toxic holiday in Cyprus than I could ever have predicted. To be honest, it's shaken me up a bit. Marriages should be like Sellotape. They should be all safely stuck down. But they're not, they peel off in the steam and sometimes they *never* stick properly again.

Suze had a wobble with Tarkie in the States, and I feared the worst. Then there was Jess looking all bleak the other day . . . and now this. Apparently Damian won't listen to reason or do counselling. At first he said there wasn't another woman – but then it turned out that there was. They work in the same company. He's in the IT department and she organizes events. Apparently they had to go to Manchester for a conference and it all kicked off in the Malmaison Hotel. (I feel I know *slightly* too many details about this, but I don't want to interrupt Steph when she's pouring her heart out.)

We're parked in a side road, and Steph keeps talking, then breaking off to check in a paranoid way if anyone's watching us. Her main concern seems to be that no one must know. Because then Harvey might get to know. And what she *really* wants is for Damian to realize he's being an idiot and come home and for Harvey never to know a thing about it.

'I mean, I suppose Damian's right,' she says, staring miserably out of the window. 'I'm not much fun these days. I don't crack a lot of jokes. If we go out for dinner, chances are I'll fall asleep at the table.' She heaves a great sigh. 'But it's hard, you know, doing the school runs and getting to the office on time, and I've had this mega project at work . . .' She rubs her forehead as though trying to massage away her thoughts. 'We moved into our house six months ago and I still haven't chosen a paint colour for the bedroom. Or even unpacked all the boxes. We rowed about that and he said I'd turned into a misery. And he was right.'

I feel a swell of fury at this guy, making someone as hardworking as Steph feel crap. I caught sight of him at school the other day and discreetly sized him up – and

I wasn't impressed. He was dressed in the faded jeans he always seems to wear and was constantly on the phone. He wasn't even *looking* at Harvey, who was clutching his hand. Plus he's got a really annoying laugh. I mean who does he think he *is*?

'Steph, you're not a misery, he's a bastard!' I say fiercely. 'You're amazing! You're strong and positive and always there for Harvey. And anyway, who has time for fun? We're all too busy making pictures out of spaghetti!'

I'm trying to make Steph smile, and at last she gives a kind of half-laugh.

'I've got three boxes I haven't unpacked since I moved out of my flat in Fulham,' I tell her, for good measure. 'I've got no idea what's in them. And anyway, if your husband wants the boxes unpacked, why doesn't he do it?'

Steph gives another sort of half-laugh, but she doesn't answer the question, and I don't feel I know her well enough to delve any deeper.

'What about your mum?' I venture. 'What does she say about all this?'

'I haven't told her,' admits Steph, after a pause. 'You're the only person I've told, Becky.'

'Tell her!' I say impulsively, even though I don't know anything about Steph's mum.

'Maybe.' Steph bites her lip, then musters a smile. 'I'd better go. You must have to go, too. Thanks.'

'I didn't do anything,' I say, a bit helplessly.

'You did.' She leans to give me a quick, tight hug. 'I appreciate it, Becky. Let me drive you to work.'

Steph drops me at the gates to Letherby Hall and I hurry up the tree-lined drive to the main house. As I enter the gift shop I'm all ready to explain away my delay to Suze – but instead it's Tarquin who greets me.

I've known Tarkie for years. He's had his ups and downs, but he's on great form at the moment. Since we all got back from the States, he's thrown himself into running Letherby Hall with real drive. He's had loads of good ideas for the business and talks to Luke a lot about it, and Luke says he thinks Tarquin is really stepping up into his role.

On the other hand, he's still quite weird. In a lovable, Tarkie-ish way. Today he's wearing a shrunken, holey rugby shirt which I'm quite sure he's had since school, and his eyes have an intense look to them as he draws breath.

'I hear we're coming to you for Christmas, Becky,' he says. 'Marvellous!'

'Yes!' I say brightly. 'I hope it'll be fun!'

'I know it's early days to talk specifics,' Tarkie presses on. 'But you're probably already thinking about entertainment on the day. I ask, because the Met is broadcasting a performance of *Parsifal* on Christmas Day.'

'Is that . . . Wagner?' I hazard, because Tarkie is a total Wagner nut.

'His most sublime, transporting opera.' Tarkie blinks at me. 'A masterpiece. And I was thinking we could gather around your television and watch it after lunch. I think it would be terribly stimulating for the children.'

A Wagner opera? On *Christmas Day*?

'Wow,' I say, trying not to give away my horror. 'That

sounds . . . You know. Fab. I mean, I love Wagner, who doesn't? Only, I'm just thinking, is it *very* Christmassy?'

'It's timeless,' says Tarkie earnestly. 'It's inspiring. The prelude alone is a Christmas gift for anyone. *Taa-daaah-daaah hmm hmm* . . .' He starts humming, his gaze fixed unnervingly on mine. '*Taa-daah-daaa-dee-daaah* . . .'

'Tarkie!' To my huge relief, Suze's shrill voice interrupts us. She's striding towards us, fixing Tarkie with a suspicious gaze. 'Are you singing Wagner? You *know* the rule: no Wagner in the shop.'

'Tarkie was just saying how *Parsifal* is being shown on Christmas Day,' I say brightly. 'That's good news, isn't it?'

'We're not watching bloody Wagner on Christmas Day!' Suze erupts and I breathe out a sigh of relief.

'I'm simply trying to help with entertainment,' says Tarkie defensively. 'Opera is a form that everyone can enjoy, young and old.'

'No it's not,' retorts Suze. 'It's a form which turns most people into rigid statues because they're so bored, but they can't leave the room because the opera-lover says "Sssh!" when they even twitch a muscle. And it goes on for six hours.'

'*Parsifal* does not go on for six hours . . .' begins Tarkie, but Suze ignores him.

'I think Christmas is all about the children.' She turns to me. 'I think we should have craft activities, finger paint, glitter, all that kind of stuff.'

My heart slightly sinks. Craft *again*? We're talking about Christmas Day here. Christmas isn't about finger-painting. It's about sitting on the sofa, eating Quality

Street and watching Christmas specials on TV while the dads try to find batteries for all the new toys and break half of them and the children end up crying. *That's* tradition.

'We could do, I suppose,' I say carefully. 'Except Jess thinks glitter is evil.'

'Hmm.' Suze bites her lip in thought. 'We could make play dough?'

'Maybe,' I say, trying to sound more enthused than I feel. 'Or just watch telly?'

'OK, well let's wait till we see what's on telly,' says Suze. 'Then we can make a plan. Oh and by the way, I can pick up Aphrodite and Hermes tonight,' she adds, changing the subject. 'The forklift truck is back from the menders. I'll bring one of the men.'

'Suze,' I say, immediately feeling bad. 'Don't take my hideous statues. You're welcome to come and spend Christmas with us, whatever. You don't want them.'

'No, I do!' says Suze eagerly. 'I've had a brilliant idea. We'll use them next Halloween. I'm going to call them Grotesque and Grotesqua.'

'Oh,' I say, feeling just very slightly insulted. 'Well, OK.' And I'm about to take off my coat when Suze touches my shoulder.

'Listen, Bex,' she says more quietly. 'Another thing. Before any customers arrive, I wanted to ask you . . . I've been thinking.' She pauses, then continues even more quietly, 'D'you think Jess is OK? Yesterday she seemed a bit weird.'

'Yes!' I exclaim. 'I thought exactly the same thing! She was tense and kind of . . . odd.'

'Exactly! She froze up when we mentioned Tom, and I thought . . . I got worried that maybe . . .'

Suze's face is all twisted up anxiously, and I know just what she's thinking.

'Khaki hotpants,' I say before I can stop myself.

'What?' Suze looks puzzled.

'I thought maybe Tom had gone off with some charity worker in khaki hotpants. Or she had. Or something.'

'Oh God.' Suze stares at me unhappily. 'That's kind of what I thought, too. Only I saw cropped chinos and a bandana.'

We lapse into silence and I find myself picturing Tom snogging a girl in cropped chinos and a red bandana. Then I change the bandana to a horrible green one and make her nose bigger, because she's too attractive. Then I make her chinos really unflattering and have her picking her nose. God, she's gross. Why would Tom prefer *her*?

'It might not be that,' I say at last. 'Maybe they just had a fight.'

'Yes.' Suze seizes on this. 'I mean, the strain of waiting for an adoption must be really stressful.'

'*So* stressful,' I agree. 'And they're all on their own out there, without any support . . . Anyway, I thought I might take Jess out for a drink. Will you come too? Then she might relax and tell us what's up.'

'She's not very talkative,' says Suze dubiously. 'And does she even drink?'

'All right, we'll go to a cooperative and eat Fairtrade oats,' I say a bit impatiently. 'The point is, she's all bottled up right now. We can help her open up and share her pain.'

I feel quite an expert on listening to marital woes after my session with Steph. I can see Suze and myself sitting at a table, eating oats and holding Jess's hands as she falteringly explains her predicament and weeps, and then says, 'But just being with you girls helps me so much, especially you, Becky.'

I mean, she doesn't *have* to say 'Especially you, Becky'. She just might.

'Poor Jess,' says Suze, as I take off my trench coat. 'I've always thought—' She breaks off mid-stream, and I look up to see her staring at my distressed tweed outfit. 'Oh my God, Bex. What happened to your *suit*?'

She doesn't seem quite as impressed by my customizing as I'd hoped. In fact, her tone sounds suspiciously close to horror.

'Oh,' I say self-consciously, tugging at my frayed jacket. 'D'you like it? I thought I'd play around with it.'

'You did that yourself? On *purpose*?'

'Yes!' I exclaim defensively. 'I customized it.'

'Right,' says Suze, after a long pause. 'Er . . . great!'

She watches as I change out of my trainers into my black riveted boots and her eyes get even bigger. 'Wow. Those are . . . fierce.'

'Do you like them?' I say, suddenly alert. Does Suze want these boots for Christmas? I have only just bought them, but then, that's what Christmas is all about: giving. 'They'd really suit you,' I add generously. 'D'you want to try them on?'

154

'No!' says Suze, recoiling. 'No thanks! I mean, they look great on you, but . . .'

'Becky, dear!' Irene bustles up, eyeing my suit with alarm. 'My goodness, what happened to your clothes? Have you been in an accident?'

Honestly. Does *no one* around here recognize the edgy look?

'It's distressed,' I explain, a bit tetchily. 'It's *fashion*.'

'I see,' says Irene faintly. 'Very modern, dear. Oh, your boots!' She claps a hand over her mouth.

'Have you got blue dye in your hair?' demands Suze, peering incredulously at my head.

'Yes,' I shrug casually. 'You know I like to mix things up. Live life dangerously.'

It wasn't actually that dangerous: it's washable non-toxic blue hair dye for children. But that's not the point. I saunter casually over to the mirror, trying to balance on my spiky heels, and stare at my reflection. I don't look like an uncool suburban mum, that's for sure. I look like . . .

Well, I don't look boring, anyway.

It's a fairly slow morning, and by eleven o'clock my feet are *killing* me, although I would never admit it to any-one. Just as I'm thinking I might sneak off for a KitKat, a group of women arrive in the gift shop, all very well dressed and holding copies of *A Guide to Letherby Hall*. They must have just been round the house.

'Well, I didn't think much of the Long Gallery,' the one with the blonde ponytail is saying as she looks at a

155

row of multicoloured tweed jackets, and I stare at her indignantly. How can she say that? The Long Gallery's brilliant. It's got loads of amazing paintings and sculptures which I'm totally intending to learn about one day. Thank goodness Suze isn't in earshot – she'd be really hurt.

'The Rodin was interesting,' ventures her dark-haired friend, but the mean blonde woman rolls her eyes.

'Clichéd,' she says disdainfully.

Clichéd? *She's* clichéd.

I want to say something rude to her, but of course I can't. My feet are agony and I'm feeling really pissed off, but both Suze and Irene have disappeared somewhere, so I force myself to approach the group with a pleasant smile.

'Hello, may I help you?'

As I'm speaking, I give Mean Blondie a quick Manhattan Once-over and realize she must have scads of money. That coat is £800 on Net-a-Porter, I've seen it.

'We're fine, thanks,' says the nice woman who liked the Rodin.

'Is that tweed suit standard?' chimes in Mean Blondie, eyeing me closely – and I realize she's just given *me* the Manhattan Once-over. 'I didn't see anything like that on the racks,' she adds, studying the fraying. 'Is it for sale?'

Hmm. Well, this woman might be mean, but at least she appreciates my artistry.

'It's a bespoke, customized outfit, actually,' I say, softening slightly. 'Here at Letherby Hall, we believe that tweed doesn't have to be boring. It can be frayed, pleated,

156

edgy, vibrant . . . it has limitless possibilities,' I finish, feeling quite inspired. I could be a spokesperson for the Tweed Promotion Board! 'Are you interested in ordering a customized suit for yourself?'

I'll customize it myself, I'm thinking in mounting excitement. I'll start a business! I'll call my label Becky's Bespoke Tweed, and people will say—

'No,' she says flatly. 'I just wondered why you look so strange.'

Strange?

My excitement collapses and I force myself not to glare at her. Instead, I say as politely as I can, 'Well, enjoy the rest of the store.'

I pretend to be busy with a display of tweed purses, but as the women walk off I eye Mean Blondie's back malevolently. If she says *one more nasty thing . . .*

They look at the soaps and the shampoos but they don't put any in their baskets. Nor any marmalade or jam. Then they stop to look at my gorgeously arranged *hygge* table.

'*Hygge Collection?*' says Mean Blondie disparagingly, reading my handwritten sign. 'For God's sake, *really*? Aren't we all *hygged* to death? Isn't it a little bit over?'

OK, that's it. I've had enough. They're not calling me 'over'.

'Oh, I'm *so* sorry,' I say smoothly, striding over and removing the *hygge* sign. 'That sign's out of date. This is actually our brand-new *sprygge* collection.'

I cross out *Hygge Collection*, turn the cardboard sign over, firmly write *Sprygge Collection*, then place it back on the table.

'*Sprygge?*' Mean Blondie stares at me.

'Yes, *sprygge*. Haven't you heard of *sprygge*?' I add in pitying tones. 'It *is* rather new to this country. Rather niche. Norwegian,' I add for good measure.

To be absolutely truthful, the word *sprygge* just popped out of my mouth before I could stop it. But now I've written it down, I think it looks really good.

'What does it mean?' asks another of the women.

'If you don't speak Norwegian, it's hard to convey,' I say, playing for time. 'But really, it's . . . a positiveness. A radiant, joyful, yet complex feeling. More intense than *hygge*. Like . . . turbo-*hygge*.'

'Turbo-*hygge*?' echoes Mean Blondie sceptically.

'Yes,' I say defiantly. 'It's the sense of euphoria and relief you feel when everything seemed as though it was going desperately wrong, but then turned out OK. It's *that* feeling.'

'I know that feeling!' says the dark-haired woman.

'There you go!' I smile at her. 'Imagine you're going to miss your train and you're utterly panicked, but then you run up the platform and you just catch it. As you're sitting there, panting, the sensation you feel spreading through your body is *sprygge*.'

'I never knew there was a word for that,' says the third woman curiously. 'Language is *so* interesting.'

'Exactly!' I beam at her. 'And these carefully curated products accompany that wonderful feeling,' I add, gesturing at the table. 'The scented candles soothe your nerves . . . the blanket reassures you that everything's OK now . . . and the chocolates say: "Well done, you made it, you deserve a treat!"'

Mean Blondie is still peering at me superciliously, but her friends seem quite transfixed.

'I'll take a candle,' says the dark-haired woman.

'I'll have some chocolates,' puts in the third woman. 'I think we do deserve a treat, don't we?'

'Well, I might have a blanket,' says Mean Blondie reluctantly.

To my slight disbelief, all three women start picking up items from the table and looking at them with more interest. *Sprygge* worked!

I turn to see both Suze and Irene watching me from the other side of the shop, and beam proudly back.

'I'll just leave you to browse,' I say to the women. 'Please let me know if you need any more help.'

I head towards Suze and Irene, mouthing 'Result!' and doing a discreet little fist pump.

'Wow, Bex,' says Suze as I reach her. 'That sounded amazing!'

'Very interesting, dear,' says Irene admiringly.

'Look, they're buying loads!' adds Suze in a whisper. 'Bex, where did you get all that information about *sprygge* from?'

I open my mouth to tell her that I made it up – then stop. I can just see a glimpse of leather jacket through the doorway. Is that . . .

Yes. It's him. Craig. Wow. I didn't expect him back so soon.

I mean, not that I was *expecting* him. I just . . . Anyway. He's here. Before I can stop myself, I toss back my hair and lean nonchalantly against the counter with a cool kind of gaze.

'What are you doing, Bex?' says Suze in surprise, and turns to follow my gaze. 'Oh. Oh!' She suddenly swivels to look at me and says 'Oh' in a completely different voice. Her gaze slowly runs from my blue streaked hair down to my edgy boots. '*Oh*,' she says a fourth time, with heavy emphasis. '*Ohhh*.'

Honestly. Can't she stop saying 'Oh'?

'What?' I say, trying not to sound defensive.

'You're looking pretty rock chick today, aren't you?' Suze is still studying me beadily. 'I *wondered* what you were doing.'

'*Rock chick?*' I try to sound baffled at the suggestion. 'Honestly, Suze. I'm just wearing . . . you know. My normal look.'

'Normal?' scoffs Suze. 'You're calling those boots normal? And your blue streak?' She lowers her voice. 'You're trying to look cool for the rock god.'

'No I'm not!' I retort in a furious undertone. 'And anyway, so are you!' I add, as I notice Suze quickly pulling out her scrunchie and smoothing down her hair. 'And ssh! He's coming! Oh, hi,' I say carelessly as Craig ambles into earshot. 'How was Warsaw? How was Blink Rage? How was the scene?'

'It was good,' says Craig in his lazy, raspy voice. 'You should have come, Becky.'

'Warsaw?' says Suze. 'I didn't know you were going to Warsaw. How did you know that, Bex?'

'Becky and I bumped into each other at the station the other night,' says Craig easily.

'Oh, *did* you?' says Suze, her eyebrows shooting up. 'Imagine that.'

160

'The cottage is awesome,' says Craig, turning his dark gaze on to her. 'The hot tub's in. I never want to leave.'

'Wow,' says Suze, going a bit pink. 'I'm so pleased you like it.'

'Love it,' he says emphatically. 'Love. It.' Then he looks at me again, with that intense dark gaze.

'So Becky, we should have a drink some time. Sink some tequila shots!'

'Oh right!' I swallow, trying to sound nonchalant. 'Yes! Tequila shots! Definitely.'

'We could meet at the Lamb and Flag? Take it from there? Bring your husband,' he adds easily. 'I'd love to meet him. Are you free tonight?'

'Er, yes,' I say, a bit flustered. 'At least, I'd need babysitting . . .'

'I'll do it if you like,' says Suze, shooting me a sardonic look. 'I can pick Minnie up when I come to get the statues. You go out partying.'

'Great.' Craig's eyes crease in a smile. 'Say . . . seven o'clock?'

'Perfect!'

'See you then, Becky.' He puts his hand on my arm and squeezes briefly, then his gaze moves downwards. 'Nice boots,' he adds with a wink.

And then he's off, loping unhurriedly out of the shop. As I watch him go I suddenly realize I'm holding my breath. I'm pretty sure Suze is, too.

'Oh my *God*,' says Suze, as soon as the door has closed behind him, and she wheels round to me. 'What was that?'

'What do you mean,' I reply defensively.

161

'*That!*' She whirls her hands expressively. 'All those sizzling looks!'

'There weren't any sizzling looks!'

'Yes there were! You totally melted under his gaze.'

'Well, so did you,' I retort, and Suze looks a bit abashed.

'OK, maybe I did a bit,' she admits. 'But that doesn't matter, because he's not interested in me. He's not asking me out for dates at the pub.'

'It's not a *date*.' I roll my eyes disparagingly. 'And he's not interested in me.'

'What was that hand on your arm, then?' demands Suze. 'There was definitely sexual tension there. I saw it.'

I feel a tiny flash of pride before I can stop it. Which is *not* because I'm interested in Craig. Of course not. It's just, if your old, mediocre-looking boyfriend unexpectedly turns into a rock god, it's quite flattering if he still . . . you know.

I mean, I'm only human.

'Have you told Luke about Craig?' Suze demands.

'Er . . .'

I pause in my own thoughts. I haven't, actually. That's strange. Why haven't I?

I rack my brain, trying to work it out. It just hasn't come up, I suppose. But there's nothing *sinister* about it. I'm not *hiding* anything. It's just that we're a busy couple and we don't tell each other every single thing, every single day.

If I admit any of this to Suze, though, she'll overreact. She'll think I'm 'keeping things from Luke'. I mean, fair enough, she's uber-sensitive, and I don't blame her. She had that wobbly patch with Tarkie and she *did* keep

162

things from him. (And me. And the world.) But this isn't remotely the same.

'Of course I've told Luke!' I say, crossing my fingers behind my back. 'He thinks it's hilarious. We've joked about it.'

'Oh.' Suze looks wrongfooted. 'Oh, right.'

It's half-true, I tell myself, because I *will* tell Luke. The minute I clap eyes on him this evening, I'll tell him all about Craig, and we'll have a laugh and it'll all be OK.

'Well, have fun tonight,' says Suze, lifting her chin. 'Enjoy.'

'Suze, d'you want to come to the pub too?' I say hurriedly. 'I'm sure you're invited.'

'Oh no!' exclaims Suze in dignified tones. 'He's your friend. Why would I want to come? Let me know if you end up in the hot tub,' she adds with that same sardonic look. 'You'd better take your bikini along.'

TEN

Honestly. Take my bikini along. What a ridiculous idea.

Although – should I? Just in case?

No. *No.* We won't end up in the hot tub, of course we won't. We're just going for a civilized drink at the village pub.

As I sit in the kitchen, colouring with Minnie and waiting for Luke to get home, I feel just very slightly apprehensive about telling Luke all in one fell swoop that 1. My ex lives in the village now, and 2. He's a rock musician, and 3. He's asked us for a drink tonight.

I mean, it's not a *problem*. It's just it's quite a lot of information, out of the blue. Suze is right, I should have mentioned Craig before. I don't know why I didn't.

As I hear the front door, I draw breath, ready to start my little explanation, but Luke strides in, full of energy, and gets in first.

'I've been thinking about your hot boots all day,' he says, coming over and surveying me with gleaming eyes. 'And they're even better than they were this morning. Is it time to put Minnie to bed yet?' He glances down at her. 'I'm sure she needs an early night. Don't you, poppet?'

His intent is so obvious, I can't help laughing. I stand up and say, 'How was your day?' intending to lead quickly on to the topic of Craig, but Luke ignores the question.

'Here's an idea,' he says, putting his arms round me. 'How about you and I get away after Christmas? If you want to go to Warsaw, Becky, why shouldn't we? I looked it up at lunchtime. Found a great hotel with a spa, right by the Presidential Palace. Couples' massages available,' he adds with a fresh glint in his eye.

'That sounds amazing,' I say, a bit breathlessly, because I'm now actually quite anxious to get on to the subject of Craig. 'So, um, a funny thing happened!' I pause, trying to get my words in order, but Luke doesn't seem to hear me.

'What you said to me the other day got under my skin,' he says, more seriously. 'You're right, we *should* stay connected. You're always experimenting with clothes and music, Becky – and you put me to shame. Why *not* go clubbing in Gdansk? Why *not* go for the weekend to Warsaw? Do you know any Polish?' He grins at me. 'I looked up "great boots" on Google translate. It's *Świetne buty,*' he says with relish. '*Świetne buty, kochanie.* That's "Great boots, sweetheart".'

'Right!' I say, desperate to stop his enthusiastic flow. 'So, anyway, I've got something to tell you.'

'What?' says Luke, running his hands down my back and squeezing the tops of my thighs. 'You bought three

165

more pairs of those boots and you've hidden them under the bed? Well, that's fine by me, as long as you bring them to Warsaw.'

'No!' I laugh nervously. 'It's just . . . um . . .'

'Yoo-hoo!' Suze's cheery voice interrupts me and we both look up to see her in the doorway, holding a big cardboard box. 'Your door was open and this was on the doorstep.'

'Oh yes,' Luke bats his forehead with his hand. 'I was intending to go back for that, but I was waylaid by my beautiful wife.'

I see something in Suze's brow soften as she surveys the pair of us. She dumps the box on the table and grins at me.

'Sorry to interrupt your love-in. I'm here to take those vile statues away.'

'Excellent!' says Luke. 'My day gets better and better. Glass of wine, Suze? We're just planning a little trip to Warsaw.'

'Warsaw!' says Suze in surprise – then her eyes light up. 'Are you going with Craig?'

'Craig?' echoes Luke.

'You know, Becky's old boyfriend,' says Suze blithely. 'Wasn't he in Warsaw this weekend? Has Becky told you about the hot tub?' she adds, with a giggle. 'I just went to check it out. It's massive. I don't *dare* tell Tarkie, he'll flip out.'

She looks at Luke expectantly, but he's standing there, holding the wine bottle, looking confused.

'Old boyfriend?' he says after a beat.

'Actually, Suze . . . I hadn't told Luke about Craig

166

yet.' I'm trying to sound casual, but Suze gapes at me in blatant shock.

'But you said you had!' she blurts out. 'You said you'd told Luke!'

I feel a jab of frustration. Why did Suze have to react like that? She's going to make this weird, when it isn't.

'It's no big deal!' I say quickly, with a little laugh, and turn to Luke. 'This guy called Craig who I used to date – *ages* ago, at uni – anyway, he's living in Suze's cottage. And he wants us to have a drink with him tonight. That's all.'

'Right.' Luke digests this. 'And what's the connection to Warsaw?'

'He was in Warsaw for the weekend. He invited you, didn't he, Bex?' Suze adds, and I see a weird little flicker pass across Luke's face.

'I see,' he says in neutral tones. 'So that's why . . . Let me get you that wine.'

'It just gave me the idea of Warsaw,' I say. 'We should definitely go, Luke! It sounds awesome!'

I'm trying to recapture the mood we had a moment ago, but I'm not sure it's working. Luke pours out three glasses and when he lifts his head he's smiling again because that's what Luke is like.

'So, why's this chap in Letherby?' he enquires.

'He's burned out after a tour,' says Suze knowledge-ably. 'He's a real . . . you know. Rock type. Leather jacket, boots, tattoos, long hair . . . A bit grungy. Nothing like you, Luke,' she says eagerly. 'He's *totally* different.'

I think Suze is trying to reassure Luke. But I kind of wish she wouldn't.

167

'I see,' says Luke again, and his gaze runs over my blue-streaked hair, then down over my frayed suit to my new boots. He looks at them for a silent moment, then back up at my face, which is growing hot, I have *no* idea why.

I stare helplessly back, thinking, 'No! You're wrong!'

But wrong about what, exactly? I don't want to second-guess what Luke's thinking. I don't want to make some tiny little nothing into a thing, when it's *not* a thing. It's *not*.

'Anyway.' I try to sound breezy. 'He's asked us to go for a drink tonight. He'd love to meet you. Suze is babysitting.'

'Great,' says Luke in the same neutral tones. 'Sounds fun.'

My head is prickling and I can sense Suze staring meaningfully at me, but I don't want to meet her gaze. I want to make the perfect, light-hearted comment that will instantly smooth everything over. Right now, though, I can't quite think of it.

As we walk through the chilly streets of Letherby to the Lamb and Flag, the village looks enchanting. All the cottages have light glowing from their curtained windows, and there's a Christmas tree on the green, all twinkly with lights. It's idyllic here and I do love it. Even if it isn't edgy Shoreditch.

I can't really savour my surroundings though, because I'm a bit nervous. Luke hasn't said much since I landed the news on him that we're having a drink with my old boyfriend. His eyes are quite distant and his jaw is tight. It's hard to tell what he's thinking.

I mean, honestly! It's no big deal. Or it shouldn't be. Luke and I are an established, happy couple. The fact that Craig is my ex-boyfriend is neither here nor there. Luke should be open-minded about it. If it were me, I'd be open-minded, I tell myself firmly. In fact, I *was* open-minded when we came across an old girlfriend of his called Venetia a few years ago. I *was*.

(Until we had a massive flaming stand-off, but that was totally provoked.)

The point is, Craig is a talented, interesting guy and he's a neighbour and we should be friends with him.

'So I expect you want to know all about Craig,' I say casually as we walk along.

'Not really,' says Luke in unreadable tones.

'Right. Oh. Well anyway . . . we hardly dated at all,' I gabble nervously. 'So. He's hardly an ex-boyfriend at all.'

'Mmm,' says Luke, as though this fact is of no interest to him.

'I mean, in some ways he's like you,' I say, after a moment's thought. 'He travels a lot, too.'

As I say the words I have a sudden image of Luke heading to the airport with his overcoat and briefcase, compared to Craig on an Instagram post, lounging in a tour bus, caption: *#hungover*. I have to admit, they're not *that* similar. But I won't go into that now.

We pause at a crossing and I tug at my amazing new skull-printed tights. I got them from the same website as the killer boots and they're a bit tight, but they look *so* edgy. In fact, my whole outfit is edgy. Under my coat,

I'm in a grey T-shirt (torn at the edges) and a black leather mini skirt. I've put on my new silver and black skull earrings, too, and I'm wearing full electric-blue eyeshadow. Plus I've tied my hair up with a leather thong.

I glance at Luke, who's still in his work suit, and feel a tiny wave of dissatisfaction. We're going out for tequila with a rock musician, but he looks as though he's about to give a presentation to HSBC.

'Why don't you unbutton your shirt?' I suggest. 'Loosen up a bit, Luke! Get into the spirit of it!'

I ruffle his hair and unbutton his top button. I'm hoping he might relax a bit, but he just gives me a look.

'Would you rather I went home and put on a slashed leather jacket?'

'No!' I say, laughing. 'Don't be silly!' I hesitate, then add, '*Have* you got a slashed leather jacket?'

He gives me another look and I bite my lip. Right. D'uh.

We walk on and still Luke says nothing. Am I imagining it or is the tension growing? I keep glancing at Luke, but his jaw is even more rigid. And suddenly, as we approach the door of the pub, I feel as if I might have made a huge, fat mistake.

Am I in denial? *Is* there sexual tension between Craig and me?

I mean OK, yes. Hand on heart, I did try to look edgier today. Because of what Craig said. But I don't *fancy* him.

Do I?

Well, maybe I do fancy him a bit, simply because he

is objectively good-looking and anyone would fancy him. (Look at Suze.) But I don't *want* him.

Do I?

Oh God. *Do I want him without realizing it*? Does my subconscious want to have an affair with Craig?

I walk along silently, feeling a bit breathless, as I probe the innermost corners of my mind. But the trouble with asking your subconscious what it wants is, it just laughs at you and says, 'Work it out for yourself, moron.'

What about Luke? He looks calm enough – but is he silently bubbling with jealousy and hatred? As we reach the entrance to the pub, I feel a lump of worry in my throat. Should I quickly cancel and say, 'Let's go home'? But if I cancel, won't that make things look worse?

What if Luke and Craig get into an argument? Or a *duel*? I have no idea where this thought has come from, but I suddenly see Luke in his Armani suit and Craig in his leather jacket, hacking at each other with swords, leaping up on to the bar of the pub and round the seats, while I cry desperately, 'Please! Don't fight over me! Your lives are too precious!'

'Becky?' Luke gives me an odd look. 'Are we going in?'

'Right.' I come to and blink a few times. 'Yes. Let's do this.'

It's warm and cosy inside, with a crackling fire. Over the sound system, Chris Rea is singing about driving home for Christmas, and there's the smell of mulled wine in the air. As I take off my coat I'm aware of the girl behind the bar eyeing up my outfit curiously.

'Going to a fancy-dress party?' she asks.

Honestly. They wouldn't ask that in Shoreditch.

'No. Just an evening out,' I reply coolly. 'With friends.'

To my own ears the word 'friends' sounds quite cryptic and mysterious. I've never felt like a *femme fatale* before – but suddenly I feel as though I'm in a love triangle in some film noir and this is the pivotal scene.

'Luke, you do know I love you, don't you?' I say, my voice suddenly low and throbbing.

'Yes,' says Luke, looking at me as though I'm an idiot.

'What can I get you, Becky?' says the landlord, Dave, in a cheery voice. But before I can answer, the pub door swings open behind me and I hear Craig's voice, accompanied by violins in my head:

'Becky.'

It's practically *exactly* like that bit in *Casablanca*. (Except in a pub. And not black and white. And not in Casablanca.)

'Craig,' I say breathlessly, wheeling round. Then I blink in slight surprise. He's not wearing leather. He's wearing a coat. And has he shaved?

He greets me with a kiss on each cheek – then I turn self-consciously to Luke.

'Luke . . . this is Craig,' I say momentously.

I don't know what exactly I'm expecting. An instant confrontation? But of course there's nothing like that. They shake hands and Luke says, 'Welcome to Letherby,' whereupon Craig says, 'Thanks, mate. Cold out there. What are you drinking?'

The whole film noir vibe has sort of ebbed away. They just sound like two blokes in a pub.

'What can I get you, Becky?' says Dave again. 'Your usual? Baileys on ice?'

I feel a flash of embarrassment. Baileys on ice is *not* my usual. I've only had it a few times.

'Tequila, thanks,' I say in my coolest voice, glancing at Craig. 'We're doing Tequila shots, right?'

'Tequila shots?' says Luke, looking astonished, but I pretend I didn't hear him.

'Not for me,' says Craig, lifting a hand, and I stare at him.

'What do you mean?'

'I wasn't serious about Tequila,' he says with a rueful smile. 'Can't do that any more, not after wrecking my stomach lining. I'll be on wine. But don't let me stop you guys,' he adds, turning to Luke.

'I'll be on wine too,' says Luke firmly. 'There's a nice Malbec here . . .'

'The Malbec.' Craig nods enthusiastically. 'That's a good wine. I had it the other night.'

Malbec? Since when did rock gods drink *Malbec*?

I watch, discomfited, as Dave pours out two glasses of wine and a Tequila shot. I feel stupid now. I don't want to do shots on my own.

'Cheers,' says Craig, clinking glasses with me and Luke. The two men sip their wine and I drain my Tequila.

Ooh. That was quite strong. The air's gone a bit blurry.

'You want another one?' says Dave, watching me curiously.

'Er . . . maybe in a minute,' I say, getting out a tissue to mop my eyes.

'So, are you into wine?' Craig is saying to Luke.

'A little,' says Luke. 'You?'

'Got into it recently,' says Craig in his raspy, laidback way. 'My mate Mark – lead singer in Blink Rage – he just bought a case of Château Lafite at Sotheby's. 1916.'

'I read about that,' says Luke, his face lighting up. 'The bidding got quite frantic, apparently?'

'It was intense,' says Craig. 'I was with Mark. He was bidding by phone, freaking out . . . Hey, you want to sit by the fire?' he adds, as a group of people get up from their seats.

'Sure.' Luke nods. 'Good idea.'

As the two of them head over to the fire I watch them, feeling affronted. When I said I wanted Luke and Craig to hit it off, I didn't mean I wanted them to start talking about wine and *ignore* me.

'Becky, are you coming?' asks Luke, looking round. 'And do you want another Tequila shot?' he adds quizzically.

Is he making fun of me?

'I'll get myself a glass of wine,' I say with dignity.

I wait for Dave to pour me my wine and order some packets of crisps, too. And I'm about to join Luke and Craig by the fire when the door opens and a girl comes in. She's about my age, wearing a coat and a very tight grey business suit, revealing quite an incredible cleavage. She has long straight hair, a biscuity fake tan and very manicured eyebrows. And she's *definitely* had her lips done with filler. (Probably twice. The first time I'm guessing she said, 'Keep it natural,' and the second time, 'I love it! Go for it! More!')

She eyes my skull tights with surprise, looks at my

174

skull earrings and bites her cushiony lip in amusement –
then scans the pub.

'Craig!' she exclaims in a nasal voice.

'Love!' Craig's whole face lights up and he gets to his
feet. 'Love, over here! Luke, Becky, let me introduce you
to Nadine, my girlfriend.'

His—

What?

Why shouldn't Craig have a girlfriend? Of course he has
a girlfriend. I don't know why it didn't occur to me
before that he would have a girlfriend. It isn't a surprise,
really.

Although what *is* a surprise is . . .

Well. Her.

If you'd said 'Craig's girlfriend' to me, I'd have pic-
tured someone cool. Rock chick. With electric-blue
eyeshadow and grungy tights, like the girls in his Instagram posts. But Nadine is nothing like that.

She's got herself a drink and come to join us, and I
can't stop staring at her in disbelief. She *can't* be with
Craig, surely? But somehow she is. She's very polished
and she drives a Fiat and apparently she hates Craig's
music. He keeps telling us that as though it's a *good* thing.

'She won't come to hear me,' he says, laughing. 'She
won't come on tour. Will you, babe? Just refuses.'

'Blink Rage!' says Nadine in return, and takes a swig
of Prosecco. 'What kind of name is that? And have you
heard the noise they make?' She runs her eyes disparagingly over my skull tights again. 'But maybe you're
into all that, Becky?'

'I'm eclectic,' I say with a casual shrug. 'I used to hang out with Craig's band at Bristol. That's how we got together, back in the day. Good times,' I add reminiscently.

I'm expecting Nadine to ask more, but she says, 'Mmm,' with a supreme lack of interest, then turns to Luke.

'Now, I know all about *your* company,' she says. 'Brandon Communications. It's famous. Where you are, that's where I want to be one day. Believe you me, you're my inspiration.'

She's leaning forward and gazing at Luke with clear blue eyes. And boosting her cleavage with one arm, I suddenly notice.

'Nadine's doing really well with her marketing company,' says Craig. 'She's got a new client. Sportswear.' He gulps his wine and pats her arm proudly.

'I'd love to learn from you, Luke,' says Nadine breathily. 'Anything you can teach me. How did you start out? What was it like at the beginning? You're such a role-model.'

Every time she speaks, she juts out her cleavage a bit more. Is she for real? I glance at Luke, wanting to catch his eye – but he seems captivated by Nadine.

'You don't want to hear my long and tedious journey into business,' he says with a laugh.

'Oh, I do!' Nadine bats her eyelashes at him. 'Believe you me, I want to know every detail. I can learn so much.'

'She does,' agrees Craig. 'She's been on at me! "Introduce me to Luke Brandon." You know, forget meeting Blink Rage. Not interested. She wants to meet you.'

'Well,' says Luke, looking amused. 'I'm flattered. Do you want another glass of wine, Craig?'

'I'll get them,' says Craig easily, getting to his feet. 'You two have your chat. Becky, you OK?' He shoots me a fleeting glance.

'I'm fine!' I say with a bright smile. 'I'm fine! All good!'

But it's not all good. An hour later, my smile has frozen solid. This evening is the *opposite* of what I expected.

Luke and Nadine have been engrossed in boring, technical talk about marketing, which nobody else can join in with. Nadine has told Luke about a thousand times how he's her inspiration, 'believe you me, Luke'. (She says 'believe you me' about every five minutes and it's driving me *nuts*.) But Luke doesn't even seem to have noticed. He just seems delighted by the attention.

Meanwhile Craig has totally ignored my attempts to make conversation. I've tried every topic, from music to Kiev (I did some research) to telling him about our brunch in Shoreditch. But each time, he's suddenly broken off mid-stream to tell Luke what a grafter Nadine is, or how she's a total tech expert and redesigned his whole website.

'Another drink, Luke?' says Nadine, seeing that his glass is empty, and he glances at his watch, then at me.

'We should probably get going,' I say, trying to sound regretful. 'I told Suze we wouldn't be long. It's been fab to meet you though.'

'Oh, you too, Becky!' says Nadine insincerely, then she looks at my spiky boots. 'Don't those kill your feet?

I can't do heels. I don't do rock music and I don't do heels over two inches. End of.' She gives Craig a satisfied look and he gazes at her admiringly.

'She knows what she wants, Nadine does,' he says with pride in his voice. 'Always does.'

'Did you go to Warsaw last weekend?' I can't help asking her.

'Warsaw?' says Nadine, flicking her hair back. 'No chance! I was working. Anyway, I don't like Craig's musician friends. Too grungy.' She wrinkles her nose. 'And I'm not much of a traveller.'

OK, I do not get this relationship. She doesn't like musicians or rock music or travel. What do they have in common? What?

'Well, see you!' I say, getting to my feet. 'It was *so* nice to catch up, and welcome to Letherby . . .'

'You must come over,' says Craig, standing up, too. 'See the cottage. Try out the hot tub.'

'Ooh, the hot tub,' says Nadine, with a flash of enthusiasm. 'Now I *do* like that. I could stay in that all day. You like hot tubs, Luke?'

I stare at her suspiciously. She's leaning very close to Luke. Does she think he's deaf or something?

'I like a hot tub,' replies Luke without flickering and my hackles instantly rise. I'm not even sure why. It's the way he said 'hot tub'. It sounded like 'hot sex'.

'I love your moustache, Luke, by the way,' says Nadine huskily, gazing admiringly at it. 'I've been meaning to say so all evening. Very Three Musketeers.'

'Oh!' Luke touches it self-consciously. 'Well, you know. It's just for charity.'

'You should keep it,' declaims Nadine.

'I've thought about it,' says Luke, looking pleased.

'It *so* suits you,' Nadine gushes. 'It looks perfect on you.'

What? No it doesn't! Shut *up*, Nadine, I think furiously. Luke's moustache is nothing to do with you.

'Oh, Luke, before you go,' adds Nadine, 'can I just ask you one more thing? I've started this website for a client and there's something I'm not sure about . . .' She starts jabbing at her phone and Luke follows her gaze while I start seething.

'Hey, Becky.' Craig's voice comes gently in my ear. 'Sorry we've been ignoring you.'

'Don't be silly!' I say with a bright, automatic smile.

'We have.' He gives me a rueful look. 'Sorry. Nadine's been so excited to meet your husband, pick his brain, all that stuff. And I guess I'm just really chuffed that Luke gets on with Nadine and you and I get on . . . We gel, the four of us. Yeah? And we live so close now. I think we could be really good mates. Don't you?'

'Well,' I say, unbending slightly. 'I suppose.'

'We want you two to come over.' Craig is only inches away and his dark eyes are fixed on mine. 'Hang out. Spend some time together. Relax. We'll enjoy the hot tub and . . . whatever, yeah? Just the four of us, nice and private.' He puts a casual hand on my arm. 'I'll play you my latest songs. Sound good?'

Play us his latest songs? OK, that would be cool. As long as Nadine didn't keep interrupting to talk about income revenue, or whatever she keeps wittering on about.

'It sounds great,' I say honestly.

'There we are then. Sorted. Nadine!' He lifts his voice. 'Becky and Luke are going to come round to us one night!'

'Wonderful!' breathes Nadine. 'I can't *wait* to see you again. Oh, and you too, Becky,' she adds.

We all kiss goodbye and say how lovely it's been – then Luke and I leave the pub. As we begin walking, Luke is silent and yet again I can't work out what he's thinking.

'So!' I say after a bit. 'What did you think? I'm sorry, I should have told you about Craig before . . .'

'No, it's fine,' says Luke. 'It's fine. Nice girl,' he adds thoughtfully, and before I can stop them, my hackles rise again.

Nice girl? Or nice *flirting*?

But then I chide myself. I mustn't be suspicious. If I can be friendly with Craig, Luke can be friendly with Nadine, even though her lips look like pillows. Exactly.

From: customerservices@gardendecorations.co.uk
To: Becky Brandon
Subject: YOUR ORDER 7654

Dear Mrs Brandon

Re: YOUR ORDER 7654

Unfortunately the following items are out of stock. Your card has been refunded.

Product	Quantity
SILVER LLAMA DECORATION	6

Yours sincerely

Customer Services Team

ChristmasCompare.com™

Supplier	Product	Price	Availability
Decorationstogo.co.uk	SILVER LLAMA BAUBLE	£6.99	**SOLD OUT**

This attractive decoration flaunts silver glitter hair and pink 'World Peace' logo.

Supplier	Product	Price	Availability
Treesandtoppers.co.uk	SILVER GLITTER LLAMA DECORATION	£5.99	**UNAVAILABLE**

Make your tree pop with this cute llama!

Supplier	Product	Price	Availability
ACuratedChristmas.co.uk	LLAMA 'WORLD PEACE' BAUBLE	£10.99	**DUE 26 weeks**

Stylish tree decoration in silver and pink with silver ribbon loop.

Chats

You created group 'CHRISTMAS!'

CHRISTMAS!

> **Becky**
> Hi everyone! I've started a WhatsApp group to organize Christmas! Any ideas or requests, let me know! Becky xxx

> **Janice**
> Love, I meant to say at brunch, Christmas isn't Christmas for us without Quality Street.

> **Martin**
> I like Matchmakers. The orange ones.

> **Suze**
> Tarkie loves the chocolates that look like shells, what are they called again?

> **Jess**
> I would like to request Fairtrade chocolates only, or perhaps a healthier substitute such as carob.

Suze
Hey Bex, there are chilli pepper fairy lights in Tesco, you should get those!

Janice
There are banana ones in Sainsbury's.

Martin
What's a banana got to do with Christmas????

Mum
Dad says, why not have an avocado theme? It's very 'now'. We've just bought avocado fairy lights for our gin and cactus social evening!!!!!

Janice
What's a gin and cactus evening?

Mum
You drink gin and show your cactuses. Everyone does it in Shoreditch, love.

Janice
I'm sure they do all kinds of things in Shoreditch.

Jess
Fairy lights are problematic.

ELEVEN

OK, so the Christmas WhatsApp group might have been a mistake.

I've had 134 notifications and we only began last night. I can't *nearly* keep track of all the millions of suggestions everyone's making. In about half an hour we went from best chocolates to best mince pies to best Christmas films to best version of *A Christmas Carol*.

(The Muppets, obviously. Dad doesn't agree – but he can't get over the fact that it's Muppets, which he calls 'puppets'. That was like, ten messages, right there.)

I keep telling myself to stay calm. I keep saying to myself, 'Whatever the Grinch can steal, that's not Christmas.' It's all details. It's white noise. It doesn't matter what kind of mince pies we have, does it? Or brandy butter?

But it's not just the requests that are worrying me, it's the tone of the discussion. I can *totally* see why the government is worried about social media causing bullying among a certain generation – because Mum and Janice are getting really quite snippy with each other.

Mum keeps telling us how they do things in Shoreditch, and showing off about how packed her schedule is and mentioning artisan gin tastings. Janice ended up replying, 'Are you sure you've got time for Christmas, dear, with your packed new social life?'

Ouch. Although Janice has got a point. Mum was supposed to be coming with me to the Christmas Style Fair on Thursday, but at 10 p.m. last night she pulled out. Apparently she's doing an experimental drama workshop and it's the only day she can do it.

I mean, fair enough, experimental drama is definitely a good idea – but what about Christmas? What about me?

As I arrive at work, my head is still whirling with WhatsApp messages, but as Suze greets me she says, 'So? *So?*' as though I must know what she's talking about.

'I'm fine with the Waitrose brandy butter,' I say, in a slight daze, and she clicks her tongue impatiently.

'I mean, so, what *happened*? How was your evening with Craig? I sent you, like, six WhatsApps last night!'

'Oh, right.' I try to focus. 'Sorry. I got distracted by all the Christmas chat. Er . . . it was fine. It was good. He's got a girlfriend.'

'A *girlfriend*?' says Suze, looking wrongfooted.

For a moment I consider saying, 'Didn't you know he had a girlfriend, Suze?' and pretending I knew all along. But I'm not sure I can carry it off – and anyway, I want to have a cosy gossip.

'I was surprised, too,' I admit. 'And guess what? She's completely different from him! She's called Nadine and she's all businessy and neat. And she hates his music and travel and everything he's about. It's bizarre.'

'Huh,' says Suze thoughtfully, as she unpacks a box of cardigans.

'I don't know *what* they have in common,' I continue. 'But we had a good time in the end. I think we're going to be friends.'

'Huh,' says Suze again. She sits back on her heels and surveys me. 'Where's your rock-chick outfit gone, Bex?'

I didn't put on my distressed tweed suit today, just because . . .

OK, to be honest, it was because I woke up, looked at it and thought, 'What was I *thinking*?' I'll have to undistress it somehow. As for the boots, Nadine's got a point. My feet were so sore today, I couldn't have worn them. Not that I'll admit this to Suze.

'Oh.' I shrug. 'I'm going for a different style today. Mixing it up.'

'Now you think Craig's into businessy women you're going for the business look?' Suze gives me a sharp glance and I gasp as the meaning of her comment hits me.

'No!' I say, stung. 'Of course not . . . No! Suze, what do you mean?'

'You know what I mean,' returns Suze darkly, and there's silence between us.

I *think* I know what she means.

But on the other hand, what if she means something else?

Or, like, a third thing?

'Say it.' I lift my chin challengingly.

'You don't even tell Luke when your ex-boyfriend turns up.' Suze counts off on her fingers. 'You dress up to impress him. You go for a drink with him. Now you're

188

telling me Craig's girlfriend doesn't have anything in common with him. But you do, Bex?' She raises her eyebrows almost accusingly.

OK, I *do* know what she means and she is *wrong*.

'Stop it,' I say indignantly. 'That is *not* what— It totally wasn't like that.'

'You're saying Craig isn't into you?' persists Suze. 'You're saying he wasn't chatting you up?'

'Yes!' I exclaim. 'That's exactly what I'm saying. If you must know, both of them ignored me most of the evening. They were all over Luke. Especially Nadine. She couldn't take her eyes off him. If anyone needs to worry, it's *me*,' I add, to emphasize the point. 'It's *me*.'

'Hmm,' says Suze, looking unconvinced.

'Suze, what are you implying?' I can't help sounding hurt. 'You think I'm going to have an *affair*?'

'I didn't say that,' Suze answers after a pause. 'I just . . .' She hesitates. 'I know how stuff can happen. You have to be careful.'

Her gaze is averted – and again I know she's referring to her own moment of madness in the summer.

'You needn't worry,' I say with dignity. 'My marriage is safe.'

For a while we're both silent. Suze is still unloading cardigans and I start putting them on the display rack.

'So are you going to Craig's Christmas party?' Suze says after a while, and I feel a little stab of guilt. Suddenly I get it. Suze feels left out. *That's* what this is.

'We'll all go,' I say firmly. 'And Suze, you *have* to come next time we meet up. Oh, and do you want to come to

189

the Christmas Style Fair with me on Thursday?' I add, suddenly remembering. 'Mum's pulled out. I'll pay for the extra cover for the shop. We can ask Irene's niece, she's always happy to do it. All my treat.'

'Oh, Bex,' says Suze, looking torn. 'I would have loved to. But I've got this big project I want to finish over the next couple of days. I'm going to have to say no.'

'What big project?' I stare at her in surprise. This is the first time I've heard of any big project.

'Just . . . something for the shop,' she says vaguely. 'You'll see.'

'What?' I demand.

'It's a secret. You'll like it,' she adds with a sudden grin. 'I promise. In fact, you'll love it. But I need all of Thursday to get it done.'

'OK. No worries.'

I think for a moment, wondering who else I can ask. Jess is in Cumbria and she wouldn't approve of the Christmas Style Fair, anyway. She'd stride around gazing sternly at the stallholders, telling them they shouldn't sell chilli pepper fairy lights, they should make candles out of recycled chillis, or just sit in the dark as Nature intended.

Then I have an idea. I take out my phone and text Janice:

Hi Janice! Do you want to come to the Christmas Style Fair on Thursday with me? I have a spare ticket. Becky xxx

Almost at once I get an answer:

**Oh love, how wonderful! Yes please! Looking forward
to it already! Janice xxx**

She sounds so excited, I feel a glow of pleasure. Janice
was exactly the right person to ask. I'll book her a nice
lunch and everything. It'll be fun!

**Will send you electronic ticket and see you in there.
Yay! Becky xxx**

I'm about to put my phone away when another text
arrives from Janice:

**Aren't you going with your mum, though? Or is she
too busy in 'Shoreditch'? Janice xxx**

Oh God. Look at those quote marks. Those are totally
snippy quote marks. I don't want to stir up any trouble
between them, so I think for a moment, then send back
a deliberately vague answer:

**She's busy! Never mind, we'll have fun! Better go
now! Xx**

As I put my phone away, Suze glances at her watch
and moves towards the shop door to open it. But I don't
feel we're quite done with our conversation.

'Suze, wait,' I say impulsively and she turns round.
'What?'

'I know you mean well,' I say earnestly. 'But you
mustn't worry. I'm not going to have an affair with Craig.'

191

'Well, just don't, will you?' she returns with energy. 'Because it would ruin Christmas.'

Ruin Christmas? OK, even though I'm absolutely *not* planning on committing adultery, I have to take issue with this statement.

'No it wouldn't,' I contradict her. 'No one would know.'

'Yes they would,' says Suze scoffingly. 'You're hopeless at keeping secrets, Bex. You'd probably come in on Christmas Day and say, "What do you think of my Having An Affair skirt? Isn't it fab?"'

I'm not even going to dignify that with an answer.

For the rest of the day we're really busy in the shop and neither of us mentions Craig, so I assume this means the subject is over. We sell a stack of Suze's homemade photo frames (on special offer), two walking sticks, a tweed coat, a couple of hampers and loads of jam. At lunchtime Suze and I help Irene find a nice jumper for her niece in Australia, after visiting about six hundred websites, tabbing them all and nearly crashing the computer. (I hadn't realized *quite* how indecisive Irene was.)

But then, as we're all walking out at the end of the day, Suze pulls me back, saying in fake tones, 'Oh, Bex, there was something I just wanted to mention.'

She waits until Irene is well out of earshot, then clears her throat and stares at me as though she doesn't know where to begin.

'What?' I say, puzzled.

'OK,' says Suze in a rush. 'Here's what happened. I googled Craig to see what kind of guy he is.'

'Suze.' I glare at her. 'Are you *still* obsessing about that?'

'I know, I know.' Suze looks abashed. 'It's none of my business. But anyway, I found this interview online, and . . . Well, I think you should see it.' She proffers her phone and I stare at an incomprehensible stream of text, accompanied by a photo of Craig.

'It's in . . .' I make a face. 'What's that language?'

'Oh sorry, that's the original,' says Suze without blinking. 'It's Latvian. You have to put it through Google translate.'

'Which I assume you've done already,' I say pointedly. 'Because you're an obsessive stalker.'

'Just look at this,' says Suze, holding out an English version. 'I've highlighted bits.'

As I take the phone I suddenly wonder if he mentioned me in the interview. Oh my God! What if he says all his inspiration is down to his first love, Becky Bloomwood, and he should never have let me go? What if I'm famous in Latvia?

But as I peer at the screen I can't see the name Becky anywhere. Instead, a different word jumps out at me: *orgies.*

'Orgies,' says Suze, pointing at it as though I can't read, and I roll my eyes at her.

'What do you mean? Suze, what *is* this? Does he mention me?' I can't help adding.

'No,' says Suze. 'But he mentions plenty of other things. Read on.'

Puffing out in exasperation, I look at the text again, my eyes landing on one highlighted phrase after another.

. . . 'don't believe in monogamy,' says Curton . . . regular member of the sex-party scene in Moscow . . . met his current girlfriend at a notorious club . . . 'experimental sex is the only way' . . . 'Since when was one-on-one enough? Never,' he laughs . . .

I lift my head and meet Suze's gaze, my mind spinning a bit.

'OK, so he leads a wild life,' I say, trying to sound nonchalant. 'What are you saying?'

'Maybe he wants a wild life with you and Luke.' Suze waggles her eyebrows meaningfully at me. '*With you and Luke*, Bex.'

'What—' I break off as I realize what she's driving at. '*No!* Suze, you're mad! Where on *earth* did you get that idea?'

'Let's look at the facts.' Suze starts striding around as if she's a barrister making a case in the Old Bailey. 'You're sitting there last night, wondering what Craig's girlfriend and he have in common. I've seen Craig flirting with you and he's pretty hot. Now they're both all over Luke. The truth is . . .' She pauses for effect. 'They're after *both* of you.'

'No they're not,' I say scoffingly, but Suze ignores me.

'I put it to you that the missing factor linking Craig and his girlfriend is nothing more than sex. Multiplayer sex,' she adds with a flourish.

'*Multiplayer sex?*' I echo incredulously. 'Is that what it's called?'

'Dunno,' admits Suze. 'But you know what I mean. I bet they met in a club and that's what they're into. And now they want to do it with you and Luke. Swinging. Multiplayer. Whatever it is.'

'Rubbish,' I say vehemently.

'What else is the hot tub for?' she retorts as though slapping down a trump card.

'The *hot tub*?' I stare at her.

'Yes! The hot tub! It's a sex-party tub! I don't know *what* Tarkie's going to say,' she adds fretfully, suddenly transforming into landlady mode. 'It's visible from the road. We'll have complaints!'

Her face is so outraged, I can't help giggling.

'OK, Suze,' I say in soothing tones. 'Well, if Craig invites us to a sex party, I'll let you know and you can call the police.'

'You think it's funny?' says Suze. 'You wait till you go round there and Craig says, "Why don't you slip into something more comfortable?" and Nadine appears and she's already in a sexy dressing gown and she goes, "Wow, Becky, you look so *hot*," and she starts slipping it off your shoulders, and— Anyway.' Suze stops dead as though that's as far as she can get with this particular fantasy.

'You're sick!' I clutch my stomach. 'Stop it!'

'I'm prescient,' says Suze, unabashed. 'I've *seen* the sexual tension between you and Craig. They're going to ask you and Luke round to the hot tub for multiplayer sex.'

'Actually, he already has done,' I admit. 'I mean the hot tub, *not* the multiplayer sex,' I hastily clarify – but Suze jabs a triumphant finger at me as though this proves everything.

'You see?'

'No, I don't see! Suze, people have hot tubs! They're not all having multiplayer sex!' I catch Suze's eye and she bites her lip as though she can suddenly see the funny side.

'Well, anyway,' she says. 'You've been warned.'

'Thank you,' I say with elaborate courtesy. 'And I appreciate your concern. See you tomorrow.'

'Be in denial, Bex,' says Suze, as we both head out of the door. 'But I'm right.'

As I'm walking down the Letherby Hall drive, I give a sudden giggle as I rewind our conversation. Honestly. Multiplayer sex. Suze is mad!

Although—

No. Stop it.

But now I can't help it – I'm remembering Craig last night, inviting us round. The way he came up so close to me. The way he said softly, 'We'll enjoy the hot tub and . . . whatever, yeah? Just the four of us, nice and private.'

The way he put a hand on my arm. The way he looked at me, kind of intent.

I mean . . . he wasn't . . . ?

That wasn't . . . ?

No, Becky. Of *course* it wasn't. Don't be ridiculous.

From: Myriad Miracle
To: Becky Brandon
Subject: Query!

Hi Mrs Brandon (née Bloomwood)

We hope you're enjoying the Myriad Miracle Training System™!

Our team have noticed your exercise activity so far is rated at 'Negligible'.

Are you having trouble with operating our interactive system?

Please contact our friendly Customer Services Team, who will help you with your settings, so that all your exercise activity is correctly logged.

Debs
(membership assistant)

TWELVE

But the idea won't go away. At 9.30 a.m. on Thursday I've dropped Minnie at school and I'm sitting at the kitchen table, cutting out fabric for her Nativity play costume, but my mind's not on it. I'm half thinking, 'Concentrate' and half thinking, 'Oh my God, I've never even *been* in a foursome.'

How does it actually work, anyway? Like, what are the *logistics*? I'm quite tempted to google *sex parties what actually happens?* only Luke might walk in and get the wrong idea. In fact, here is Luke, coming into the kitchen. Should I mention it to him?

No, because it sounds crazy. It *is* crazy.

'How's it going?' He surveys the ocean of dark blue silk filling the table. 'Looks good.'

'Oh, right.' I force my attention back to Minnie's costume. 'It's going pretty well. Thanks!'

I don't want to boast, but I've chosen fabulous material for Minnie's costume. It's the most sumptuous midnight blue silk, embossed with gold spots. And OK,

198

it wasn't the cheapest option – but then how often is your little girl a king in the school Nativity? I bought some gold velvet ribbon, too, and sequins. Minnie's going to look spectacular.

'Just cutting out the pattern,' I add briskly, picking my scissors back up and trying to sound like a sewing expert. I won't mention that I'm cutting it out for the second time. *Total* disaster first time round – but I bought some pins this time. They're so nifty! Someone should have told me about them before. And at least I had plenty of spare material. (I got a bit carried away in the fabric shop and thought maybe I'd make a matching dress for myself. Which is looking a *tad* less likely, to be honest.)

'I'm going to make a coffee to go,' says Luke. 'You want one?'

'Yes, please,' I say absently as I resume cutting. I love the metallic sound the scissors make as they slice through the material. It makes me feel like a total pro. I work carefully round the curve of the sleeve, then look up to see Luke watching me, a fond expression in his eyes.

'What?' I say.

'Nothing. Just, lucky Minnie.'

'Oh,' I say, feeling a tiny glow inside. 'Well, you know. I want her to have the best costume she can. Although she might not be lucky,' I add honestly. 'It might be a disaster. I'm not exactly brilliant at all this craft stuff. Not like Suze.' I can't help a gusty sigh. 'You should see the stuff she makes—'

'Becky.' Luke cuts me off firmly. 'You're you. Other people are other people. This is going to be an awesome costume, and Minnie's going to be an awesome king. Has she got any lines to learn?' he adds with sudden interest. 'Should we be practising?'

'No,' I say with a sudden giggle. 'They have to make it up. Miss Lucas is into improvisation. She thinks it makes the children creative.'

'*Improvisation?*' Luke raises his eyebrows. 'Isn't that a high-risk strategy at that age?'

'You'd think. Apparently at the last rehearsal one of the shepherds told his sheep to hurry up or he'd wallop him.'

Luke laughs. 'Well, rather Miss Lucas than me.'

He puts a coffee in front of me, picks up his own takeaway cup (bamboo, present from Jess) and kisses me. 'Have fun at the Christmas fair today.'

'I will!'

I watch Luke leaving and when he's almost through the door I say impulsively, 'Hey Luke. You know Craig and Nadine?'

'Yes?' He turns back and I hesitate, not sure how to continue. What I really want to say is, 'D'you think they want a foursome with us in their hot tub?'

But I can't. I mean, it's *ridiculous*.

'Nothing,' I say at last. 'Just . . . It was nice hanging out with them.'

'Yes.' He nods. 'It was fun. See you later.'

The Christmas Style Fair is being held at Olympia, and as I travel there I give myself a stern talking-to. I've been spending too much time thinking about Craig and sex parties and hot tubs. It's all nonsense and it's distracting me from the issue at hand, which is that I'm *hosting Christmas*. And it's only a month away now. I need to focus.

On the tube I leaf through another Christmas magazine to reassure myself – but it does the opposite. It keeps asking tricky questions which I can't answer, like, 'Why not make lace-printed paperchains?' and 'Why not fill a Scandinavian dresser with festive crockery, ready to greet your guests?'

I'm already googling *Scandinavian dresser delivery before Xmas*, before I realize that we don't have room for a Scandinavian dresser, and nor am I ever going to persuade Luke we need three life-size stuffed reindeer to stand in front of it, like in the photo spread. I must stay down to earth, I tell myself firmly. Be realistic and practical and think about what I *need*.

And yes, OK, I know Christmas is about family and friends – but it turns out my family and friends are quite demanding. Janice keeps asking me what my 'table theme' is and I keep dithering. Should I go Scandi? Modern metallic? Highland tartan? Every time I turn a page of a magazine and see a new photo I think, 'Ooh, *that* looks nice,' and change my mind.

Anyway, I've got a list, which begins 'Tablecloth, napkins, candles'. I've decided I'm going to pick a theme today and stick to it. I'm *not* going to get distracted and I'm *not* going to make pointless purchases that I don't need. Exactly.

But oh *God*. As I step into the massive hall, I can't help feeling dazzled by the sheer . . . *festiveness*. There are stalls as far as the eye can see, all decked out with decorations. There are gifts and garlands and baubles and puddings and already people are milling everywhere with a contagious sense of urgency. I text Janice to say 'Let's meet in row A,' then plunge into the mêlée, feeling breathless with excitement.

It's all very well focusing on what you need. But sometimes you don't know what you need until you see it right in front of you. I mean, look at that stall with festive aprons! They're made from rustic linen with adorable printed motifs like holly leaves and robins. I *have* to get a whole family set. Surely we'll host Christmas better if we have matching festive aprons?

I spend a bit of time looking at all the different designs before I decide on holly for me, robins for Minnie and Christmas puddings for Luke. There's a discount if you buy three, which is even better, and as I walk away with my linen tote, I feel a spring in my step. I've begun!

The next stall is selling 'tiered mince pie display stands' made out of recycled vintage crockery. I didn't know I needed one of those, either, but I definitely do.

'Shall I send that to the collection area?' asks the stall-holder as I pay, and I beam at him.

'Yes please!'

This is even better. I don't have to lug the bloody thing around with me. I *love* this place.

As I'm taking my collection ticket, I glimpse Janice in the crowd and wave frantically at her.

'Becky!' She comes hurrying up, wearing a belted coat with a fur collar which I know used to be Mum's, and a new virulent mauve lipstick.

'Janice!' I exclaim, kissing her. 'Isn't this fab? Have you bought anything yet?'

'Yes!' She brandishes her tote at me. 'Edible gold dust and chocolate-dipped orange peel. And I've seen a *super* wreath, made of red jingle bells.'

Ooh. Should red jingle bells be my theme? I'm about to ask Janice where the wreath is, when I notice that her eyes keep swivelling longingly to a nearby café area, so I say, 'Shall we fuel up with some coffee and a mince pie?'

'Super idea!' she exclaims and bustles me towards an empty table. Soon we're sitting with a cappuccino and mince pie each, and I gaze around happily at the Christmassy hubbub.

'Well, thank you for inviting me, Becky,' says Janice. 'Although, as I say, I'm surprised your mum couldn't make it.'

'Oh well,' I say. 'You know. One of those things.'

'She's very busy these days,' says Janice, gazing off into the middle distance. Her eyes are flickering, and I feel a tweak of apprehension.

'Yes,' I say carefully. 'Have you seen much of her?'

'Not to speak of,' says Janice. 'She's got her new life to keep her busy, hasn't she? In the famous "Shoreditch". Posting photos on WhatsApp all the time, showing off about everything. She's forgotten about all of us in Oxshott.'

She dabs at her nose with a tissue, although I can't tell if she's upset or angry or a bit of both.

'Mum said she was going to invite you to lots of events,' I venture. 'Hasn't she done that?'

'She asked us to a poetry reading,' says Janice after a pause. 'And she mentioned some sort of dance class. But we didn't go.'

'Why not?' I say in surprise.

'Oh, love, it's not our scene,' says Janice fervently. 'They're all young. They have a different outlook. All these new foods and new words and new views about life . . . We'd never fit in, Martin and I. We're not "artisty gin" people.'

'Yes you are!' I say encouragingly. 'You could be!'

'It's not us, love.' Janice seems so determined, I don't know what to say. 'But luckily, I have a new friend in Oxshott,' she adds distantly. 'Her name's Flo. We've started having a coffee together after Zumba. You can tell your mum *that*.'

I stare at her in dismay. This is even worse than the snippy WhatsApp messages. Are Mum and Janice actually *falling out*? They can't. Mum and Janice have been friends since before I was born. If they split up, I'll be from a broken home!

'Janice . . .' I begin – but I don't know how to carry on. I can't speak for Mum. I don't know how to patch things up. I just know that this isn't right.

'Anyway!' Janice says briskly, before I can gather my wits. 'Let's not talk about that any more. How's your Christmas preparation going, Becky? I've had my delivery of cosmetics for the festive makeovers, so that's one thing ticked off, although they sent the wrong highlighter stick, would you believe . . .'

As she continues talking about all her online orders, I gradually calm down. I'm overreacting. Mum and

Janice can't possibly fall out! They've been friends for too long. It's just a little spat. I'll talk to Mum about it and it'll all be—

Hang on. What was that?

I've just seen a glimpse of familiar-looking silver fronds. I whip my head round and peer through the crowd, eyes narrowed. They're poking out of a woman's shopper. Is that . . . ? Could it be the must-have llama bauble?

I squint desperately, trying to see, but a moment later the woman is out of sight in the crowd and I subside. Maybe it was just a bit of tinsel. Guiltily I turn my attention back to Janice, who seems to be on to a new topic by now.

'He simply wasn't thinking!' she's declaiming. 'I mean, *you* understand why I got cross, Becky.'

'Er, sorry, Janice,' I say. 'I just missed that last bit. What did you say?'

Janice heaves a sigh. 'I was saying how Martin messed up my present cupboard. All my labels, ripped off, all my lists, vanished . . . What am I supposed to do now?'

'Have you put labels on your presents already?' I say in surprise. 'That's very efficient.'

'I do the labels every year on Boxing Day, love,' says Janice.

'Boxing Day?' I stare at her.

'While we watch *Oklahoma!*' Janice nods. 'Christmas Day we unwrap the presents.' She counts off on her fingers. 'Boxing Day I label them and put them in the gift cupboard. Then the next December, I reassign them and wrap them again. It's my system, love. And Martin *knows* that.'

Reassign?

'You mean . . . you regift them?'

'Well, yes, love.' Janice seems surprised that I'm asking. 'Everyone regifts.'

'Everyone regifts a *bit*. Do you regift every single present you get?'

Janice thinks a moment, sipping her cappuccino, then says, 'Not the perishables.'

'But everything else? You regift *everything else*?'

'It makes sense!' says Janice defensively.

'Oh my God, Janice.' I stare at her. 'You're a regiftaholic! I had no idea.'

'I'm very careful, Becky,' says Janice, looking a tad sheepish. 'I wear cotton gloves and I always check them for wear and tear. No one receives a sub-standard gift.'

The ramifications of this discovery are gradually dawning on me. I knew Janice liked to 'get ahead on her Christmas cards' – i.e. buy them half-price on Christmas Eve, write them out on 1 January and keep them in a drawer for the rest of the year. But this is worse.

'So you mean, all those presents I've given you over the years went straight in the cupboard for regifting?' I can't help sounding hurt.

'Oh, love.' Janice pats my hand. 'I do appreciate them. Every present I receive is one less to buy next year, you see?'

'But that's not the point of presents! What about the Bobbi Brown *Makeup Manual* I got you?'

'It went to my sister Anne,' admits Janice.

'And what about the cocktail shaker?' I stare at her, crestfallen. 'Didn't you make a single cocktail?'

'Ah,' says Janice, lifting a finger triumphantly. 'Now

206

that *did* work out well. We gave that to Martin's niece Judy. She uses it all the time!'

Maybe she does, I think, a bit resentfully. But I didn't want Martin's niece Judy to use it, I wanted Janice and Martin to use it. (And by the way, no wonder her make-up technique hasn't improved.)

'Janice, people give you presents because they want to,' I say earnestly. 'Because they love you. They want you to *enjoy* their gifts. Presents are enjoyment and love, not just something to fill a cupboard.'

'I know, Becky.' She gives me a rueful smile. 'I know I should enjoy my presents, but I just can't help being practical.'

I'm not going to give her a lecture, because people can't *help* being regiftaholics, can they? It's probably a genetic thing which they'll do scientific research about one day. But this year, I vow, I'm giving Janice something she *can't* regift. Some kind of luxury perishable food, perhaps. Ooh, maybe a lobster. I can't help grinning at the idea of presenting Janice with a live lobster, and at once she says, 'What is it, love?'

'Nothing.' I put down my cup. 'Come on. Let's shop!'

We head into the food section, which has the massive advantage that they give away stuff. Every single stall has something to taste, from cinder toffee to Christmas cake to festive vodka.

'Is festive vodka a thing?' I say uncertainly to Janice, but she's already got us two little sample glasses.

'Of course it is, love!' she says, swigging hers in one go. 'Look, there's tinsel on the bottle. Shall we try all the flavoured ones? There's lemon. And cinnamon!'

Actually vodka does feel fairly festive, if it's spiked with cinnamon and you drink it singing along to Mariah Carey. We move on to festive gin and then festive traditional 'mead' and then Janice starts going back and asking for seconds. If I don't say something, she'll stay in the booze section all day.

'Janice,' I say at last. 'We have to move on! We'll try the mulled wine another time, OK?'

As I'm tugging at her arm, I spot a nearby stall selling smoked salmon, which is actually on my list. There's a massive queue, which is a good sign, so I quickly join it. And I'm just craning my neck to read the sign about applewood smoking when another glimpse of silver fronds catches my eye and I swivel round in hope—

Yes! It's the silver llama must-have bauble! It's hanging from the handle of a toddler's buggy and I bet you *anything* his mum bought it here.

I'm *not* missing it this time.

'Janice,' I say hurriedly. 'Could you possibly buy my smoked salmon for me? Here's my credit card.' I hand her my Visa card and add in a whisper, 'The PIN's 4165. Just pay whatever it costs. I just need to make a quick purchase.'

'Of course, love!' says Janice brightly. 'How much? I don't know what the prices are like . . .'

'Don't worry about the price, just get lots. Or at least, why not see if there's a special offer?' I can see Janice drawing breath to ask something else, but I hastily add, 'Thanks!' and dash into the crowd. I've *got* to track down that llama bauble.

I jog along, fighting my way past groups of people

until I see the mother with the buggy. And there it is! The silver llama, hanging on a velvet ribbon loop. It has long glittery hair and WORLD PEACE is beautifully embroidered on the side. I can *totally* see why it's this year's must-have bauble.

'Excuse me!' I gasp, touching the woman on the shoulder, and she wheels round.

'Yes?'

'Did you buy that here?' I gesture at the llama bauble.

'Yes,' she says. 'Stall over there.' She jabs a finger towards the far corner of the hall.

'Thanks *so* much,' I say, as she starts wheeling the buggy off. 'It's this year's must-have bauble, you know!' I add over my shoulder. 'Sold out everywhere! Very rare!'

As I'm hastening in the direction she pointed, my phone bleeps with a text.

Love, do you want oak smoked, applewood smoked or cold smoked? Janice x

I pause, and type a reply:

Don't mind! Applewood, maybe? Bx

Then I start hurrying on again, but at once my phone rings and **Janice** pops up on the display screen.

'Hi, Janice!' I say breathlessly. 'Is everything OK?'

'There *is* a special offer, love!' she says triumphantly. 'They do bundles, twenty, thirty or forty pounds. Only

I know you said don't worry about the price, but I don't feel I can make that decision—'

'Thirty, please!' I hastily cut her off. 'Perfect! Thank you so much.'

I dash on as quickly as I can and manage to get to the next corner before Janice pings back another text:

Sorry, my mistake, they can't do 30 in the applewood smoked, love. Janice x

Honestly. As if anyone will tell the difference after a few glasses of Buck's Fizz. Trying not to give away my impatience, I text:

Get any bundle any kind. Thanks so much Janice, really appreciate it!! Bx

The path ahead has miraculously cleared so I increase my pace to a sprint, not even pausing when my phone bleeps again. It'll be some random question about packaging or something. Janice will have to decide that on her own.

I reach the far corner of the hall, look around wildly – and there it is! It's hanging on the side of a stall: a silver llama with WORLD PEACE in pink on its side. Yay!

Regaining my breath, I approach the stall and beam at the woman behind it, who smiles sweetly in return, while polishing her gold spectacles. She has a lanyard around her neck and I notice that she's called Yvonne Hanson.

'Hello, Yvonne!' I greet her. 'Lovely stall.'

'Thank you,' she says complacently. 'I do my best. How can I help you?'

'Could I please have a silver llama bauble?' I say, trying not to sound too urgent. 'In fact . . . several? In fact . . . all your stock?'

'I'm afraid the llama's sold out,' says Yvonne pleasantly, replacing her spectacles. 'I'm so sorry.'

Sold out? But there's one right in front of me.

'Could I buy that one, please?' I ask politely, pointing at it.

'Ah.' Her brow creases. 'I'm afraid not. That one is for display purposes only.'

I stare at her in bewilderment. 'But you've sold out.'

'Exactly.' She nods in agreement. 'As I say. Sold out.'

'So . . . couldn't I buy it?'

'This is a *display* llama,' she says in slow, distinct tones. 'For *display*.'

'I don't understand,' I say, trying to stay patient. 'If it's sold out, why are you displaying it?'

'Because it's part of the range.' She smiles. 'Very popular.'

'But no one can buy it!' I say in frustration. 'It's sold out! So this is misleading. You're luring people to your stand like a mirage in the desert! You're toying with people's hopes! Is that fair? Is that just? Is that *human*?'

Abruptly I realize I've raised my voice, and a few people are staring at me, including Yvonne, whose smile has become a little rigid.

'I'm afraid the llama's sold out,' she says politely, as though beginning the conversation again. 'Would you like a turtle instead? Lovely sequins, very popular.'

I glance briefly at the sequinned turtle – which isn't a patch on the llama – then back at Yvonne. For a few moments I'm silent. I'm not a vengeful person, but I have totally taken against Yvonne, with her gold spectacles and power trips.

'May I *look* at the llama bauble, please?' I ask, after a few moments.

Yvonne's eyes narrow, but I can tell she can't think of a reason to say no, so eventually she replies, 'Certainly you may.' She lifts it off its nail and places it in front of me on the stall, adding, 'As I say, it's sold out.'

'Of course.' I match her pleasant tone. 'I *absolutely* understand that it's sold out and you can't sell me this one, even though it's right here in my hands. It makes *total* sense.'

Yvonne doesn't reply, but as I dart a glance at her I can see it plain in her face. We're enemies.

'It's lovely, isn't it?' I say, running my hand gently over the silver metallic hair. 'So beautiful. How strong are these fronds, I wonder . . . ?' I run my fingers through the metallic strands a few times – then carefully snap one off. At once I gasp in apparent horror. 'Oh no, I've broken it. How could I be so careless?'

'What?' Yvonne makes a grab for the llama, but I swoop it out of her reach and open my eyes wide.

'What a terrible accident! I do apologize. And now it's damaged, of course you won't be able to display it, so I simply *must* buy it, to repay you.' I meet her gaze innocently. 'At full price, naturally. I insist.'

'It doesn't look damaged to me,' chimes in an elderly lady who has just joined me at the stall – but Yvonne and I both ignore her. This battle is *mano a mano*.

212

'How much is it?' I add, reaching for my purse, but Yvonne doesn't reply. As I look up, I see a kind of glinty triumph in her eyes and feel a sudden qualm.

'Oh, I would never sell a damaged item,' she says, her smile even sweeter than before. 'I'm afraid it will have to be removed from display altogether. Could you give it to me, please? I would rather not have damaged goods on view, as they compromise my high standards.'

She holds out her hand and I glare at her, trying to think of a response, before reluctantly handing over the llama.

'It looks perfect!' says the elderly lady – but neither of us flickers. I can't *believe* Yvonne outwitted me.

'May I not buy it as damaged goods?' I make a last attempt. 'Surely you don't just waste damaged items?'

'But it's not damaged!' says the elderly lady, sounding perplexed.

'I will be holding a damaged goods sale in June,' snaps Yvonne with an air of finality. 'You may consult my website for details.'

She drops the llama into a nearby cardboard box and Sellotapes it shut for good measure, shooting me a victorious look as she does so.

'Fine. Well, Happy Christmas,' I say darkly, hoping that she can detect my subtext message: *You don't deserve one.*

'And to you!' she replies breezily, clearly meaning, *I won, so I don't care what you think.* 'Can I help you?' She turns to the elderly lady and I give her a final resentful glare before moving away. Christmas shopping is brutal. *Brutal.*

I walk disconsolately away, and I'm about to text

Janice to see where she is when I hear her cheery voice hailing me:

'Becky, *there* you are. Good news, love! I've ordered the smoked salmon and bought mince pies *and* I've got us some festive brandy!'

She proffers two little cups and I practically grab one from her. When you've had a run-in with a bureaucratic despot, festive brandy is definitely the solution.

'Delicious!' I say, draining it in one gulp. 'Just what I needed. Let's go and get some more.'

From: malcolm@christmaswholesale.co.uk
To: Becky Brandon
Subject: Re: Llama bauble crisis

Dear Mrs Brandon (née Bloomwood)

Thank you for your email.

I'm sorry to hear that you have been unable to purchase a silver llama bauble. Unfortunately, we do not have any in stock here at head office, as this product has been very popular.

I wish you every success with your Christmas decorations, and suggest that you browse the attached catalogue, showing our full range of tree baubles.

With all best wishes for the festive period

Yours sincerely

Malcolm

From: malcolm@christmaswholesale.co.uk
To: Becky Brandon
Subject: Re: Re: Re: Llama bauble crisis

Dear Mrs Brandon (née Bloomwood)

Thank you for your email.

I assure you that we are not deliberately withholding supply of the silver llama bauble in an attempt to create a 'South Sea bubble' situation.

We are therefore not 'playing a dangerous game', as you put it. Nor do we agree that our actions will 'probably threaten the economy and cause global havoc'.

With all best wishes for the festive period

Yours sincerely

Malcolm

Chats

CHRISTMAS!

Martin
Becky, my back's playing up, so might I bring along my orthopaedic stool on Christmas Day?

Becky
Of course!

Jane
Martin, so sorry to hear about your back! In our street in Shoreditch, there's a super new therapist called the Tantric Back Cooperative. Shall I book you an appointment?

Janice
In Oxshott we prefer qualified medical professionals, love.

Jane
What are you trying to say, Janice?

Janice
Nothing, Jane.

Jane
Yes you are.

Janice
No I'm not. What are YOU trying to say?

Martin
Ladies, ladies.

Janice
Be quiet, Martin.

THIRTEEN

Oh my God. My *head*.

It's throbbing so hard, I've been forced to put sunglasses on. It was that festive brandy that did for me. Unless it was the festive pina coladas, which Janice found from some stall. What was she *thinking*? (Actually, they were so delicious, I ordered a bottle.)

I slept through my Black Friday alarm, so I haven't got a single online bargain and now I'm running late. Even worse, I've just had a quick look through my purchases from yesterday – and I went seriously off-piste.

Items I intended to buy:

Tablecloth

Napkins

Candles

Wrapping paper

Items I actually bought:

Family Christmas aprons

Mince pie display stand

Smoked salmon

Festive pina colada (one bottle)

Festive mojito (two bottles)

Inflatable mistletoe wreath

Twelve musical baubles which play 'Jingle Bells'

Felt Christmas tree with padded felt candy canes (adorable)

White Christmas tree with LED lights and diamanté decorations (stunning, I mean, *everyone* was stopping to look at it)

Papier mâché Christmas tree covered with red-foil-wrapped chocolate stars (how can you not buy a Christmas tree covered with red shiny chocolate stars?)

So that's three Christmas trees. Plus I've already ordered a massive premium Norwegian spruce, which I can't cancel because Luke keeps saying the smell of the tree is his favourite bit of Christmas. And I need an eco tree for Jess.

Which makes . . . five Christmas trees in total.

I pause in my hair brushing, thinking hard. Can I have five Christmas trees? I try to imagine telling Luke we're having five Christmas trees and bite my lip. It just sounds . . . you know. Quite a lot.

I could spread them about the house a bit and maybe no one would notice?

Or . . . yes! I won't call them Christmas trees. I'll call the real one our Christmas tree and the rest can be 'Christmas shrubs'. I'll have a Christmas shrubbery. Genius. And then—

Oh God, look at the time. I need to hurry.

Luckily it's a bright, crisp day with one of those unreal, shiny blue winter skies, so no one questions my sunglasses as I drop Minnie off at school. And by the time I'm walking to Letherby Hall, I'm feeling a bit more human. As long as no one makes a loud noise—

'Stop! Bex, stop!' I'm jolted out of my reverie by Suze charging towards me, her hands waving frantically.

'Ssh!' I recoil. 'Quiet! What's the problem? Is there a fire?'

'No!' says Suze breathlessly. 'But I want to show you the surprise!'

Oh God, the surprise. I'd forgotten about that. It's probably just a new way of displaying handbags or something. But I must be supportive. So somehow I gather enough energy to smile at Suze and say, 'Of course! I can't wait! Show me!'

'OK, shut your eyes,' says Suze excitedly. 'I *bet* you can't guess . . .'

I close my eyes (which is actually quite a relief) and let Suze lead me into the shop, stumbling over the step.

'Ta-daah!' she cries – and I open my eyes dazedly to see a large banner reading, *Thank Sprygge It's Friday!*

I stare at it for a confused few moments, wondering if this is some weird hangover delusion.

'Wh-huh?' I manage at last.

'Look!' Suze gestures excitedly at the display table beneath. 'Look at everything!'

Dumbly I lower my eyes to the display table, which has a brand-new sign reading *EXCLUSIVE – NEW 'SPRYGGE' COLLECTION*. There's a stack of greetings cards with bold type announcing *We wish you a sprygge Christmas!* Next to it is a cushion on which is emblazoned *Don't worry, be sprygge!* There's a row of mugs with the slogan *Keep spryggering on* and a basket full of key-rings, with fobs printed with *#sprygge*.

I can't quite speak. But Suze doesn't seem to have noticed.

'It's our new *sprygge* range!' she enthuses. 'That's what I've been working on in secret. Oh Bex, it's *so* popular. It was flying out of the shop yesterday! Only you need to write down exactly what *sprygge* means,' she adds as an afterthought, 'because customers were asking us yesterday and Irene and I couldn't quite remember. It's like, feeling happy, basically, isn't it?' She blinks at me. 'Something like that? I tried googling it but I couldn't find it.'

'Oh, Becky, you're here!' says Irene, bustling up. 'Now, is it "sproog-uh" or "sprigg-uh"? You'll have to give us lessons in Norwegian! It's been *such* a success,' she adds. 'So novel. Are we the first *sprygge* stockists in the UK?'

'I think we must be,' says Suze happily. 'So many customers said they'd never even heard of *sprygge*!'

222

'We're ahead of the game,' nods Irene. 'Trust Becky to know the latest thing.'

'Oh, Bex always knows about new stuff,' says Suze confidently. 'She's a real trend-setter.'

My stomach has started to churn, and not just because of the festive brandies.

'Suze . . .' I begin, but my words dry up on my lips. I don't know how to tell her. Oh God. I *can't* tell her.

But I have to. Somehow.

'Suze, come here.' I hustle her away from the *sprygge* table, to a corner well away from Irene.

'Suze, listen,' I say in a desperate undertone. 'I made *sprygge* up.'

'What?' She stares at me uncomprehendingly.

'I invented *sprygge* just to annoy that snotty woman. I just plucked it out of the air. It's not a real word.'

Slowly I see the truth dawn on Suze's face.

'No,' she falters. 'You mean . . .' Her eyes dart to the *sprygge* table and back a few times. 'You mean . . . Oh my God.' She swallows. 'Bex, you're joking.'

'I'm not,' I say in agonized tones. 'Sorry.'

'But you gave a whole speech about it! You were so convincing! We all thought it was real!'

'I know! I was *going* to tell you it was made up, but . . .' I wrinkle my brow, trying to recall why I didn't – then suddenly remember. 'Craig came in and I forgot,' I confess shamefacedly.

Suze's gaze is fixed on the *sprygge* table. I can see from her eyes that thoughts are crashing into her head, and not in a good way.

'I can't believe you'd make something like that up,'

223

she says. 'How could you *do* that?' She turns on me with an accusing gaze.

'I didn't think you'd go and make a stack of cushions saying *Don't worry, be sprygge!*' I retort defensively. 'How could I have predicted that?'

'But then this is against the Trade Descriptions Act!' says Suze, gesturing around the shop in agitation. 'We've been telling everyone it's Norwegian! We could be sued! We could be prosecuted! We'll have to pulp the whole collection.' Her head descends into her hands and I feel an almighty wave of guilt.

'Suze, calm down.' I put my arms round her shoulders. 'No one's going to *sue* you.'

We both watch as our first customers of the day come in: two middle-aged women. They head straight to the *sprygge* table and I can hear them exclaiming with interest.

'I need to go and tell them it's all fake,' says Suze in dispirited tones.

'Suze, don't!' I say impulsively. 'Don't pulp the collection. It would be *such* a waste. It's only a word. And you've made such gorgeous things. Does it really matter if a few people have cushions saying *sprygge* in their house?'

'But we're saying it's Norwegian,' says Suze in hopeless tones. 'We're not being honest.'

'Well then ... let's not say it's Norwegian,' I suggest after a moment's thought. 'Let's say, "Some people believe it comes from Norway." That's true enough. All the customers from yesterday believe that, for a start. And anyway,' I continue, suddenly hit by a new idea, 'language is constantly evolving. It's fluid. There are new words in the dictionary every year! Why shouldn't one of them be *sprygge*?'

'What do you mean?' Suze stares at me suspiciously.

'If we start using the word *sprygge* a lot, then maybe other people will too, and then it'll get into the language. That's what language *is*,' I impress on Suze. 'That's how language *develops*. If anyone asks, we can say it's practically Norwegian. We can say it's "pending" Norwegian.'

One of the customers is filling her basket with *sprygge* mugs, her eyes sparkling.

'My daughter will love these,' she's saying to her friend. 'So different!'

'So original!' agrees her friend, reaching for a cushion. 'I've not seen them anywhere else.'

'You see?' I say to Suze. 'They both look so thrilled. If we tell them the truth, we're total spoilsports, and is that the Christmas spirit? No. It's not. Here's what I think: if the word *sprygge* makes people happy, then who are we to curtail that happiness?'

'It *is* a good word,' allows Suze reluctantly.

'It's a brilliant word,' I agree, trying to imbue her with confidence. 'It's a positive, joy-spreading word and it doesn't matter where it came from.'

I'm about to go and help the customers with their purchases when my phone buzzes with a text. I open it up and read it. Then I read it again, swallowing hard.

'What?' says Suze, watching me.

'Um. Nothing. Just, um, Craig, asking me and Luke to go round, later on, for a glass of wine.' I attempt a

225

casual tone. 'He says, "Let's have a special evening, the four of us."'

Suze's eyes widen dramatically. 'A "special evening, the four of you"?' she echoes, looking scandalized. 'Bex, you *know* what that means!'

My mind has already jumped to exactly the same thought, but I'm not admitting it to Suze. Or even myself.

'No I don't,' I say robustly. 'Suze, you have way too much imagination.'

'*Do* I, Bex? Or maybe you're just too naive to see what's right in front of you.' She puts both hands on my shoulders and gives me an earnest look. 'Just promise me you'll have a safe word, OK?'

'A *safe word*?' I can't help bursting into laughter. 'I'm not choosing a safe word! What, you think he's going to lock us in a dungeon?'

'I wouldn't be surprised,' she says darkly. 'You don't know what he gets up to.'

'Does the cottage have a dungeon?'

'Well, no,' she admits, after a moment's thought. 'But he might have made a sex room out of the second en suite.'

'Suze, you're mad! We're going round there for a civilized glass of wine and that's all. End of discussion. And now I'll go and help our customers, like I'm *paid to do*,' I say pointedly.

As I stride off towards the *sprygge* display, my phone buzzes again. I glance down to see a second message from Craig and gulp inwardly.

Bring your swimmers and we can all enjoy the hot tub together!
Or go au naturel . . . ? ;)

I don't think I'll mention that to Suze.
Oh God . . .

By six thirty, I've chosen an outfit to wear for our evening at Craig's. I've chosen black trousers, together with a very high-necked, tightly tied pussy-bow top. Plus a buttoned-up evening cape. (I bought it in the sales and then thought, 'Oh God, what a mistake. When will I ever need a cape?' Well, now I know.)

I'm sitting at the kitchen table as Minnie drinks her milk, tapping words into my phone, feeling like I lead some sort of torrid double life. There's my innocent child, drinking her milk – and here am I, choosing safe words. I've got about ten options so far, including 'Chanel', 'Dolce' and 'Gabbana'.

Then it occurs to me that they might not be very easy to work into conversation. Maybe a safe word should be something more nondescript like 'hello' or 'water'.

But then what if I want a drink of water?

Honestly. How do safe words work, anyway? Surely the safest word is 'Stop'? Or 'I'm going home now, I've had enough, and actually I'm not into multiplayer sex, I prefer shopping.' (OK, so that's more of a safe sentence.)

As Luke strides into the kitchen I jump with nerves and blurt out, 'So we're really going, are we?'

'What?' Luke gives me a puzzled look. 'Of course we

are. Unless – have you changed your mind? Aren't you feeling well?'

'I'm feeling fine!' My voice rises shrilly. 'It'll be super fun! Can't wait! Um, Craig said something about going in the . . . um . . .' I clear my throat. 'The hot tub.'

'The *hot tub*?' Luke chuckles. 'Well, let's see if we get that far.'

I stare at him uncertainly, wondering what exactly he means by 'get that far'. Oh God. Is Suze right and I'm really naive and everything has a double meaning that I've never understood before?

Luke wouldn't be into multiplayer sex.

Would he?

Just then the doorbell rings and Luke lets in the baby-sitter, Kay, who is a cheery lady in her sixties full of local gossip. Between us we get Minnie into bed, whilst hearing all about Kay's neighbour's dog's operation. And then, before I know it, we're walking along the dark, chilly village road towards Lapwing Cottage.

Luke is talking about the bottle of wine he's bringing and how we should think about going over to France one day to tour some vineyards and I'm nodding and saying, 'Yes, yes, burgundy, fab,' without any idea of what I'm on about. With every step I feel more jittery. I'm being ridiculous, I keep telling myself. Nothing is going to happen.

But what if it did? What would I *do*? Oh God, we're nearly there. Should I quickly say something to Luke?

Lapwing Cottage is off the main village road, down a little unlit lane. It's not completely dark though – there's a glow ahead, which must be the cottage. As we get

228

closer the glow gets brighter and brighter, until I blink in surprise. Wow. The cottage has been covered all over in fairy lights, some white, some multicoloured and some flashing. Minnie would *love* it.

We're nearly at the house now and Luke whistles.

'There's the hot tub.' He gives a small chuckle. 'Look. That's quite something.'

He's pointing over the hedge into the back garden. I follow his gaze – and stare, taken aback. There's not just a mammoth hot tub on the terrace, there's also a Hawaiian-looking bar, three sunbeds, about six patio heaters and some palm trees in pots.

'Did they bring those palm trees with them?' Luke is saying incredulously. 'And the sunbeds? It's hardly the right time of year. As for the patio heaters, I read a piece the other day about those . . .' He starts talking about global warming, but I can't listen, because I'm staring in slight terror at the palm trees.

Palm trees. Isn't that the sign? Isn't that what swingers have in their gardens to alert other swingers?

My heart is thumping hard as we walk up the path to the front door. It's on. It's real. Suze was right. I have to tell Luke, quick.

As he lifts his hand to the doorbell, I grab his arm.

'Luke,' I say in a desperate whisper. 'I'm not sure they want to talk about wine. It's all a front.'

'What?' Luke stares at me.

'I think they want . . . you know,' I gulp, then whisper even more quietly, 'An orgy.'

'*What?*' Luke gives a bark of laughter, then peers at me again. 'Becky, are you being serious?'

'Yes! Craig is into threesomes and foursomes and . . . everythingsomes. Suze saw it online. He goes to sex parties all the time. And look at the palm trees.' I gesticulate wildly towards the back garden. 'It's the sign! Swingers!'

'I'm fairly sure the sign for swingers is pampas grass,' says Luke calmly.

'Palm trees . . . pampas grass . . . it's all the same. We need a *plan*,' I add urgently. 'We need *signals*.'

'Hi guys! You made it!' Craig's raspy voice greets us, apparently out of nowhere, and I jump. He's leaning out of an upstairs window, wearing an open-necked shirt and beaming.

Oh God. Did he hear us? No. I don't think so.

'Hi!' I say in a strangled voice. 'We were just . . . Hi!'

'Hi there!' Luke hails him easily.

'I'll be down in a sec . . .' Craig's head disappears and I hear him calling, 'Nadine, they're here!'

I can already hear high heels approaching on the other side of the door. Shit.

'Our safe word is *sprygge*,' I gabble in panic. 'OK?'

'What?' Luke looks baffled.

'*Sprygge!* Safe word! *Sprygge!*'

I don't have time to say any more before the door swings open and there's Nadine, wearing a smart silk shirt which displays her amazing cleavage and wafting some musky perfume.

'Guys,' she says, embracing Luke, then me. 'Welcome!'

'Hi,' says Luke easily. 'We brought a little something.'

Nadine takes the bottle and our coats and ushers us into a nice big room with a fire blazing in the hearth and fairy lights decorating the mantelpiece. The look is kind of half-country cottage, half-music studio. There are linen-covered sofas and chairs, but there are also three guitars on stands and a couple of massive amps.

'Guys!' Craig comes striding in, wearing his usual ripped jeans and clutching what looks like an expensive bottle of wine. (The label's really old and torn, that's how I know.)

He kisses me and shakes Luke's hand warmly. Soon we're sitting on the linen sofas, listening to the fire crackle and watching the fairy lights round the mantelpiece flash on and off. Nadine passes round olives and nuts and Craig puts on some music and I start to relax a bit. It doesn't *feel* like a sex party. Not that I've ever been to one.

'What do you think of the wine, Luke?' Craig asks. 'Can I pour you some more?'

'Luke, come nearer the fire,' chimes in Nadine. 'Is that sofa comfortable for you? Can I get you another cushion? More olives?'

Instantly my radar starts to prickle. They're both all over Luke, just like they were in the pub. But maybe they're just trying to be friendly.

'The house looks amazing!' I say, to make conversation. 'All the fairy lights! Beautiful!'

'I made Craig do those,' says Nadine with satisfaction. 'I was like, babe, get up on your ladder, *now*.'

'She's the boss,' agrees Craig with a chuckle. 'You should see her manage her team at work. More wine, Luke? What are you up to for Christmas?'

'We're hosting for the first time,' says Luke. 'Becky's the mastermind.'

'Hosting Christmas for the first time!' says Nadine with a sympathetic eye-roll. 'I remember doing that. I nearly went mad. All my family were like, "Can we have this, can we have that?" In the end, I was like, "Enough! We're doing it my way!"'

'Oh my God!' I exclaim, feeling a bond with Nadine for the first time. 'Same! I've started a Christmas Whats-App group and it's sending me demented. Everyone wants different chocolates and mince pies and traditions. My sister's vegan and my best friend wants to do children's crafts, and her husband wants to watch opera and our neighbour Janice wants a piñata. You can't make everyone happy.'

'How many did you invite?' asks Nadine sympathetically, refreshing my wine glass.

'Well actually, they all kind of invited themselves,' I reply, after a moment's thought.

'Invited themselves?' Nadine opens her eyes wide.

'I mean, I *wanted* them to come,' I explain hurriedly. 'I love them all to bits. It'll be great! It's just . . . you know. Quite a lot to do.'

'I hear you,' says Nadine, nodding. 'Believe you me, Becky, you have to put your foot down.'

'It's just so full-on.' I take a gulp of wine. 'And now my mum's fallen out with Janice, and they're both supposed to be coming . . .'

'Oh no!' exclaims Nadine, wrinkling her nose. 'That's not ideal.'

'No. It's not.' I emit a gusty sigh. I hadn't realized how

much all this Christmas business had been stressing me out. It's quite a relief, sharing it with someone on the outside. 'All I want is a lovely day, you know? Everyone just enjoying being with each other, and not *caring* about how we cook the Brussels sprouts.'

'Don't have Brussels sprouts, that's what I say,' says Nadine briskly. 'Brussels sprouts can fuck off.'

'Christmas isn't about sprouts,' says Craig seriously. His voice sounds so raspy and rock-star-like, it sounds like he's declaiming a lyric from a really bad Christmas song, and I can't help laughing.

'I keep telling myself that,' I agree. 'None of the details really matter, do they? All that matters is that we have everyone gathered round the table. Friends. Family. *That's* what Christmas is all about.'

'Here's to that,' says Craig, raising his glass.

'Hear, hear,' agrees Luke.

'I couldn't agree more,' says Nadine. And she sounds so warm and friendly, I find myself unbending towards her even more.

'We've adopted this motto,' I confide. ' "Whatever the Grinch can steal, that's not Christmas." '

'I like that,' says Craig, nodding sagely. 'Yeah, I like that. Plus, you know, sprouts are rank.'

I can't help giggling again and Nadine pats my knee.

'You'll get your Christmas with your family and friends, Becky,' she says soothingly. 'Just make sure you enjoy the day, too.'

Enjoy the day? I hadn't even thought about enjoying it, just making sure it wasn't a total catastrophe. But I smile at her and say, 'Yes, I will, thanks.'

There's a pause while we all munch some olives and Craig turns down the lights a little. I'm enjoying this, I realize. I'm starting to relax.

'And now . . .' He sits back down on the sofa, stretching out his legs. He shoots a raised-eyebrows look at Nadine, then turns to Luke. 'Well. You guys have probably guessed. There's a bit of an . . . agenda tonight.'

At once I stiffen all over. Agenda?

Slowly Craig leans forward, gazing seriously at Luke, and so does Nadine. The atmosphere is suddenly charged and my head starts prickling. It's real. They're coming on to us. I should *never* have relaxed, I should *never* have let down my guard . . .

'Agenda?' says Luke easily. 'I thought this was a social engagement.'

'Yeah well.' Craig laughs again. 'You get into bed with someone, you want to know them socially first, don't you?'

Get into bed. Oh God . . .

'I don't know how open you are to this kind of thing . . . ?' puts in Nadine huskily, swishing her hair back and looking at Luke directly. The light is shining on her lipgloss and her cleavage and her sheeny shirt, and she looks pretty spectacular.

My heart's thudding frantically, but I don't seem able to speak. I feel surreal. Also: what's Luke going to say?

'I'm not, I'm afraid,' says Luke flatly, and I feel a whoosh of relief.

(I mean, obviously I knew he would say that.)

'Right,' says Nadine, without missing a beat. 'That's

disappointing. But maybe we can persuade you to another view.'

'I learned a new word today,' I say, finding my voice. '*Sprygge*. It's Norwegian. *Sprygge*.' I gaze desperately at Luke. '*Sprygge!*'

But no one even turns their head.

'I thought you were open-minded, Luke,' Nadine says huskily, leaning even further towards him, her breasts gleaming. 'And I'm going to be honest with you, OK? I really want this. I *really* want to pitch you.'

I stare at her, aghast. 'Pitch'? What does *that* mean? Is 'pitch' some weird sexual fetish slang I've never even—

Then my thoughts break off abruptly as I see the word 'PITCH' on a printed-out document at Nadine's feet, half under the sofa.

Hang on. Pitch as in . . . *pitch*?

OK, wait, *what* is going on here?

'I can give you advice,' Luke is saying smoothly to Nadine. 'But I'm not an investor.'

'You've got funds, though,' says Nadine, batting her eyelids at him. 'You've got a company that could expand. You've got the experience, I've got the talent.'

'You want *money*?' I say in astonishment, and Nadine swivels her head, looking annoyed.

'I want a *partnership*,' she says. 'It's not about money, it's about meshing talent and ideas. It's about channelling my energy and drive into greater pathways.' Then her eyes narrow at me. 'What did you think I wanted?'

'Sex!' I blurt out before I can stop myself.

There's a startled silence. Craig's eyes have widened.

235

Luke has turned to look at me with an expression I'm too flustered to read.

'*Sex?*' says Nadine at last. She's staring at me with such an amused gaze, I feel nettled. She needn't act like I'm a total moron for even thinking it.

'My friend read online that you're into sex parties,' I say defensively to Craig. 'In Moscow and stuff. Threesomes and . . . things.' If Nadine didn't know about the sex parties in Moscow, then too bad. Welcome to the sisterhood.

But she doesn't even flicker. In fact, she rolls her eyes impatiently as though I'm distracting her from the task in hand.

'Yeah, yeah, we're into that.' Craig shrugs, as though he's saying he likes a bit of golf at the weekends. 'But that's not what tonight is about.'

'What we get up to is our own affair,' says Nadine, a bit snippily. 'But if you think that's why we invited you . . .' She breaks off and runs her eyes over my high-necked top as though enjoying a private joke. 'Let's say . . . you're not the type.'

Not the type? At once I feel offended to my core. They're *rejecting* us? On what grounds? Why aren't I the type?

'I'm brilliant in bed,' I retort indignantly. 'And Luke's even better!'

'Sweetheart,' says Luke, his mouth twitching. 'Thanks for the recommendation. But . . . too much information? It's been a great evening,' he continues politely, putting his wine glass down. 'And thank you both. But maybe—'

'You're not *leaving*?' Nadine's voice has tightened. 'You're not even giving me a chance! Why do you think—' She stops herself mid-stream and smiles again. 'I've got the pitch ready. I've prepared it all. I think I deserve this opportunity.'

I glance at Luke and I can tell he feels a bit stuck.

'All right,' he says after a moment. 'I'm happy to listen.'

'Let's go next door,' says Nadine, getting to her feet and swishing her hair back. 'I've got my presentation ready there. Why not bring your drink?' As she ushers Luke to a door behind us, she shoots me a sidelong glance. 'Don't worry, Becky, I won't *jump* him.'

Ha bloody ha.

When Luke and Nadine have closed the door behind them, Craig pokes the fire, and it crackles a bit, and then we sit in silence. I feel unspeakably awkward – but Craig doesn't seem to be awkward at all. In fact, he seems barely aware of my presence.

'How's the music going?' I say at last. 'Have you got any new songs you could play us?'

'What?' he says absently. 'No, not really.'

'So ... where are you going to travel to next? Any more weekends in Warsaw?'

'Not sure,' says Craig in the same distracted tone.

'So ... er ... what d'you think of the situation in Venezuela?' I try in desperation.

'Venezuela?' He looks blank.

How can he look blank? Venezuela's, like, his special-ist subject! I want to exclaim, 'You used to bang on about Venezuela all the time! And you used to play the

237

guitar all the time! And you used to be able to make conversation!' But I'm not sure he'd even hear me.

If Suze could see us, she'd have to take back everything she said. Sexual tension? Flirting? What a joke! He's not even *looking* at me. Instead, he keeps glancing at the door behind which Luke and Nadine have disappeared, and taking deep swigs of wine.

'Wonder how it's going,' he says, his tone a little tense. 'She's so talented, Nadine. She deserves a break, you know? She works so hard at her business plans. I say to her, "Babe, have a rest," but she won't. She's driven, you know? Driven.'

'She's quite different from you,' I venture.

'Yeah, that's what I admire.' Craig's eyes shine. 'She's got her shit together. She's got a plan. First woman I've ever met who had a plan.'

At once I want to object to this. I always had plenty of plans! He just never listened to them. But actually, I'm a bit tired of talking to Craig. Once you get past the leather and the raspy voice, there's not much to him.

'You want to watch telly?' he says suddenly, and I gape at him. This is the last straw. He's invited us round for drinks and now he's putting on the *telly*?

But actually, I'm pretty bored, sitting here, so why not?

He turns it on to a Christmas movie where a stressed-out city girl called Rae has got stuck in a gorgeous small town on Christmas Eve: all snow and hot chocolate and a handsome stubbled lumberjack called Chris. She's just deciding to go in for the 'best decorated tree' competition and Chris is offering to help her chop down a tree . . . when the door opens and Nadine appears, followed by Luke.

I blink at them, still slightly lost in the Christmas movie world, and say, 'Oh, hi. Have you finished?'

'As I say, Luke,' says Nadine, ignoring me, 'there are plenty of other ways we could go. Believe you me, one of my strengths is being open to the future. All versions of the future. Because today *is* the future.'

'Absolutely,' says Luke in unreadable tones.

'So you'll give me a call?'

'What do you think?' chimes in Craig eagerly. 'She's talented, isn't she, Nadine?'

'Very much so.' Luke smiles politely at Craig. 'But there's a lot to think about. Maybe we should leave it there for now and pick up again in business hours.'

'I'm flexible on figures, too,' Nadine adds quickly. 'I should have made that clear . . .'

'Great,' says Luke. 'That's good to know.'

Craig has turned the sound down on the TV, and is following this conversation intently, but I'm still half following the action onscreen. Rae and Chris are having a row. She's brandishing the wood chopper at him as her hair blows around picturesquely in the wind. Why? What happened?

'Anyway,' says Luke, in a decisive voice which makes me come to. 'It was great hearing about your ideas, Nadine, and thanks for the wine – delicious – but I think our babysitter needs to leave early, am I right, Becky?'

Ah. He wants to go.

Ooh, if we hurry, we can watch the rest of the Christmas movie at home!

'What about the hot tub?' protests Nadine. 'We could carry on our conversation there, pour some more wine . . .'

'Yeah, you have to try the hot tub,' says Craig.

'I think we'll pass,' says Luke, glancing at me. 'Yes?'

No *way* am I ever getting in a hot tub with Nadine. So that's a yes.

'That's right,' I say, getting to my feet. 'We'd better go, but thanks for a *lovely* time,' I add insincerely.

A lovely time. Pah. Listening to business pitches and watching TV and being told we don't cut it as foursome partners? I'd rather just have gone to Pizza Express, at least we'd have got pizza.

This evening is the absolute opposite of what I expected. And the biggest disappointment is Craig. He's gone from mesmerizing charmer to . . . blah.

We make our farewells and both Craig and Nadine say 'Thanks' over and over to Luke and pump his hand, and Craig even gives him a long, heartfelt hug. (He doesn't hug me, I notice.)

But soon enough we're outside again, walking back through the village, with a bright moon overhead and owls hooting in the distance. The whole evening feels like a surreal dream.

'Weird,' says Luke at last.

'Weird,' I agree. 'What did you think of her business pitch?'

'*Awful*,' says Luke, so definitively that I can't help laughing. 'It was *painful*. I still have no idea quite what her proposed business is, except that it involves Brandon

Communications giving her large amounts of money and setting her up with a staff and a car.'

'Oh my God.' I can't help giggling. 'Did you say no?'

'I'll say no when we talk again,' says Luke. 'I really just wanted to cut her off. I'll let her down gently,' he adds in a kinder voice. 'There are some people she could usefully talk to. I'll make her a list, give her some contacts. I mean, kudos to her, wanting to pitch. She just needs some stronger ideas. She has a lot to learn.'

I squeeze his hand because that is so him – to want to help her anyway. How could Nadine not want to have sex with him? I think indignantly – then hastily amend my thoughts. Obviously I wouldn't *want* them to have sex. But still. She has zero taste.

As we near home, I pause underneath an overhanging holly bush and impulsively draw Luke into a long kiss. I know it should be mistletoe – but I don't know where to find any. (I should really carry my inflatable mistletoe wreath around with me.) Kissing in streets is sexy. It reminds me of when we first got together. We should kiss in streets more.

The moustache is still not ideal, hand on heart. But other than that, this is pretty perfect.

'I think we're a hot couple, anyway,' I say at last, as we finally draw apart. 'I would *totally* want to have sex with us.'

'Me too,' says Luke. 'They lost out.' He tugs at the bow on my blouse. 'Does this untie?'

'Might do.' I glint teasingly at him as he loosens the bow. All this thinking about foursomes has kind of got me going. As soon as Kay leaves, we'll light some candles . . . pull up the sheepskin rug in front of the fire . . . put on a sexy playlist . . . mmm . . .

Oh, but what about the Christmas movie? I suddenly remember. What about Rae and the lumberjack? I *have* to know what happens . . .

No, it's fine, we can get it on Catch-up. God, technology is great.

Chats

SUZE & BEX

Suze
So??? Are you all tangled up in the hot tub with Craig and Nadine??!!

Bex
No!!! I'm watching a Christmas movie with Luke actually.

Suze
Watching a Christmas movie?? What happened??

Bex
They didn't want a threesome. Or a foursome. Or any kind of -some.

Suze
Really??? I swear I read Craig's into that kind of stuff.

Bex
He is. They are. But not with us.

Bex
They said, 'You're not our type.'

Bex
Suze? Are you there????

Suze
Sorry. I was laughing so hard I dropped my phone.

BECKY & JESS

Becky
Hi Jess! Just wondering, will Tom definitely be back in England in time for Christmas??

Jess
Yes

Becky
Only you've been apart quite a while, haven't you?

Jess
Yes

Becky
That must be really hard for you.

Jess
Yes

Becky
Anyway, Suze and I wondered if you'd like to meet up some time? Shall we go to Waste Not Foods? It's a packaging-free shop with a vegan café! Doesn't that sound perfect??!!

Jess
Yes

Becky
And you're sure everything's OK with you and Tom?

Jess
Yes

Becky
Because you can confide in me about anything, you know that?

Jess
Yes

Becky
So you and Tom really are OK???

Jess
YES

246

From: Tom Webster
To: Becky
Subject: FYI

Dear Becky

Jess shared with me your recent WhatsApp exchange. Clearly you think we've got some sort of problem. I would like to let you know:

There is nothing wrong with our marriage.

To repeat:

THERE IS NOTHING WRONG WITH OUR MARRIAGE!!

Best

Tom

From: Anders Halvorsen
To: Becky Brandon
Subject: Re: An exciting new word for your dictionary – 'sprygge'!

Dear Mrs Brandon née Bloomwood

Thank you for your email. I must admit, I found it confusing.

In answer to your question: no, I cannot put 'sprygge' into the Norwegian National Dictionary. This word is unfamiliar to me.

I do not believe it has 'passed into everyday Norwegian'. Nor is it 'on the tip of everyone's tongue these days'.

What exactly do you believe it means?

Yours sincerely

Anders Halvorsen

Editor
Norwegian National Dictionary

FOURTEEN

A week has passed and I've put Craig and Nadine out of my mind. Because the best thing to do in life is move on from embarrassing encounters and not look back, even when your husband keeps teasing you about them. He sent me a text yesterday:

> **John at work has invited us for dinner in the New Year with his wife. NB Fairly sure he means dinner, not a foursome in a hot tub.**

Ha, ha, *hilarious*.

But I'm also quite preoccupied with Jess, because Tom's email troubled me. No one sends an email like that if their marriage is fine. Tom actually sounds a bit deranged, if you ask me. Although, let's face it, he's never been what you might call 'standard issue'. It's not so long ago that he was building a monster summer house in Janice and Martin's garden and announcing he was going to live there.

As I ice Minnie's birthday cake on Saturday morning, I'm feeling quite concerned – although I'm even more concerned by the stupid cake. The sponge keeps falling apart every time I try to smear the buttercream on. I thought this job would take about ten minutes and I could get it all done while Minnie was at her ballet lesson, but this is a disaster.

'Suze, help,' I say desperately as she strides into the kitchen. 'My cake keeps falling to bits when I try to ice it.'

'Did you cover it with a crumb coat first?' she enquires.

'Of course not.' I stare at her. 'Crumb what? How did you know about that?'

Suze shrugs vaguely, which probably means she learned it at finishing school. She's always coming out with some life tip that she learned there, like how to lay a table for six courses or address an envelope to a bishop. I'm about to say, 'Is it too late to do the crumb-whatsit thing now?' when Luke walks into the kitchen.

'Jesus,' he says, and breathes out hard.

'What?'

'I've just been on the phone to Nadine.'

'Nadine?' I put down my smearing knife and stare at him. 'How come?'

'She called me about her business pitch.'

'On a Saturday?'

'She said she'd been waiting impatiently for my call.' He winces. 'She seemed to have . . . let's say, the wrong idea about how things had gone when we met.'

'In what sense?'

'In the sense that she thought I was about to write her

a cheque, give her a car and rename my company "Bran-don and Nadine's Communications".'

'Oh my *God.*' I stare at him, half horrified and half wanting to giggle. 'But that's ridiculous! You didn't prom-ise anything. You just said, "There's a lot to think about." I heard you with my own ears.'

'Of course I didn't promise anything!' says Luke. 'She's a chancer. Or deluded. Or both. Hi, Suze,' he adds.

'Hi, Luke,' says Suze blithely. 'So Craig and Nadine aren't your new best friends after all? Shame.'

I shoot a suspicious glare at her. I can sense a big old 'Told you so' in her voice, although if I confront her, she'll say, 'Whatever are you talking about?'

'Tell you what,' says Luke, starting to make some cof-fee. 'Nadine got quite nasty on the phone. She implied they need the money.'

'Need the money?' I stare at him. 'How can they need the money?'

'She pretty much implied that Craig is broke.' Luke shrugs. 'I'm just going on what she said.'

'But he's a rock star!' I say, bewildered. 'He went to Warsaw! He can't be broke!'

'That's right, Bex,' says Suze in a deadpan voice. 'Because rock stars never go to Warsaw when they're broke. They take in extra washing and cut coupons.'

'Ha ha.' I roll my eyes.

'Poor Bex.' Suze suddenly relents. 'I see you've washed the blue dye out of your hair. And where are your killer slutty boots? Are you ever going to wear them again?'

'They're upstairs,' I say with dignity. 'And of course I'll wear them again, upon the right occasion.'

251

'I like the killer slutty boots,' says Luke cheerfully. 'Don't knock the killer slutty boots. Does anyone want coffee?'

'No thanks,' I say. 'We're about to go and meet Jess for lunch. You're picking up Minnie, remember?'

'Actually, *those* boots are really nice,' says Suze, her eyes suddenly focusing on my feet. 'Are those new?'

'Yes! Brand new!'

They're a pair of caramel ankle boots which I'd actually forgotten I ordered until they arrived this morning. I turn this way and that to show them off to Suze – then it hits me. Is this a hint?

'Suze, have them,' I say impulsively.

'Have them?'

'For Christmas!' I start tugging one off. 'Try them on!'

'No! I'm not having your brand-new boots that you've never even worn!' says Suze, almost crossly. 'Put that back on, Bex. We should get going. What are you going to do with your cake?'

'Dunno,' I admit, squirming my foot back into its boot.

'That's a *cake*?' says Luke in astonishment, peering at the misshapen pile of sponge and buttercream on the counter. 'I thought—' He stops himself. 'I mean, Minnie will love it, whatever.'

'Put it in the freezer,' advises Suze. 'Then make some more buttercream and pile it on top. You can't have too much buttercream. And spray it with edible glitter,' she adds airily. 'It'll be fine. Come on, let's go.'

I've been really looking forward to visiting a packaging-free shop – and as I walk into Waste Not Foods I feel a blinding revelation. *This* is where we should shop. All the time! Here!

I mean, *look* at it. There are rustic wooden boxes filled with earthy potatoes and carrots. There are eggs with feathers still on them. And there are loads of big glass jars, like in old-fashioned sweet shops, all filled with nuts and oats and stuff like that. You just help yourself! It's genius!

'Hi,' says a girl behind the till. She has a nose ring and hair tied up with twine and is wearing one of those brown linen artist-type tops that I always half want to buy but *actually* make me look like a sack.

Not that she looks like a sack.

I mean OK, she does a tiny bit, but she probably doesn't mind looking like a sack.

'Hi!' I beam back. 'Fab shop!'

There are festive brown hessian stockings hung up by the door, each containing a Fairtrade chocolate bar wrapped in recycled paper, an eco coffee cup and a copy of a book called *How We're All Doomed*. I am *so* coming back here to buy one for Jess. She'll love it!

'Are you going to buy anything?' I say to Suze.

'Yes, I need rice,' she says, pulling two plastic ice-cream tubs out of her tote. 'And maybe some pasta. And the sweet potatoes look good, don't they?' As she speaks, she produces an extra cotton shopping tote and shakes out a couple of brown paper bags.

I stare at all her bags and tubs, feeling discomfited. 'Did you bring those with you?'

'Well, yes,' says Suze, looking surprised. 'Of course I did. There isn't any packaging, Bex. You have to bring your own receptacles.'

Right.

I mean, obviously, I knew that. It's just . . .

Oh *God*. Why didn't I bring a few tubs and things? I haven't even got a Bag for Life with me, I realize with a jolt of horror. But I'm not going to admit that. No way.

As I wander around the jars of spices and pulses, I feel both inspired and stressed out. I want everything here! Only I need some packaging. I need a tub or bag or *something* . . .

Then, thankfully, I spot a shelf behind the till holding some glass wide-necked jars. Excellent. I'll buy a load of jars and pretend that's what I intended to do all along.

'Hello!' I say, approaching the girl at the till. 'Your shop is so inspiring. I'm *totally* giving up on packaging.'

'Oh good,' she says.

'So, could I have thirty jars, please? Fifteen tall and fifteen short?'

'*Thirty jars?*' She stares at me.

'To put stuff in,' I explain.

I'm never having packets again, I've decided. I can just see my kitchen, looking like something out of *Livingetc*, with labelled matching jars lined up neatly. It'll be amazing!

But the girl is frowning dubiously.

'I don't even have thirty jars in stock,' she says. 'Can you *carry* thirty glass jars?'

Oh. I hadn't thought about that.

'Most people bring old plastic tubs,' she continues. 'We encourage recycling as much as possible. Didn't you bring anything?' She looks at my empty hands. 'Nothing at all?'

She doesn't need to sound so condescending.

'I'm plastic-free, actually,' I retort in a supercilious voice. 'All right, I'll have six jars, please. For now.'

The girl raises her eyebrows, which I think is needless, but reaches behind her and puts six glass jars on the counter.

They are quite bulky. But they'll look fab!

I pick up a wicker shopping basket, load it up with the glass jars, head to a big container full of pulses and fill up a jar. Then I check to see what I'm buying. Mung beans! I have no idea what to do with mung beans, but I can find a recipe.

I'm about to fill up a second jar with barley when I get a text from Luke: Can you buy some eggs? We're out. I quickly text back No problem and head to the rustic feathery eggs in their tray. I pick up two – then wonder what to do with them. They aren't in boxes, so how do you carry them?

'Did you bring an egg box?' says the girl behind the till, who's watching me. 'We ask all our customers: if they want to buy eggs, please bring an old egg box. Otherwise you *can* buy a reusable bamboo one for a pound, but obviously we encourage recycling. Did you want to buy a bamboo one?'

I can read her snide expression exactly. She means 'Do you want to pollute the planet even further, you moron who couldn't remember an egg box?'

'No thanks,' I say, lifting my chin. 'I have receptacles already.'

'You can't carry eggs in jars,' she says as though I'm an idiot.

'Yes I can,' I contradict her.

I gently put two eggs into a glass jar and put the lid on, then do the same with three more jars. I'll just have to carry them carefully.

'Hi, Becky.' Jess's voice greets me and I whip round.

'Hi, Jess!' I give her a hug. 'This place is amazing!'

'What are you doing?' She peers at my jars, looking puzzled.

'Buying eggs.' I manhandle my glass jars to the counter, where the girl stares at them. 'Hi,' I say in a nonchalant manner. 'I'd like to pay for these, please.'

'Why didn't you buy an egg box?' says Jess incredulously.

'Because I don't want to ruin the planet with hollow consumption,' I reply, raising my eyes. As if she needs to ask.

'But half of your eggs are already broken,' says the girl, looking through the glass.

Drat.

'They're for scrambled eggs,' I say briskly. 'So it's fine. How much is that?'

'£45.89,' she says. 'Have you got a bag or do you need to buy one?'

For a moment I'm silent. No *way* am I admitting I forgot to bring a Bag for Life.

'I don't believe in bags, actually,' I say at last. 'My rule is, "Buy only what you can carry."'

'But you can't carry all that,' says the girl.

'My sister will help me,' I say without missing a beat.

'You'll help me get all this out to the car, won't you? And Suze?' I raise my voice. 'I don't want to wreck the planet, so could you help me too?'

Between us we get all my jars into Suze's boot and go back into the shop for Suze to pay.

'Excuse me?' says the girl at the till to me. 'You forgot to take your last jar.' She holds out the empty jar and I take it nonchalantly, wanting to impress Jess in some way.

'Thanks,' I say. 'Maybe I'll fill it with . . . black turtle beans.'

I have no idea what you do with black turtle beans but they sound totally worthy.

'I love black turtle beans,' I add to Jess. 'They're so *vegan*.'

I saunter over to a massive glass dispenser labelled 'Black turtle beans', place my jar underneath and twist the handle. At once, small dried black beans start pouring out in a gush, and I smile at Jess. When the jar is nearly full I casually twist the handle back – but it won't go. I try again, but it's stuck. Shit.

Shit.

To my horror, beans have started cascading over the top of my jar and clattering on to the floor. I desperately yank at the handle, but I can't shift it and the beans are coming faster and faster.

'What the *hell*?' says the girl behind the till, as everyone turns to stare at me and the torrent of beans. 'Turn the handle back! Quick!'

'I'm *trying*!' I say, my face boiling. 'What do you think I'm *doing*?'

The girl leaps up from her seat and hurries towards

me, but even before she gets there, it's too late. The clattering has come to an end. The dispenser is empty. There are beans all over the floor. I hear a sudden snort from Suze's direction and look up to see her hand clamped over her mouth.

'I'll buy them, obviously,' I say quickly, before the girl can utter a word. 'All of them. They'll be so useful for . . . dishes.'

'You'll buy them *all*?' The girl in the sack eyes me in disbelief.

'Of course!'

'Uh-huh.' She thinks for a moment, then lifts her eyebrows. 'How do you intend to transport them? Do you need a bag, by any chance?'

She sounds so snotty, I feel a flare of indignation.

'No, I do not need a bag,' I say coolly. 'As I mentioned before, I'm an ethical, bag-free consumer. I will therefore carry them . . . er . . . in my skirt,' I say in sudden inspiration.

'In your *skirt*?'

'Yes!' I say defiantly. I make a hammock out of my Rixo midi skirt – which is ideally shaped – and start to scoop beans into it. 'See?'

Suze gives another sudden snort and comes over to where I'm kneeling on the floor.

'Bex,' she says, 'that's a great plan. Obviously. But if you didn't mind compromising your ethical principles just a tad . . . we *could* just use a cardboard box?'

Hmph. I still think I could have got those beans out of there in my skirt. I could have stored some in the glove compartment and some in the boot. The car could have been our black turtle bean storage facility.

On the other hand, I guess it *was* quicker just to sweep them all into a box, pay for them and head into the café. Now we're sitting at a window table, all cosily together. We've ordered our food and we're sipping our water, and Suze and I keep glancing at each other. It's time to tackle Jess, with as much sensitivity and empathy as we can muster.

'*Wait* till you see your vegan turkey on Christmas Day,' I say to Jess as a preamble. 'It's going to be amazing!'

'Great,' says Jess.

I glance yet again at Suze and wonder how to proceed. Our plan was to help Jess 'open up' – but how?

'So . . . how's life in Chile?' I begin cautiously. 'It must be hard. How's . . . Tom?'

'He's fine, thanks,' says Jess shortly. 'Everything's fine.'

But at once I can see the muscles in her neck twitching. And she's clenching her water glass. Does she really think we're fooled?

'Jess, you're really strong and independent,' I say earnestly. 'I've always admired that. But I want you to know . . . we're here for you.'

'We're totally here for you,' affirms Suze.

'In case there was anything . . .' I trail off uncertainly.

'The whole adoption thing must be a real strain on both of you,' Suze says softly. 'Isn't it?'

There's a much longer pause and I can barely breathe, because Jess's eyes are starting to shimmer. Jess's eyes *never* shimmer. I always thought they were made of granite, like her abs.

'Yes, it's quite a strain,' she says at last, and her voice sounds choked. 'It's harder than we predicted. You think you're patient, you think you're philosophical . . . but . . .'

She breaks off into silence. Oh God. We need to tread so carefully. I look nervously at Suze, who makes an encouraging face back.

'Is it . . . I mean . . .' I hesitate. 'Do you . . .'

I don't even know what I want to ask. *Actually*, what I want is for Jess to blurt out all her feelings spontaneously and then I'll say something wise in return and we'll all hold hands.

But already she's gathering herself. The shimmer has gone from her eyes.

'Maybe we should order some bread as well,' she says, glancing at the café counter.

'Jess, don't talk about bread!' I say as supportively as I can. 'We're here. Just the three of us in a safe space. Why not talk about . . .'

'What?' She narrows her eyes at me.

'Anything!' I wave my hands vaguely. 'Anything at all! Chile . . . Tom . . .'

As I say the word 'Tom', Jess inhales sharply.

'What *is* this?' she demands, looking from me to Suze. 'You're on about Tom again. I thought he emailed you and said that everything was OK?'

'Well,' I say after a pause. 'Yes, he did.'

I don't want to add, 'And his email made me more concerned than ever!' Nor do I want to ask yet again, 'When *is* he coming back to the UK?'

'Everything's fine.' Jess glowers at me. 'What are you expecting me to say, Becky? What are you implying?'

'Nothing!' I backtrack hastily. 'No! I'm not . . . Just . . . if there's anything to share . . . I'm your sister, after all . . .' I put a gentle hand on her arm and try not to notice her recoiling.

'And I'm your friend,' chimes in Suze, putting a hand on Jess's other arm and fixing her with earnest blue eyes. 'So if you did want to share . . .'

'She doesn't *want* to share!' comes the sardonic voice of the girl in the sack, who seems to have moved on to waitress duty and is walking past. 'Jeez! Leave the poor woman alone!'

'It's none of your business!' I say indignantly, but Jess has already moved her arms out of our grasp. She thrusts them under the table, looking supremely uncomfortable.

'I'm sorry, Becky, but she's right,' she says in a tense, low voice. 'Just leave it. Stop inventing problems with my life.'

'But—'

'Leave it.' Jess cuts me off, and I exhale in frustration. How can we talk . . . if Jess won't talk?

I open my mouth – then shut it. I'm desperate to say more, but Jess's resolute expression puts me off. She'll only get angry, and that's the last thing I want.

'If there's anything you should be worried about, it's not my marriage,' Jess continues robustly. 'It's your mum and Janice. *That's* the relationship gone south. They're not even speaking, as far as I can work out.'

'What?' says Suze in shock, and I realize I haven't filled her in on the whole situation.

'Oh yes, Mum and Janice have kind of fallen out,' I admit. 'It's not great.'

261

'But why?' demands Suze. 'What happened?'

'Janice feels ignored,' says Jess bluntly. 'She feels as if your parents have moved on and forgotten all about her.'

'Mum and Dad *have* invited Janice and Martin to things in Shoreditch,' I say, wanting to stick up for them.

'Oh, I know.' Jess shrugs. 'I'm not taking sides. Janice doesn't help herself. She's got a mental block about Shoreditch. Her new thing is looking up knife crime stats. She keeps saying things like, "Well, I *hope* poor Jane and Graham don't get mugged by a drug runner on a moped," and "Well, I *hope* poor Jane and Graham don't get caught up in gang warfare."'

Jess does such a good imitation of Janice's quavery voice, I can't help grinning.

'Still, she's upset,' Jess concludes.

'Not too upset to find herself a new friend though?' I can't help retorting.

'Oh God.' Jess rolls her eyes. 'Flo.'

'Flo?' Suze looks intrigued. 'Who's Flo?'

'Janice's new best friend,' I explain. 'In Oxshott.'

'I can't even *imagine* Janice having a new best friend,' says Suze in wonderment. 'That's extraordinary!'

'It's gruesome,' says Jess, shaking her head.

'You're not a fan of Flo?' says Suze with a giggle. 'Sorry,' she adds. 'I know it's not funny.'

At that moment, the waitress brings over our food, so we break off our conversation. And I'm just reaching for my napkin when my phone bleeps with a text. I glance at it to see if it's Luke making any more shopping orders – but as I read it, I clap my hand over my mouth.

'No *way*,' I say, when I can find my voice.

'What?' says Suze.

'It's Janice,' I say, and turn my phone round so the others can both read it:

Can't wait for Minnie's birthday tea, Becky love, and I'll be bringing my new friend, Flo, if that's OK. Love Janice xxx

---

Dear Mrs Brandon née Bloomwood

Thank you for your email.

Your definition of 'sprygge' means nothing to me.

I do not recollect any old Norse 'sprygge' myths as you suggest, nor any 'rhymes learned at my mother's knee', nor any jokes involving the word 'sprygge'.

I must reiterate my previous answer: that I cannot put 'sprygge' into the Norwegian National Dictionary. Thank you for your offer of a T-shirt reading 'We'll always have sprygge', which I decline.

Yours sincerely

Anders Halvorsen

Editor
Norwegian National Dictionary

FIFTEEN

I mean, basically Janice is declaring war. I know that sounds extreme, but that's what it is: bringing a new friend on to our territory. She *knows* Mum will be there. She *knows* there's tension between them. She's doing this to stir up trouble.

Not that I have time to think about that right now, because I'm too busy piling buttercream on to Minnie's birthday cake. I've made quite a lot. Like, two bowlfuls. I peer at the cake, which is still a bit wonky, and add another inch of buttercream. Then another. Then I think, 'Oh, sod it,' and heap the rest up in the middle. As Suze said, you can't have too much buttercream. And now it's about a foot high and it looks fab.

Minnie has had a lovely birthday morning, happily opening all her cards and playing with her new monster truck and interactive fluffy kitten. (She saw it on a TV ad and begged for it, but I haven't admitted that to Suze.) Now Suze and her children have arrived, and it's mayhem. Minnie and Wilfie are running monster trucks up and down the sitting-room floor while Ernest plays a piece on the ancient piano (which came with the house and is totally out of tune). Meanwhile Clemmie has found the 'Jingle Bells' baubles and keeps setting them off at different times.

'That kitten is amazing!' says Suze, coming into the kitchen with Jess. 'It purrs and drinks milk and everything! Where did you find it?'

'Oh . . . just came across it,' I say vaguely. 'I looked for a sustainable wooden version, obviously,' I add quickly, glancing at Jess. 'At Sustainable Wood Toys Dot Com. But they didn't have one. Shame.'

'The toy industry has a lot to answer for,' replies Jess austerely.

'And you know something? Minnie still wants a hamper for Christmas,' I inform Suze, trying not to sound smug. 'I asked her last night. That's all she wants, a picnic hamper. I knew she wouldn't swerve.'

'Don't be so complacent,' says Suze, rolling her eyes. 'There's still time for a major swerve.'

'No there isn't.' I glare at her. 'Don't freak me out.'

'Christmas is still weeks away. *Loads* of time for a swerve.' Suze puts on a childish, breathless voice. '"Mummy, all I want is a talking mermaid! If Father Christmas really loves me, that's what he'll bring me. He knows I've changed my mind because he's magic!"'

'Stop it. You're just winding me up.'

'"Does Father Christmas . . . *not* love me?"' continues Suze, in a broken, gulping voice. '"Wasn't I good, Mummy? Is that why he brought me this grotty old picnic hamper that I've lost all interest in?"'

'Shut up!' I can't help giggling. 'You're evil!'

'Nice pinny, by the way,' says Suze, finally relenting and gesturing at my new festive apron.

'Oh,' I say, mollifed. 'D'you like it? I got it at the— Ooh!' I interrupt myself. 'D'you want it for Christmas?'

'Bex, stop it!' Suze exclaims in exasperation. 'Stop trying to give me all your new stuff! We're giving each other Christmas presents from our own possessions,' she explains to Jess. 'You know, to be non-consumerist and everything.'

'Sound idea.' Jess nods.

'Only Suze won't even *hint* at what she wants,' I say reproachfully.

'In some cultures, if you admire another person's possession, they immediately give it to you,' says Jess.

'Oh my God,' says Suze with a giggle. 'Can you *imagine*? Bex and I would be constantly stripping off and swapping everything we own. "Nice shoes, Bex." "Have them!" "Nice lashes, Suze." "Have them!"'

I can't help smirking at the idea of Suze standing in the middle of a drinks party, peeling off her fake lashes and holding them out to me.

'Lashes?' says Jess, puzzled. 'You mean false eye-lashes?'

'Well . . . yes,' says Suze.

'You wear *false eyelashes*, Suze?' Jess seems appalled and I hastily back away before she asks me if I do, too.

'Sometimes,' says Suze cautiously, and Jess fixes her with a concerned stare.

'Don't you think it a tragedy that you feel the need to

augment your own body according to inherently sexist stereotypes?'

'Just for parties,' says Suze. 'They're organic, I think,' she adds evasively, gazing at the ceiling.

She's crossing her fingers behind her back. They are *so* not organic.

'Ooh,' Suze adds hastily as the doorbell rings. 'Is that your mum and dad, Bex?'

Thank God, because I feel like Jess was about to start quizzing me on why I brush my hair because hairbrushes are sexist, or something. As I quickly sprinkle pink edible glitter all over the buttercream, I hear Luke's footsteps in the hall and a moment later the distinctive sound of Mum's voice:

'Luke! Minnie, darling, happy birthday!'

I thrust a model of a sparkly fairy on top of the cake, then cover the whole thing up with a giant-sized wooden salad bowl that I ordered slightly by mistake.

(OK, totally by mistake. This is the trouble with online shopping: you can't tell how big anything is. I mean, I know they *say* '54cm'. But who knows what 54cm looks like? No one. Exactly.)

I take off my apron, then hurry out of the kitchen to find Mum and Dad taking off their coats in the hall.

OK. Wow. I blink a few times, trying to get my head round their appearance. Somehow I'd forgotten about my parents' whole new look. I'd imagined them arriving today in traditional Oxshott clothes. Maybe a blazer; maybe a floral shirtwaister.

But oh no. Mum's in a psychedelic print dress and weird necklace extending down to her navel, woven out of . . . is that *cassette tape*? Instead of her usual handbag she has a satchel slung over her shoulder which reads 'Postal Worker'. Meanwhile Dad is wearing a strange black woollen draped hat, together with a graphic *Rick and Morty* T-shirt and skinny stonewashed jeans. Every item makes me wince. The skinny jeans frankly look uncomfortable and I don't believe Dad's ever watched a *Rick and Morty* episode in his life.

But I must be supportive.

'Hi!' I greet them each with a warm hug. 'How's everything? How's Shoreditch?' I stop and stare downwards. 'Wait, what happened to your *foot*?'

Dad's left foot is all wrapped up in a bandage. And there's a crutch propped up against the wall, I suddenly notice.

'Oh, nothing much!' says Dad at once, giving his coat to Mum and picking up the crutch. 'Just a little . . . ahm . . . encounter with the ground. Now how's that lovely granddaughter of mine?'

As Dad hobbles after Minnie into the sitting room, I turn to Mum.

'What happened?'

'Oh, love,' she says, lowering her voice. 'Dad's a bit sensitive about it. He fell off his unicycle.'

'Oh no!' I say in horror.

'It wasn't his fault,' adds Mum defensively. 'He's getting very good. But he was practising in the Green Space on the roof and one of the community bees stung him. He got such a shock, he fell off.'

'Poor Dad!' I say, wincing. 'Well, I've made some avocado sandwiches, that'll cheer him up.'

'Oh Becky, love.' Mum lowers her voice even further. 'I haven't told you the bad news, have I?' She pauses and I feel a flutter of fear. 'Dad's discovered he's intolerant to avocado.'

She looks so distraught, I have a sudden urge to laugh, which is *wrong*.

'Yes.' She exhales. 'He went to the doctor. He's had to give it up. I've given up too, in sympathy.'

She scratches her neck and adjusts the cassette-tape necklace, which I have to say does *not* look comfortable.

'Mum, is that necklace making you sore?' I say, suddenly seeing a red patch of skin on her neck. 'Why don't you take it off?'

'Oh,' says Mum, looking defeated. 'Well . . . maybe. It is a super piece, though. It was made by Lia in our building. It represents Chaos.'

'It's lovely!' I lie. 'So . . . artistic!'

As Mum takes the necklace off and puts it in her new satchel, I detect a slightly crestfallen expression. I mean, it's no wonder. The bees, the unicycle *and* the avocados have let them down. Next they'll discover they're allergic to artisan gin.

'Mum, are you OK?' I squeeze her arm. 'Are you still enjoying Shoreditch?'

'Oh *yes*, love,' says Mum emphatically. 'It's such an adventure. Dad and I wake up every morning and think, "What today?"' She pauses, then adds, 'But we do miss our old friends.'

'Right,' I say cautiously. 'I think Janice has missed you, too.'

'Really? She hasn't exactly visited much.' Mum smiles,

270

but I can see the hurt in her eyes. 'I don't blame her – Shoreditch is a bit of a journey from Oxshott. I would have thought she'd return my calls, though.'

'What?' I peer at her. 'What calls?'

'Oh, I've left her a few voicemails, but she's never responded.' Mum gives me a bright smile. 'Anyway, she's probably been busy.'

'I think she thinks you're too busy for *her*,' I venture. 'You're always putting up pictures on WhatsApp showing how eventful your new life is.'

'Well, that's what WhatsApp's *for*,' says Mum in surprise. 'Sharing photos.'

I stare at her for a moment before something clicks. 'Mum, are you thinking of Instagram?'

'Oh, they're all the same thing, love,' says Mum airily.

I'm about to explain that really they're not, when the doorbell rings again and I feel a nervous lurch inside. Does Mum know that Janice is bringing her new friend? Does Mum even know that Janice *has* a new friend? I open the door – and sure enough, it's Janice, standing on the doorstep, holding a bunch of lurid pink flowers.

As soon as she sees Mum in the hall, she lifts her chin defensively.

'Hello, Becky,' she says tremulously, ignoring Mum altogether.

'Janice!' I exclaim. 'You made it!' I'm about to add, 'Where's your friend?' when Mum barrels up to the doorway and pushes past me.

'Janice, love!' she says, clasping Janice in a warm hug. 'It's been too long! Oh love, I've *so* much to tell you. Did you not get my voicemail about the theatre trip?

Anyway, I'm sorry you missed it, but we'll do it another time, and you *must* tell me what you think about my dahlia idea.' She breaks off and looks expectantly at Janice, who seems bewildered.

'Dahlia idea?' she echoes at last.

'I left you a voicemail, love!' says Mum blithely. 'I was on the treadmill at the time, so I might have sounded a *bit* breathy . . .'

'I didn't get a voicemail.' Janice seems flummoxed.

'But I've left you loads!' says Mum. 'No *wonder* you didn't tell me what you thought of the new Poirot adaptation. Far too shabbily dressed,' she adds, wrinkling her nose. 'Poirot was never shabby. Where's Martin?'

'At a . . . golf-club lunch,' stammers Janice. 'Jane, I didn't get *any* voicemails from you. None.'

Meanwhile Luke has wandered into the hall behind us, and he chimes in, 'A lot of voicemail is malfunctioning at the moment. Happened to a guy at work. He lost them all. Janice, is your voicemail backed up in the cloud?'

Both Mum and Janice peer at him, looking blank – then Mum says fretfully, 'Did I do it wrong?'

'No, it's not you, Jane, it's the system.'

Luke starts trying to explain, when Janice interrupts in an anxious voice, 'Flo's just parking the car.'

'Flo?' Mum crinkles her forehead. 'Is that one of your friends, Becky?'

'No, she's my friend,' says Janice, her voice trembling. 'You weren't there, Jane, and I never heard from you and I thought . . . Anyway, Flo's . . . my new friend.'

There's a long, hideous pause. I glance at Luke, then

at Jess, who has also walked into the hall and is watching, agog.

'Your new friend,' echoes Mum after a pause, in the weirdest, tightest voice I've ever heard her use. 'I see. Your new friend. Well . . . how lovely, Janice! I can't wait to meet her!'

Oh my God. The tension in this hall is unreal. I glance at Luke, who makes a face I can't read, then at Jess, who draws a finger across her neck, then at Mum, who has still got a bright smile plastered on her face, but underneath, *God* knows what she's thinking.

When the doorbell rings we all jump a mile.

'Right,' I say too heartily. 'I'll just . . . get this.'

I open the door and a thin woman in a beige coat and hat peers at me through rimless glasses.

'Oh, hello,' she says in a timid, wispy voice I can barely hear. 'Is it Becky? I'm Flo.'

OK. I know I shouldn't be taking this personally. But Flo? Over *Mum*?

I agree with Jess wholeheartedly. Flo's gruesome, in a totally wet, floppy way. As I usher her, Janice and Mum into the sitting room, Minnie yells, 'Waniss! Grana! It's my *birthday*! Look at my *presents*!'

As Janice and Mum exclaim over the kitten, Suze appears with a tray of hot drinks that she's just rustled up in a brilliant Suze-ish way.

'Hello,' she says to Flo with a broad, friendly smile. 'I'm Suze, a friend of Bex's. Would you like some tea or coffee? The blue cups are tea and the white cups are coffee. Milk's in the jug.'

'Oh,' says Flo. 'Well. Goodness.' She looks around the room uncertainly, as though searching for a second opinion. 'Yes. Please. If it's not too much trouble . . . But really, it doesn't matter. Don't mind me.'

'It's right here on the tray,' says Suze, looking a bit flummoxed by Flo's speech. 'Tea or coffee? Please do help yourself.'

'Whatever's easiest,' says Flo with a helpless smile.

'Well, we've got both, so they're both easy.' Suze holds out the tray of cups. 'Tea? Coffee?'

'I really don't mind,' says Flo with a little gasp. 'Either way.'

'You decide,' says Suze pleasantly.

'Oh . . .' Flo extends a hand, then withdraws it. 'I'm not sure . . .'

I can see Suze starting to lose patience and I'm not surprised. All the tea and coffee's getting cold while Flo stands there peering at it.

'Well!' Suze says briskly. 'Why not have tea, then? Bex, why don't you take a cup of tea for Flo?'

We exchange brief looks as I take the cup, then usher Flo towards the sofa.

'Please have a seat,' I say politely.

'Oh. Goodness.' Flo looks at the empty sofa as though it's a minefield. 'Where should I sit down?'

'Anywhere!' I say, trying to sound as friendly as I can.

'I see.' Flo edges to the corner of the sofa, then stops as though marooned. 'Where does everyone else want to sit? Please don't let me get in the way.' She gives me her helpless smile again, and I quell a desire to say, 'Just sit down, you drip!'

274

'I'll put your tea here,' I say kindly, placing the cup on the coffee table, 'and you can decide.'

Then I feel bad at calling Flo a drip, even inside my head. Maybe she's just feeling awkward in a new crowd of people. As she finally takes a seat, I make another effort.

'So, did *you* see the new Poirot on TV, Flo?'

'Yes, I did,' says Flo in uber-cautious tones, as though she suspects I might use her answer somehow against her in court.

'And what did you think of the adaptation?'

'I don't really know,' says Flo, looking blank. 'It's up to the experts, isn't it?'

'Right. Well . . . did you enjoy it?' I persevere.

'I couldn't say, really.' She gives me that helpless smile yet again.

Oh my God. I was right first time. She is a drip. *How* can Janice hang out with her?

As though reading my thoughts, Janice comes over to the sofa with a cup of tea herself and sits beside Flo. A moment later, Mum sits down opposite, and everyone sips their tea without talking. Everyone's just staring into the middle distance. It's all so awkward, I can't bear it.

'Cake!' I say shrilly. 'Let's have Minnie's birthday cake!'

I dash into the safety of the kitchen, carefully put the candles on the birthday cake, light them, and carry it back into the room, calling out to the children to gather. We sing 'Happy Birthday' and Minnie looks beside herself with joy as she blows out her candles. Then I set the cake on the coffee table to cut it, while Luke goes for some plates and forks.

275

'What a large cake!' says Janice as I start cutting into it. 'And what an interesting shape, Becky. Did you use a dome-shaped baking tin?'

'Er . . . no . . .' I can't really answer properly, because I'm too preoccupied by trying to cut the cake. It's weird. My knife keeps going through the buttercream without seeming to *slice* anything.

'Is there a problem, love?' says Mum, watching me. 'Let me try.'

She takes the knife from me, briskly slices through the buttercream, then peers at it, puzzled. 'Love, where's the cake?'

'It's in there somewhere,' I say desperately, taking the knife back from her and prodding at it. 'I *know* there's a cake in there. I saw it. I made it!'

'What proportion of buttercream to cake did you use?' enquires Jess, which is *so* like her.

'You might need a spoon,' says Suze helpfully. 'And we could eat it with spoons, too. We could think of it as . . . a mousse?'

'Here,' says Luke, handing me a spoon. 'Serve it with this.'

'I can't serve everyone solid buttercream!' I whisper desperately to Luke. 'They'll all have heart attacks! I don't know *what's* happened.'

'Cake!' says Minnie, holding up her plate, and all the other children join in, yelling, 'Cake! Cake!'

I stare anxiously at the cake – or rather, mound of buttercream – and Luke says quickly, 'I'll take it out to the kitchen and have a proper look at it.' As he picks it up, he addresses the room: 'Becky's been making a wonderful costume for Minnie's Nativity play. You should see it.'

I feel a swell of love for him because he's so obviously trying to make me feel better – and everyone at once follows his lead.

'Wow,' says Suze. 'Awesome, Bex!'

'Well done, darling!' says Dad.

'Show us now!' suggests Suze, but I shake my head.

'I want to keep it a surprise. Um, I'll just see to this cake . . .'

I hurry out to the kitchen, where I find Luke attacking the buttercream with a spatula.

'There *is* some cake in there,' he says, peering closely at it, 'but not very much. Shall we dig it out and give it to the children?'

'I don't know *what* went wrong,' I say dismally. 'Has the cake dissolved into the buttercream?'

'*Does* cake dissolve into buttercream?' enquires Luke.

'I have no idea!' I say, just as the doorbell rings. 'Oh God, what now? You get the door and I'll dig out the cake.'

I scoop out as much cake as I can find and arrange it in four splodges on plates. At least children don't care about presentation. I plonk the plates on a tray and I'm carrying it out into the hall when I hear a nasal voice it takes me a moment to recognize.

Oh my God. Is that *Nadine*?

I put the tray on the floor and hurry towards the front door, which is ajar. Luke and Nadine are on the door-step, and Nadine is talking in a quick, urgent way, while Luke tries to chime in. As I step outside, he's saying, 'Nadine, I'm sorry. It's not going to happen.'

'Just take this.' She brandishes a thick, printed document at him, then shoots me an unfriendly look. 'Oh hi, Becky.'

She's all dressed up in a suit, even though it's the weekend, and her perfume is overpowering. This is all a bit weird.

'Hi!' I say cautiously. 'What a surprise to see you!'

'Nadine came round to talk business,' says Luke, sounding a bit strained. 'But as I'm trying to explain, I really don't see a future for us in any kind of partnership.'

'You haven't given me a chance.' Nadine barely seems to be listening. 'You can't just write me off. You can't just *dismiss* me.' Her voice is steady but her chest is heaving, I notice.

'I'm not dismissing you,' says Luke at once. 'Absolutely not. But—'

'It's an opportunity for both of us,' she interrupts. 'This is my only chance. You can't just say no.'

'Well,' says Luke, after a tiny pause. 'I can. And this is certainly not your only chance—'

'Just read this.' Nadine tries to hand him the document again. '*Read* it. It's different from the version you saw before. I listened to you. I've changed it. Already. See?' She turns to the second page and jabs at a paragraph with an immaculate pink nail. 'This is what you said. Word for word. You said it wasn't focused enough, not businesslike enough. *This* is businesslike—'

'Nadine, *this* isn't businesslike!' Luke erupts, gesturing at her. 'You can't just come to people's houses at the weekend with no warning! I told you I was happy to speak on the phone—'

'Brush me off, you mean.' She glares at him. 'What was it you said? "Maybe after Christmas."'

'I'm travelling before Christmas and I'll be out of regular contact, as I explained,' says Luke evenly. 'But I'm happy to talk in the New Year and give you some pointers—'

'Oh, *pointers*.' She echoes the word so savagely, I feel an inward shiver. This woman is actually a bit loopy and it's Minnie's birthday party and I don't want to be listening to this.

'Nadine, we have to go,' I say. 'We're in the middle of something.' I glance at Luke, who nods.

'I'm still happy to talk to you by phone at an agreed time,' he says. 'But now you need to leave.'

There's silence and I can see Nadine's chest heaving harder than ever. She looks like she might pop out of her tight jacket. It would be funny, if her eyes weren't so hostile.

'Why do you think we rented that bloody cottage in the first place?' she suddenly bursts out savagely. 'To meet *you*.'

'*What?*' I stare at her, staggered.

'What did you think? That we *wanted* to live in this back-of-nowhere shit-hole?'

'Excuse me!' I say indignantly, but Nadine's on a roll.

'We were doing the "old boyfriends, old girlfriends" chat. Craig tells me about some old girlfriend called Becky Bloomwood. It rings a bell. Isn't she married to Luke Brandon? Can I get to Luke Brandon through a personal connection? Is *this* my big opportunity? You know, I already wrote to your company,' she adds to Luke. 'Got the brush-off from some bloody minion.'

Oh my God. She's a stalker.

'Nadine, you have to go,' I say carefully. 'It's Minnie's birthday. We have all our family and friends here.'

'Oh, that's right.' She swivels her gaze to focus on me. 'Your precious *family and friends*.'

'Yes,' I say robustly. 'My precious family and friends.'

Nadine surveys both of us in turn with her scary eyes – then seems to give up.

'Well, I'm sorry to disturb the happy occasion,' she says, her voice edged with sarcasm. 'Have a super day. Have a super life.'

She turns and picks her way back down the garden path, while Luke and I watch in silence. I feel quite shaken.

'Wow,' says Luke as she disappears from view, and I feel my whole body sag.

'Bloody hell.'

'Didn't see that coming,' he says thoughtfully.

'How could anyone see that coming?' I exhale and for a few moments we're both silent. Then I turn to Luke, feeling hot with mortification. 'Oh God, Luke, I'm *so* sorry. I should *never* have introduced you to Craig, I should *never* have brought them into our lives . . .'

I should never have dressed up in edgy clothes to impress my old boyfriend, I silently add.

'Don't be silly!' Luke looks surprised. 'You couldn't have predicted any of this. And she's gone now. No harm done.'

He's so reasonable and fair and calm, I feel an

immense surge of love for him. Our marriage is Sello-taped down and it's never going to unstick, *ever*. I put my arms around Luke, gazing up at the man I adore, and, with a fresh wave of emotion, hear myself saying, 'I love your moustache.'

Wait. Where did *that* come from?

'Really?' Luke looks supremely taken aback and touched. 'Oh, darling.'

He kisses me and I clasp him even more tightly, while my brain says, *Hang on. Why did I say that?*

He'll never get rid of it now. What was I *thinking*? I was just feeling so generally loving, the words came out of my mouth.

We draw apart and Luke gazes at me, his face soft-ened with affection.

'My darling Becky,' he says, running a finger gently down my cheek. 'I love you.'

'I love you too,' I say, a bit breathlessly.

Shall I quickly add, 'Except I didn't mean the bit about the moustache'?

No. No. Not a good idea.

At last Luke turns back towards the front door.

'We'd better rejoin the party,' he says. 'Shall we keep this little exchange between ourselves? If anyone asks, we'll say it was someone collecting for charity.'

'Yes,' I agree fervently. 'Good idea. Everything's quite tense in there already.'

I want to add, 'What do you think of Flo?' but we need to get back, and anyway, I'm sure I know the answer.

Luke picks up the tray of cake splodges, eyes them for a moment, then says, 'Well, they look delicious, anyway.'

Instantly my heart melts. Oh God, he's so kind. He's such a good husband. I'm *never* going to tell him the truth about the moustache, I resolve. What I'll do is . . . I'll get hypnotized to like moustaches. Yes! Excellent plan. I'll google it.

I'm just opening the door to the sitting room when my phone rings. *Honestly.* Can't I just have a birthday tea party in peace? I'm considering ignoring it but I glance at the display just in case – and see **Edwin**.

Hmm. Maybe I'd better take this.

'I'll be two secs,' I say apologetically. 'It's just a . . . a Christmas-related thing.'

As Luke takes the cake into the sitting room, I hurry back into the kitchen and shut the door.

'Hello, Edwin,' I say quietly. 'How are you?'

'Very well, thank you!' come Edwin's well-modulated tones. 'And you?'

'Oh, I'm fine, thanks!'

'Just a quick one, my dear. Unfortunately I've been called away to the south of France, *terrible* bore, and it means I won't have time to write your speech for the meeting after all. Can you rustle it up?'

I stare at the phone in dismay. Do *what*? The whole point was, *he* was going to write the speech.

'Right.' I clear my throat. 'Well . . . I suppose so. What should I say?'

'Oh, I'm sure you know the sort of thing,' says Edwin airily. 'Your enthusiasm for billiards, how shut out you feel as a woman, that kind of thing. Social justice. Discrimination. Make the blighters squirm with guilt. I never asked, *did* you have a deprived childhood?'

'Er, well . . .' I prevaricate, thinking guiltily that Mum and Dad are sitting only yards away and you can't really call a detached house in Oxshott 'deprived'. 'I mean, I suppose some bits were a *bit* deprived . . .'

'Splendid! Lay that on thickly, too. Now I must go, my dear, but I'll see you there?'

'Absolutely!' I say. And I'm about to add, 'What shall I say about billiards, exactly?' when he rings off.

I stand motionless for a few seconds, thinking this through. A speech about billiards. *Can* I make a speech about billiards? Oh God. Is this all getting a bit much? Shall I just get Luke his normal old aftershave, which will take thirty seconds online, and forget all about the portmanteau?

But then my determination hardens. Come on. I can do this. I *will* do it. For Luke. How hard can it be to talk about billiards? It's only a game with six balls.

Or maybe eight balls.

Some number of balls, anyway. I'll look that up. But now I'd better get back to the party.

Thrusting my phone in my pocket, I hurry back into the sitting room, where all the children have buttercream smeared round their mouths and Flo is saying in a pained voice, 'I must say, cake has never really been my thing,' and Mum looks like she wants to explode.

As I look around, I try to get into a nice relaxed party mood. I want to smile and enjoy the moment. But somehow I can't. I feel too hassled. By Flo . . . by my disaster cake . . . by Nadine . . . by having to make a billiards speech . . . and that's not even *mentioning*

Christmas, which hangs over everything like some sort of glittery exam I have to pass.

'You could have a garland here,' Suze is saying to Jess, pointing at the mantelpiece. 'Or maybe here.' Then she turns to me. 'We were just wondering when you were going to decorate for Christmas, Bex.'

And I know it's just a question, I know it's just Suze being artistic and creative . . . but somehow I can't help feeling criticized.

'I was waiting,' I explain. 'I thought we'd have Minnie's birthday first and *then* get into Christmas decorating.'

'Ah! Speaking of Christmas, love.' Mum looks up. 'Did you see the recipe for stuffing I sent you?'

'Um . . .' I wrinkle my brow, trying to remember which of her million WhatsApps was about stuffing.

'I've already sent Bex a brilliant recipe for stuffing,' objects Suze. 'Apricot and hazelnut. It's delicious.'

'Mine's cranberry and chestnut,' counters Mum. 'Much more Christmassy.'

'But what about sage and onion?' says Janice. 'And Becky, will we be able to have a bracing walk on the day, even though Graham's hurt his foot? Because I was thinking, *first* bracing walk, *then* piñata.'

'A piñata is cultural appropriation,' says Jess disapprovingly. 'I keep telling you. And Becky, you're not planning a wood fire, are you? Because it *is* catastrophic for the planet—'

'You could have a fabulous decoration in this alcove,' Suze interrupts, still appraising the room. 'Where are you putting your tree?'

'Er . . .' I haven't decided where to put the tree yet, but I don't want to admit it.

'And have you sorted out your carols yet, Becky?' enquires Janice. 'Only I *do* love "Good King Wenceslas"—'

'D'you want me to come round some time and help decide about the tree?' Suze cuts across her. 'And make a plan for your garlands?'

'No!' I exclaim, suddenly rattled by all the voices coming at me. 'No, thanks! I'll decorate myself, in my own way. And I'll choose the stuffing. And we won't have a fire. And everything you all want, I'll order, OK?'

As I break off, breathing hard, I realize how stressed out I sound. 'Sorry,' I add, trying to calm down. 'I'm just a bit . . . It's all a bit . . .'

'Of course!' says Suze, shooting a look at Mum. 'Bex, don't worry about a thing! Have some tea and relax.'

I sit down next to Flo, take a few deep breaths and gradually feel my heart rate slow down. I'm overreacting, I tell myself. It'll all be fine. I'm aware that Mum and Suze are exchanging looks with Janice – but I don't care. Let them exchange looks.

'So,' I say at last, forcing myself to be polite and turning to Flo. 'Where are you spending Christmas, Flo?'

'Oh, Christmas,' she says, crinkling her brow dubiously. 'I never was much of a one for Christmas.'

For real? OK, that's it. Someone has to tell Janice: Flo's got to go.

SPEECH TO LONDON BILLIARDS CLUB

By Prospective Member Rebecca Brandon
(née Bloomwood)

Copyright Rebecca Brandon (née Bloomwood)

STRICTLY CONFIDENTIAL

Embargoed till 11th December

FIRST DRAFT

~~Billiards is very~~
~~Billiards are very~~
Billiards is very

Oh God.

From: Myriad Miracle
To: Becky Brandon
Subject: Re: Re: Query!

Hi Mrs Brandon (née Bloomwood)

We hope you are enjoying the Myriad Miracle Training System™!

Thank you for checking your interactive settings on the app. We have monitored your progress and it seems that your current exercise activity has moved from 'Negligible' to 'Negligible to Zero'.

It is part of the Myriad Miracle Training System™ philosophy that we provide extra, boosting content for clients whose activity has decreased.

We would therefore like to offer you a complimentary real-time health and exercise Skype session with our trainer, Olga Ritsnatsova. Olga comes to us from training Olympic weight-lifters. She will be calling you soon to arrange your complimentary three-hour session, including:

- high-intensity strength work
- endurance hour
- nutritional chat
- ice bath to facilitate recovery.

Happy health-seeking!

Debs
(membership assistant)

From: Myriad Miracle
To: Becky Brandon
Subject: Re: Re: Re: Re: Query!

Hi Mrs Brandon (née Bloomwood)

Thank you for your quick response.

I'm sorry to hear that you have broken your leg.

Olga is looking forward to hearing from you and organizing your complimentary three-hour Skype session as soon as you have recovered.

Happy health-seeking!

Debs
(membership assistant)

Chats

CHRISTMAS!

> **Janice**
> Dear Becky, it was such a lovely day yesterday. Thank you so much for hosting. I have a small request: Might I bring Flo to our festivities on Christmas Day?

> **Suze**
> OMG Bex have you SEEN what Janice has asked? She wants to bring Flo to Christmas!!! That miserable drip!!!

SUZE & BEX

> **Bex**
> Suze!!!! Wrong thread!!!!!

> **Suze**
> Shit. D'you think Janice has seen it?

> **Suze**
> Oh God. Two blue ticks. Yes she has.

CHRISTMAS!

> **Suze**
>
> Oh. Janice. Gosh. I'm sorry, I didn't mean to post that message. Actually, I was talking about someone else called Flo that I met at a different party altogether. That Bex and I were at, but not you. Isn't that a hilarious coincidence? Just to confirm, it was a different Flo. Not your friend.

> **Suze**
>
> Janice???

> **Suze**
>
> Hello??? I know you've read my message.

> **Suze**
>
> OK, forget that. I WAS talking about your new friend because we all think she's FRIGHTFUL.

SIXTEEN

OK. Don't panic. Don't *panic*, Becky. It's only Christmas. That's what I keep telling myself – but the trouble is, I don't believe myself any more. There's no such thing as 'only Christmas'.

Everything is sliding out of control. For example: 1. My garlands keep falling off the mantelpiece, even though I've tried Sellotape and Blu Tack and string and, in desperation, my gym weights anchoring them down. 2. My giant snow globe of a Christmas village leaked all over the floor yesterday. 3. My Alexander McQueen dress still doesn't fit, even though I did twenty crunches before I tried to put it on, *and* I breathed in.

(Should I do the three-hour Skype session with Olga, after all?)

(No. I mean, an ice bath? Are they *kidding*?)

But the thing that's most out of control is: 4. My guests.

It's all kicked off between Suze and Janice. After her WhatsApp faux pas, Suze decided to defend Mum and tell Janice she shouldn't have got a new best friend so quickly. Whereupon Janice took umbrage and threatened not to come to Christmas. But then she changed her mind and said she *believed* that the invitation had come from 'dear Becky', so it was nothing to do with Suze and maybe *Suze* should rethink her Christmas plans instead.

Argh.

Mum is playing the total martyr and saying things like, 'It's up to Janice, if she wants to move on and ignore my phone messages, good luck to her, I can easily return her Christmas present.'

(Point of information: Janice didn't ignore her phone messages, they were lost in the cloud, but no one's listening to facts any more.)

Jess won't take sides, in fact she won't communicate. She's totally monosyllabic and unhelpful these days. I sent her a two-page email asking her what I should do and she literally replied, 'I don't know.'

When I appealed to Dad, he said, 'Oh, it'll sort itself out.' Then I asked Luke what he thought and he pretty much said the same. (He spoke for longer, but it essentially boiled down to 'Oh, it'll sort itself out.') He also thinks I shouldn't get involved. He said last night, 'Becky, you can't do everything. You have a hard enough job organizing Christmas without organizing everyone's emotions, too.'

Which is fair enough. But maybe I don't have any choice. Maybe 'emotions' is something else a hostess has to put in order, along with napkins and canapés. Because maybe if I don't, we won't *have* any Christmas.

All the fretful voices and WhatsApps are jangling in my head and I keep thinking, 'There *must* be a way to unite everyone.' But I don't have time to ponder on it right now. Because amid all this, I've got to give a speech about bloody billiards.

I'm walking up St James's Street in a smart dress and carefully blow-dried hair, giving myself a last-minute test on random billiards facts. The stick thing is called a cue. I already knew that. But everything else about the game is gibberish. There's 'baulk' and 'winning hazard' and 'cannon'. If you play a seventy-sixth consecutive cannon it's a foul, I know that. Only I can't remember what a cannon is.

I keep telling myself they won't actually quiz me on billiards facts. And I've prepared a few remarks to make in conversation, so I'll sound like a pro. Like, 'I was double baulked the other day, *total* nightmare.' But on the whole, I'm hoping I can just slip in, make my speech and slip out again with the portmanteau. Anyway, Edwin will look after me. He can make conversation about double baulks or whatever.

And yes, it has occurred to me to give up on the idea. What Luke said last night is true: you can't do everything. I know sod-all about billiards. Luke doesn't even know about the portmanteau. I could buy him an aftershave gift set and he'd be delighted and life would be easier.

But all this Christmas hassle has made me even more resolute. Maybe I can't reconcile Mum and Janice right now. Maybe I can't make my garlands stay up. But I can give a speech about billiards to a load of men with elbow patches.

As I arrive at the club it's all lit up with extra candles in brass holders and members are milling around with glasses in their hands. It looks almost alive and kicking. I approach the ninety-three-year-old behind the desk, and he gives me his familiar 'go away' look.

'Hello,' I say politely. 'I believe Lord Edwin Tottle is expecting me?'

'Lord Tottle has been delayed,' replies the man, reaching for a note on a piece of paper and surveying it. 'He will arrive presently.'

My heart sinks in dismay. Edwin's not *here*? I thought he would usher me around and tell me what to do.

'No problem!' I reply, trying to sound assured. 'Did he have any other message?' I add, seeing that the note is full of writing.

'Yes,' says the man reluctantly. 'He asked me to relay the following: "Give 'em hell, I know you can do it, Becky. I'll be there as soon as I can."'

'Thank you,' I say. 'So . . . can I go in?'

'Special dispensation has been granted to you,' says the man in tones of supreme disapproval. 'By Sir Peter Leggett-Davey himself.'

He hands me a cardboard slip reading 'Guest Pass' and I put it into my pocket.

'Thanks!' I say, feeling a bit more bouncy. 'Well, here's to a lovely evening. What's your name?' I add.

'Sidney,' says the man distantly.

'Hi, Sidney! I'm Becky, but you knew that. And what time is the AGM?'

'The AGM commenced at four o'clock this afternoon,' says Sidney, pointing at the wooden double doors. 'I

294

believe your . . . *item* is number fifty-six on the agenda. Please help yourself to sherry.'

I collect a drink and head through the double doors to find that the massive room with the fireplace has been rejigged for the AGM. There's a big long table, at which five ninety-three-year-olds are sitting facing the audience. Then there are rows of chairs, mostly empty, with a few ninety-three-year-olds sitting here and there, sipping sherry and listening. Or sleeping, in some cases.

As I sit down, I'm not surprised. Some guy with a white beard is intoning in the most boring voice I've ever heard, 'Item fifty-four: the works in the Lower Middle Dining Room. The Works Committee has reported back on the quotation and I would like to draw attention to the following points . . .'

He drones on a bit about woodworm and I tune out, looking around the room. I suddenly notice that the prizes for the raffle have been arranged on a table. There's the portmanteau and a case of sherry and a book about billiards. As soon as I become a member I'm buying my tickets, I resolve. That *very minute.*

My eye moves along the row I'm sitting in and I suddenly blink in astonishment at a familiar face. It's . . . who *is* that? A dad from school? I rack my brains for a moment, till it comes to me. It's the guy! It's Annoying Mr Blue Scarf from Selfridges! What's he doing here? He's not ninety-three!

As he sees me looking at him, his face registers astonishment too, and he moves along the row to sit nearer.

'Hello again,' he says in an interested undertone. 'You must be the woman.'

'What woman?'

'The woman trying to change two hundred years of tradition.'

'Oh,' I say proudly. 'Yes, I am, actually. Are you a member?'

'No, I'm here as a proxy,' he says. 'My father sent me along to vote against you.'

Against me?

'You haven't even heard my case!' I hiss indignantly, because we're getting some looks from a few nearby ninety-three-year-olds. 'How do you know you want to vote against me?'

'I hadn't given it any thought.' He shrugs. 'It's my father's club, not mine. I'm only here to do him a favour.'

'Well, think now!' I snap. 'I've come here in the spirit of modernity. The spirit of fellowship. The spirit of *billiards*.'

I eye him significantly, just as the white-bearded guy at the front says, 'Item fifty-five: Members' News. Any information for the London Clubs' Newsletter should be submitted to Alan Westhall by this Friday. Item fifty-six: Membership of Rebecca Brandon, née Bloomwood.'

It's me! I'm up! My heart gives the most almighty bound of nerves and I get to my feet, scrabbling for my speech.

My speech.

Where the hell is my *speech*?

'Something wrong?' says Annoying Mr Blue Scarf, as I delve furiously in my bag.

'Nothing,' I say, looking up, my face hot. I know my speech is in my bag. I know it. But I've tried every compartment and I can't find it. I should *never* have bought a bag with compartments, I think murderously. It's *much* better when it's all just one giant mess.

Suddenly I notice the double doors opening and a surge of ninety-three-year-olds appears, all holding glasses of sherry and chatting. They start to fill the seats, most of them giving me some sort of pointed glance.

'What's going on?' I say, bewildered. 'Why are they all arriving now?'

'They've all come here to vote on you,' says Annoying Mr Blue Scarf. 'You're the only item of interest. Good luck,' he adds casually. 'Knock 'em dead.'

My legs are a bit wobbly, but I can't give up now. I make my way up to the front and a ninety-three-year-old in a velvet smoking jacket suddenly claps me on the shoulder.

'Becky!' he says. 'I was looking out for you! I'm Edwin's friend John. I'm one of the chaps who seconded you. Best of luck. Edwin says you'll do *splendidly.*'

'Oh well, let's hope so,' I say, with my most confident smile. 'Thanks!'

At least I have some support. I approach the man with the white beard and lift my chin.

'How do you do,' I say politely. 'I am Rebecca Brandon née Bloomwood. First of all, I think your club is *fabulous—*'

'Thank you,' says the man, cutting me off coldly. 'I am Sir Peter Leggett-Davey. You'll have your turn to speak. Sit there, please.'

He points at a chair to the side, and I sit down on it, prickling with resentment. He doesn't have to be so snooty. I feel all the more determined to get into this stupid club. I might even learn billiards.

'Good evening, to those who have just arrived,' says Sir Peter, surveying the audience. 'Now we come to the most contentious item of the day. The application of this female person to join the club, supported by several members with us here today. This membership would, of course, require a change in our constitution, which has been proposed by Lord Edwin Tottle – please see the document now being circulated. And may I start by saying I think this a *disgraceful* idea.'

Disgraceful?

I feel a surge of indignation as he carries on talking about how special the club is and how females would ruin it and how Lord Edwin Tottle has always had a grudge against him, Sir Peter, as members will recall from the painful incident in 2002 regarding the sherry trolley.

OK. He *really* needs to get a life.

At last he stops speaking and one after another of the ninety-three-year-olds stands up, saying all the same stuff, about tradition and sanctity and 'facilities', by which they mean loos. After a while I give up listening and google *billiards cannon what is it?* – although I'm not sure *exactly* how I'm going to work it into my speech.

'Mrs Brandon, would you like to make a reply?' Sir Peter's voice interrupts my thoughts and my head bobs up. Shit. It's my turn already.

'Yes!' I say in dignified tones. 'Thank you so much. I am yours etc.'

I make one more hopeless thrust into my bag,

hoping I'll find my speech – but it's not there. I'll have to wing it.

I walk slowly to the centre of the space, turn to the audience and say, 'Good evening. I am Rebecca Brandon, née Bloomwood, fellow billiards lover.'

The whole room is silent, waiting for me to say more. I can even see Sidney, loitering at the doorway to listen.

'I could talk about . . . cannons.' I spread my arms nonchalantly. 'I could talk about how I was double baulked the other day. Nightmare!' I give a knowing little laugh. 'However, today I want to talk about . . . billiard balls,' I say in sudden inspiration. 'Consider billiard balls. We polish them. We respect them. We play our beloved game with them. But we should *learn* from them.'

'What? What's that?' barks a man in the front row who looks about 103, and his ninety-three-year-old neighbour says loudly, 'She says we should learn from *billiard balls*, Sir Denis.'

'After all, what is one billiard ball hitting another, if not *connection*?' I continue. 'Billiards balls don't discriminate. Billiards balls are tolerant. They're happy to roll anywhere on the table, see all sides, interact with any other ball, male or female. Or intersex,' I add after a moment's thought.

'What's she talking about?' demands Sir Denis, and his ninety-three-year-old neighbour practically shouts back, 'Sex, Sir Denis!'

'*Sex!*' echoes Sir Denis, looking impressed.

'Billiards balls want to connect without prejudice,' I continue, trying to ignore them. 'But billiards clubs do *not*.' I fix Sir Peter with my sternest gaze. 'Billiards clubs say, "No, the red balls may not interact with the white balls, because red balls are male and white balls are female." And what happens? *Nobody* wins. The world is a worse place.'

'Thank you very much, Mrs Brandon,' begins Sir Peter in icy tones, but I lift a hand to stop him.

'I haven't finished yet,' I say firmly. 'I stand before you, a passionate, female billiards aficionado, not to mention lover of parlour music, who has been shut out of the greatest experience a billiards lover could know. To be a member of this hallowed club. And why? Because of an outdated, prejudiced rule that has no place in any true billiards lover's heart. You don't *really* want to turn me away. I can see it in your eyes. All of you.'

I move along the rows, catching the eye of each ninety-three-year-old in turn, and lingering especially in front of Sir Denis, who beams up at me.

'What are you scared of?' I say, more gently. 'Be brave. Be true to what you really believe. And let me into this club, where I will do my best to be worthy of it. Thank you.'

I make a little bow and a smattering of applause breaks out. Sir Denis even exclaims, 'Hear, hear!'

'Well, if that is all,' says Sir Peter, as I take my seat, 'then I propose—'

'Wait!' A voice interrupts him. 'I'd like to speak.'

There's a kind of crumping sound as a hundred tweed jackets turn round to look – and to my utter astonishment, it's Annoying Mr Blue Scarf, standing up in the back row. He winks at me, then says, 'Let me introduce myself. I'm Simon Millett and my dad sent me here today to cast a proxy vote against this application. D'you know what else he said in the same breath? He said, "I do wish you'd think about joining, my boy, we need some younger blood."' Simon pauses. 'To be frank, I haven't joined this club because it seems stuck in the Dark Ages. Full of attitudes and people I don't relate to. But here's a chance for you to change that. So here's my advice to you . . .' He looks around the crowd of agog ninety-three-year-olds. 'Do something to make your grandchildren proud of you. You might find they want to join. That's all.'

He sits down and I mouth, 'Thank you!'

There's a kind of commotion among the audience members and then Sir Peter says, his mouth tighter than ever, 'Well, let us proceed to a vote. All those in favour of amending the constitution and allowing Mrs Rebecca Brandon, née Bloomwood to become a member.'

A forest of hands shoots up, and I start to count, but I keep losing track. Then suddenly everyone's voting against, and there's another forest of hands and I can't count those either. Oh God. I can hardly breathe for the tension. It's really stressful, voting! No wonder MPs are all so wrinkled and grim-looking.

For a few moments there's silence as the committee members confer. Then Sir Peter draws a long breath.

'The motion is carried,' he says in sepulchral tones, and someone grabs my hand and says 'Congratulations!' and it's only then that it properly hits me – I won! I'm in!

'I need some raffle tickets,' I say in a gasp. 'I want to go in for the raffle, please.'

'Never mind the raffle, dear girl!' exclaims Edwin, who has materialized out of nowhere, in a shocking-pink tie and reeking of brandy. He clasps my hand and shakes it about a hundred times. 'You won! You turned this place upside down! I heard you speak! Tremendous stuff! If in doubt, go for sex!'

Honestly, what are these people like? My speech was *so* not about sex. But I don't contradict him, because I'm too anxious about the raffle.

'That's one in the eye for Sir Peter,' Edwin is crowing. 'Did you see his face?'

'The raffle,' I say again. 'Who's selling tickets?'

'Ah, now that'll be Leonard,' says Edwin. 'Chap in a burgundy smoking jacket. Not sure where he's got to . . . John, isn't it marvellous?' He turns to greet John, who has just made his way towards us – and I take the opportunity to slip away. I need to find this Leonard. I can't see a single burgundy smoking jacket, so I hurry out of the room, as ninety-three-year-olds alternately congratulate me or give me baleful looks. There are no burgundy smoking jackets in the hall, either, but I can see some ninety-three-year-olds on the stairs, so I quickly head up there.

The landing is empty. Where the hell is he? I head to another immense door and push it open – to find myself in a massive room containing a billiards table and Simon, all on his own, playing what I guess is a billiards shot.

'Oh, hi!' I say. 'Thanks so much for your speech. What you said made all the difference.'

'No problem,' he says, then nods at his cue. 'Thought I'd try out the famous table while I'm here.'

'Right,' I say. 'Absolutely. The famous table.'

I'm about to ask him if he's seen Leonard, but Simon gets in first.

'Looking forward to your exhibition shot?' he says, potting a ball expertly.

'Huh?' I look at him blankly.

'You know. Club tradition. The new member plays their first shot on this table. Big deal. People take photos. Usually there's a bunch of new members, but tonight it's just you.'

'Wow!' I say, trying to conceal my dismay. 'Um . . . no one told me about that.'

OK. I have to leave. Enter the raffle, then leave. Smartish.

'People practise all year to have the perfect shot ready. Usually some kind of fancy trick shot.' He raises his head from lining up a ball. 'What have you got up your sleeve?'

'Oh . . . you know,' I say vaguely, 'a little shot I invented myself . . . Actually, what I *really* need is some raffle tickets. Have you seen someone called Leonard in a burgundy smoking jacket?'

'Sorry, no. Have a practice.' He hands me the cue and automatically I take it. 'Didn't mean to hog the table.'

I try to hold the cue naturally, but it's quite heavy, and longer than I thought. I should have played pool at uni. Why didn't I learn pool? I have literally never held one of these in my life.

'*There* you are!' Edwin's face suddenly appears round the door. 'Got your cue, I see. Marvellous! Stay there, Becky, and I'll gather the crowd for your exhibition shot.'

What? No!

'All yours,' says Simon, standing back from the table.

I stare at the endless green baize, trying to think very quickly. What do I do now?

'Not wanting to put you off,' adds Simon, 'but you're pretty much representing women in billiards at this point. So my advice is, don't go too ambitious. Keep it simple and nail it.'

My stomach heaves. I can't represent women in billiards. This is mad. I need to put down the cue, run down the stairs and escape. Go *on*, Becky.

But somehow my feet don't move. If I escape now, I'm giving up on Luke's present, and I just can't. Not after all this effort.

Could I do an exhibition shot? Do I maybe have a natural talent for billiards that I never realized?

Experimentally I approach the table, and try to line up the cue like I've seen them do on TV. But it keeps wobbling everywhere. It's too *long*, that's the problem.

'Just getting used to the cue,' I say quickly, as I notice Simon staring at me. 'They're all different.'

'That's . . . the wrong end,' he says in a strange voice.

'Oh.' My face flames and I peer at the cue. 'Of course! Just got confused there for a moment . . .' I quickly turn the cue round, nearly hitting Simon in the face as I do so.

'Jesus!' he says, lifting a hand to protect himself. 'What the hell? You're not a billiards player, are you?' He glares at me accusingly.

'Yes I am!' I begin robustly – then realize there's no point. 'OK, I'm not,' I concede in a lower voice, 'but you can't tell anyone.'

Simon looks at me for a silent moment, then goes to the door, reaches for a door stop and wedges it shut.

'Speak fast,' he says. 'Why have you made all this fuss about joining this club if you can't play billiards?'

'To win the raffle,' I admit after a pause.

'The raffle?' He stares at me as though I'm insane. 'The *raffle*?'

Honestly. He needn't look like that. What's wrong with wanting to win a raffle?

'For my husband's Christmas present!' I explain, a bit sniffily. 'There's this amazing portmanteau as first prize and you can only win it if you're a member, so I needed to join.'

Simon makes a snorting sound.

'Is this for real? I thought you were getting him aftershave.'

'I gave up on aftershave,' I confess. 'You were right, he didn't want a surprise. But I didn't want to give him something, you know, *predictable*, so . . .'

'So you decided to change the history of a two-hundred-year-old institution instead,' supplies Simon. 'Does your husband know any of this?'

'Of course not!' I say, shocked. 'It's his *Christmas* present! You don't tell people about their—'

I'm interrupted by a rattling at the door and Edwin's voice calling out, 'Hello? The door's jammed! Finch? Where's Finch?'

Shit. They're coming. What am I going to do?

'Have you ever played snooker?' demands Simon. 'Pool?'

'No. But I *do* know how to do it – look.'

305

I approach the billiards table and make what I think is quite a good attempt at a shot, except I miss the ball and the tip of the cue brushes the green baize.

Simon winces and grabs the cue back from me.

'Listen,' he says sternly. 'If you rip this table, I can't guarantee your safety. If I were you, I'd claim sudden illness and leave.'

'*Here* we are!' The door bursts open and Edwin appears, followed by a crowd of ninety-three-year-olds. 'All ready, Becky, I see! We just need to wait for Sir Peter.'

'Right,' I say, my heart leaping in panic. 'Um, what I *really* want is a raffle ticket. Is Leonard around?'

'Not sure,' says Edwin vaguely, as Sir Peter strides into the room.

He glares at me as though I'm some form of low-life, then announces, as though each word makes him ill, 'Welcome to today's Membership Ceremony. I am pleased to welcome our newest member, Mrs Rebecca Brandon, née Bloomwood. Mrs Brandon: the table.' He takes a step back and gestures at the billiards table, and Edwin gives an excited whoop.

I feel weak. The cue's all slippery in my hand. There are more and more ninety-three-year-olds pressing into the room to watch. Edwin's produced a phone and seems to be filming me. Should I just run away?

Then I glimpse a burgundy smoking jacket in the throng, and feel a stab of renewed resolve. Come on. The prize is still within my grasp. I *can't* give up. I just have to get through this moment . . .

And then an idea hits me.

'Good evening,' I say, addressing the crowd of ancient

306

men. 'And thank you for the warm welcome that many of you have extended to me. I would like to say a few words.'

I wait until silence falls, then draw breath.

'Tonight I have ended a long tradition,' I proclaim. 'I would like to thank you, as a club, for your flexibility, willingness to change, and support. Now we are gathered for my exhibition shot.'

I lean casually against the table, putting a hand proprietorially on the green baize as though I'm a shit-hot billiards player.

'However, this is another tradition I want to challenge. I do not wish to celebrate my membership by "potting balls in holes" or "claiming my territory", which seems frankly a bit sexist, in this day and age.'

'*What?*' splutters Sir Peter, looking outraged.

'She's on about sex again,' says Sir Denis to his neighbour. 'I *like* this girl.'

'Instead, I would like to make a speech of commitment,' I continue hurriedly. I hold up my cue and gaze at it momentously for a few seconds. 'With this cue, I vow to thee my billiards club,' I say in sincere tones. 'In the dawn's early light. Or . . . at dusk. Billiards for ever!' I hastily conclude, and bow to the crowd.

There's a flabbergasted silence, then a hubbub breaks out, above which I hear Edwin calling, 'Billiards for ever! Well *done*, my dear!'

'Ridiculous!' Sir Peter is exclaiming angrily to his friends. 'Absolutely *ridiculous*.'

Ignoring him, I hurry towards the burgundy smoking jacket, which is inhabited by a man with a purple face. (He should really choose a different-coloured jacket.)

'Hello!' I greet him. 'Are you Leonard? May I buy five raffle tickets, please?'

At last! At last! I'm already pulling the notes from my purse – when Leonard shakes his head.

'My dear, I'm sorry, but the raffle's closed,' he says comfortably.

'*Closed?*' I freeze, my money in my fingers.

'I'm about to draw the numbers in the hall,' he explains. 'The raffle will be drawn in two minutes!' he calls out loudly and all the members start heading out of the room.

For a moment I stand still in disbelief – but then I rouse myself. It's fine. I can still do this. I'll just see who wins and persuade them to sell the portmanteau to me. As I go to replace the cue in the rack, I see Simon grinning at me.

'Nice speech,' he says. 'You've really struck a blow today. What's the hurry?' he adds as I thrust the cue away.

'I need to go and watch the raffle,' I say distractedly. 'I need to buy the portmanteau from whoever wins it.'

'You're still on that?' he says, shaking his head.

'Of course I'm still on that! It's why I'm *here*. It's the whole *point*.'

Something odd passes across Simon's face and he surveys me for a moment.

' "Some people are happy to go the extra mile for their husband's Christmas present," ' he says. 'D'you remember saying that? It kind of stuck with me.'

'Yes.' I lift my chin defensively, wondering where he's going with this. 'And it's true.'

'I'd call this about a hundred miles.' His expression is suddenly kind. 'If not more. I hope your hubby appreciates it.'

'Well.' I give a slightly awkward shrug. 'You know. I don't like giving up on things.'

'Good for you.' With a flourish he pulls a fan of tickets from his pocket and proffers them. 'I bought these earlier. They're yours, all ten of them. Hope you win.'

'Oh my God!' I gasp. 'Thanks *so* much!' I hurry out, along the landing and on to the wide carpeted staircase, which is full of members, gathered to hear the raffle.

In the hall, Leonard is holding a big silver bowl. Sidney is next to him in his waistcoat and chalk-stripe trousers, poised to draw the tickets.

'And for the portmanteau, the top prize in this year's raffle . . .' Leonard is announcing. 'Sidney, please do the honours.'

Sidney thrusts a hand into the silver bowl, rummages around, and pulls out a folded ticket.

'Number 306,' he reads aloud. 'Bought by . . . Simon Millett.'

For a moment I can't quite process what I'm hearing. Simon Millett? Annoying Mr Blue Scarf?

'That's me!' I squeal. 'Me! Me! I won!'

In utter euphoria, I push my way down the stairs, squeezing between all the scratchy jackets and walking sticks. I won! I can give Luke the portmanteau for Christmas!

'Hi!' I say, arriving breathlessly in the hall, brandishing all the tickets. 'It's me! It's my ticket! I'm *so* thrilled, thank you *so* much—'

'Wait!'

The stentorian voice of Sir Peter Leggett-Davey interrupts me, and he steps forward on the patterned tiles, a look of utmost hostility on his face.

'Mrs Brandon, I fail to see how you can be the winner,' he says in clipped tones. 'The name on the ticket is Simon Millett.'

'Yes, but he gave me his ticket,' I explain eagerly.

'It's true, I gave it to her,' comes Simon's voice from the stairs and I give him a grateful wave. But Sir Peter's expression doesn't shift an iota.

'Leonard,' he says coolly. 'Did you sell this raffle ticket to Simon Millett? He is not a member, therefore he cannot enter.' As he speaks, Sir Peter rips the ticket into tiny pieces. 'Please refund Mr Millett his money. All his tickets are null and void.'

'What?' comes Simon's irate voice from the stairs. 'That's bollocks! I'm here as a proxy—'

'There are no proxy raffle tickets,' Sir Peter cuts him off, unmoved. 'Draw again.'

No. *No.* He can't do this.

'But I won the prize!' I say desperately. 'It's not fair! I'm a member. I *won*.'

'For shame!' Edwin's voice comes loyally from the back of the crowd, but no one else seems at all bothered.

'Draw again,' repeats Sir Peter to Sidney.

'With pleasure, Sir Peter,' says Sidney, shooting me a totally needless look of triumph. He pulls out another

310

ticket, unfolds it and reads out in loud throaty tones, 'Number 278. Sir Peter Leggett-Davey.'

'Well!' says Sir Peter. 'How very pleasing.'

Sir Peter won?

I stare at his smug face in despair. That's it, then. It's all over. He'll never sell me the portmanteau in a million years. I've lost. After all that effort, I've lost.

As Sidney draws the next raffle ticket, I turn away, sagging a little. What Simon said just now was true. It does feel like I've gone a hundred miles for Luke's present. But for what? I got *so* close . . . and then I failed.

Search history

Portmanteau for sale

Portmanteau eBay

Best Christmas present for husband

Best Christmas present for husband not aftershave

Best Christmas present for husband not socks

Llama bauble available now

Llama bauble in stock

Llama bauble eBay

Sprygge

Sprygge is new hygge

Ice baths

Ice baths bad for you research shows

How to host Christmas when guests not talking

Does cake dissolve into buttercream

SEVENTEEN

It's over a week later and things are . . . how are they? Good and bad, I suppose. Let's say they're patchy.

First of all, the good. I don't want to jinx it . . . fingers crossed . . . but my preparations are actually going to plan. Five days to go and *finally* I feel like I have Christmas in hand. I've finished Minnie's costume. I've decorated the house and my garlands are actually staying put. I've got all the presents wrapped up, including the picnic hamper. The vegan turkey arrives tomorrow and the proper turkey arrives on the 23rd. I've got scented candles everywhere. I've got a playlist of carols and Christmas songs on a constant loop. I've been hanging up Christmas cards from strings (most of them are from people like estate agents, but never mind) and I've put holly behind the pictures. The 'Christmas shrubbery' is clustered in the bay window of the dining room, where it looks fantastic (only I must stop eating the chocolate stars or there'll be none left).

And last night we decorated the actual, proper

Christmas tree, which looks amazing and makes the whole house smell like a forest. It's all twinkly with lights and decorations and is just perfect. Who cares that we don't have some stupid old must-have llama bauble? Not me!

(OK. Maybe I have been checking every hour if the llama bauble is available online. But it's not. So I totally don't care about it.)

So that's the good. Here's the less good: I still don't have a present for Luke. In fact, just thinking about it makes me feel despondent. I haven't got over my terrible defeat, and somehow I can't now picture buying anything that *isn't* a portmanteau from the London Billiards and Parlour Music Club.

I know I'm being stupid. It's only a Christmas present. And last night I found a navy jumper that I bought ages ago for Luke's birthday and forgot about – so I could give him that. He'd be delighted. I should just wrap it up and it would be done. But I can't help myself – I'm still holding out for something mindblowing and spectacular. Even though I don't know what.

So that's the less good. And here's the really bad: all my friends and family are still at daggers drawn. No one's speaking on our WhatsApp group. It's gone from vitriol to completely dead with tumbleweed blowing around. The last message was Janice saying, 'Yes, and I DO NOT AGREE,' replying to Suze asking if she'd read her email. (What email?) And since then, nada.

Suze has been away at some pre-Christmas family get-together in Norfolk with no signal, so I haven't been able to talk to her properly about it. Meanwhile, the minute I try to talk to Mum she starts saying prickly-voiced things like, 'Well, maybe I'll never return to Oxshott at all,' and 'Well, maybe my entire friendship with Janice was a sham, Becky.' And when I called Janice for a chat, Flo answered her phone. Flo! I was so appalled, I just asked Janice what kind of gravy she likes and hastily rang off. I can't even remember what she said. In fact, I don't think there are different types of gravy, are there?

(Are there? Oh God. I should *so* not be hosting Christmas.)

In desperation, I've been watching one Christmas movie after another, and feeling genuine withdrawal symptoms in between. They're like Valium – not that I actually know what Valium is like, but I'm guessing. They make me feel calm and happy and hopeful, because in all of them, without fail, Christmas spirit brings everyone together. Divorced workaholic dad and neglected child? Christmas spirit. Curmudgeonly guy who hates 'new-comers' and immigrant neighbour? Christmas spirit. Factory owner and all his downtrodden workers? Christmas spirit. (And in that one they sang a song, too, while he dressed up as Santa and gave them all pay rises.)

Every time the credits roll on another movie I sit back with a contented sigh and think, 'It'll be OK – because of Christmas spirit!' But then I consider the actual facts, and my optimism fades away. It's all very well when you're in a picturesque New England town and you can rely on snow to fall at exactly the right moment. In *actual* England the snow never falls except at a totally crap moment, like when you're about to drive on the

315

A3. Nor are we all planning to gather at the carolling party or log-splitting contest, so how are we all supposed to reconcile and hug each other in Christmas jumpers and say, 'We've all learned something here'?

Stupid real life. Why isn't it like a Christmas movie?

I had thought Minnie's Nativity play might be a nice meeting point ... but my parents can't even come, because Dad has a foot appointment. So much for that bright idea. Hmph.

I'm sitting in the kitchen, finishing my breakfast coffee, while Minnie sings 'Hark dah herald angel king' at the top of her voice. (I've tried correcting her, but she's adamant it's 'king'. She's quite stubborn, my daughter.) She woke up at five o'clock this morning and came running into our room yelling, 'Nativity! Nativiteeee!'

'Are you excited?' I give her a hug. 'I'm so excited! I can't *wait* till this afternoon.'

I can't stop admiring her costume, all ready on its hanger. It nearly killed me making it, and I don't want to boast ... but it's fantastic. The silk hangs down in gorgeous ripples and the sequins are sumptuous and if Minnie doesn't get Best King then there's something wrong with the world. (OK, I know there isn't really Best King. But in my head.)

'Well,' says Luke, striding in. 'The house looks great, Christmas tree up, we're all set.'

'Except no one's talking to each other,' I point out.

'Oh, that'll blow over,' says Luke dismissively and I feel a prickle of resentment. He doesn't ever go on WhatsApp, so what does he know?

'What if it doesn't?' I object.

'It will.'

'But what if it *doesn't*? God, I wish life was like a Christmas movie, don't you?' I add with a gusty sigh.

'Hmm,' says Luke carefully. 'In what sense?'

'In every sense!' I say in astonishment.

In what possible sense could you *not* want life to be like a Christmas movie?

'Every sense?' Luke barks with laughter. 'In the saccharine, manufactured and totally unrealistic sense?'

I glare at him. He needs to watch more Hallmark Channel, that's his problem. If he was in a Christmas movie he wouldn't laugh, he'd say, 'Oh honey, let me pour you some hot apple cider.'

'OK.' Luke relents. 'What would happen in a Christmas movie?'

'Everyone would get together at some lovely festive event, and they'd all wear Christmas jumpers, and they'd hug each other, suddenly realizing that the Christmas spirit is more important than—' I break off, inspired. 'Wait! That's it! Luke, we need a festive event!'

'We have a festive event,' he says, looking baffled. 'It's called Christmas.'

'A *pre*-Christmas event! Where everyone can come together and wear Christmas jumpers and feel the Christmas spirit and make up. I'm organizing one,' I add firmly. 'And we *won't* ask Flo.'

I can see Luke opening his mouth to make some objection, but I ignore him, because whatever he's going to say, I'm right. This is the answer.

* * *

317

Not a carolling party, because none of us can sing. Not log-splitting, because ... really? Not a sleigh ride, because we're not in Vermont.

Then, as I'm arriving at school with Minnie, the answer comes to me. We'll make gingerbread houses! It'll be fun and it doesn't matter if they're crap because everyone can just eat the gingerbread.

'Minnie,' I say, 'shall we have a gingerbread-house-making party?'

'Yes!' says Minnie enthusiastically, and I beam down at her. At last I feel as though I'm taking control. I have a plan.

As we arrive at the classroom, there's a buzzy group of parents bringing in their costumes, and children saying 'Look at *mine*, look at *mine*!' to Miss Lucas.

'Yes!' she's saying, beaming round the faces. 'Marvellous! Oh Zack, look at your donkey mask!'

Ha. Midnight-blue silk and sequins beats a donkey mask any day. For the first time ever, I feel like I'm the one with the really great craft project. I'm the one who went the extra mile. I can see Wilfie's and Clemmie's coats on their pegs, which means Suze has already been and gone – which is a shame, because I was looking forward to showing off my handiwork to her. But she'll see the costume in the play. In fact it's better if she sees it for the first time in the performance. I can't *wait*.

Through my happy reverie I suddenly spot Steph walking along the pavement towards school, and my stomach drops in horror. She looks terrible. Her skin has a grey tinge and her hair is greasy and her gaze is distant. Harvey keeps pulling at her arm and trying to get her attention, but she obviously can't hear him. She's lost in a place in her head. A bad place.

I need to talk to her – but not here in front of everyone. I hurry back out with Minnie, into the playground, and meet Steph coming in through the gates.

'Steph!' I greet her. 'I haven't seen you for a while. Are you OK?'

Steph's eyes jolt with shock as though I've woken her from a nightmare.

'Oh, hi, Becky,' she says, her voice dry and scratchy. 'Hi. Sorry I haven't been around much. I've been dashing in and out.'

'Don't apologize!' I say. 'I just wanted to, you know. Check in. See how you're doing.'

'Yeah.' Her voice descends to a whisper and she takes a deep, shuddery breath as though fending off tears. 'Yeah. Not great.'

'Right. Is there . . . Are you . . .' I hesitate anxiously, wanting to be there for her but not to pry. 'Is it . . .'

'He's been to a lawyer,' she says, her voice so low it's barely audible. 'He wants a divorce.'

'Already?' I say, shocked.

'I'm spending half the day on the phone to my lawyer. It's nuts. I just don't have the time to get divorced. Like, I'm late for a meeting right now, but the lawyer's just called. And *Christmas*,' she adds despairingly. 'How do people have *time*?' She gives a weird laugh, then breaks off abruptly as Eva's mum comes past, holding a huge fluffy sheep costume.

'Look at my costume!' shouts Eva. 'My mummy made it!'

319

Steph freezes and turns even more ashen. Her eyes start flitting about wildly, taking in all the excited children arriving with their costumes.

'Costume,' she says, and swallows hard. 'Costume. I never . . . Oh God. The pattern. I put it . . . I don't know where I put it . . . It's today, isn't it?'

Reluctantly I nod, and see panic consume her face.

'Where's my costume?' says Harvey, and he looks up at her so trustingly my heart squeezes.

'Oh, Harvey. Oh, darling. Don't worry!' Steph looks as if she might throw up. 'I'll go to the . . . I'll get you . . .' She glances at her watch. 'Oh God, but I'm late . . .' She actually totters slightly on her high heels, and I feel a jolt of alarm.

'I've got a spare,' I hear myself saying hurriedly. 'Have this one.'

'A *spare*?' Steph stares at me.

'Yes!' I say as convincingly as possible, and hold up my carrier bag. 'This one didn't fit Minnie in the end, so I brought it to school to see if anyone else could use it and . . . how perfect is this? It's still got Minnie's name on it, but you can change that. Harvey, *here's* your costume!' I say brightly.

'Becky, are you sure?'

The expression of gratitude on Steph's face is kind of unbearable, because she looks so exhausted and ground down, too. I wish I could sort out *everything* for her.

But anyway this is something, at least.

'Of course! Don't wait for me,' I add, 'if you're in a rush.'

'Thanks.' Steph puts her hand on my arm and squeezes hard. 'Thanks *so* much, Becky.' Then she hurries towards the classroom, gripping Harvey with one hand and the carrier bag in the other.

'That's my costume,' says Minnie, who has been watching alertly. 'My costume.' She raises her voice. 'My costuuuuuuuuume!'

Oh God. It's been a while since Minnie had a melt-down. I'd forgotten how ear-splitting her voice could be.

'Give it baaaaaack!' she yells. 'That's my cos-tuuuuuuume!'

'Minnie, it was *going* to be your costume,' I say quickly, crouching down so we're eye to eye. 'It was *going* to be. But we gave it to Harvey. That's what Christmas is about, giving things. You like giving presents, don't you? Well that's . . . what we did!'

As I say the words, it hits me for the first time what I've done. I worked so hard on that costume. Cutting out and sewing and re-sewing. Stitching on those endless sequins. It took for ever. And now I won't ever see Minnie perform in it. I keep on smiling brightly at her little face, but behind my eyes I feel a ridiculous hotness.

Then I force myself to stand up straighter and shake my hair back. It's no big deal. It's fine.

'Sweetheart, we just need to pop home quickly,' I say. 'We're going to get your other costume. Your *even better* costume,' I add as convincingly as I can.

I hurry her out of the school gate and into the car, racking my brains for something that will make a king costume in five minutes. As soon as we arrive home I dash upstairs and start rooting through all my drawers for anything glittery or sequinned. Scarf? Shawl? Could I repurpose some costume jewellery?

Minnie watches me silently for a minute, then starts grabbing for things, too.

'Kings wear neckwisses,' she tells me, taking a diamanté necklace from my drawer. 'Kings wear *two* neckwisses.'

The doorbell rings, and I curse and dash downstairs again. I open the door to see the postman peering over a pile of brown boxes.

'You're here!' he exclaims. 'Only I was going to pile them up where I normally do . . .'

'Thanks!' I say breathlessly as I take them and close the front door with my hip. I'll open them later. They're hardly the priority right now.

Or, actually, maybe I'll open them now. Just to check what they are.

I rip open the first box to find vests for Minnie. The next box has got A4 printing paper in it. Booooring. But the last package is a large padded envelope, containing something soft and tissue-wrapped—

Oh my God. It's my Denny and George scarves! At last!

I tear them eagerly out of their tissue paper. One's turquoise silk, one's pink tulle and one's deep burgundy velvet. It's massive – almost a shawl – and I suddenly realize that it's perfect.

I hurry up the stairs, clutching the scarves, calling out, 'Minnie! Sweetheart! You're going to have the most stylish costume in the whole play!'

I find a dark red cotton dress that Minnie wore last summer to be a base layer. Then I drape the velvet scarf around her, fixing it with brooches and safety pins, feeling sentimental whenever I catch sight of the iconic Denny and George label.

'You know, you wouldn't be here if it weren't for a Denny and George scarf,' I tell Minnie. 'It was Denny and George that brought Mummy and Daddy together.'

As I tweak and pin her costume into shape, I somehow find myself relating the whole story of Luke lending me the money to buy a Denny and George scarf. I'm pretty sure she doesn't follow a word – but it's soothing to me, anyway.

'OK,' I say at last, sinking back on my heels and assessing the finished look. 'Amazing. We can use a crown from the dressing-up box – and now you just need a casket of gold.'

Briefly my mind flashes to the cardboard casket I spent two evenings painting and decorating. But Harvey needs that. We can improvise.

'Here we are,' I say, delving in my bottom drawer and bringing out a golden cardboard Gucci Premiere perfume box. 'Here's a *lovely* casket. This can be your gold, sweetheart. It says Gucci, and that begins with G, just like gold.' I point at the embossed G. 'See? "Guh" for gold . . . and "guh" for Gucci.'

'Gucci,' repeats Minnie, looking a bit confused.

'Gucci.' I enunciate it clearly. 'Gu-cci. Gucci is very special and expensive, just like gold. They do amazing shoes and belts, and bags, of course. Mummy has a gorgeous Gucci bag somewhere . . .' I stop mid-flow. Not the point. 'Anyway, you'll look like a *brilliant* king, poppet.' I kiss her on the forehead. 'You'll be the King in the Denny and George Scarf.'

At last I've named the costume, packed it in a bag, delivered Minnie to school and arrived at work. I feel knackered, and the day has hardly begun. The trouble with Christmas is, it never seems to end. I still need to find Luke a present and organize this gingerbread-house-making party and reconcile my guests and fit into my Alexander McQueen dress and do a thousand other things. I feel like going back to bed, to be honest.

By contrast, Suze greets me at the door with a relaxed and radiant smile.

'Guess what?' she says.

'Dunno,' I say. 'How was Norfolk?'

'Oh, fine.' She waves an airy hand. 'You know. Same old family stuff. I won the backwards rafting race,' she adds as an afterthought.

The backwards rafting race? I'm about to ask her what that is, except I can already guess – it's an eccentric English family all on rafts, yelling and wearing weird clothes and laughing hilariously at jokes no one understands while they all fall in freezing-cold water.

'Guess what?' she says again. 'Takings are up! Like, *way* up. This is our best year ever! It's the *sprygge* effect,' she adds confidently.

'Really?' I say, distracted momentarily. 'How do you know?'

'It's all in the numbers! *Sprygge* is our star section! You're so clever inventing it, Bex!'

'Well, it was you who made all the products,' I point out.

'But you inspired me,' says Suze generously. 'And we all sold them. So I thought everyone should have a bonus. And a present. I've got the Hotel Chocolat catalogue. Come and have some coffee and help me choose nice things. Are you OK?' she adds, looking at me more closely. 'You seem a bit . . . stressed.'

'Oh, I'm fine,' I say, trying to sound upbeat. 'Apart from . . . you know.'

'What?' she says, as though she has no idea.

'*Christmas*, of course!' I can't help sounding just a tad resentful. Here am I, stressing about her row with Janice, and here Suze is, going on rafts and buying chocolate and behaving as though nothing's wrong.

'Christmas will be OK, won't it?' says Suze in surprise as we go into our tiny staffroom.

'Not if no one's talking to each other!'

'Oh, Bex, you're overreacting,' says Suze, raising her eyes to heaven. 'It's only a spat. There's always a spat at Christmas. One Christmas at my Uncle Mungo's, things were so bad between some of my relations, it was all written out on the seating plan.'

'What was written out on the seating plan?'

'Who was talking to who,' explains Suze. 'And who wasn't. My cousin Maud refused to even *look* at my Aunt Elspeth, so her chair had to face the other way. And my father had just tried to get Uncle Mungo ex-communicated from the Church of Scotland, so Uncle Mungo threatened him with the carving knife. But it was fine,' she concludes comfortably. 'Just family stuff.'

'It doesn't sound fine,' I say in horror. 'It sounds awful! And I don't want my Christmas to be like that, I want it to be *harmonious*. So I'm organizing a Christmas Eve bonding event.'

'A what?'

'A gingerbread-house-making party. Everyone has to come and wear Christmas jumpers and make up their differences. I'll make hot chocolate and we'll have a fire and—'

'Bex, you're nuts,' interrupts Suze, and I stare at her, hurt. I thought she'd love the idea. 'You look stressed out already,' she continues firmly. 'You're doing so much already. Why on earth would you try to organize *another* thing? Just relax. It'll all be OK.'

'What if it *isn't*?' I shoot back – and I know I sound scratchy, but it hasn't been the most wonderful day so far, and now here's Suze dissing my Christmas movie idea. Also, I ordered twenty gingerbread-house-making kits on my phone on the way here.

'Bex,' says Suze. 'Listen.' She takes a breath as though about to impart some advice – but before she can continue, Irene's head appears round the door.

'Oh, Suze,' she says, sounding anxious. 'There's a customer here, asking to see the manager. She's asking about *sprygge*.'

'Oh, OK,' says Suze easily. 'I'll come out. What does she want to know?'

'Well, everything, really,' says Irene.

'Have you given her the spiel about "People say it comes from Norway"?'

'Well, that's the thing,' says Irene, looking even more nervous. 'She's the Norwegian ambassador.'

I have never seen Suze more like a terrified cat. She practically leaps off her chair and stares at Irene, her eyes like plates.

'*Norwegian?*' she hisses.

'The Norwegian ambassador,' Irene nods unhappily. 'And she says she's never heard of *sprygge*, and she wants to see the manager.'

'Oh God, oh God.' Suze looks faint. 'Oh God. We'll be prosecuted.' Her eyes dart towards the window as though she wants to climb out and escape – and I grab her arm.

'No we won't!' I say, more firmly than I feel. 'People don't get prosecuted for saying things are Norwegian. Come on. Let's just go and . . . and say hello.'

As we emerge from the staffroom we see her at once – a well-dressed blonde woman in a very cool parka. Suze looks as though she might run away any moment, so I nudge her in the ribs and she advances gingerly, holding out her hand.

'Hello,' she says to the woman in a quaking voice. 'And welcome to Letherby Hall Gift Shop. I am Susan Cleath-Stuart, manager and proprietor of . . .' She swallows. 'How may I . . . um . . .'

'My name is Karina Gunderson,' says the woman in cool, pleasant tones. 'I'm interested in your display.' She gestures at the *sprygge* table. 'The assistant says it's supposed to be Norwegian?'

Suze seems unable to answer. She opens her mouth and closes it again, shooting desperate looks at me.

'Hello!' I come to her rescue and approach Karina Gunderson in my most confident manner. 'Let me introduce myself. I'm Rebecca Brandon, née Bloomwood, the member of staff who first brought the *sprygge* concept to the store. *Sprygge* for us is an overpowering form of happiness and wellbeing. It's radiant and joyful.' I spread my arms. 'Euphoric and sublime. Yet complex. Yet in other ways, simple.'

I smile at Karina, hoping that we've wrapped up the subject of *sprygge*, but she seems unmoved.

'Yet not Norwegian,' she says. 'As you claim.'

'I don't think we've *exactly* claimed that,' I say, after thinking for a moment. 'Have we, Suze? What we've said is that *some* people think it originates from Norway.'

'Which people?' asks Karina Gunderson at once.

'I don't think we specify which people,' I say, after another pause for thought. 'Just, you know, some people.'

'Exactly,' says Suze, finding her voice. 'Some people.'

'Some people,' affirms Irene eagerly.

'Which is true,' I add in casual tones. 'So.'

There's a long silence. Karina Gunderson's unreadable blue eyes are resting on me, making me feel a tad uncomfortable.

'Although, obviously some people *don't*,' I say, suddenly thinking of a way out. 'There's another school of thought that believes it's, um . . . Finnish.'

'*Finnish?*' echoes Karina Gunderson disbelievingly.

'Exactly.' I avoid her eye. 'It's one of the big unanswered questions in life. Whither *sprygge*?' I allow myself a small dramatic flourish. 'Research hasn't confirmed the truth one way or another. But while the *sprygge* debate rages on in journals and . . . other places . . . we in our humble way simply want to bring happiness to the world. Through cushions and other gift products.'

'The mugs are popular,' adds Irene nervously. 'Very popular, aren't they, Becky? And the wall signs sold out.'

'Please have a complimentary mug,' says Suze in a rush, picking up a mug and proffering it. 'Or . . . not,' she adds as Karina Gunderson makes no move to take it. 'Either way.'

She looks at me and winces and there's another long, prickly pause. I can't quite tell if Karina Gunderson is going to smile or call the police.

'Actually,' I continue cautiously, '*here's* a funny coincidence. We've recently considered suspending the sale of *sprygge* products until the research on its origins has been concluded one way or the other. Haven't we, Suze? And that might be wise. All things, um, considered.'

'Yes,' says Karina Gunderson. 'It might.' She takes the mug from Suze and looks at it, her mouth twitching. ' "Don't worry, be *sprygge*",' she reads aloud, her tone giving nothing away. She gives us all a long look – then turns to Suze. 'Goodbye. Your house is very beautiful.'

'Oh! Goodbye, then!' says Suze, her relief so obvious I want to laugh. We all watch as Karina Gunderson makes her way out of the store, then Suze collapses in my arms.

'Oh my *God*,' she says.

'I know.' I hug her back. 'Don't worry, she's gone.'

'Bex, we have to stop this,' says Suze fervently. '*Sprygge* has to end. Right here, right now. Or we really are going to get into trouble.'

'I hate to say it,' I say sorrowfully, 'but I agree. How much stock is left?'

'Not much,' says Irene. 'Only ten or so mugs, three cushions, a few keyrings . . .'

'Well, we'll keep them as souvenirs,' says Suze, sounding resolute. 'Everyone help yourself to what you want. But no more selling them. In fact – let's get rid of the whole display.'

Irene starts gathering up the keyrings and putting them into a cardboard box, while Suze and I pack away the mugs.

'It was fun, though, wasn't it?' I say wistfully, pausing to run my finger along the words. 'And now *sprygge* will never be in the Norwegian language.'

'I know, Bex,' says Suze, rolling her eyes. 'But nor will we be in prison for fraud.'

Honestly. Suze always exaggerates. We were never going to go to *prison*. (Were we?) On the other hand, she's ordered each of us a massive box of Hotel Chocolat truffles to celebrate the brief glory that was *sprygge*, so there's always a silver lining.

She and I have both taken the afternoon off for the school Nativity play and I decide to pop home beforehand. The temperature has plummeted and as I look up at the solid white sky I find myself thinking: will it snow?

Maybe it will! I mean, why shouldn't it? It's got to snow sometime. Imagine if there's a massive snowfall and it'll be like we really *are* in a Christmas movie. We can make a snowman in the front garden and everyone will say, 'D'you remember Becky's Christmas? It was amazing! There was *snow*.'

As I open the front door I feel more optimistic than I've been for a while. Maybe Suze is right, maybe I need to relax. Do positive visualizations. I'm just picturing a perfect Christmas table, with all my friends and family gathered around a spectacular turkey and saying, 'Becky, this Christmas is the best *ever*,' when a noise from the sitting room draws my attention. I head in and stop dead. My happy thoughts vanish and I stand, breathing fast, consumed by Christmas rage.

My bloody garlands have fallen down again. *Again*. That noise was the sound of my lovely twiggy one flopping down into the hearth, bringing the gold one with it. It slipped out yet again from under my gym dumbbells. *How?*

I mean, what does it take to make a Christmas garland stay up? Concrete? Steel bloody girders?

Next time I buy a house, I'm buying one with built-in garlands, I tell myself feverishly, as I grab the golden twiggy mess out of the hearth. I don't care if it looks weird. I'm not doing this every December.

I shove the garlands on the sofa to be dealt with later – then try to regain my calm, optimistic mood. It's OK. I'll find a solution. I'm just googling *garland stay up device never fails* when my phone rings and I jump.

'Hello?' I answer it, wondering madly if it's a garland company who somehow saw my googling and have the solution.

'Oh, hello,' comes a woman's voice down the line. 'Is that Mrs Brandon? It's Ve-Gen Foods here. Just a courtesy call to let you know that unfortunately the vegan turkey you ordered is unavailable. Would you like to order another product instead or would you prefer a refund?'

It takes me a moment to digest the horror of what she's telling me. She's cancelling my vegan turkey? She can't do that!

'But I need a vegan turkey!' I say. 'My sister's vegan and I've promised her a vegan turkey for Christmas.'

'A lot of customers have opted for the mushroom risotto,' replies the woman blandly. 'It contains similar ingredients and is equally festive.'

I stare at the phone, my Christmas rage rising again. What kind of travesty is this? Mushroom risotto is *not* equally festive.

'Why isn't the vegan turkey available?' I say. 'Because I really, really need one.'

'I can't say, I'm afraid,' says the woman. 'Was that a refund, then?'

'Do you have maybe *one* vegan turkey?' I say, unwilling to give up. 'Like just *one*, around the place, that nobody needs?'

'No,' says the woman flatly. 'I'll be refunding your card, then. Sorry for the inconvenience and have a merry Christmas.'

'*Merry?*' I retort, hoping she can detect my sarcasm, but she's already gone.

My chest is rising and falling, but there's no point feeling bitter, vengeful hatred, even though I do. I'm just starting another Google search – *vegan turkey last minute available no shortage next day* – when the doorbell rings. I peer out of the window. There's a delivery van outside. Well, at least *something*'s arrived on schedule.

'Hello!' I say as I swing open the front door to a beaming man in white overalls.

'Good afternoon!' he returns cheerily. 'I'm here with your fish.'

I stare at him blankly. Fish?

'Smoked salmon,' he clarifies, consulting his clipboard. 'Bundle order. Rebecca Brandon.'

Of course. The smoked salmon from the Christmas Style Fair. I'd forgotten about that.

'Great!' I say, smiling back. 'Perfect! Just in time for Christmas.'

'Absolutely! Where do you want it?' he adds, and I peer at him, a bit puzzled. Where do I *want* it?

'What do you mean?' I hold out my hands. 'Can't you just, you know, give it to me?'

The man shoots me an amused look. 'Fifteen sides of salmon? Not likely.'

'*Fifteen sides?*' I echo blankly.

'Thirty pounds.' He nods. 'I'll just go and get my trolley,' he adds over his shoulder as he heads back to the van. 'Show me where the freezer is, I'll load it in for you.'

I can't quite speak. Thirty pounds? As in *weight*? What's he *talking* about? This has to be a mistake.

Frantically I summon up my Visa bill on my phone and scan down the entries, trying not to look too carefully (£49.99 in M&S? I *so* did not spend that, it must have been Luke), until I suddenly see it. Whitson Fish. £460.

I feel a bit cold. *Janice spent £460 on smoked salmon?*

Desperately I try to recall her asking me all those

random questions as I was chasing after the silver llama bauble. Maybe she did say something about 'thirty pounds'. But I thought she meant thirty quid. Thirty *quid*! Never in a million *years* did I think she meant thirty pounds in weight. Who can eat thirty pounds of fish?

And oh God, here he comes, wheeling a trolley up the path, piled high with polystyrene boxes.

'Nice lot of fish,' says the man with satisfaction as he reaches me. 'Good-quality stuff, this.' He pats the top container, which is labelled *Cold smoked salmon – frozen*.

'Right.' I lick my lips nervously. 'Actually, there's been a very, *very* slight mistake. I didn't mean to order quite so much. Could you take it back?'

The man's expression immediately changes to one of wariness, and he starts shaking his head.

'Oh no, no, no. We don't process returns. You want to sort something out with the company, that's your business. You got a freezer space we can load it into?'

Oh God. The only freezer we've got in this rented house is one drawer of the fridge, full of Minnie's fish fingers.

'Not . . . exactly.' I swallow.

'Best leave it outside for now, then,' says the man. 'Where d'you want it? Here?' He nods at the tiny patch of grass in our front garden, and when I don't reply, starts briskly hefting the boxes off the trolley and unpacking sides of frozen smoked salmon, shrink-wrapped in plastic.

'Can't you leave the boxes?' I say in consternation, but he shakes his head.

'We take them away. Part of our contract. Sustainable packaging.'

Soon all the fish is heaped up on the lawn and I've scribbled on the man's paper, and he's driving off in his van. I gaze at the pile, feeling a bit unreal. I have a front garden full of frozen salmon. What do I do?

My phone bleeps with a text and I peer at it distractedly to see a message from Suze:

Seats are filling up, have bagged two for you and Luke, but you should hurry!!!

Oh *God*—

Insulation, it suddenly hits me. That's what I need.

I dash upstairs, grab Minnie's Paddington Bear duvet off her bed and run back down to the garden with it. I hastily tuck it round the sides of salmon, patting and squashing it down to ensure the fish is fully protected. Then at last I stand up, to see an old woman staring at me from across the road.

'Is that a *child*?' she says, in tones of horror.

What? I mean, *what*?

'No!' I snap. 'It's fish!' I glare at her till she starts walking on, then grab my coat and bag, feeling totally hassled.

Come on, Becky, I tell myself firmly. It's all fine. I'll go to the Nativity and I'll enjoy watching Minnie . . . and *then* I'll deal with this. And the vegan turkey. And the garlands. And Luke's present, it suddenly crosses my mind. And oh God, I *still* haven't decided which stuffing to make . . .

No. Stop it. Be calm. Be mindful.

I stride quickly through the village, nearly bumping into about six people because I'm simultaneously ordering an online chest freezer, next-day delivery, plus some 'instant champagne coolers' which were in a bundle offer, and a book called *100 Ways with Smoked Salmon*.

The school hall is already full of parents and there are hardly any seats left, but I spot two chairs with sheets of paper taped to them, on which Suze's handwriting reads: *Reserved for the Brandons*. I sink into one of them, relieved, and look around for Suze, but I can't see her so I quickly text:

Thx for seats!!! Where are you??

A moment later she replies:

I'm on the other side.

Then, a few seconds later, a follow-up appears:

Can't wait to see Minnie's costume!!!

I stare at my phone, suddenly realizing I never told Suze what happened. Slowly I start typing, **Actually, I gave it to Steph Richards**, but then stop, feeling torn. Suze has no idea I even *know* Steph. She might ask awkward questions, like 'Why?'

I look around for Steph – but I can't see her either. I think for a moment more, then delete the text. I'll tell Suze later. But first I'll ask Steph if I can let Suze into her secret. After all, the more heads the better, and I know Suze will be totally supportive—

'Hi!' Luke's voice interrupts me. He's taking his place beside me, a cheerful look on his face. 'The great occasion at last!'

'I know!' I say, beaming back. 'Isn't it exciting?'

Shall I quickly add, 'By the way, there's thirty pounds of fish on the lawn, but don't worry, I've just ordered a freezer'?

No. Not the moment.

'What I'm looking forward to *most* of all is seeing Minnie's costume,' says Luke with relish. 'I've seen you put in all those hours of work, Becky,' he adds before I can reply, 'and I hope Minnie knows how lucky she is to have you. Because *I* do,' he adds gently. And there's something about his warm, loving expression that makes me catch my breath. 'I've brought my camera,' he adds more matter-of-factly, taking it out. 'Thought the occasion warranted it.'

Luke hardly ever brings that camera. It's the high-spec one he uses for special moments, when he thinks his phone isn't good enough. And suddenly my throat feels clogged.

'Luke,' I say into his ear. 'I need to tell you something. Minnie . . .' I swallow. 'Well, she won't be in the costume I made. I gave it to another child to wear.'

'What?' Luke freezes in shock. 'You *gave* it— *Why?*'

'Ssh!' I try to hush him. 'They needed it. It's . . . there's a story. It was the right thing to do.'

Luke is still staring at me in disbelief.

'So what's Minnie going to wear?'

'It's fine. I cobbled something together. She doesn't mind.'

'But do *you* mind?' says Luke at once – and I can't quite answer. I thought I wouldn't mind at all. But sitting here in the hubbub of anticipation, it's hard not to feel just a *tiny* bit . . .

Anyway. It's fine.

Luke is silent for a moment, gazing at me with his dark eyes.

'You worked every night on that costume, Becky,' he says at last, his voice so low I can barely hear. 'It meant so much to you.'

'I know.' I hesitate. 'But I'm very lucky. And they're not so lucky. I can't say any more than that.'

Luke doesn't reply, but takes my hand and squeezes it tight. And I think: I am lucky. Whatever else goes wrong, I'm lucky.

Although half an hour later I'm not feeling quite so lucky. I'm sure improvisation is great for creativity and all that. But it's really, *really* bad for putting on a children's Nativity play.

The story is all over the place. Some children have obviously been coached by their parents, whereas others clearly have no idea what they're doing. One has started crying and one has told the Angel Gabriel he needs the toilet.

My legs are numb, sitting on this plastic chair. We seem to have been watching this play for ever. Jesus has been born and the shepherds (including Wilfie and Clemmie) have been and gone and everyone's sung

'Away In A Manger' and 'Let It Go'. (Huh?) But now all the children seem a bit stuck.

'We have nowhere else to stay,' intones Mary mournfully, clutching the plastic baby Jesus in her lap. 'There are no hotels.'

She's said that line about thirty times.

'The donkey is tired,' ventures Joseph, although the donkey left the stable twenty minutes ago and changed costume into an angel.

'We have nowhere else to stay,' says Mary a bit desperately. 'There are no hotels.'

'Kings!' I can see Miss Lucas hissing and beckoning enthusiastically. 'Kings! Come on!'

A moment later Minnie and two boys walk on to the stage, all dressed up in their bright shiny costumes. The audience is so calcified with boredom that everyone seems to wake up, and wild applause breaks out, as though the three kings are celebrities appearing in a pantomime.

I can't help gazing wistfully at Harvey, because he looks *amazing*. The midnight-blue silk is spectacular and the gold sequins are gleaming under the lights and even his casket is all iridescent and magnificent.

But Minnie looks good, too, I tell myself defensively. In more of a bohemian, thrown-together way. At once she beams and waves at us, looking delighted to be the centre of attention.

'I have myrrh for the baby Jesus,' announces the first king in a monotone. He's a stolid boy called George, who clearly has had his line drummed into him by his mum.

'I have frankincense for the baby Jesus,' says Harvey,

enunciating clearly, and sending a sweet smile to the audience.

And now it's Minnie's turn. I'm quite nervous, I suddenly realize. My daughter, on stage in a play! I glance at Luke, and he grins back.

I can see Minnie peering at Harvey's glittery casket – the one I made for her and which we practised with at home – then at her own box with the golden Gs. She frowns, looking confused, draws breath, then pauses.

'I have Gucci,' she says at last. 'For the baby Jesus.' At once there's a series of snorts along our row.

'Gucci?' says Luke, beside me. 'Myrrh, frankincense and Gucci?'

'Gold!' I mouth desperately at her, hoping she can read my lips. 'Gold! Not Gucci!'

Minnie looks at me uncertainly.

'I have Gucci,' she repeats more firmly, brandishing the Gucci box. 'Mummy has a Gucci bag,' she continues and there are more snorts of laughter. 'Mummy bought the scarf,' she adds conversationally to the audience. 'Daddy had the money. In his pocket.'

Oh God, she's remembering all the stuff I told her about that first Denny and George scarf. What else is she going to say?

I can see shoulders heaving everywhere and hear the odd splutter of mirth. On stage, George looks a bit put out that Minnie's hogging the show.

'I have myrrh,' he repeats loudly.

'I have *Gucci*,' Minnie cuts across him defiantly.

'The vicar's sitting over there,' says Luke to me, nodding to the left. 'Just in case you were wondering.'

'Stop it.' I bite my lip. 'Concentrate on the play.'

By now Minnie has run out of steam. Silence falls on the stage and Mary rouses herself.

'We have nowhere else to stay,' she repeats in doleful tones. 'There are no hotels.'

I can see something waking up in Minnie's mind at the word 'hotels'.

'No minibar,' she says sternly. She turns to Joseph and jabs a finger at him. 'No minibar. No sweeties. It is *too 'spensive.'*

At once the entire place erupts in laughter.

'Quite right!' calls out one dad.

'Don't eat the Toblerone!' joins in another.

'Stick to the all-inclusive buffet!' shouts a third, and there's another huge gale of laughter.

Everyone's turning to grin at me and Luke, and I smile back, even though my head is boiling. Our daughter just stood in Mary and Joseph's lowly stable and told them not to use the minibar. I want to *die*.

After the play has finished there's mulled wine and mince pies for parents in the dining room. Luke and I sip our steaming drinks while the word 'minibar' floats on every conversation, amid gusts of laughter. I can hear people exclaiming about Harvey's 'wonderful costume', too, and every time they do, Luke squeezes my hand. I haven't spotted Steph anywhere, but I'm guessing she's here; everyone comes to the Nativity play.

'Oh my *God*, Bex.' Suze arrives at my side, her face flushed from laughing. '"No minibar." That is classic! And Minnie had an *amazing* costume,' she adds carefully.

'Well done, Bex! How did you make it – with a scarf? Is it Denny and George?'

I know Suze. She's being as sweet as she possibly can about a costume which was obviously thrown together in five minutes with safety pins. And I appreciate her tactfulness. But part of me is burning inside with frustration. I want to retort, 'Do you really think I worked for weeks on that? I made the *good* costume! The one everyone's talking about!' But I can't risk it here, with the other parents all milling around.

'Thanks,' I say tightly, and swig my drink, as Luke answers a call on his phone. He talks for half a minute, then turns to me, looking puzzled.

'Becky, that was the council. They say there have been some calls about a homeless person in our front garden. Apparently they've made a camp, with a duvet. D'you know what they're on about?'

Oh, for God's *sake*.

'It's not a homeless person!' I erupt. 'It's fish!'

'*Fish?*' Luke seems staggered.

'I bought some fish and I put it under a Paddington Bear duvet,' I explain, a little impatiently. 'That's all I did. And everyone jumps to the wrong conclusion.'

'You put fish . . . under a duvet?' echoes Luke.

'I had to!' I say defensively. 'What else was I supposed to do with it?'

There's silence and I see Luke exchanging perplexed glances with Suze.

'Bex, don't take this the wrong way,' says Suze carefully. 'But you seem a bit . . . tense.'

'I'm not tense,' I counter at once. 'That's ridiculous. I'm fine. I'm totally chilled. Aren't I, Luke?'

'You're a little bit tense,' he says, and I glare at him. Traitor.

'You are, Bex.' Suze puts a hand on my arm. 'In fact, you've seemed tense ever since you agreed to host Christmas. Let me help. Please. I'm *longing* to help. Or . . . let me host! Change of plan!'

What?

I stare at Suze in disbelief as she turns eagerly to Luke. 'Maybe that's the answer. I could easily do it, everyone could come to Letherby Hall—'

'What, so you think I *can't* host Christmas?' My distressed voice cuts across hers. I shake her hand off my arm and she flinches. 'You think I can't do it, Suze?'

'No!' Suze backtracks hastily. 'God! Of course you can! I'm just saying . . . you seem a bit hassled . . . I only want to help . . .'

'Well, you could help by having faith in me! You could help by *supporting* my idea for a gingerbread party.'

'I do!' says Suze warily. 'Of course I do, Bex! We can totally do that if you want. I just—'

'Good,' I cut her off, a little shrilly. 'Because if you really want to know, everything's fine. It's all on track, and I'm super-relaxed and it's going to be an amazing Christmas Day.' I drain my mulled wine. 'So there's no need for anyone to worry.'

Chats

CHRISTMAS!

Becky

Dear all, I cordially invite you to come and make gingerbread houses on Christmas Eve. Let us bond as friends and family, forget all disagreements, drink mulled wine and be merry. Dress: Christmas jumpers! Love Becky xxx

From: customerservices@ramblesons.com
To: Becky Brandon
Subject: UNAVAILABLE ITEM

Dear Mrs Brandon

We apologize that the following item

Free range turkey

is unavailable.

We have endeavoured to substitute an item as close as possible to the original order. We hope you are happy with our choice of substitution.

Yours sincerely

Customer Services Team
Ramblesons Online Groceries Ltd

ORDER: TSK67468675

Unavailable item:	Quantity
Free range turkey 7kg	**1**

Substituted item:	Quantity
Reconstituted Turkey Slices Pack 200g	**35**

EIGHTEEN

I was lying. Everything is not fine, and everything is not on track.

I haven't got a turkey and I haven't got a present for Luke and yesterday needles started dropping off the Christmas tree (why?) and I still don't know what I'm giving Suze and I keep bumping into the new chest freezer in the kitchen, so I've got a massive bruise on my thigh.

Thank God I made a backup online order. Thank *God*. I've added turkey to the list, so it'll arrive tomorrow. But it hasn't made me feel any calmer. What if I hadn't booked two deliveries? How can they substitute turkey slices for turkey on December 23rd? How? Are they *sadists*?

My Christmas stress keeps spiking, like one of those machines in medical dramas that starts bleeping and everyone runs around madly. Only there's no one to run around madly here, because Luke is away on business till tomorrow afternoon and Minnie is at a playdate. It's just me and six pounds of mushrooms. As a last resort I've decided to *make* a vegan turkey. I've found instructions online and this is my third go, only it's collapsed again.

I peer in mounting despair at the construction in front of me. It looks nothing like a turkey, it looks like a pile of mushrooms and chickpea flour. I rewind the YouTube video – and watch in frustration for the tenth time as the lady says cheerily, 'Now mould your mixture into drumsticks.' I've *tried*. But my drumsticks won't *stay* as bloody drumsticks.

I stare at my gloopy mess, thinking desperately. Maybe I could use . . . cardboard? I know vegans don't usually eat cardboard, but it could be like bones, couldn't it? I could say casually 'Watch out for the cardboard!' like you say 'Watch out for the fish bones!'

I grab an empty loo roll from Minnie's craft box, and stuff it full of mushroom mixture. It doesn't look anything like a turkey drumstick, but I could . . . paint it, maybe? I reach for Minnie's bottle of brown poster paint (non-toxic) and a paint brush. I briskly slather on some paint, then put the 'drumstick' on a plate and stare at it.

No. I cannot serve painted loo rolls as my Christmas vegan option.

My head is all fuzzy from staring at the same YouTube video over and over and I decide I need some fresh air. I'll go to the supermarket. Maybe I'll suddenly find a brand-new range of vegan turkeys for sale, I think in a sudden burst of optimism. I mean, it's possible, isn't it?

The supermarket is only a ten-minute drive away and I head through the glass doors to see a big display of wrapping paper beneath a sign: *Gift wrap all 50 per cent off*. Which is really annoying, because I bought wrapping paper last week but this is much nicer. It's got red and green glittery candy stripes, *and* it's reduced. In fact, I can't tear myself away. Maybe I need some more wrapping paper? (I don't. I really don't.)

Wait! I have the answer: I'll buy some for *next* Christmas. And the Christmas after. Yes. It makes absolute financial sense. I mean, we'll always need Christmas wrapping paper, won't we?

Feeling better already, I fill my trolley with twelve glittery rolls and six reels of reduced holly-printed ribbon and some festive pom-pom decorations. And I'm just deciding whether I should buy a bumper pack of five hundred snowflake gift tags (they'll always come in handy) when I hear a voice greeting me:

'Hi Becky.'

My head jerks up and I stiffen in shock. It's Craig, coming towards me with a trolley full of shopping bags, smiling easily at me. *Smiling*. As though we're best friends and everything's fab. What an absolute nerve.

'Hi Craig,' I say coldly. 'So, your girlfriend came round to our house unexpectedly the other day.'

'Oh. Yeah. I heard.' Craig winces, and I wait for him to say, 'I'm so sorry, that was highly inappropriate of her.' But instead he sucks his teeth and shakes his head ruefully. 'Yeah, Nadine wasn't pleased. She thought Luke should have given her more time. More respect, you know?'

What? Is he for *real*?

'We were having a family party at the time,' I say.

'And Luke doesn't usually hold business meetings with no notice. At home. On a Sunday. On his daughter's *birthday*.'

I couldn't be more pointed, but Craig seems oblivious.

'Yeah,' he says, in the same musing tones. 'Nadine was quite pissed off. And you don't want to get on the wrong side of Nadine.' He shoots me a rueful glance. 'I'm afraid Luke's made a business enemy there.'

Luke's made a business enemy of Nadine? Oh my God, we're all terrified. I'm sure Luke's quaking in his boots. I expect they'll have a showdown across some massive board table with views over the Shard.

Not.

'What a shame,' I say. 'Well, have a good Christmas.' I make to push my trolley on, but Craig puts a hand on it.

'You're still invited to our Christmas party,' he says. 'Maybe Luke and Nadine can make up there, under the mistletoe.' His eyes gleam wickedly at me and I bristle. What's *that* supposed to mean?

'I doubt it,' I say in off-putting tones. 'I think we're busy.'

'Last chance to use the hot tub before we move,' says Craig, waggling his eyebrows tantalizingly, and I stare at him in surprise.

'Move?'

'Yeah, we're leaving. Renting another place. Bit quiet for us here. Bit nothing.' He hesitates, then adds, 'Plus, Nadine's found out where Lord Alan Sugar lives. Reckons she might get to know him.'

Oh my God, she's even madder than I thought.

'Brilliant plan,' I say, somehow keeping my face serious.

'That's the way to do it. I'm sure she'll be a tycoon really soon. Any time now.'

I'm fairly sure Craig doesn't realize I'm being sarcastic, because his face softens.

'She's got drive, Nadine,' he says admiringly. 'So much drive.'

Yes, I answer silently. And the sooner she drives herself out of Letherby, the better.

'Well, good luck with that,' I say politely. Two women are coming in through the glass doors and I see them eyeing up Craig and nudging each other. I suddenly view him through their eyes: long hair, stubble, mesmerizing eyes. The sexiest rock god Letherby has ever seen.

And I give a wry, inward laugh. That was me, melting under his dark, smouldering gaze. What an *idiot* I was.

Even so, I feel a slight pang as he says, 'Well, bye then, Becky, and Happy Christmas.' I may never see him again. And after all, he was an important part of my life. (Sort of.) Plus, I have some unanswered questions.

Well, one unanswered question, anyway.

'Wait, Craig,' I say. 'Before you go, I've always wondered something.' I hesitate, then blurt out, 'Did you ever write a song about me? Or at least . . . mention me? Refer to me at all?'

Craig's slow, sexy smile creeps across his face again – then he nods.

' "Girl Who Broke My Heart",' he says succinctly, and I stare back, gripped.

'Wow. But the girl in that song is French. Was that,

like, camouflage? Is it really *me*? Am I that girl?' My voice suddenly trembles with the drama of the moment. 'Craig . . . did I break your heart?'

'No,' says Craig, looking amused. 'And you're not that girl. But you're in verse three, first line. See you.'

He pushes his trolley out of the supermarket and I stare after him, transfixed, then spring to life. I hastily summon Google on my phone and search *Lyrics girl who broke my heart Craig Curton*. I'm in a song! I'm actually in a song! This is so cool! What does it say?

After a few seconds the lyrics appear on my screen. I breathlessly scroll down to the third verse and read the first line:

'She had better hair than the one before.'

For a few moments I peer blankly at the words, trying to make sense of them. Where am I in this? Did I have better hair than someone? I can't make head nor tail of it. Typical Craig, to write something incomprehensible.

OK. Let's start from first principles. The song is about a French girl. And 'she had better hair than the one before'.

Wait. I frown as the horrible truth hits me. As in . . . the girl he dated before? Is that *me*? I'm 'the one before'? With *inferior hair*?

I gasp in sudden outrage. Is he saying I had bad hair? I did *not* have bad hair. Everyone wore their hair like that at uni. And *he* can talk. And who was this French girl anyway? Who says her hair was so great? I bet it was a boring old bob.

I glance out of the supermarket, half tempted to go after him and demand furiously, 'What d'you mean,

351

bad hair?' but he's gone. Hmph. I'm *never* dating a rock musician again.

I mean, obviously I'm not, I hastily add in my head.

That goes without saying.

For about the millionth time since I met Luke, I hope he can't somehow read my mind. Because, to be frank, that would be a disaster.

Still bristling all over, I start to push my trolley round the supermarket. What I'm *really* hoping to see is a sign saying, 'Get your vegan turkeys here!' But it's all reduced mince pies and Advent calendars. Hmph again.

Then I hear a familiar, annoying laugh. I can't place it at first, but feeling curious I follow the sound around a pile of tins. And oh God, of course. Paunch: tick. Faded jeans: tick. Greying beard: tick. It's Steph's husband Damian, talking to someone in the baked-goods section.

Great. Another super-annoying man. Is this Super-Annoying Man Day?

Then, as he moves, I see to my shock that the person he's with is Steph. Does this mean . . . are they back together again?

As I glimpse Steph's face, I decide it's unlikely. She's hissing words at him miserably and gesticulating, while he eye-rolls and checks his watch and even gives her a patronizing pat on the shoulder. I'm fuming on her behalf – and I can't even hear what he's saying.

At last he lifts up both hands as if to say 'Enough' and walks away while Steph slowly slumps. I hesitate at the corner of the aisle, feeling torn. Every impulse is telling me to go and hug Steph – but what if it's intruding on her privacy? What if she didn't want anyone seeing that scene?

As I watch anxiously, she heads to the café and sits down at a table. That decides me. I'll give her five minutes before I approach her. And meanwhile, I can't resist it – I'm going to follow Damian.

I casually walk in the direction he went, and turn a corner just in time to see him join a woman holding a trolley and plant a kiss full on her lips. *Argh*. It's her! It has to be. The one who works in events. The one he got together with in the Malmaison, Manchester.

I stare at them, gripped. She's got to be in her twenties. Expensive highlights, but a pinched face. She's going to be *so* mean to him, I predict with inward satisfaction. Once the lustre's worn off. She's going to be horrible, you can just tell. And he totally deserves it. He had Steph and he went for *this* pinchy-faced woman instead?

His hand keeps fondling her bum, I notice with revulsion. Is that appropriate in the frozen pizza section? I'd quite like to make a complaint to Customer Services. I'd like to see a person in a suit approach him and tell him not to be so gross.

I should get on with my shopping, I know I should – but somehow I can't tear myself away from the awful pair. When they head to the dairy section I follow, at a distance, fixated by the sight of her showing him low-fat yogurts and him fondling her bum again. Their entire relationship appears to be based on him fondling her bum. Well, I hope he gets carpal tunnel syndrome.

My whole body is throbbing with indignation. (To be

absolutely honest, this is also partly a lingering outrage towards Craig.) I want to punish him for being so vile. Even though it's nothing to do with me, and I'm supposed to be finding a vegan turkey and how would I punish him anyway?

I should just let this go, I tell myself several times. I should stop trying to be the Christmas Fairy of Vengeance. But somehow I can't stop following the pair of them at a distance, wondering what on earth I could do.

Then, as I'm tiptoeing up the cooked meats aisle, I see an official supermarket fleece slung over a crate. It's green, with a logo, and no one seems to be using it right now. And as I stare at it, a sudden, fully formed idea lands, pow, in my brain. The kind of idea that makes you think, *What?* And then, *Nooo. I can't.* And then, *Yesss! I can!*

I put on the fleece and at once feel invisible. I'm no longer Becky, I'm an anonymous, nameless store-worker. Abandoning my trolley, I walk past Damian to be sure – but he doesn't flicker. Even though we're fellow parents at school, he totally doesn't recognize me. Of course he doesn't. He's one of those guys who lives in the bubble of their own starring role, and everyone else is just chorus.

Which suits me fine.

I swiftly walk towards the stationery section and gather some props. Clipboard. Notepad. Reading glasses for extra disguise purposes. In my bag is an old lanyard that I keep for Minnie to play with. It's from a play centre, but I put it on and turn it round – then screw my hair into a bun, using an elastic band.

Then, before I can lose my nerve, I approach Damian

with an ingratiating smile, my pen poised over my clipboard.

'Hello, sir,' I greet him in sweet, singsong tones. 'Everything all right for you in store today?'

'Fine,' says Damian, barely looking round.

'Only I'm here to assess our facilities for the elderly,' I press on. 'Are you managing all right today, sir, or are there any problems you'd like to highlight?'

'What?' Damian frowns at me, confused.

'We understand the challenges facing your age group,' I reply soothingly, 'and we're here to help with mobility, larger signs for the visually challenged, hearing aids . . . Are you finding everything you need?'

Ms Pinchy Face suddenly gives a snort of laughter.

'I'm not *elderly*,' says Damian, looking livid.

'Of course you're not! "Age-challenged" is what I meant to say.' I nod. 'I understand, it's a sensitive topic . . .'

'I'm fifty–four!' barks Damian. 'Fifty-four!'

'As I say, we *do* want to help your generation have the most effective shopping experience for your needs.' I look at Ms Pinchy Face and add brightly, 'Oh, is this your carer? Did you have any comments or suggestions? He's a lovely old gentleman, isn't he?'

'Carer?' Damian appears apoplectic. '*Carer*? Can I talk to your superior? What's your name?' He makes a swipe for my lanyard and I hastily back away.

'My apologies, sir. I can tell you don't want to participate in our study, so I'll leave you in peace. Just *one* more piece of information . . .' I add in my most helpful manner. 'Incontinence aids are on special offer this week, if that's of interest to you?'

Before he can draw breath, I hastily walk around the corner, rip off the fleece and glasses and undo my hair – then sprint to where I left my trolley. By the time I glimpse Damian and Ms Pinchy Face appearing from the next aisle, I'm a shopper with a trolley again, looking firmly the other way.

'I mean, it was quite funny, babe,' Ms Pinchy Face is saying in mollifying tones. 'I think it was an honest mistake.' At once I feel an inward giggle. It wasn't just funny, it was bloody hilarious, and I *wish* Steph had been there to see it.

I walk briskly round the whole store, but I can't see any vegan turkeys and I don't want to miss Steph. So as soon as I'm sure that Damian and Ms Pinchy Face have left, I pay for my shopping, head for the café and wave at her as I'm queuing for a cup of tea.

'Hi! Becky!' Her face lights up, and she waves back. 'Come and join me.'

As I head to Steph's table I'm relieved to see that she looks a lot more cheerful than she did before.

'Christmas shopping?' I say, nodding at her bags, and she grimaces.

'Kind of. I mean, it's just me and Harvey, and Harvey's not wild about turkey. I'm definitely not cooking a whole turkey for myself, so . . .' She shrugs. 'We'll be having sausages.'

'Cool!' I say, although the picture of Steph and Harvey on Christmas Day, just the two of them, makes my heart contract. 'You couldn't get together with your family?' I venture.

'Too far. They're in Leeds. And work's manic at the

356

moment. I've got to go in today, even though I'm supposed to have the day off.'

'On a Saturday?' I make a face.

'I know,' she says resignedly. 'I just nipped in here
to stock up. Harvey's at the childminder's for the day.'

'Have you told your mum about Damian yet?' I ask,
even though this is really none of my business.

'Not yet,' says Steph after a pause, and I bite my lip.
Because it's not for me to tell her what to do. But it's
Christmas. And her family doesn't even know she's on
her own.

'If I were your mum I'd want to know,' I venture, and
I see something flicker across Steph's face. Then I worry
that I've overstepped the mark, so I quickly add, 'Did I
see Damian just now?'

'Yes.' Steph's face falls. 'With *her*.'

'I thought she looked really ugly,' I say seriously, and
Steph bursts out laughing.

'Becky, you're deluded.'

'I'm not. She's gross.'

'She's about twenty-three and she's stunning. Did you
see her hair? Did you see her *bum*?'

I want to say, 'No, Damian's big fat hand was in the
way,' but that would be unhelpful. Instead I decide to
change the subject.

'Harvey was *amazing* in the play,' I say. 'He's got such
a gorgeous smile!'

'Oh, was he?' A wistful light comes over Steph's
face. 'I couldn't go. I've taken too much time off work
recently. But there'll be a DVD, won't there?'

I stare at her, stricken. She didn't even go. And there I

357

was, feeling sorry for myself because I didn't see Minnie in my costume.

'Steph, what are you doing tomorrow?' I ask on impulse. 'Would you and Harvey like to come to my gingerbread-house-making party?'

'Really?' Her face brightens. 'We'd love to!'

'Great!' I say. 'I'll text you the details. We're wearing Christmas jumpers and making gingerbread houses and . . . well, that's it.'

'Is it a family tradition?'

'Not exactly. It's . . . a new tradition.'

I won't add, 'Which I've just invented to reconcile my warring Christmas guests.'

'It's really kind of you to include us.' Steph suddenly reaches across the plastic table and clasps my hand. 'Thanks, Becky. For everything. Can I bring something tomorrow?'

'Nothing,' I say. 'Just yourselves.'

Steph shakes her head firmly. 'People always say that, but there must be something. What's the thing you most want, right now? And *not* world peace.'

'A vegan turkey,' I say honestly. 'If you've got one of those I'd be super-grateful.'

Steph stares at me in surprise. 'Are you vegan?'

'No, but my sister is,' I explain. 'And I ordered her a vegan turkey. But they cancelled, so I thought I'd make one . . .' I relate the whole sorry story and by the time I get to the painted loo rolls, Steph is laughing so hard she spurts tea down her nose.

'What are you *like*?' she says. 'Just serve risotto like the woman said! Have an easy life!'

358

'I don't want to have an easy life,' I say stubbornly. 'I want to serve a vegan turkey.'

'Well then, make it out of ...' Steph casts around. 'What can you make a turkey out of?'

'Exactly! That's the problem! I tried mushrooms and cardboard. That didn't work.'

There's silence – then Steph suddenly exclaims, 'Wait!' She plucks a packet of doughnuts out of her bag, peers at it, then jabs her finger at it triumphantly. 'Thought so. These are vegan. Use them!'

I follow her gaze and see a sticker printed with 'NEW RECIPE – NOW VEGAN!'

'Doughnuts?' I say, bewildered. 'I can't make a vegan Christmas turkey out of *doughnuts*.'

'Why not? What's wrong with doughnuts? Everyone loves doughnuts.' Steph starts giggling and that sets me off – and for a moment neither of us can talk for hysterics.

'OK, I'll do it,' I say at last, still snuffling. 'I'll do it. Why not?'

'And I'll help,' says Steph. Her face is flushed from laughing and she looks more positive than I've seen her for ages. 'I'll come early tomorrow and I'll bring the doughnuts – and we'll make the most kickass vegan doughnut turkey you've ever seen.'

NINETEEN

As I wait for Steph to arrive the next morning, I actually feel buoyant. The house looks utterly Christmassy. The Christmas tree lights are twinkling and all my garlands are firmly in place and I've hung the piñata up in the sitting room.

I'm also wearing a fantastic Mrs Santa outfit that I spotted in the supermarket yesterday. It's bright red with white fur and even has a little cape with a brilliant mobile-phone-sized pocket. Meanwhile, Minnie looks *adorable* in her Christmas jumper. It's decorated all over with satin ribbons tied in bows, just like a gift.

'You *are* a gift,' I say, giving her a tight hug, whereupon she wriggles free and says, 'Doughnuts?'

OK, so it was a mistake to tell Minnie about the doughnut turkey. She woke up at 5 a.m. and ran into the bedroom, demanding, 'DOUGHNUTS! Where are the DOUGHNUTS?'

'They're coming!' I say. 'Harvey and his mummy will be here soon.'

At that moment the doorbell rings, and there they are on the doorstep, both with festive jumpers and massive smiles and – oh wow, is that a *snowflake* drifting through the air?

'I know!' says Steph, following my excited gaze. 'Snow! Well . . . snow-ish,' she amends. 'I've seen about five snowflakes.'

'Five is better than none!' I say. 'Look, Minnie, snow! Snow at Christmas!'

The two children both peer obediently up at the sky and we all wait breathlessly . . . but it looks like the sky has shut up shop.

'Maybe the snow will come later,' I say at last. 'You can go and play.'

'Nice costume, Mrs Santa!' says Steph, as we go inside.

'What, this old thing?' I pluck at my red and white outfit with a grin. 'I just, you know, threw it on.'

Soon I'm making coffee for Steph while she rips the packaging off what looks like a million packets of doughnuts. She's also brought wooden skewers and cocktail sticks to fix them together.

'Happy Christmas,' she says, toasting her coffee cup with mine. 'We're going to nail this bastard.'

While Minnie and Harvey run around playing hide and seek, Steph and I start creating a doughnut construction, which it turns out is an incredibly calming and therapeutic activity. After we've used about forty doughnuts we stand back to assess our work.

'It's quite good,' I say, wanting to be positive. 'Except it doesn't look *that* much like a turkey.'

It doesn't look anything like a turkey, is the truth. It could be the Easter Bunny, or Mount Everest.

'It doesn't look much like a turkey *yet*,' rejoins Steph. 'But we haven't done the finishing touches. Have you got any Play-Doh?'

Within about ten minutes, Steph has commandeered all Minnie's Play-Doh and put the two children to work, rolling out shapes on the table. Soon she's adding orange Play-Doh wings to the doughnut turkey. Then black claws. And then big googly eyes.

'Oh my *God*,' I say, staring at it in a mixture of horror and admiration. 'It's looking at me.'

'And a beak . . .' says Steph, carefully adding a big pointy red Play-Doh shape. 'There. Behold . . . the vegan turkey!'

I must admit, it definitely looks like a turkey now. Or at least a bird. A creepy, freaky doughnut/Play-Doh bird that will probably give us all nightmares for life.

'Result!' I say, and lift my hand to high-five Steph. 'You've got a new career if you want it.'

'Purveyor of vegan turkeys,' says Steph with a nod. 'Yes, I think I'd do well.'

Her face is pink and there's a piece of Play-Doh stuck to her cheek and she looks like she's having the time of her life. 'What shall we call it, kids?' she adds.

'Peppa Pig,' suggests Harvey promptly, and I snort with laughter.

'OK, Peppa Pig it is,' I say. 'Peppa Pig the vegan turkey.'

'Is this your one and only turkey for Christmas?' asks Steph, suddenly looking a bit concerned. 'Or have you got a real one, too?'

'We've got a real one, too,' I say. 'At least, we haven't *got* it yet, but it's coming at five p.m. today.'

And if they substitute thirty jars of turkey paste, I add to myself, I will literally murder someone.

I carefully move the turkey to the counter and cover it with a cardboard box so that none of the guests will see it. Then I start laying out gingerbread kits all round the kitchen table. I can see the odd snowflake out of the window, and suddenly I *do* feel like I'm in a Christmas movie. God bless us every one. All that. Surely all my guests will feel the same?

There are still a few minutes till everyone's due to arrive, so I make some more coffee and pile some left-over doughnuts on to a plate. Then I adjourn with Steph to the sitting room while Harvey and Minnie start pushing monster trucks up and down the hall.

'So, let me fill you in on who's coming today,' I begin. 'There's Suze and Tarkie and their three, who you already know. There's my parents and their neighbours Janice and Martin. And there's my sister Jess, plus her husband Tom, *if* he's made it back from Chile. He's also the son of Janice and Martin,' I add. 'That's how Jess and Tom met.'

'Wow,' says Steph, taking all this in. 'So you're a pretty close-knit group.'

'I suppose so,' I nod.

'Nice big Christmas table.' She smiles.

'It will be.' I nod, then lean forward impulsively. 'Steph, please come too. You and Harvey. Come here for Christmas. There's plenty of room, we'd all love to see you . . .'

I break off as Steph shakes her head, smiling.

'Becky, you're very sweet,' she says, 'and I appreciate the offer . . . but I'm fine.' Her face suddenly shines. 'My parents and my sister are coming down. They'll be here later. They're bringing a turkey and we're all having Christmas together.'

'*What?*' I stare at her in delight. 'That's fantastic!'

'I know.' Steph pauses, then adds in a lower voice, 'I told them about Damian. After what you said yesterday. I went home and I called Mum straight away and . . .' Her eyes suddenly fill with tears and for a moment she can't speak. 'I don't know why I didn't tell them before,' she manages at last. 'It was stupid.'

'Because it's hard,' I say understandingly. 'Telling your family when you're in trouble is really hard.'

'It's the hardest.' She nods. 'You just don't want to admit it. I kept thinking, "If I don't hear it said aloud, maybe it's not true."'

'Oh, Steph.' I bite my lip.

'But the minute it was out, I felt better. I felt *stronger.*' Steph sips her coffee. 'So anyway, we'll be doing our own thing tomorrow. I'm glad I'll get to meet your family today, though. They sound great.'

'They are,' I say, a bit distracted, because Steph's words have struck home. She's confided in me so much – and now I want to confide in her.

'You know my sister Jess?' I say cautiously. 'The vegan one? I think she might be having problems in her marriage, too. But she won't say anything either. She's a very private person and she just clams up. It's really hard, when you want to help her.'

'Just be patient,' says Steph, nodding understandingly.

'If she's anything like me, she probably feels really vulnerable. I felt so ashamed that Damian had left.'

'*Ashamed?*' I say, appalled. 'Steph, *he* should be ashamed, not you!'

'I know.' She gives an abashed smile. 'It's not rational. But you want things to work, don't you? And you blame yourself if they don't. I'm sorry to hear about your sister,' she adds. 'That's really tough.'

'I know. So I was actually wondering . . . maybe if you get a chance while you're making the gingerbread houses, you could talk to her? Really discreetly?'

'Of course I will,' says Steph. 'I don't have any answers, but I sure as hell understand the problems. What time's everyone arriving, by the way?'

'Oh,' I say, glancing at my watch. 'Actually, I was expecting them by now.'

I'm just about to get out my phone to see if I've missed any messages when the sound of a text forestalls me. I take my phone from my pocket and find a new message from Jess.

Dear Becky

Sorry, but I won't be coming either today or tomorrow for personal reasons. I'm sorry if you have gone to a lot of trouble.

Happy Christmas
Jess (and Tom)

What?
She . . . *What?*

365

I almost can't breathe for disbelief. I've just spent all morning making a vegan turkey for Jess ... and she's not coming? She's *not coming*?

'Becky!' says Steph in alarm. 'What's happened? Are you OK?'

'Not really,' I say, trying to smile but utterly failing. 'No. I'm not really OK. You know my sister Jess, who I just mentioned? The one we've been making the vegan turkey for? Well, she's pulled out. She's not coming today *or* tomorrow. No warning. No good excuse. Just "personal reasons".'

Steph's hand flies to her mouth and she's silent for a few moments. 'Is she normally the flaky type?' she asks at last.

'No! She's totally unflaky! She's solid. She's ... she's *granite*. She never lets anyone down, ever.'

'Right.' I can see Steph thinking hard, and at last she meets my eyes. 'She's hurting. That's my guess. She can't face everyone, it's just too hard, it's too painful, so she's avoiding you all.'

'Oh God,' I say, stricken. 'What do I do? Should I go over there right now?'

'That might freak her out,' says Steph warningly. 'She has to be ready to talk about it, otherwise you'll make her clam up even more.'

'But she can't spend Christmas Day on her *own*!' I say in dismay, just as my phone rings.

'Is that her?' asks Steph at once, but I shake my head.

'It's my mum. I wonder if she knows.'

'Hi, Mum,' I say hurriedly. 'Are you on your way? Listen, I just got this weird text from Jess—'

'Oh love,' Mum interrupts before I can continue. 'Dad and I are both in the wars. Nasty virus. We can't come after all, I'm afraid.'

'Oh,' I say, taken aback. 'Well . . . will you be all right tomorrow?'

'I don't think so, love,' says Mum regretfully. 'We wouldn't want to give the children our germs. You have a lovely peaceful day without us. We'll do our Christmas presents another time.'

I stare at the phone, feeling a bit blindsided. Another time? But it's Christmas *tomorrow*. We're all ready. I've bought the Quality Street and the *Radio Times* and everything.

My lips are trembling. But I mustn't let Mum know how disappointed I am. It's not fair, when she's ill.

'Right,' I say, in the most upbeat tones I can manage. 'Well, that's a big shame, but the important thing is, you get better. So rest up, give my love to Dad, drink lots of fluids . . .'

'Of course we will, darling,' says Mum. 'And you have a super day tomorrow.'

'Mum, about that,' I say. 'I've just had this text from Jess, saying she's not coming either—'

'Love, I'd better go.' Mum cuts me off before I can say any more. '*So* sorry not to see you, darling, but have a happy Christmas!'

Before I can utter another syllable, she's rung off, and I stare into space, a bit dazed. Why did she have to hurry away like that?

'Becky?' says Steph after a few seconds. 'Becky, speak to me. What's happened?'

'It was my mum,' I say, forcing myself to focus. 'She's pulled out of Christmas too. She's ill. And so's my dad.'

'Oh *no*,' says Steph in horror. 'What bad luck.'

'I know.'

My phone bleeps with another text, and I look down to see if it's from Jess – but it's from Janice.

Dear Becky, I'm so sorry for the late notice, but Martin and I have decided to spend Christmas quietly at home, if that's all right, but I do hope you have a lovely day. Janice xx

I stare at the words, my head reeling. I don't understand. What's happening?

'Tell me,' demands Steph. 'Becky, you look dreadful.'

'I *feel* dreadful,' I gulp. 'Everyone's pulling out of Christmas. On Christmas Eve. With no warning. For no reason.'

'Oh Becky.' Steph looks dismayed. 'After all your hard work. I mean . . . could you reschedule? Have a gathering when everyone's feeling better?'

'You don't understand,' I say desperately. 'Why are they all pulling out?'

'Well,' says Steph warily. 'Your parents are ill . . . your sister's feeling sensitive, we're guessing . . .'

'What about Janice?'

'I don't know Janice.' She grimaces apologetically. 'Sorry.'

'Does everyone think I can't host Christmas?'

'What?' Steph stares at me. 'Don't be ridiculous!'

'Suze thought I couldn't do Christmas,' I say, barely

hearing her. 'She said maybe she should host it instead. Has she told everyone it's going to be a rubbish Christmas?'

'Becky!' Steph sounds staggered. 'You're being paranoid! People get ill. They pull out of things, OK? These things happen.'

'People don't all pull out of the same thing within five minutes,' I retort, my voice rising in distress. 'That doesn't happen! It's not statistically possible. OK? It's not statistically *possible*.'

I can see Steph opening her mouth to object, but then she seems to think better of it.

'Suze is going to pull out too,' I say miserably. 'I know she is.'

'You're mad,' says Steph robustly. 'Of course she's not. This isn't some secret plot, it's just bad luck. You've got an amazing group of family and friends, they all sound really supportive and loving—'

'They're not loving!' I admit in despair. 'They're at each other's throats! Everyone's been fighting! That's why I threw this gingerbread party, to try to reconcile everybody.'

'Oh,' says Steph, halted. 'Right. I didn't realize.'

'Maybe *that's* why everyone's pulling out.' I feel a fresh wave of despair. 'They can't face sitting round the same table. But don't they understand, I was trying to bring about peace?'

My phone rings and we both jump a mile. And even though I was expecting it, my stomach crashes down as I see *Suze* on the display. Silently I turn it so that Steph can see.

369

'Answer it,' she says, looking anxious. 'It might not be that.'

I let the phone ring twice more, while I try to compose myself. Then I press Answer and say, in a fake, high-pitched voice, 'Oh hi, Suze, are you on your way to the gingerbread party?'

'Oh hi, Bex,' Suze replies, sounding flustered and fake, too. 'Um, sorry, I'm not sure we can make it. I've got this last-minute Christmas-shopping emergency that just came up.'

I was right.

My chest has started to ache. I hadn't realized how much I was hoping *not* to be right.

'No problem,' I say numbly. 'It doesn't matter. It was only a . . . you know. Doesn't matter at all.'

'And, um, about tomorrow.' Suze sounds really uncomfortable, as though she's standing on one leg and twisting the other around it, which she probably is. 'About Christmas. Tarkie suddenly said he really wants us to go to his Uncle Rufus after all. Sorry to pull out so late, Bex, but . . . You don't mind if we do that instead?'

And then there were none.

My chest starts to ache even more, and my eyes are hot, but somehow I keep my composure.

'Right.' I swallow. 'No, of *course* I don't mind. You must go! Have fun!'

'You really don't mind?' she says anxiously.

'Of course not!' I say shrilly. 'In fact, it's a relief. You're right, hosting Christmas is a total stressmare, so this way . . .'

370

'Exactly,' says Suze, sounding relieved. '*Much* easier for you.'

She didn't think I could do it. I can tell from her tone of voice. She didn't think I could host Christmas. Two tears suddenly slide down my cheeks, but I try to ignore them.

'Absolutely!' I say brightly. 'It'll be great! So, have a wonderful day with Uncle Rufus and let's catch up . . . whenever. Happy Christmas, give my love to everyone . . . Bye!'

I turn the phone off, then stare ahead, my head prickling, unable to speak.

My entire Christmas has just disintegrated in the space of ten minutes.

TWENTY

Steph does her best. She hugs me hard. She tells me that it's all just random coincidence and that my friends and family *do* love me, of *course* they do. She relates the story of a disastrous childhood Christmas when her uncle got stuck in Wales, and makes me (sort of) laugh.

Then we get a notification that the school has uploaded the Nativity play video on to the website and Steph quickly suggests we watch it on her iPad as a distraction.

It is a distraction. Kind of. But it's also a painful reminder of what Christmas is all about. As I watch all the adorable children lisping their way through 'Away In A Manger', I start to feel unbearably sentimental. And sentimental is quite close to sad. And sad is quite close to weeping uncontrollably, sinking to your knees and crying out to the heavens, 'Whyyyyyy?'

Meanwhile Steph is riveted by the play. As Minnie, Harvey and George appear for their three kings act, she gazes at Harvey as though she wants to eat him up.

'He was brilliant,' I say, as eventually the three kings make way on stage for a throng of angels.

'They were all brilliant,' says Steph. 'Minnie was priceless! Shall we watch their bit again?'

We rewind and start again from the kings' entrance, and this time I can see Steph taking in the details more closely.

'Wait,' she says suddenly. 'Wait.' She presses Pause and stares intently at the screen. 'Becky, you said the costume you gave me was a spare.'

'Oh,' I say, taken off-guard. 'Yes. Totally! It was.'

'But look, Minnie's just wearing a scarf you've pinned on to a dress,' says Steph, squinting even more closely. 'Whereas Harvey's costume is a bloody work of art. I mean, *look* at those sequins.' She turns to me in sudden distress. 'You gave me Minnie's costume, didn't you?'

'No!' I say automatically. 'God! I mean . . . It doesn't matter. The costumes aren't the point. It was a lovely play! Let's keep on watching.' But I'm not sure Steph even hears me.

'I was so frazzled that day,' she's saying, almost to herself. 'I didn't even *think* . . . But why would you have a spare costume just waiting in a carrier bag? It makes no sense. I'm such an *idiot*. Minnie should have been in that costume.'

As though reading our minds, Minnie looks up from the game she's been playing with Harvey and comes over to look at the iPad.

'That is *my* costume,' she says with deliberate emphasis, jabbing her finger at the frozen image of Harvey. 'Myyyy costume. We gave it to Harvey.'

Honestly. Remind me never to try to escape from the Nazis with Minnie in tow. I meet Steph's eye and give a sheepish shrug.

'I know you did,' Steph says to Minnie. 'And we're very grateful, aren't we, Harvey? Because your mummy worked hard on that costume. She sewed it for you, didn't she?'

Minnie thinks for a moment, then shakes her head and says, 'Mummy *pinned* it. The pin went in *me*. And I said "Ow!"'

'Ow!' echoes Harvey sympathetically.

'Ow! Pin!' yells Minnie, her face lighting up with glee, poking her finger at Harvey. 'Pin! Pin!'

My daughter is such a drama queen. I grazed her lightly with a pin, once, when I was fitting her. *Grazed* her.

Still yelling, 'Pin! Pin!' Minnie and Harvey chase each other out of the room, and Steph exhales, long and hard.

'Becky,' she says jerkily. 'I don't know what to say.'

As I look up, I see to my horror that her eyes are full of tears. No. No. She cannot start, or I'll collapse in a soggy mess.

'It's no big deal,' I say in a rush. 'Forget it.'

'It *is* a big deal. It's one of the most generous things anyone's ever done for me.'

'Well,' I say, looking furiously out of the window. 'I mean, anyone would have done it. So.'

'You don't deserve this.' Steph sounds suddenly impassioned. 'You *so* don't deserve this, Becky.' Her phone bleeps with a text and she looks at it with an impatient sound – then winces. 'Oh God. My family are here. Early. They're outside my house. But I don't want to leave you.'

'You must go!' I say at once. 'Go! Have a wonderful Christmas.'

'Is there anyone you could call? Like . . .' She trails away awkwardly and I know what she's thinking. Who can I call? My closest friends and family? I feel a fresh spasm of pain but force myself to smile.

'It's fine. Luke's on his way back. He'll be here soon. Steph, you need to go and see your family. Enjoy them.'

Steph gives me a last, agonized look, but then gets to her feet and scoops up Harvey. I can hear the excitement in her voice as she says, 'Gran's here, darling! At our house!'

After a tight hug, she's gone, and it's just me and Minnie, waiting for Luke. I put on *The Snowman* and snuggle down beside Minnie on the sofa, trying to feel cosy. But my head feels all hot and heavy.

I suddenly see Minnie's Grinch book lying on the floor, and pick it up, hearing Luke's voice in my head. *Whatever the Grinch can steal . . . that's not Christmas.* I flip through the copy until I reach the page with all the Whos holding hands and singing. The page that represents happiness. Togetherness. Christmas spirit. I stare at it until the illustration blurs and the words swim and my head feels heavier than ever.

I've got the presents and the decorations and even the vegan turkey. But I haven't got the friends and family. I haven't got the one thing that Christmas is all about.

And now I can't keep up the pretence any more. My

head sinks down and I sob silently into my knees so Minnie won't see that anything's amiss.

How can my first ever Christmas at home be like this? Where did I go wrong?

My shoulders are heaving and my nose is running and my eyes are squeezed shut . . . and when I hear Luke's voice it's as though in a dream.

'Becky?' I feel his arms come around me. 'Becky! Oh my God! What's happened?'

'Oh. Hi.' I hastily lift my head, rubbing my face. 'It's all fine. You know. It's just . . . um . . . Everyone's pulled out of Christmas, so I was a bit disappointed. But it'll be fine.'

'Pulled out?' Luke stares at me blankly.

'Cancelled.'

'Who's cancelled?'

'Everyone. Mum and Dad, Janice, Suze . . . Jess . . .'

For a moment, Luke seems incapable of speech. Then he says, in the polite parental voice we use in front of Minnie, 'Becky, could you come into the kitchen for a moment?'

I follow him in and we close the door. Then Luke wheels round.

'What the fuck? What the *fuck*? Start from the beginning. What happened?'

'Well,' I falter, 'first Jess sent a text saying she doesn't want to come to ours for personal reasons. And then Mum said she and Dad are ill. And Janice said she wants to spend a quiet day with Martin, and Suze said she's going to Tarkie's Uncle Rufus.'

'This is beyond belief,' says Luke in quiet, ominous

tones. 'This is beyond *belief*.' His face has actually gone white. I don't often see Luke this livid. 'You don't pull out of Christmas on Christmas Eve. You don't treat people like that.'

'If they don't want to come, it's their choice,' I say miserably.

'Fuck that!' explodes Luke. 'They need to explain themselves. I'm not having this, Becky. I'm not having it. You have worked bloody hard at this Christmas and they are *not* treating you like this.'

'You helped too,' I say, to be fair, but Luke shakes his head.

'I haven't taken it on like you've taken it on. It's your shout. It's your creation. It's your dedication. You *don't* deserve this.'

Already he's taking out his phone and dialling. After a moment he frowns and says, 'Voicemail . . . Hi Jane,' he says shortly. 'Luke here. I'd be grateful if you'd call me.'

He leaves the same message for Suze, Janice and Jess, then puts his phone away, taut-faced. The kitchen seems very flat, suddenly. Not Christmassy at all.

'D'you want a coffee?' says Luke at last. 'Or a drink?'

I shake my head, feeling out of energy. Luke nods, then turns on the kettle. As he does, his attention is caught by the cardboard box. He lifts it and recoils at the sight of the doughnut turkey.

'Jesus. What the hell's *that*?'

'A vegan turkey,' I say dispiritedly. 'It's called Peppa Pig.'

'Right.'

I can see Luke attempting to process this, then abandoning the attempt and replacing the box. He makes a cup of coffee and stirs it slowly.

'So you didn't speak to any of them? Take me through it again.'

'I spoke to Suze and Mum. Suze sounded weird. Kind of shifty. Not like Suze at all. Luke, I think something's up,' I say despairingly. 'I know it sounds paranoid, but I do. They all phoned up within about ten minutes of each other. It was like . . . a coordinated strike.'

Luke exhales slowly, his eyes distant. His rage has abated and his face is creased with thought.

'But what the *hell* would make everyone cancel Christmas?'

'I don't know!' I raise my arms hopelessly. 'I've been trying and trying to think. Is it still because of Flo? Or some other row? Have they all got a secret WhatsApp group I don't know about? I feel like everyone knows something I don't,' I conclude desperately. 'That's how I feel. And no one will tell me.'

Luke sips his coffee silently for a moment, then meets my eyes.

'OK,' he says. 'Who's the straightest-talking person in your family?'

'Jess,' I say without hesitation.

'Exactly. Jess. We'll get it out of Jess.' He takes out his phone again and dials. 'Voicemail. What's her landline?'

'It's home,' I remind him. 'Mum and Dad's number in Oxshott.'

'Of course.' He dials again, listens intently – then says, 'The line's busy. She's home.' He strides to the door of the kitchen and calls out, 'Minnie! Sweetheart! Get your shoes on. And your coat . . . We're going to see Jess right now,' he says to me, his jaw set. 'And we're not leaving till she tells us what's up.'

It takes half an hour to reach Oxshott and as we near the house, my stomach is jumping. I keep expecting the worst. Except what *is* the worst?

Everyone's having Christmas together, without us, because they suddenly hate us. No, they always did hate us. Our whole life has been a lie and a sham. Oh God, no, that can't be it. I feel a bit deranged, to be honest.

When we arrive, we get out of the car silently, approach the house and Luke rings the bell. I'm secretly half hoping no one will answer, but after a while the front door opens and Jess stares at us.

'Hi.' She looks from me to Luke and back again. 'I didn't expect to see you here.'

'No,' says Luke curtly. 'Well, we didn't expect everyone to pull out of Christmas. May we come in, please?'

'Yes,' says Jess after a pause, and she silently shows us into the sitting room.

It looks the same as it always does. Jess hasn't imposed anything of her own, as far as I can see, apart from some geology books on the coffee table and a gym mat rolled up in the corner with the heftiest-looking dumb-bells I've ever seen. We all sit down and I resume playing *The Snowman* on the iPad for Minnie. Then Luke glances at me as though encouraging me to speak.

'Jess,' I begin. 'I know you said you had personal reasons for not wanting to spend Christmas with us. And I respect those reasons. I do. But we find it quite coincidental that everyone pulled out of Christmas at the same moment.' My voice trembles. 'We find it weird. And . . . and hurtful. And what I want to know is, why?'

There's silence, and Jess peers at me as though trying to read my expression.

'You're upset,' she says at length.

'Yes! Of course I'm upset!'

'You're not relieved?'

'Relieved?' I gape at her. 'My whole Christmas is ruined! Why would I be *relieved*?'

There's another long silence, during which Jess's eyes flicker between me and Luke as though she's performing some internal algorithm. Then she frowns and says, 'Luke, things have clearly misfired. You need to speak up. Tell Becky what you did. Be honest.'

'Luke?' I say blankly, then turn to face him. '*Luke*?'

'I don't know what you mean, Jess,' says Luke, looking perplexed. 'What did I do?'

'Your email,' says Jess flatly.

'What email?'

'To Suze. She forwarded it to all of us. We've all seen it.'

'What email to Suze?' expostulates Luke. 'What are you *talking* about? I haven't sent any emails. I've been away, I came back to find Becky devastated and that's all I know. What's going on?'

There's another silence, and Jess's eyes flicker between us again. Then she reaches for her phone, scrolls down for a few moments and passes it to Luke.

'You didn't write this email?'

As Luke peers at the screen, his eyes nearly pop out.

'Lukebrandonwork@LBC.com,' he says, aghast. 'That's not my email address, for a start. What the *hell*?'

I'm not looking at the email address, I'm feverishly scanning the text.

Dear Suze

I don't know how to put this, but I'm going to ask you to withdraw from Christmas, as tactfully as possible. Please find an excuse, any excuse. Becky is beyond frazzled, miserable and dreading the day. We always planned a quiet Christmas, just the three of us, until everyone invited themselves over. Since then, Becky has been so stressed out I'm worried about her, what with all your demands and WhatsApps. She's tearful, exhausted and resentful of you all . . .

I lift my head in agitation, my cheeks burning. Is that what everyone thinks?

'Jess, I'm not resentful,' I say. 'I'm not exhausted. I don't know what this is, but it's not me . . .'

'I didn't write this.' Luke flicks it angrily. 'I did *not* write this, this is absolute bollocks . . .'

I'm already scrolling down to read the ending:

Above all, do NOT contact Becky or let her know I have emailed. She is very proud and will deny everything, thus jeopardizing her health. Believe you me, what Becky needs is for Christmas to be discreetly cancelled. I will leave it with you.

Best,
Luke

I stare at the words, my heart beating hard. Something's chiming . . . something's ringing a bell . . .

Believe you me . . . believe you me . . .

'Oh my God!' My head jerks up. 'Nadine! Nadine sent this!'

'Nadine?' Luke stares at me, astounded. *'Nadine?'*

'Isn't that your new friend?' Jess crinkles her brow, looking puzzled.

'She's not our friend,' I say fervently. 'She's our enemy. She hates us. And she knew.' I suddenly turn to Luke. 'She *knew* this was the way to get back at us. We talked about Christmas, remember? She knew I was stressed out.' I feverishly count off on my fingers. 'She knew everyone had invited themselves for Christmas. She knew about the WhatsApps.' I jab at the email. 'No one else says "Believe you me". *And* she's into tech. It was her. Didn't you see the way she glared at us before she left? She was out for revenge.'

'Jesus.' Luke breathes out.

I suddenly recall Nadine's syrupy voice, that evening at the cottage. *You'll get your Christmas with your family and friends, Becky.*

She knew what was most precious to me – and she tried to take it away. We underestimated her.

'She's worse than the Grinch,' I say darkly. 'She's Grinchier than the Grinch. The Grinch only stole stuff. She stole *people.'*

'But we shouldn't have let ourselves be stolen!' exclaims Jess, in sudden distress. 'Becky, I'm so sorry—'

'So, what happened?' I swing round to her, sounding

382

hurt. 'You read this email and all just said, "Oh, OK, let's cancel"?'

'No!' says Jess, looking shocked. 'Of course not. We talked about it extensively. For days. But in the end we all agreed to pull out of Christmas, using different reasons so you wouldn't guess the truth.'

'You might have decided not to all contact Becky at once,' says Luke dryly. 'Slightly gave the game away.'

'But why did you *believe* it?' I demand, my voice almost a wail.

'Because it seemed . . . plausible,' says Jess uncomfortably. 'You have seemed stressed recently, Becky. You seemed rattled at Minnie's birthday party. And Suze said you were babbling about putting fish under a duvet . . .'

'I was rattled at the party because Flo was a nightmare!' I say defensively. 'And my cake was a disaster and Nadine had a go at Luke on the doorstep. *That's* why. And the fish under the duvet had a totally reasonable explanation. And anyway,' I add, gathering steam, 'even if I have been a bit stressed out, *everyone* gets stressed out by Christmas! It doesn't mean you *cancel* it! I mean, didn't anyone try to call Luke?' I can't help sounding accusing, and Jess flinches.

'Yes!' she says. 'Of course! Suze did. But he was out of reach.'

'Nadine knew I'd be travelling,' Luke puts in wryly.

'Suze left a message for you though, Luke,' adds Jess – and I stiffen.

'Message? What message?' I swivel to face Luke. 'Did you get a message?'

I can see a kind of light dawning in Luke's face.

'Ah,' he says evasively. 'Right. Yes. There might have been a message from Suze. But it began "Luke, about Christmas", and I thought I could probably leave it till I got back.'

I half want to exclaim, 'So this is all *your* fault!' But of course it's not. Nor Suze's fault. Nor any of theirs. I look up to see both Jess and Luke watching me anxiously, and feel a sudden prickle in my nose . . .

'When everyone pulled out, I felt . . . I thought . . .' I swallow hard. 'I didn't know what to think.'

There's silence, then Jess comes and puts a hand on my shoulder.

'We didn't know what to think, either,' she says. 'If it's any consolation, we've all been beating ourselves up.' She summons WhatsApp on her phone and shows me a group entitled 'IS BECKY OK??'

I knew it! I wasn't paranoid. There *is* a secret WhatsApp group.

I begin to scan the messages – and feel little prickles of shock as I read them.

Janice

This is all my fault. I should NEVER have invited Flo to Becky's house. I blame myself.

Jane

It's MY fault, love. We shouldn't have moved to Shoreditch.

Janice

We don't need a piñata!!! Why couldn't I see what I was doing with my endless unreasonable demands???

Suze

We all put so much pressure on Becky. I feel REALLY bad that we invited ourselves for Christmas, I never even thought about it.

Jane

It's come back to me now – when I asked Becky to host Christmas she said she was terrified by the idea. She said it would give her sleepless nights. Those were her ACTUAL WORDS, Janice, love. 'Sleepless nights'.

I pause, puzzled. I'm sure Mum's invented this. I'm sure I didn't say it would give me sleepless nights.

Jane

I didn't listen to my OWN DAUGHTER IN HER TIME OF STRESS.

Janice

Love, don't feel bad. We're all guilty.

'Jess . . .' I raise my head. 'This is insane. We have to put everyone right.'

'Yes.' Jess nods and takes the phone. She swiftly types a message, then looks up. 'You've had enough hassle, Becky. We'll sort it. And just to double check . . .' She hesitates. 'We're back on for Christmas at yours, yes?'

'Yes,' I say firmly. '*Yes!*'

As Jess types a follow-up message, I watch her fingers, feeling a bit overwhelmed that all these conversations have been going on.

'On the plus side, at least everyone's talking again,' I say as she finishes, and Jess meets my eye with a little grin.

'Even better, your mum and Janice have totally bonded over fretting about you. Flo's out of the picture.'

'Really?' I say, my spirits lifting. 'Well, there's a silver lining!'

'I'll make some tea,' says Luke cheerfully. 'Come on, Minnie, you help me. You can bring the iPad,' he adds, as she opens her mouth to protest.

'This Nadine character sounds . . .' Jess shakes her head wonderingly. 'Vindictive.'

'I think she's just a really, *really* entitled person,' I say, frowning in thought. 'She thought she was entitled to Luke's money. When she couldn't get that, she decided she was entitled to us having a miserable Christmas. Anyway,' I add hastily, as Jess winces. 'Let's not dwell. We found out in time, so . . . No harm done.'

'Thank God you came round.' Jess gives a sudden massive yawn and claps a hand over her mouth. 'Sorry. *Sorry.*'

'Oh God,' I say, suddenly stricken by remorse. 'Are you tired, Jess? Are you not well?'

I've been so obsessed by Christmas I haven't paid proper attention to Jess. But now I survey her, she looks terrible. Pale and thin. And kind of agitated. Her eyes keep flicking away from mine, as though there's some massive distraction in her head.

'Jess, speaking of wellbeing . . .' I say in softer tones, 'how *are* you?'

Jess gazes at me silently. 'You're still worried about me, aren't you?'

There are huge shadows under her eyes, I notice with a twinge. Just like under Steph's. Oh God, here am I, selfishly worrying about Christmas, when it's *Jess* who looks as if she's on the edge.

'Yes,' I say bluntly. 'I am. Jess, I know it's none of my business, but I was just talking to a friend who's had . . . difficulties. She said you might be feeling so vulnerable you couldn't open up. And I just want you to know that if you're hurting—'

'You think I'm hurting.' Jess cuts me off in a weird, constricted voice. 'Because of Tom's infidelity.'

I stare back at her, breathless. Is she going to lower her defences, finally?

'Becky,' she continues in the same weird voice. 'Haven't the events of today taught you *anything* about making assumptions?'

'What?' I say, not following, and there's another strange beat of silence – then she seems to relent.

'I've got something to show you.' She gets to her feet and beckons me to follow. 'We're coming upstairs,' she calls.

'Who are you calling to?' I ask, puzzled, as we begin to mount the stairs.

'Tom.'

'Tom?' I echo, flabbergasted. 'Tom's *here*?'

'Of course he's here. I told you he was coming home for Christmas.'

'Right,' I say hurriedly. 'Of course.' But my mind is flailing. I can't catch up.

'You're astute, Becky,' says Jess, reaching the top of the stairs. 'I have been keeping something from you. From all of you. We were just so anxious not to jinx it.'

'What?' A breathless hope is growing in me that I don't even want to articulate, just in case— 'What is it, Jess? *What?*'

'Hi, Becky.' Tom greets me from the doorway. He's tanned and smiling, although there are shadows under his eyes, too. 'Come and see.'

Oh my God . . . *oh my God . . . it can't be . . .*

Tom leads me into the spare room, and I stop dead, tears flooding my eyes. In the double bed, fast asleep, is a child with dark curls.

'This is our new son, Santiago. We arrived late last night. Long flight.' Tom grimaces. 'But worth it.'

I realize I've grabbed Jess's hand without even meaning to. I can't take my eyes off Santiago. He's about four or five, I guess. He has long lashes and golden skin and he's dressed in a beige T-shirt with *Recycled* printed on the back.

'I had no idea it was so imminent,' I manage at last. 'Congratulations. *So* many congratulations.'

I fling my arms round Jess and then Tom, and as I draw back we're all a bit shiny-eyed.

'We had no idea either,' says Tom. 'We had almost no notice. The news came through, Jess flew straight out . . .'

'You've been to Chile and back?' I stare at Jess.

'Of course,' she says, without a flicker.

'We did the paperwork,' continues Tom, 'had all the meetings that needed to be had, then got pretty much straight on a plane, and . . .'

'We haven't had any sleep.'

'We don't need sleep.' Tom puts an arm round Jess.

They both look shattered and joyful. They look

exactly like parents with a new baby. *How* did I not realize this the minute I set foot through the door?

'So, how long have you . . . I mean how did you . . . ?' I'm floundering to even know what question I want to ask.

'We were matched a while ago, but we didn't know when it would be finalized. And we didn't want to tell anyone,' Jess adds a little defensively. 'Not until it was definite.'

'Jess already had her lectures booked.' Tom takes over the story. 'So we agreed she would go back to the UK and I'd stay, just in case there was some news before Christmas.'

'We were just trying to wait patiently,' says Jess. 'Wasn't easy.'

That's why Jess has been so tense. It wasn't anything else. I'm an utter *moron*.

Also, I blame Suze. She totally encouraged me in the whole khaki hotpants theory.

'Jess, I'm so sorry,' I stutter. 'I know I slightly got the wrong end of the stick . . .'

'Did you think *I* was having an affair or *Jess* was having an affair?' asks Tom wryly. 'We weren't quite clear.'

He meets eyes with Jess and she rolls hers expressively. Oh God, this is mortifying. Partly because Jess and Tom look more in sync and in love with each other than I've ever seen them.

'What did Janice and Martin say?' I hastily change the subject. 'They must be overjoyed.'

'They don't know yet,' says Jess, after glancing at Tom.

'They went out first thing before we could catch them, and we didn't want to tell them by phone. So . . . you're the first person to meet Santiago, Becky.'

'I'm the *first*?' My throat is suddenly thick. 'Well . . . I'm honoured.'

I put out a hand and touch one of Santiago's curls, not wanting to wake him, but unable to resist.

'Welcome, Santiago,' I say softly.

'He can't hear,' says Jess matter-of-factly. 'He's profoundly deaf.'

'Oh,' I say, halted. 'Right. I see. Well . . . we'll learn sign language then. We'll teach him. We'll do everything he needs. Just let me know what I can do.'

As I stand up, I'm blinking hard, because a moment ago I didn't even know Santiago existed, but now I'm determined to smooth his path for him, throughout his life, whatever it takes.

'It's wonderful.' I gaze at Jess and Tom. 'I'm so happy for you. And just in time for Christmas,' I add with a sentimental sigh. 'That makes it so much more special.'

'I disagree,' says Jess calmly. 'It would have been equally special on any other day of the year.'

I bite my lip, trying not to laugh. That's *so* Jess. And she's right, of course she is. But I think I'm a bit right, too.

Chats

SUZE & BEX

Suze
Bex!!! OMG!!!!! I feel TERRIBLE!!! Xxxxxxxx

Suze
I can't believe I believed that email!!

Suze
I'm never believing ANY emails, EVER again.

Suze
We thought you were having a breakdown!!

Suze
Nadine's EVIL.

Suze
I can't believe you were going to have multiplayer sex with her.

Suze
You didn't have multiplayer sex, did you? Or did you actually? You can tell me. I won't judge.

TWENTY-ONE

As we arrive home later, I feel emotionally drained. I've been trading WhatsApps with Suze all the way back in the car, assuring her that yes, I will forgive her and that yes, Christmas is still on. And no, we didn't have multi-player sex and yes, I would tell her what it's like.

As we get inside the door, Luke turns to Minnie.

'Sweetheart, I need to do some last-minute shopping for Mummy. So in a moment we'll go out while Mummy puts her feet up and watches a Christmas movie. Sound good, Becky?'

'Sounds great,' I say in heartfelt tones.

I walk into the sitting room and look around at all the festive decorations, lights and presents, feeling content for the first time in ages. The cancelled Christmas is uncancelled. Everything's OK after all. Maybe I really can put my feet up and relax. And I'm just wondering idly where I left the remote, when a flash of grey shoots past my field of vision.

What?

Surely that wasn't—

It scuttles past again and this time I can see it properly and I gasp in petrified horror. A mouse. An actual *mouse*. In our *house*? On Christmas *Eve*?

'Didn't you get the memo?' I address it furiously. '"Not a creature was stirring, not even a *mouse*." Argh!' I can't help shrieking as it runs about an inch from my foot. I'm quite freaked out by mice, actually.

At that moment Minnie comes in and my heart sinks. I *really* don't want her going to school and telling everyone we've got mice. But too late, she's seen it.

'HAMPER!' she yells, her whole face suffused with joy. 'Look, Mummy, a HAMPER!'

Hamper? I peer at her with a confused frown. What's she on about?

The mouse scurries near my foot again and I resist the urge to shriek, because shrieking at mice is not feminist.

'Hamper!' Minnie runs after the mouse. 'HAM-PER! Father Christmas will bring me a hamper,' she adds chattily. 'He will bring a hamper in the chimney. HAMPER! Come here!' As the mouse dashes past again, she holds her arms out as though to hug it while I stare at her, unable to move, her words slowly unravelling in my mind.

Hamper. Not picnic hamper. But *hamster*. She's been asking for a hamster, all this time, steadfastly, without swerving. A *hamster*.

As the frightful truth dawns on me I feel icy all over. It's Christmas Eve and the shops are about to shut and only now am I realizing what my daughter wants for

393

Christmas. The number one nightmare of all Christmas nightmares is coming true.

As calmly as I can, I walk out of the room into the hall – then grab Luke and pull him frantically into the coat cupboard.

'Luke,' I gabble. 'Disaster. Minnie wants a hamster for Christmas.'

'A *hamster*?' He stares at me. 'But I thought—'

'I know,' I cut him off desperately, 'I know. No time. I'll go and get one while you take her out. Also, we *need* to work on this baby talk of hers,' I add – and I see the truth suddenly hit him.

'Shit.' He bites his lip. 'Shit. Actually, that's quite funny.'

'It's not! Because we don't have a hamster! At least – you haven't bought me one, have you?' I add in a gasp of hope, because Luke once joked that he would buy me a hamster for Christmas and call it Ermintrude.

'No, I haven't, I'm afraid.' Luke looks amused. 'Becky, *relax*,' he adds, putting his hands on my shoulders. 'The shops are still open. There's that pet shop in Ellerton Road.'

'OK,' I say, nodding feverishly. 'Yes. I'll go there. But what if they don't have one?'

'They will. All pet shops have hamsters. Or shall I get it?'

'No, you can't! You're taking Minnie out! She'll see! I'll get it. I'm going. Now!'

'Dressed as Mrs Santa?' queries Luke.

'*Now* you're interested in my clothes?' I hurl back at him. 'They're not exactly the priority right now, Luke!'

I grab my phone and bag, and leg it to my car. A hamster. I can't believe it. A bloody hamster.

As I drive to Ellerton Road, my heart is racing. This should not be happening. It's all wrong. I started Christmas shopping *early*. I was *organized*. Buying Minnie's present was the first thing I did! The first bloody thing! Yet now here I am racing around on Christmas Eve in a panic, exactly like I *didn't want to be.*

I park the car, sprint along the pavement to the pet shop and stop dead with shock. Closed. *Closed.* It can't be closed. How can they close a pet shop on Christmas Eve? What about all the last-minute hamsters?

I rattle the door, just in case, but I know it's fruitless. As I turn away, I'm almost gibbering with panic and an old lady with a shopping trolley looks at me curiously.

'There's a pet shop in Bickersly, dear,' she says. 'Woodford Street. You could try that.'

'Right!' I say. 'Thanks!'

I don't even know where Bickersly is, but I can find it on sat nav. I follow a weird route through villages I've never seen before, and find myself in a small side road with three shops in a tiny parade. One's called Pete's Pets and the lights are on. Thank God, thank *God.*

As I dash in, I can't help feeling dubious. The only pet shops I've been in before, with Suze, have been large and open plan and wholesome looking. This one is staffed by a guy covered with tattoos who looks like he probably breeds the hamsters for use in Satanic rituals. But I don't exactly have a choice, so I approach him with a polite smile.

'Hello, Mrs Santa,' he says with a smirk, eyeing my outfit up and down.

'Hello,' I say. 'I'd like—'

'We're closing soon,' he interrupts flatly. 'You better be quick.'

'No problem. I'd like a hamster. And a cage. And food,' I add as an afterthought. 'And whatever a hamster needs.'

'OK.' He nods. 'What kind of hamster?'

'The . . . hamster kind.'

He gives me a look and leads me to a plastic cage, full of hamsters in individual partitions, all squirming about and eating food and doing hamster things. 'Take your pick.'

'Right,' I say, trying to sound keener than I feel.

I mean, they're basically rodents. I'm choosing to introduce a rodent into my house. But Minnie will love it, I remind myself. I have to focus on that.

I wonder what colour she'd like. Maybe Luke could subtly find out? I get out my phone to call him – but there are no bars on my display. Drat.

'Yeah, our signal's dodgy,' says the guy. 'So which one do you want?'

I peer at the hamsters, trying to see them through Minnie's eyes.

'Maybe that one,' I say, pointing to a beige one.

'That's a male Syrian hamster. Want to have a closer look?'

He picks it up and proffers it to me – and I try to suppress my revulsion. 'You ever looked after a hamster before?' he adds with a narrowed glance.

'Er . . . no. But I'll follow all the guidelines,' I say hurriedly. 'I'll take good care of it. I promise.'

He gestures for me to take the hamster, and gingerly I do so. It's furry and snuffly and scrabbly, with really sharp claws.

'Argh!' I say, as the hamster suddenly ends up on the table and starts running away.

'Don't bloody let *go*!' says the guy in consternation, scooping the hamster back up.

'I didn't mean to!' I say, mortified. 'Sorry. It just took me by surprise.'

'You shouldn't buy it if you can't handle it,' he says disapprovingly, and I feel a spike of panic. Is he going to say I'm not fit to be a hamster owner? Is there some test and I've just failed?

'I can,' I say fervently. 'I can handle it. I promise.'

'OK, so hamster, cage, bedding, food . . .' He pauses. 'You want any accessories?'

My head pops up in sudden interest. Ooh. Accessories?

The guy shows me to a shelf of stuff, and I get quite excited. Who knew hamsters had so much gear? I choose an exercise ball, a 'hamster cottage' and a really cool tube contraption for the hamster to scamper about in. And I'm just dithering over a hamster see-saw when a terrible thought strikes me: my shopping delivery. My turkey. *Shit*. In all the flurry, I totally forgot. It's coming in half an hour. I need to get home, pronto.

'OK,' I say hastily. 'I've chosen. Done.'

I pay for everything, then take it all out to the car in several journeys, because it's pretty bulky. The last thing to take out is the hamster itself, in its cage, and I'm about to lift it up off the floor when I have a sudden idea. I'll take a quick picture and text it to Luke! I need to practise handling it, anyway.

I get down on my knees, reach for the squirmy little thing and get it out, trying not to flinch. There. I'm better at this already. I mean, he's quite cute, with his snuffly little nose. We need to think of a good name for him.

I take a photo, and I'm carefully lowering him back into the cage when the guy suddenly bellows, 'Piss *off*!' on his landline to someone.

Which makes me jump. Which makes my grip on the hamster loosen for a nano-second.

Just a nano-second. But it's enough. To my utter horror, before I can grasp him again, the hamster wriggles out of my hand and runs off over the floor. He stops and looks at me as though to say, 'Ha, ha!' (OK, I may be projecting) and I stare back, my heart beating hard.

I *can't* admit I've dropped the hamster again. The guy will say I'm irresponsible and will never let me buy him. I'll just quietly catch him myself, I decide. I reach gingerly for the hamster, but he deftly evades my grasp. I make a bolder swipe, but this time he scampers right away, through an open side door.

Shit.

Crawling silently, I follow the hamster through the door and find myself in a dimly lit little stock room. I hastily pull the door shut and look around. It's only a small space. It's contained. I've *got* to find this bloody hamster.

I listen for scrabbling but I can't hear anything. So I

put on the torch function on my phone and swing it around the space, searching for the flash of two beady little eyes. Nothing.

I suddenly notice a box of 'hamster treats' on a nearby shelf, and have a flicker of inspiration. I wrench the box open, telling myself that I'll buy it, and find some revolting little pellets which are presumably like caviar for hamsters.

There's a big empty cardboard box nearby, too. I turn it on its side and make a big pile of treats on the cardboard floor. Then I retreat to a squatting position, poised to move like lightning and trap the hamster. I feel like one of David Attenborough's team, waiting to capture the Serengeti lion at the waterhole.

Except sometimes those teams wait for weeks, I suddenly recall.

No. Don't think like that. I expect sometimes they only wait five minutes and the lion turns up. Exactly.

A few unbearable minutes pass. My thighs are hurting a bit from my squatting position. But I don't dare move. David Attenborough's team don't complain when their noses get frozen off or whatever, do they? So I shouldn't complain either.

Even so, I can't help feeling disconsolate. How has it come to this? This was supposed to be an *organized* Christmas. A *smooth* Christmas. Not a Christmas where you end up squatting in a dingy back room waiting for a hamster to get hungry.

I'm just wondering if this is an utterly stupid idea and I should just go and 'fess up to the guy when suddenly I hear a tiny scrabbling noise and I stiffen. I peer through the gloom – and I can see two beady eyes glinting at me! Yes! It worked!

As the hamster nears the pile of food, I have to restrain myself from cheering. I did it! I'm a hamster whisperer! All I need to do now is—

Wait, *what*?

I peer at the hamster in disbelief as it edges on to the box. It's a different hamster. It's the wrong hamster. This one is half beige, half white. It must have been hiding somewhere in the stock room and smelled the food.

What now? My brain whirls uncertainly as I watch the hamster pick up a treat between its paws. (Actually, that is quite cute.) What do I do? Do I trap this one? But I don't want this one, I want *my* one. Where's *my* one?

As I'm trying to decide how to proceed, another hamster suddenly joins the first. But this is the wrong hamster, too. It's a darker grey-brown colour. How many bloody hamsters *are* there in this stock room?

I'm quite tempted to go and tell the pet-shop guy he's overrun by hamsters, only I can't bring myself to move. Because if *those* hamsters were lured out by the food, then maybe . . . just maybe . . .

I stiffen as I hear a new scrabbling sound on the stone floor – and my heart suddenly leaps. Yes! It's the beige one! He's approaching cautiously, but then stops dead.

Go on, I silently will him. *Go and get the food. You know you want to.*

He pauses, and I gaze at him, using every single psychic hamster power I possess. *Go on . . . go on . . .*

After an unbearable minute or two he starts to move

again. Forward . . . forward . . . Yes! He's on the side of the box! In one seamless movement I reach forward and tilt the box on to its base, whereupon all three hamsters, plus the treats, land on the bottom. They're well and truly contained.

I sink back on to my heels, my heart pumping and my legs feeling twingy with pins and needles. OK. Panic over. I have my hamster. I glance at my watch and feel a wave of relief. I've still got time to get home before the turkey arrives. So it's all good. In fact it's all great, because now I have a hamster *and* a story to tell Luke. (You always have to think of the plus side.)

'I've got your hamsters!' I say, marching out of the stock room, clutching the box – then stop dead.

The place is dark. It's empty.

I look around in disbelief, clocking the dead till. The sign on the door. The metal grille across the frontage. It's *closed*? They *closed* it? With me *inside*?

Thoughts start thudding into my head like missiles. What do I do? What do I *do*? The turkey's arriving in fifteen minutes. If I'm not in, they'll take it away again. I need to get out. But how? Call someone. But there's no signal.

I switch on all the lights, then hurry over to the till to use the landline phone that the guy was using earlier – but the phone's vanished from the counter. Where is it? *Where's the bloody phone?* I try the drawers, but they're all locked. Oh God . . .

I hurry to the door and start banging on it, yelling, 'Help! Help! Let me out!' But the street is empty. After five solid minutes of shouting and banging, my throat feels hoarse, but no one has appeared, let alone come to help me.

And now a series of even worse thoughts starts to thud into my head. What if no one walks past the shop? What if no one sees me? Luke doesn't know I'm here. No one knows I'm here. I could be trapped here over Christmas. I could miss Christmas altogether, trapped in a shop, with only small animals for company.

As I peer out at the empty street, I feel surreal and a bit faint. I was wrong before. *This* is the number one Christmas nightmare. And I'm in it.

Five o'clock comes and goes. Half past five comes and goes. Six o'clock comes and goes. It's dark outside, and I haven't seen a single passer-by and I'm starting to resign myself to my nightmarish fate. (If I'd known I'd be stuck in a shop over Christmas, I'd at least have chosen one with *clothes*.)

I've started marking lines on my hand with biro – five for every half-hour. Because you have to keep your morale up somehow. You have to give yourself structure – otherwise the insanity gets to you. I've seen *Castaway*, so I know these things. I don't want to end up painting a face on a hamster ball.

I've also made a careful note of my supplies and thankfully there's a water cooler in the corner. I can survive on sunflower seeds – and if they run out there's always hamster food. If it comes to rationing, so be it.

And in a funny way, the animals are keeping me going, with their brave and comradely spirit. I've made friends with them all – the hamsters, the gerbils, the fish – and when this is all over, I think we'll be bonded for life.

Every five minutes I hammer on the door, shouting my head off – then sink back in despair. This is the emptiest road I've ever known. Or maybe it's just that everyone's inside, in their cosy homes, watching *The Muppet Christmas Carol* and singing along, so they can't hear my cries.

My throat tight, I reach for a handful of sunflower seeds and crunch them miserably. Thinking about *The Muppet Christmas Carol* reminds me of all the Christmas films I could be watching right now, snuggled up on the sofa. *Elf*. Or *It's A Wonderful Life*. Or, if it's Luke's choice, *Die Hard*, which he always claims is a Christmas film and I say it's not and we argue about it.

It's time to bang on the door again, so I summon all my energy, crash my fists against the glass and yell as loudly as I can. There's no response from the empty street. But as I eventually come to a pause, my mind is whirring in a weird way.

Die Hard. I can't stop thinking about *Die Hard*. Why? I don't usually think about *Die Hard*, but now I can't stop.

I keep seeing Bruce Willis, crashing through windows, shooting six people at once. Refusing to take no for an answer. Knowing what the right thing to do is, and just doing it.

And suddenly I know why these images are in my head. I know what my brain is telling me. I feel ashamed at my total feebleness. Why have I resigned myself to my fate? Why am I thinking *Castaway*? I should be thinking

Die Hard! If Bruce Willis was trapped in a pet shop on Christmas Eve, he wouldn't just sit there and put up with it, would he? He'd climb up the vents with a gun, or explode his way out or something.

I'm not a *Castaway* victim, I tell myself firmly. I'm not a prisoner. I'm not going to moulder away here, eating sunflower seeds for Christmas lunch and hoping to be rescued. My jaw set, I survey the hamsters.

'I'm going to spend Christmas with my family,' I tell them, in a growly Bruce Willis-y voice. 'And no one can stop me.'

I can escape from this place, of course I can. It's only an unfamiliar building, with a locked metal grille barring the front entrance and a heavy bolted door at the back. Come on, Becky, don't be wet.

For the first time since I entered the shop, I look upwards – and there's a trapdoor in the ceiling. It must lead somewhere. Oh my *God*. Why didn't I think of this before?

It takes me a few minutes to locate a pole with a hook on the end of it, and soon I'm hauling down a folded-up loft ladder. I hastily climb up to a kind of attic room with grotty carpet and piled-up boxes, and search for an easy way out, maybe labelled 'Way Out'.

OK. So there isn't an easy way out labelled 'Way Out'. But there's a skylight. I can use that. The catch is stiff, but I finally manage to wrench it open, find an old chair to stand on and poke my head into the cold air. I'm out! Kind of. I breathe in the evening air greedily, surveying the street below, feeling almost emotional. I will never take my freedom for granted again. Never.

The only thing is, the skylight's pretty narrow. But maybe I can squeeze through it on to the roof. And then get down from the roof . . . somehow.

With an almighty effort, I lift myself up so that my head and shoulders are protruding through the skylight. I squeeze and squash, desperately edging myself up . . . but it's no good. My hips definitely won't fit through. Stupid Myriad Miracle workout.

At last I decide to go back inside and think of a different plan. But as I try to descend . . . somehow I can't. After a lot of huffing and desperate pushing I realize the awful, embarrassing truth: I'm stuck. I'm wedged in the skylight, half in, half out.

OK, don't panic, I tell myself firmly. So I'm stuck in a skylight on Christmas Eve and no one knows where I am. There'll be a solution. There's always a solution.

I wait for the solution to present itself – but it's obviously feeling shy. And I'm starting to lose my optimism. And hang on . . . was that a *snowflake*?

I stare up in disbelief as tiny dots of white fluff start drifting down, falling on my hair and down my neck. *Really*, sky? You're choosing *now* to present me with my *White Christmas* fantasy? What if I get frostbite? What if I freeze to death? I should never have listened to my inner Bruce Willis, I'm an idiot . . .

And then a sudden thought comes to me. There's one more tiny, weeny, outside possibility.

My heart thumping with hope, I retrieve my phone from my pocket. I lift it up, as high as I can, stretching my arm out and squinting at the display . . . and it's a miracle! It's a miracle on Woodford Street! I have one bar of signal! I immediately type a text:

Luke! At Pete's Pets. Stuck. Woodford Street in Bickersly. Help!!! Xxx

I press Send and stare at it breathlessly – then see 'Delivered' appear. And every particle in my body collapses in relief. He'll see it. It's all OK. I'm saved.

Now that I'm in signal, a whole bunch of texts and messages start arriving in my phone and as I read them, my face grows a little hot.

Becky, can we talk?

Becky we feel terrible!!!

Becky love, your dad and I are coming over, we need to explain everything

Bex, WHERE ARE YOU??? We're WORRIED!!!!

If ever I thought my friends and family didn't care about me, this is the proof that they do. And I know you shouldn't need proof. But even so . . . I'm not going to delete these any time soon.

As I'm reading, a noise attracts my attention, and as I look up, I gasp. People! Actual people, in this street! My saviours! It's a couple and a little boy, on the other side of the road, and they're pointing and smiling at me. I stare back at them resentfully. Why are they *smiling*, for God's sake?

'Help!' I yell, but I don't think they can hear me, because they just smile again, and the father lifts up the little boy to see me better. For a moment I don't get it at all – till it hits me. I'm in my Mrs Santa outfit. They think I'm some kind of festive stunt!

'I'm *stuck*!' I call. 'I'm not Mrs Santa, I'm *stuck*!'

But they're too far away to hear me properly. They smile and wave back and the dad takes a photo of me – bloody nerve – then they all wave cheerily again and walk on.

Great. Just *great.* So you see someone dressed in a Santa costume, on the roof on Christmas Eve . . . and it doesn't occur to you to save them? What kind of twisted world do we live in?

I'm just composing a tetchy letter to *The Times* about it when a car screeches to a halt below me and out gets Luke. He strides to the pet shop and bangs on the door. 'Becky?'

'Hi!' I shout. 'Luke! Up here! On the roof!'

'*Becky?*' He takes a pace or two back and stares up at me, his jaw slack. 'What the *hell*? I've tracked down the owner, someone's coming to let you out . . . are you OK?'

'I'm fine!' I call back, just as another car screeches to a halt and disgorges Suze, Janice, my parents and Minnie.

'Becky!' screams my mum in horror as she sees me. 'Be careful, love! Don't fall! Graham, look, she's on the roof!'

'I can see that!' replies Dad testily. 'I'm not blind. Becky, hold on, darling!'

'Bex, I'm *so* sorry,' calls up Suze. 'We never meant to hurt you!'

'We all want to spend Christmas with you, love!' calls Janice, her thin voice carrying up on the evening air. 'Oh Jane, will she be all right?' She grabs Mum's hand and then Suze's too, as though for comfort. 'What if she falls to her death?'

'Don't worry!' I call down. 'I'm just glad everything's sorted out!'

'That Nadine character is a monster!' shouts Dad. 'Shocking behaviour!'

'We got everything wrong!' chimes in Suze, at top volume. 'We're such morons!'

'We're all coming tomorrow!' adds Mum. 'Everyone! And we don't care about the food or any of that, love. We only care about you! Can you hear me, Becky, love? YOU!'

They all gaze up at me, standing in a row, holding hands, snowflakes falling on their heads, looking for all the world like the Whos in Minnie's Grinch book. And suddenly there's a kind of expanding feeling in my heart which blocks out all my worries. I haven't got a turkey. Nothing's going to be perfect. But gazing down at the people I love . . . I realize I don't care.

TWENTY-TWO

I *have* got a turkey!

As I haul it out of the oven, all golden and crispy and succulent, I can't quite believe it. I'm here. On Christmas Day. With everyone. And the lunch looks good. And everyone's in a brilliant mood . . .

And I'm wearing an Alexander McQueen dress *that fits*!

Luke presented it to me this morning, just after we'd watched Minnie greet her hamster with wondrous joy. He handed me a gift-wrapped parcel, saying, deadpan, 'I know we're doing presents later, but I understand you like this style of dress?' I stared at the package in confusion, then ripped it open and my jaw dropped.

It was exactly the same gorgeous dress I bought in the sale – only two sizes bigger! (Luke said he 'tracked it down', which must have been almost impossible, but of course he downplayed that.) It's such a fantastic, thoughtful present.

And OK, yes, maybe I would *slightly* have preferred to

fit into the teeny one. But one must remember the point of Christmas, as the vicar so wisely told us in church this morning. The point of Christmas is not being a size minus-6. Or squishing into a dress and not being able to breathe and dying and everyone saying, 'Oh no, and on Christmas Day, too.' The point of Christmas is wearing a dress you can breathe *and* move your arms in, because it turns out you need to do both on Christmas Day – what with all the hugging and exclaiming and cooking and toasting each other.

It was while I was admiring myself in the mirror that Luke gave me the best Christmas present of all. He came out of the bathroom, freshly showered, and I peered at him, thinking, 'Something's different . . . something's changed . . .' Till it hit me. The moustache was gone!

'Your moustache, Luke!' I exclaimed cautiously. 'It's . . . Did you . . . ?'

'You don't mind, do you, Becky?' Luke said. 'You're not too upset? I know you loved my moustache, but I just don't think it's *me*.'

'It's fine,' I said in generous tones. 'You need to do what makes *you* feel happy, Luke.'

'You *did* love it?' he added, meeting my eye – and there was suddenly a teasing note in his voice.

'Of course,' I replied with dignity. 'I said so, didn't I?'

'Yes, my love,' he said, looking amused. 'You did say so.'

I still don't know how he worked it out – but I don't care. I have a husband with no moustache! Result!

And now it's 2 p.m. and I feel as if we've already done a million things. We've heard the vicar's carol medley, which went disastrously wrong but was covered up by spirited tambourine playing. The children have bashed at the piñata and screamed with delight as sweets cascaded down. Mum and Janice have put candles on their hair to sing Swedish songs, although that only lasted thirty seconds, because they both got a bit unnerved. Then Janice gave us all our Christmas makeovers, so everyone now looks a bit shiny and streaky and weird.

We've served champagne, Baileys, sweet sherry, festive mojitos and organic kombucha (Jess). I've passed around a selection of canapés, consisting of smoked salmon on bread, smoked salmon on crackers, smoked salmon on blinis and smoked salmon on cocktail sticks.

And now it's time for our big turkey lunch and I feel . . . what do I feel?

'I feel *sprygge*,' I say, realizing it only as Suze comes into the kitchen. 'Totally, utterly *sprygge*.'

'Me too,' says Suze in heartfelt tones. 'You know, we thought you'd been kidnapped last night! I think my heart's only just stopped juddering.'

I tuck tin foil round the turkey like Mary Berry says to do, and say, 'OK, it's resting,' in my most knowledgeable Christmas-hostess manner. (I'm not sure what this whole 'resting' thing is actually, but I would trust Mary Berry with my life.)

'*How* many kinds of stuffing are you doing?' asks Suze, peering into the oven.

'Three. Plus spicy falafels,' I add, pointing at the top baking tray.

'Spicy falafels?' Suze stares at me.

'Everyone likes spicy falafels for Christmas,' I say

defensively. 'And they're ethical. Come on, time for some presents.'

'Well, the turkey looks wonderful, Bex,' says Suze as we head out of the kitchen, back to the sitting room. 'It all looks wonderful. Thank God for Steph!'

Because it was Steph who saved the day on the turkey front. When we finally got back home from the pet shop, all feeling a bit hysterical (and bruised in my case, because being hauled out of a narrow skylight isn't as much fun as you would think), there she was. Sitting on the front doorstep. With the massive turkey next to her and Minnie's costume on her lap.

'I took delivery!' she called out as we came in the garden gate. 'Don't worry, no substitutions!'

'Steph!' I exclaimed, feeling staggered. 'You're amazing! Thank you so much! But . . . your family . . .'

'It was the least I could do,' said Steph. 'Luke called to say you were missing and ask if I'd heard anything from you. He said he was heading out to find you – and I thought, "Well, at any rate I can make sure they get their turkey." So I came straight round. My mum agreed I should, when I told her. She's . . . we're all grateful to you, Becky.'

'Bex, why is Steph Richards at your house?' said Suze, looking bewildered. 'What's she talking about?' And for a moment I didn't know how I was going to explain our friendship without giving too much away.

But I needn't have worried, because as we got near, Steph stood up and said resolutely, 'Hi, Suze. I don't know if Becky's mentioned it, but my husband's just left me.'

'Oh,' said Suze, looking taken aback. 'Right. No. I had no idea. I'm so sorry to hear that.'

'Well, I was keeping it secret,' said Steph. 'But I'm not any more. Anyway, Becky's been kind of a rock, in recent weeks, so I'm glad I could give something back.' Then she held out the blue silk costume and added, 'Minnie should wear this for Christmas Day. It's hers. You made it, Becky. You should enjoy it.'

Whereupon Suze's eyes got even wider and she said, 'That's Minnie's? But . . . Bex . . .'

So it all had to be explained. Whereupon Suze said she *knew* I must have made a better costume than that Denny and George one. But then she instantly backtracked in case I was offended, and started saying how actually, in many ways she *preferred* the Denny and George one, it was terribly imaginative.

At last Steph said she'd better go, but she gave me a tight hug and said in my ear, 'Let's have happy Christmases, shall we?' And as she drew away, for the first time she looked as if she actually might.

As for me, I'm having the happiest Christmas I can remember, despite the fact that all the snow has vanished. (Typical.) Carols are playing. The food smells sensational. Minnie is in seventh heaven. Mum and Janice are best friends again, and Mum's even wearing one of Janice's old two-pieces, with a tinsel necklace. She said over a Buck's Fizz this morning, 'We do *enjoy* Shoreditch, love. Like you enjoy a holiday. But it's not . . .' and she bashed her heart. She didn't say any more, but I think I knew what she meant.

Although, having said that, Janice has mentioned

413

about a hundred times how keen she is to start visiting Mum more, and going to 'workshops and events', and 'Maybe Martin and I will look at an apartment in Shoreditch too!' So I have no idea how that might pan out. As for Flo, the subject hasn't even been mentioned. It's as though she never existed.

The star of the show, of course, is Santiago. We're all pretending to be interested in each other's stories and jokes, but really, no one can keep their eyes off him. Right now he's playing with all the others in some new game of Clemmie's involving pictures of hats. And the other children are being so sweet and careful to include him that it melts my heart.

'He's amazing,' I say to Jess every five minutes, because he is. He really is.

He's also the most ethically dressed child I've ever seen, in bamboo and recycled cotton and vegan leather shoes. *Plus* he's been the only child to show any interest in my eco tree, so he gets extra points, unlike my godson Ernest, who just said flatly, 'What's that? Shall I take it to recycling?' To be fair, it's not the *most* impressive sight. It's a branch from the garden decorated with three spoons. But Santiago stroked the spoons and smiled – he's got the most ravishing smile – and as Jess watched him, I could tell she's absolutely besotted.

In fact, she must be on some sort of cloud nine, because an hour ago, we all realized Minnie had decorated a beaming Santiago in wreaths of tinsel and fairy lights. But when I rushed in horror to rip them off him, thinking, 'Oh God, evil plastic, evil tinsel, Jess will get totally offended and leave,' she put up a hand to stop me. And, looking sheepish, she said, 'Wait. He looks so sweet. Let me take a quick photo.'

She actually took a photo of her son adorned with plastic decorations! Jess, who hates plastic! It's being a new mother, I reckon. It's addled her brain.

I'm about to tinkle a fork in my glass and suggest we open some presents when Suze arrives by my side breathlessly and says, 'Bex. Come here a sec.'

She leads me into the hall and shows me a large cardboard box, covered in rain stains and bird droppings. 'This was in your front garden!' she says. 'I just took out some recycling and I spotted the corner of it, behind your rose bush. I think it must have been dumped there a few days ago.'

'Oh God,' I say guiltily. 'It must be something I bought online.'

'What?' says Suze expectantly. 'It's quite big.'

'No idea. Don't tell Luke.'

I hastily rip it open, so that I can go and hide whatever it is under the bed – but the sight that greets me makes me momentarily freeze. It's leather. Dark-brown leather. As I tear the cardboard further, my heart thumping, I see a handle. A brass 'LB' charm. I rip the rest of the covering off in a frenzy – and it is. It's the portmanteau. I can't *believe* it.

'Wow!' exclaims Suze. 'That's phenomenal! Where did you get that from?'

I can't speak. I'm searching for an envelope, a note, something – and suddenly I see it. I rip open the expensive, lined envelope and find myself looking at a correspondence card, with a handwritten note:

Dear Mrs Brandon (née Bloomwood)

I gather that you have pioneered women's membership at the London Billiards Club. My husband, Sir Peter Leggett-Davey, is most put out.

As a result of his rage, I have been wishing heartily that I had done the same thing many years ago, and admire your courage and determination.

Simon Millett told me that you had set your heart on winning this item in the raffle. I am delighted to send it to you with my very best wishes and congratulations.

Lady Rosamund Leggett-Davey
(née Wilson)

'Who's it from?' says Suze and I lift my head, feeling almost giddy.

'Just . . . someone,' I say at last. Then, as I hear the sound of Luke laughing, I snap into action. 'Quick. Suze. Help me wrap this up.'

Within five minutes we've got it wrapped and man-handled under the tree, and I'm tinkling my fork in my glass.

'Let's do some presents before lunch!' I say, as everyone gathers around the tree. 'And Luke, I want to start with this one. Happy Christmas.'

'But I've seen my present,' says Luke, looking confused. 'It was a lot smaller.'

'That was . . . a decoy,' I quickly improvise. 'Ha! Fooled you!'

It's fine. I'll give him the jumper for his birthday.

Luke tears off the paper and I watch, biting my lip, as

he stares, blinks, then looks more closely, rubs his hand over the leather, opens and shuts it, takes in the lining, the 'LB' charm, the sheer amazingness of it ... then finally lifts his eyes to mine. He looks quite overcome.

'Becky,' he says at last and comes over to kiss me. 'This is incredible. Where on *earth* did you get it from?'

'Er . . .' I hesitate. Maybe I'll tell Luke the whole story one day – but not right now. 'I just saw it in a window,' I say, which is true. 'And it was so perfect, I had to get it. So!' I add, hastily moving the conversation on. 'Let's all give Janice her presents, to say thank you for the lovely makeovers she's given us.'

I can't help glancing around the others with a grin, because the truth is, we've coordinated on this. In fact, we've had our own secret WhatsApp group called 'Janice's presents' – and I can't *wait* to see her face.

Suze's present is an insulated carton of fresh crab meat. 'I know you love crab, Janice,' she says earnestly. 'But it's *very* perishable, so you *must* eat it very soon.'

Mum's present is a flat parcel, and Janice opens it to find a drawing of her house in Oxshott. 'Look, love!' says Mum cheerfully. 'It's got every detail. I do hope you and Martin enjoy it!'

My present is a hairbrush with 'Janice' engraved on the back. Tom gives her a personalized 'Janice' teapot, while Jess gives her a box of chocolates printed with 'To my mother-in law, Janice'.

'Goodness,' says Janice, looking quite flustered. 'What lovely presents. Absolutely super.'

'But Janice,' says Martin, the penny clearly just

417

dropping. 'What about your cupboard? You can't regift any of these.'

'Martin!' snaps Janice, her cheeks colouring.

'Oh Janice!' I say, clapping my hand to my mouth. 'I guess you'll have to *enjoy* your presents instead.' I grin at her to show I'm teasing, and Janice's colour deepens.

'Yes!' she says, fluffing out her hair, looking embarrassed. 'Well. Thank you. Thank you all.' She picks up the teapot and suddenly looks delighted. 'I *will* enjoy using this,' she says. 'I really *will*.'

'So, next up, my present for Suze,' I announce. 'Jess told us how she was giving everyone a zero-waste present, and we were really inspired. So we're giving each other things from our own possessions. Only I just couldn't decide, so . . . wait a sec . . .'

I head out of the room, grab the sack I've hidden in the coat cupboard, tied with a big red bow, and drag it back into the room.

'Suze, here's a load of my stuff. Just have what you want. Honestly. I think it would all suit you.'

'Bex!' gasps Suze. 'I did the same!' She reaches behind the sofa and hauls out three bin bags, and I stare at them in sudden excitement. Three bin bags full of Suze's stuff? This is the most perfect Christmas present ever! I can't resist reaching into one of them and pull out her pale-pink slouchy cashmere jumper.

'I've always loved this,' I say in elation.

'I've always loved this!' rejoins Suze, pulling out my Ally Smith cardigan with the signature button. 'Oh my God, Bex, are you sure?'

'Of course! Put it on! Let me see!'

418

'Maybe you should sort it all out after lunch,' says Luke hurriedly. 'Or . . . after Christmas, even. Is it lunchtime, perhaps? Shall we do the rest of the presents later?'

'Yes,' I say reluctantly, putting back a feather boa. 'Or actually . . . no!' I suddenly sit up, struck by an idea. 'I think Jess and Tom should give out their presents before lunch. Are you still giving us all words?' I say curiously to Jess.

'Yes,' says Jess, flushing faintly. 'We have a word for each of you.'

I can't wait to hear these words. I've never been given a word before in my *life*.

'Well . . . fab,' I say. 'Bring it on.'

Jess and Tom stand up and walk over to Dad, who says, 'Me?' and laughs nervously – then lapses into silence under the steady gaze of Tom and Jess. They look at him in silence for a few more moments, and I start to feel prickly. This is actually quite magical. As I glance around the room, I think everyone feels the same way – kind of overawed and wondering what's going to happen next. It's as though we're at some special ceremony, all of a sudden.

'Graham,' says Tom seriously at last, 'we would like to give you the word . . . "Wise".'

'Goodness,' says Dad, looking taken aback. 'Well . . . thank you. Thank you very much!'

As if they've practised this (which they probably have), Tom and Jess move in sync towards Clemmie and give her the same grave look.

'Clemmie,' says Jess softly, 'we would like to give you the word "Nightingale".'

Nightingale! That's genius, because Clemmie has actually got a lovely singing voice.

'Thank you,' says Clemmie, looking a bit nonplussed, then Tom and Jess move to Tarkie.

'Tarquin,' says Tom, 'we would like to give you the word "Dynamic".'

That's really clever for Tarkie, too, because I can see how chuffed he is. And now they're heading towards me, their faces both intent – and in spite of myself I feel a giant spasm of nerves. *Please* not 'Overdraft'. Or 'Flaky'.

'Becky,' says Jess seriously, 'we would like to give you the word "Joy".'

Joy? I got joy? I feel ridiculously pleased, and shoot a delighted smile at Luke. I got joy!

As Jess and Tom move around the room, I'm mesmerized. In fact, everyone is. Janice gets 'Beauty', which makes her pinken with pleasure. Luke gets 'Integrity', which I know will make his day. At last, everyone has received a word, and Tom and Jess face each other, with Santiago standing between them, his eyes huge and solemn.

'Tom,' says Jess, her face serious, 'I give you "Strength".'

'Jess,' says Tom, 'I give you "Resolute".'

Then they both turn to Santiago and start doing what I guess is sign language, while he watches wide-eyed. They finish and there's a tiny pause before they draw breath and say gently, in unison, 'Santiago. Our son. We give you "Cherished".'

Cherished. Oh my *God*. My throat is all choked up, and I decide instantly that I never want anything for

Christmas again except a word. Words rock. Words rule. Words are the best present, *ever*.

As we gather around the table twenty minutes later, everyone is still a bit bowled over by all their amazing words.

'My word is "Valiant",' Ernie keeps telling everyone proudly. 'It means brave. It means I'm very brave.'

'Oh Becky!' Janice suddenly exclaims. 'I nearly forgot. I've got another tiny thing for you. Nothing much really, but I picked it up at the Christmas Style Fair. I meant to give it to you on the day as a thank-you, but I forgot. Quite fun, I thought.' She pops out to the hall, then hands me a little gift bag. 'As I say, it's just a tiny thing . . .'

I reach into the gift bag, expecting a lipgloss or something – but my hand closes over a soft object, wrapped in tissue paper. I pull it out and see a flash of silver. And my heart catches.

No way, *no way* . . .

I rip off the remaining tissue – and it is! It's the silver llama bauble! I can't believe it. Janice *had one all the time*?

'As I say, it's not much,' Janice is saying apologetically, 'but it did catch my eye . . .'

'Janice!' I fling my arms around her. 'I *love* it!'

'Well!' she says, looking pleased. 'Goodness. Happy Christmas, love!'

I can't resist hurrying to the sitting room and hanging the llama on the tree, that very moment. I put it right at the front, then stand back and regard it admiringly. Our entire tree is transformed!

Then I head into the kitchen, to find Luke standing motionless, staring at his phone.

'How's the turkey?' I say. 'Does it look well rested? Luke?' I add, as he doesn't seem able to respond. '*Luke?*'

Finally Luke raises his head and just gazes at me for a few seconds.

'Becky,' he says in an odd voice. 'I've just had an email from someone called Simon Millett, wishing me happy Christmas and filling me in on a few things.'

What? He emailed Luke? That sneak.

'Oh,' I say hastily. 'Well, I wouldn't listen to him—'

'According to him, you did a bit more than just "see my present in a window". He's sent me a link to the London Clubs' Newsletter. Which actually I *do* receive,' he adds, in an even odder voice, 'but never bother to read. Because I never expect to see a picture of my wife in it.'

He turns around his phone and I see a photo of me addressing the ninety-three-year-olds, my hands aloft and my mouth wide open. *Who* chose that awful shot? I bet it was Sir Peter.

'Oh right,' I say, as Luke seems to be expecting an answer. 'Yes. I've joined a club.' I try to sound casual. 'I was going to mention it. You can come along as my guest, if you like.'

'Becky . . .' Luke trails off, appearing almost speechless. 'A *billiards* club?'

'Well, I wanted the portmanteau!' I say defensively. 'It had your *initials* on it.'

'So you changed the laws of one of the oldest clubs in town,' Luke says, gazing at me as though there's a

422

thousand other things he wants to say, but doesn't know where to start. 'You swept the floor with them, according to this chap Simon Millett. I *wish* I'd been there.'

'Well, you know.' I shrug. 'I wasn't just going to get you boring old *aftershave*—'

And then I can't speak because Luke has enveloped me in a tight hug. In fact, so tight I can hardly breathe.

'There's no one like you, Becky,' he says against my neck, his voice husky. 'No one in the whole wide world.'

This is something Luke says to me quite a lot. And sometimes I'm not sure if he means it in a good way or a bad way. But right now, I'm fairly sure it's in a good way.

At last we draw apart and take a few deep breaths and remember what we're *supposed* to be doing, which is serving Christmas lunch. Luke carries in the turkey and I follow him with Peppa Pig the vegan turkey. The whole dining room erupts into cheers and Tarkie exclaims throatily, 'And so say all of us!'

The next few minutes are a blur of carving and spooning and passing dishes along. But at last everyone has a plate of food and we've pulled the crackers (sustainable, handblock-printed by Nepalese women) and everyone's wearing a paper hat – and Christmas lunch is underway. The table looks fab, with its Highland ribbons and neon table confetti and Scandi candlesticks. (My theme in the end was 'eclectic'.) Martin has piled his plate with sprouts, Suze has piled hers with broccoli and everyone has taken at least one doughnut. Peppa Pig is a massive hit – I think we might have to have a vegan doughnut turkey every year, now.

'Well!' says Mum, whose word was 'Source' and has

just revealed to me she thought at first Tom and Jess meant 'Sauce' and was quite confused and had to have it explained. 'What a wonderful Christmas!' She rises to her feet and bangs her pudding spoon on her plate until there's quiet around the table. 'Everyone! I would like to make a speech. We all know that Becky hasn't had it easy, these last few days, what with one thing and another. But here we are, enjoying a wonderful Christmas, in this beautifully decorated house, and I would like to say to you, Becky and Luke and Minnie . . . thank you!' She raises her glass. 'To the Brandons!'

'The Brandons!' everyone echoes, rising to their feet, and Suze chimes in, 'Née Bloomwood!' and everyone bursts into laughter and then sits back down again to dig happily into their food.

I sit back in my chair and watch everyone for a moment, just absorbing the happiness of it all – Mum cutting up Minnie's turkey and Suze checking out her paper hat in the mirror, and Jess suspiciously reading the leaflet about the sustainable credentials of the crackers. Christmas is the best. Even if it goes wrong, it's the best. Then I turn to Luke, who's sitting on my left, at the head of the table.

'What did you think of the words, by the way?' I say to him, under the cover of conversation. 'Tom and Jess's present, I mean.'

'Pretty impressive,' says Luke. 'Not what I expected, somehow.'

'Me neither.' I nod, before adding in my most casual manner, 'So . . . what word would you give me?'

'Oh, I don't know,' says Luke with an easy laugh.

'Go on, Luke, give me a word. Give me a word for Christmas.' I'm half joking – but half serious, too. I suddenly want to hear his word. The word he would choose for me.

As though sensing this, Luke puts down his knife and fork. He turns to me, and his dark eyes lock on to mine for what seems an endless span of time, before he says, quietly,

' "Beloved".'

My face flashes hot and I feel a prickle in my nose. Beloved. That's his word for me, beloved.

I love my new dress. Of course I do. But this is the present I'll always remember.

'That's a good one,' I say, trying to keep my composure. 'Thank you.'

'It's my pleasure.' Luke takes his knife and fork back up and resumes eating. 'Now you give me a word,' he adds. 'Something good, mind.'

I'm silent for a moment, thinking hard. Then I draw a slightly shaky breath and say, 'OK. I'll give you a word.'

'Excellent!' Luke wipes his mouth. 'Will I like it?'

'I think you'll like it,' I say, my heart thumping hard. 'I really think you will. Ready?'

I wait until he puts down his knife and fork. I wait until he turns his head to look at me directly. I wait. And wait.

Then I lean forward and whisper gently into his ear, ' "Pregnant".'

THE LONDON BILLIARDS
AND PARLOUR MUSIC CLUB
EST. 1816
ST JAMES'S ST
LONDON SW1

Dear Mrs Brandon née Bloomwood

Thank you for your recent letter, requesting use of the Prince of Wales room for your 'baby shower', an American term, I believe.

I am afraid that this will be impossible. It is an unsuitable purpose for the room in question. Further, there can be no question of your filling a room in this club with 'zillions of balloons' as you put it. Some of our members are very elderly, and such a sight might prove alarming, if not fatal to them.

Yours sincerely

Sir Peter Leggett-Davey
Chairman

THE LONDON BILLIARDS
AND PARLOUR MUSIC CLUB
EST. 1816
ST JAMES'S ST
LONDON SW1

MINUTES FROM MEMBERS' QUARTERLY MEETING
(CONT'D)

MOTION 6

That Mrs Brandon (née Bloomwood) should be permitted
to:

1. Host a 'baby shower' event in the Prince of Wales room;
2. Furnish the Prince of Wales room with inflatable
   balloons;
3. Create a 'tier of cupcakes';
4. Serve Prosecco and
5. Play amplified music by the popular artist known as
   'Beyoncé'.

Proposed by Mrs Rebecca Brandon (née Bloomwood)
Seconded by Lord Edwin Tottle

Carried: 56 votes to 3.

Acknowledgements

I'd like to thank my wonderful readers – in particular, all those who have enquired so kindly after Becky. Your enthusiasm and love were a massive inspiration in writing this book.

Also, special thanks to Linda Evans for coming out of retirement for Becky's sake!

Don't miss Sophie Kinsella's
irresistible new stand-alone novel.

Read on for an extract from

Love
Your
Life

ONE

As I reach for the doorbell, my phone bleeps with a text and my head instantly fills with a roll call of possibilities.

– Someone I know is dead.

– Someone I know won the Lottery.

– I'm late for an appointment I'd forgotten about. Shit.

– I was witness to a crime and now I need to give very specific, detailed evidence about something I can't remember. *Shit*.

– My doctor was looking back through my notes. (Why? Unclear.) And she found something. 'I don't want to worry you, *but . . .*'

– Someone sent me flowers and my neighbour took them in.

– A celebrity just tweeted something I need to see. Ooh. What?

But as I take out my phone, I see that it's from Seth, the guy I had a date with last week. The one who said nothing, the whole evening. *Nothing*.

Most guys have the opposite problem. They drone on about themselves and their brilliant achievements and as you're paying your half they ask as an afterthought, 'What do you do, again?' But Seth stared at me silently with his close-set eyes while I babbled nervously about the butternut-squash soup.

What does he have to say? Does he want another date? Yikes. My stomach cringes at the very thought, which is a sign. One of my major rules of life is: you should listen to your body. Your body is wise. Your body *knows*.

It's fine. I'll let him down gently. I'm pretty good at letting people down.

Hello Ava. After consideration I have decided our relationship is not something I can continue with.

Oh. Hmph. I see.
Whatever.

I eye-roll very deliberately towards the phone. Although I know he can't see me, I have this very slight theory that you can somehow convey emotions through your phone. (I haven't shared this theory with anyone, because most people are quite narrow-minded, I find. Even my best friends.)

You may have thought I was contacting you to ask for another date, in which case I'm sorry to have raised your hopes.

My hopes? My *hopes*? He should be so lucky.

433

You'll want to know why.

What? No. I don't, thanks very much.

I mean, I can guess.

No, scratch that. I can't.

Why should I have to guess, anyway? Who wants to *guess* why someone doesn't want to date them? It sounds like some awful TV game show called *Is It My Bad Breath?*

(It's not my bad breath. Whatever it is, it's not that.)

I'm afraid I cannot date anyone who thinks butternut-squash soup has a soul.

What?

I stare at the phone, incensed. He has *totally* misrepresented me. I did *not* say butternut-squash soup has a soul. I simply said I thought we should be open-minded about the way the physical and spiritual interlink. Which I do. We should.

As if he can read my mind, Harold gives a sympathetic whine and rubs his nose against my leg. You see? If that doesn't prove the world is interconnected, then what does?

I want to text back, 'Sorry not to be closed-minded enough for your limited outlook on life.' But that would indicate that I've read his texts, which I haven't.

Well, OK, I *have*, but the point is, I'm deleting them from my mind. All gone. Seth who? Date? What?

Exactly.

I ring the doorbell, then let myself in with the key

Nell's given me. It's what we all do, in case Nell's having an episode. It's been a while, but they can flare up viciously out of nowhere.

'Nell?' I call.

'Hi!' She appears in the hall, grinning widely, her hair pink and spiky.

'You've gone back to pink!' I exclaim. 'Nice.'

Nell's hair colour has changed about 106 times since we were at uni together, whereas mine hasn't changed once. It's still the same dark auburn, straight down to my shoulders, easy to swish into a ponytail.

Not that hair is really on my mind right now. I was distracted momentarily by Seth's texts – but now that I'm inside the house, my throat is starting to tighten. My stomach feels heavy. I glance down at Harold and he turns his head inquiringly towards me in that adorable way he has, whereupon my eyes start to prickle. Oh God. Can I really do this?

Nell squats down and holds out her hands to Harold. 'Ready for your holiday?'

Harold surveys her for a moment, then turns back to me, his liquid brown gaze fixing mine piteously.

If anyone thinks dogs can't understand everything we say and do, then they're *wrong*, because Harold *knows*. He's trying to be brave, but he's finding this as hard as I am.

'I can't take you to Italy, Harold,' I say, swallowing hard. 'I've told you that. But it won't be long. I promise. A week. That's all.'

His face is crunched into a heartbreaking 'Why are you *doing* this to me?' expression. His tail is gently

435

thumping on the ground in an encouraging, hopeful way; as though I might suddenly change my mind, cancel my flight and take him out to play.

I've sworn I won't cry, but tears are brimming as I gaze at his bright, intelligent face. My Harold. Best beagle in the world. Best dog in the world. Best *person* in the world.

'Harold can't *wait* to stay with me,' says Nell firmly, ushering us both into the living room. 'Can you, Harold?'

In answer, Harold screws up his face still more and gives a soul-shattering whine.

'That dog should go on the stage,' says Sarika, glancing up at him from her laptop with an amused look. Sarika isn't really a dog-person – she admits as much – but she's a Harold-person. You can't meet Harold and not be a Harold-person.

I found Harold at a rescue centre four years ago when he was just a puppy, and it was instant, utter devotion. He looked up at me, his eyes bright, his breath all snuffly and excited, and he seemed to be saying, 'There you are! I knew you'd come!'

I'm not saying it was plain sailing. I'd never owned a dog before. I'd longed for one as a child, but my parents were the types who keep vaguely promising, then it never happens. So I was a beginner at looking after a dog. And Harold was a beginner at being looked after. Because, believe me, he was *not* looked after by the people who abandoned him on the side of the A414. That was *not* looking after him. Just thinking about it makes me feel hot and bothered.

Anyway, it's been a learning curve. When Harold first arrived at my flat, he had a freak-out. He was quite clearly saying, 'What have I *done*, agreeing to live with you?' And I had similar wobbles. There was quite a lot of howling, on both sides. But now I can't imagine life without him. Yet here I am, planning to leave him for a week.

Maybe I should cancel. Yes. I should cancel.

'Ava, stop stressing. You realize he's *trying* to make you feel bad?' says Nell. She turns to Harold and surveys him sternly. 'Listen, mate, I don't fall for your hammy act. Ava can go on holiday without you. *It's allowed*. So stop giving her a hard time.'

For a long moment Harold and Nell lock eyes – two huge personalities confronting each other – then at last Harold subsides. He gives me another reproachful look, but pads over to the hearth rug by Nell's chair and settles down.

OK, maybe I won't cancel.

'Do *not* apologize to him,' says Nell to me. 'And do *not* waste all week mooning over videos of Harold instead of writing your book.'

'I won't!' I say defensively.

'We'll be fine,' she reiterates. '*Fine*.'

I don't have many life tips. But one of them is: if you're ever feeling sorry for yourself, visit Nell. She's tough in all the right places. She bounces back stupid thoughts at you. Her matter-of-fact attitude whips through you like a gust of sharp, cold air.

'Here's all his stuff.' I dump my massive bag on the floor. 'Bed, water bowl, blanket, food . . . Oh, his essential oils!' I suddenly remember, taking the bottle from my bag. 'I've made him a new blend, lavender and cedarwood. You just have to spritz his—'

'Bedding.' Nell cuts me off. 'Ava, relax. You've already sent me five emails about this, remember?' She takes the bottle from me and scrutinizes it briefly before putting it down. 'That reminds me, I've been meaning to ask. Whatever happened to your aromatherapy qualification?'

'Oh,' I say, halted. 'I'm still . . . doing it. Kind of.'

My mind flicks back to my aromatherapy books and bottles, shoved to one side in my kitchen. I'm doing an online course, and I *must* get back to it, because I'm definitely still interested in become a part-time aromatherapist.

'Kind of?' queries Nell.

'It's on pause. It's just, with work, and writing this book . . . You know.' I heave a sigh. 'Life gets in the way.'

My job is writing pharmaceutical leaflets and online copy, which I can pretty much do in my sleep by now. I work for a drug company called Brakesons, based in Surrey. It's fine, I like the firm and they let me work mostly from home. But I'm always trying to expand my horizons. If you ask me, life's too short *not* to expand your horizons. You should always be thinking: 'This is OK . . . but what *else* could I be doing?'

'All the more reason to go to Italy and focus on writing your book,' says Nell firmly. 'Harold *wants* you to do that. Don't you, Harold?'

In answer, Harold emits a soulful 'wahoo!' – sometimes he sounds just like a wolf – and Nell laughs. She ruffles Harold's head with her strong stubby hand and says, 'Idiot dog.'

We've been friends since Manchester uni. Nell, Sarika, Maud and I all met in the university choir and bonded on a tour to Bremen. Sarika had barely spoken a word till then; all we knew about her was that she was studying law and could sing a top C. But after a few drinks she revealed she was secretly sleeping with the conductor and their sex life was getting a bit 'dark'. So now she wanted to dump him but also stay in the choir and what did we think? We spent a whole night drinking German beer and discussing it, while also trying to elicit what 'dark' meant, exactly.

(In the end, Nell crashed her glass down and said, 'Just bloody *tell* us, OK?')

(It was a bit gross. Not worth repeating, or even thinking about.)

Anyway, Sarika did dump the conductor, and she did stay in the choir. That was fourteen years ago now (how did *that* happen?) and we're still friends. Of the four of us, only Sarika still sings in a choir – but then, she was always the most musical one. Plus she's constantly on the lookout for a man whose interests chime with hers, and she reckons London choirs are a good place to start. Along with cycling clubs. She joins a new choir every year, and switches cycling clubs every six months, and there's been a pretty good yield of guys.

I mean, three serious possibilities in two years. Not bad, for London.

We all live near each other in north London, and even though our lives are different in a lot of ways, we're

439

closer than ever. We've been on a few rollercoasters, these last few years. We've shrieked and clutched each other's hands, both literally and . . . whatsit.

Not-literally.

Metaphorically? Figuratively?

Great. I'm going on a week-long writing course tomorrow and I don't know what the opposite of 'literally' is.

'What's the opposite of "literally"?' I ask Sarika, but she's tapping intently at her laptop, her dark shiny hair swishing the keys. She's often to be found tapping intently at her laptop, Sarika, even when she's round at Nell's. (We tend to gather at Nell's place.)

'No smokers,' Sarika mutters, then presses a key and peers closely at her screen.

'What?' I stare at her. 'Is that work?'

'New dating site,' she says.

'Ooh, which one?' I ask with interest. Sarika has more cash than any of us, being a lawyer, so she's the one who can afford to join the expensive dating sites and then report back.

'No psychics,' replies Sarika absently and presses another key, then looks up. 'It's called Meet You. Costs an arm and a leg. But then you get what you pay for.'

'"No psychics"?' echoes Nell sceptically. 'How many psychics have you dated, exactly?'

'One,' says Sarika, swivelling towards her. 'And that was more than enough. I told you about him. The one who reckoned he knew what I *really* liked in bed and we argued about it and I said, "Whose body is it anyway?" and he said, "It's for both of us to enjoy." '

'Oh, *him,*' says Nell, light dawning in her eyes. 'I

didn't realize he was a psychic, I thought he was an arsehole. Is there a "no arseholes" filter?'

'Wouldn't work,' says Sarika regretfully. 'No one thinks they're an arsehole.' She turns back and taps at her keyboard again. 'No magicians,' she types briskly. 'No dancers . . . What about choreographers?'

'What's wrong with dancers?' objects Nell. 'They're fit.'

'Just don't fancy it,' says Sarika, shrugging vaguely. 'He'd be out every night, dancing. We should keep the same hours. No oil-rig workers,' she adds as an after-thought, typing again.

'*How* does this site work?' I say, baffled.

'It starts with all your deal-breakers,' replies Nell. 'It shouldn't be called Meet You, it should be called Fuck Off You. And You. And You.'

'You're making it sound really negative,' protests Sarika. 'It's not about telling people to fuck off, it's about being super-specific, so you won't waste time looking at unsuitable people. You keep honing your target match until you've got the perfect shortlist.'

'Let me see.' I head round the sofa to look over her shoulder. The screen of her laptop is filled with male faces, and I blink at them. They all look nice to me. The guy with the stubble in the right-hand corner looks particularly cute. His expression says, 'Pick me! I'll be kind to you!'

'He looks sweet.' I point at him.

'Maybe. OK, what next?' Sarika consults a typed list on her phone. 'No vegetarians.'

'What?' I stare at her in shock. '*No vegetarians?* What are you saying? Sarika, how can you be so narrow-minded? Your sister's vegetarian! *I'm* vegetarian!'

441

'I know, she says equably. 'But I don't want to date my sister. Or you. Sorry, babe. You know I love your halloumi crumble.' She reaches out an arm to squeeze my waist affectionately. 'But I want someone I can roast a chicken with.'

She clicks on 'Filters' and a box appears with four headings: *Yes Please!*, *Don't Mind*, *Not Ideal* and *Deal-breaker*.

'Deal-breaker,' says Sarika firmly, starting to type 'Vegetarian' in the box. After two letters, the word *Vegetarian* auto-fills and she clicks on it.

'You can't rule out all vegetarians,' I say in utter horror. 'It's prejudiced. It's . . . is it even *legal*?'

'Ava, lighten up!' retorts Sarika. 'Now watch. This bit is fun. "Apply filter".'

As she clicks, the photos on the screen start to shimmer. Then, one by one, big red crosses appear in front of faces, scattered over the screen. I glance at the cute guy – and feel a nasty lurch. There's a cross in front of his face. He looks as though he's been sentenced to execution.

'What's going on?' I demand anxiously. 'What is this?'

'It's called "Last Chance",' explains Sarika. 'I can reprieve any of them by clicking on them.'

'Reprieve him!' I say, pointing to my favourite. 'Reprieve him!'

'Ava, you don't know anything about him,' says Sarika, rolling her eyes.

'He looks nice!'

'But he's vegetarian,' says Sarika, and presses 'Done'.

The screen shimmers again and all the guys with

442

crossed-out faces disappear. The remaining guys swirl around the screen, and then assemble again in neat rows of photos, with new ones taking the place of the vanished.

'Great,' says Sarika with satisfaction. 'I'm getting somewhere.'

I stare at the screen, slightly traumatized by this culling process.

'It's brutal,' I say. 'It's heartless.'

'Better than swiping,' puts in Nell.

'Exactly!' Sarika nods. 'It's scientific. There are more than eight hundred possible filters on the site. Height, job, habits, location, political views, education . . . The algorithms were developed at NASA, apparently. You can process five hundred guys in, like, no time.' She consults her list again. 'Right, on to the next. No one over six foot three.' She starts typing again. 'I've tried super-tall. Doesn't work with me.'

She presses 'apply filter', three red crosses appear, and within seconds a new selection of guys is gazing out from the screen.

'Apparently one woman kept on applying filters until there was only one guy left on the screen, and she contacted him and they're still together,' Sarika adds, scrolling down the typed list on her phone. 'That's your ideal.'

'It still feels wrong,' I say, watching the screen in dismay. 'This can't be the way.'

'It's the only way,' Sarika contradicts me. 'Basically everybody dates online now, right? *Eve-ry-bo-dy*. Millions of people. Billions of people.'

'I guess so,' I say warily.

'Everybody dates online,' Sarika reiterates clearly, as though she's giving a TED talk. 'It's like going to a cocktail party and there's everybody in the world standing there, trying to catch your eye. That's never going to work! You need to narrow it down. Ergo.' She gestures at the screen.

'ASOS is bad enough,' puts in Nell. 'I searched for "white shirt" yesterday. You know how many I got? One thousand, two hundred and sixty-four. I was like, I don't have time for this shit. I'll take the first one. Whatever.'

'Exactly,' says Sarika. 'And that's a shirt, not a life partner. "No more than ten minutes from Tube station",' she adds, typing briskly. 'I've had enough of schlepping to flats in the middle of nowhere.'

'You're ruling out guys who *live more than ten minutes from the Tube*?' My jaw sags. 'Is that even a *thing*?'

'You can create your own filters and if they like them they add them to the website,' Sarika explains. 'They're considering my one about hair-washing frequency.'

'But what if the perfect guy lives eleven minutes from the Tube station?' I know I'm sounding agitated, but I can't help it. I can already see him, drinking his coffee in the sunshine, wearing his cycle shorts, listening to his Bach CD, longing for someone just like Sarika.

'He'll lie about it,' says Sarika comfortably. 'He'll put "ten minutes". It's fine.'

She's really not getting the point.

'Sarika, listen,' I say in frustration. 'What if there's an amazing guy who's six foot five and vegetarian and he lives twenty minutes away from Crouch End . . . and you've ruled him out? This is nuts!'

444

'Ava, stop freaking out,' says Sarika calmly. 'You have to have *some* deal-breakers.'

'No, you don't,' I say adamantly. 'I don't have any deal-breakers. I want a good man, that's all. A decent, civilized human being. I don't care what he looks like, what his job is, where he lives . . .'

'What about if he hates dogs?' says Sarika, raising her eyebrows.

I'm silenced.

He couldn't hate dogs, because only really strange, sad people don't like dogs.

'OK,' I concede at last. 'That's my only deal-breaker. He has to like dogs. But that's the only one. Literally.'

'What about golf?' chips in Nell craftily.

Damn her.

Love Your Life

'Love is the ineffable, mysterious connection that happens between two humans when they connect, and they feel it . . . and they just know.'

Ava is sick of online dating. She's always trusted her own instincts over an algorithm, anyway, and she wants a break from it all. So she signs up to a semi-silent, anonymous writing retreat in glorious Italy.

Then she meets a handsome stranger . . . All she knows is that he's funny, he's kind and – she soon learns – he's great in bed. He's equally smitten, and they pledge their love without even knowing each other's real names.

But when they return home, reality hits. They're both driven mad by each other's weird quirks and, as disaster follows disaster, it seems that while they love each other, they just can't love each other's lives.

Can they overcome their differences to find one life, together?

Coming autumn 2020 in hardback, ebook and audio

The Secret Dreamworld of a
Shopaholic

**The perfect pick-me-up when life is hanging
in the (bank) balance!**

Meet Rebecca Bloomwood.

She has a great flat, a fabulous wardrobe, and a job
telling other people how to manage their money.
She spends her leisure time . . . shopping.

She knows she should stop, but she can't. She tries Cutting
Back, she tries Making More Money. But neither seems to
work. The letters from the bank are getting harder to ignore.

Can Becky ever escape from this dreamworld, find true love,
and regain the use of her credit card?

Out now in paperback, ebook and audio

I Owe You One

'Love means all debts are off.'

Fixie Farr can't help herself. Straightening a crooked object, removing a barely-there stain, helping out a friend . . . she just has to put things right. It's how she got her nickname, after all.

So when a handsome stranger in a coffee shop asks her to watch his laptop for a moment, she not only agrees, she ends up saving it from certain disaster. To thank her, the laptop's owner, Sebastian, scribbles her an IOU – but of course Fixie never intends to call in the favour.

That is, until her teenage crush, Ryan, comes back into her life and needs her help – and Fixie turns to Seb.

Soon the pair are caught up in a series of IOUs – from small favours to life-changing ones – and Fixie is torn between the past she's used to and the future she deserves.

Does she have the courage to fix things for herself and fight for the life, and love, she really wants?

Out now in paperback, ebook and audio

Remember Me?

'Women need chocolate. It's a scientific fact.'

Lexi wakes up in a hospital bed after a car accident, thinking she's twenty-five with crooked teeth and a disastrous love life. But, to her disbelief, she learns it's actually three years later – she's super-toned with straight teeth, she's the boss of her department – and she's married to a good-looking millionaire!

She can't believe her luck – especially when she sees her stunning new loft apartment. And with the help of the 'manual' her husband has given her, she'll soon have the marriage to match!

But she quickly realizes her perfect life isn't all it seems. All her old friends hate her. A rival is after her job. Then a dishevelled, sexy guy turns up . . . and lands a new bombshell.

What the **** happened? Will she ever remember? And what will happen if she does?

Out now in paperback, ebook and audio

I've Got Your Number

'There are moments in life that the white chocolate Magnum ice cream was invented for, and this is one of them.'

A couple of glasses of bubbly with the girls and Poppy's life has gone into meltdown. Not only has she lost her engagement ring, but in the panic that followed she's lost her phone too. When she spots an abandoned phone in a bin it seems it was meant to be . . . Finders Keepers!

Except the phone's owner, elusive businessman Sam Roxton, doesn't agree. He wants his phone back, and doesn't appreciate Poppy reading all his messages and wading into his personal life. Can things get any *more* tangled?

Out now in paperback, ebook and audio

Can You Keep a Secret?

'Mummy always told me, you should never let a man see your true feelings or the contents of your handbag.'

Nervous flyer Emma is sitting on a turbulent plane fearing this might be the end. So naturally, she starts telling the man sitting next to her all her secrets.

How she scans the backs of intellectual books and pretends she's read them.

How she's not sure if she has a G-spot.

How she feels like a fraud at work . . .

She survives the flight, of course, and the next morning the famous founding boss of her company visits the office. As he walks around, Emma looks up and realizes . . .

It's the man from the plane.

What will he do with her secrets? He knows them all – but she doesn't know a single one of his. Or . . . does she?

Out now in paperback, ebook and audio

My ^not so^ Perfect Life

'As long as I can remember, I've wanted out of Somerset. I've wanted London. I never had boy bands on my bedroom wall, I had the Tube map.'

Katie Brenner has the perfect life: a ~~tiny~~ flat in London, a glamorous ~~admin~~ job, and a super-cool ~~staged~~ Instagram feed.

Fake it till you make it, right?

Then her London life comes crashing down when her boss, Demeter, sacks her and she has to move home to help her dad with his new glamping business.

So when Demeter and her family book in for a holiday, Katie sees her chance to get revenge on the woman who ruined her dreams. But does Demeter – the woman who has everything – actually have such an idyllic life herself? Maybe they have more in common than it seems.

And what's wrong with not-so-perfect, anyway?

Out now in paperback, ebook and audio

Surprise Me

'If love is easy . . . You're not doing it right.'

After being together for ten years, Sylvie and Dan have a comfortable home, fulfilling jobs, beautiful twin girls, and communicate so seamlessly they finish each other's sentences. They have a happy marriage – until it's casually mentioned to them that they could be together for another *sixty-eight years* . . . and panic sets in.

They quickly decide to create little surprises for each other, to keep their relationship fresh. But in their pursuit of Project Surprise Me mishaps arise with disastrous and comical results.

Gradually, the surprises turn to shocking discoveries. And when a scandal from the past is uncovered, they begin to wonder if they *really* knew each other after all . . .

Out now in paperback, ebook and audio

Visit

www.sophiekinsella.co.uk

The official website of

sophie kinsella

- New book announcements
- Updates from Sophie
- Enter competitions
- Read book extracts
- Sign up to the newsletter

You can also join Sophie on her official Facebook fan page

f **facebook.com/SophieKinsellaOfficial**

or follow her on Twitter 🐦 **@KinsellaSophie** and

Instagram 📷 **@sophiekinsellawriter**